"This set of four novellas stars one Lucius Hutchfield, a character who might make you think of someone out of Faulkner or Walker Percy . . . the kind of hero our mothers warned us against, knowing that we wanted nothing more than to be him. As always, Madden is both wise and winking here. Some people say life's the thing, but David Madden reminds us that art is always the better choice." DAVID KIRBY | author of *Get Up, Please*

"Over the course of these novellas, Madden delivers four distinct episodes from Lucius's life, spanning late youth to middle age. *Marble Goddesses and Mortal Flesh* is equal parts comic, heartbreaking, suspenseful, meditative, erotic, romantic, nostalgic, and masterfully rendered end to end. Just read it. You'll see what I mean." MICHAEL KNIGHT | author of *The Typist: A Novel*

"I've always admired David Madden's work for its keen music and instinct for time and place. These novellas will add to and strengthen his reputation as an observer of the enigmatic and the legendary." —Phil Schultz, Pulitzer Prize-winning poet for *Failure*

"*Marble Goddesses and Mortal Flesh*, David Madden's collection of four linked novellas, is a singular achievement. . . . Madden's mastery of the novella, an often misapprehended and elusive form, is complete—and here I league him with the writers whose craft and precision in the novella I most admire: Katherine Anne Porter, Alan Sillitoe, Jim Harrison, and Glenway Wescott." JOSEPH BATHANTI | Author of *The Life of the World to Come* and North Carolina Poet Laureate (2012–14)

"David Madden has long since joined the pantheon of great fiction writers, but in *Marble Goddesses and Mortal Flesh*, he has outdone himself. By turns hilariously funny and tenderly romantic, his young narrator Lucius Hatfield astounds the reader with both his fearlessness and intelligence, making him unforgettable, and one of the more original and endearing characters ever to grace Southern literature." ROSEMARY DANIELL | author of *Fatal Flowers: On Sin, Sex and Suicide in the Deep South,* and seven other books of poetry and prose

"I could continuously cite inventions, details, and felt connections that I admire in this collection of four extraordinary novellas. 'Only connect,' E. M. Forster says. There are no unconnected elements in this gathering of tales— Madden seamlessly weaves insight, imagination, implication, inflection, and innuendo." ALLEN WIER

"If you read these novellas in the order in which they are presented, you will enjoy the rare treat of seeing how an artist over his lifetime comes into the full use of his materials." GAIL GODWIN | author of *Publishing: A Writer's Memoir* and *Flora*.

"David Madden is one of the great storytellers of our day—his dialogue is pitch-perfect, his characters memorable, his plots ageless. Gather round and listen!" EDMUND WHITE | author of *Our Young Man* and *Inside a Pearl: My Years in Paris*

"'Too much James Joyce and not enough Jesse James?' ponders the narrator of these magical, luminously connected tales. He needn't worry. Madden writes with a masterful contrariness that is unique in American literature, and gets it just right" TERRY BISSON | author of *Any Day Now*

"In the title novella, Lucius Hutchfield, takes us on a riveting journey through his life by way of the Bijou Theatre where he worked as a young man. His ruminations and —reflections on sex and love and art create a wonderful time capsule of the world as reflected on the silver screen, as well as life in Knoxville, Tennessee, and all that goes into the heart of a young man as he moves toward his future. At one point he asks: 'What do you see that can be remembered later?' For Lucius, there is an encyclopedia's worth and for the reader this is a welcome treasure". JILL MCCORKLE | author of the novel *Life after Life*

MARBLE GODDESSES AND MORTAL FLESH

Marble Goddesses & Mortal Flesh

Four Novellas

DAVID MADDEN

The University of Tennessee Press | Knoxville

Library of Congress Cataloging-in-Publication Data

Names: Madden, David, 1933– author.
Title: Marble goddesses and mortal flesh : four novellas / David Madden.
Description: First edition. | Knoxville : University of Tennessee Press, [2017]
Identifiers: LCCN 2016053320 (print) | LCCN 2017000559 (ebook) |
ISBN 9781621903390 (softcover) | ISBN 9781621903406 () | ISBN 9781621903413 ()
Subjects: | BISAC: FICTION / General.
Classification: LCC PS3563.A339 A6 2017 (print) | LCC PS3563.A339 (ebook) |
DDC 813/.54--dc23
LC record available at https://lccn.loc.gov/2016053320

*For
Robbie,*

WHO WAS THERE FROM THE START, 1956,

AND REMAINS

Thou still unravish'd bride of quietness,
    Thou foster-child of Silence and slow Time,
Sylvan historian, who canst thus express
    A flowery tale more sweetly than our rhyme:
What leaf-fringed legend haunts about thy shape
    Of dieties or mortals, or of both,
        In Tempe or the dales of Arcady?
    What men or gods are these? What maidens loth?
    What mad pursuit? What struggle to escape?
        What pipes and timbrels? What wild ecstasy?

—*"Ode on a Grecian Urn," John Keats*

Contents

Preface: The World's One Breathing *xiii*

The Hero and the Witness *1*

To Play the Con *31*

Nothing Dies, but Something Mourns *75*

Lucius Hutchfield Meditates on
Marble Goddesses and Mortal Flesh *129*

Preface
The World's One Breathing

One morning in 1968, the first year of the 41 in which I lived, taught, and wrote in Baton Rouge, Louisiana, a voice, perhaps not my own, woke me, saying, "The world's one breathing may at first attain true time."

Of course, I understood what it meant only intuitively, but I was glad not to get it out of my head, not even after naming one of my stories "The World's One Breathing." In time, it became my mantra. As I understand it now, partially, five decades later, it expresses my long-held belief that since the beginning of time all the world breathes together in one breathing. "Time" is merely our useful way of referring to no time. Metaphysically, I am convinced that what is imagined contributes to some extent to what happens in "reality." For me, personally, more simply, I have always believed that in all my roles—lover, husband, father, teacher, activist, writer in all genres—I move upon a single, unbroken flow of creative energy.

The Southern Appalachian oral storytelling tradition and the movies and radio drama influenced my craft before Thomas Wolfe, Ernest Hemingway, William Faulkner, Virginia Woolf, and Joseph Conrad took hold of me.

The history of the creation of the four novellas in *Marble Goddesses and Mortal Flesh* is one expression of that single flow of creative energy in the process of the world's one breathing. Despite William Faulkner's well-known practice, a writer's re-use of previously published material is not always in the view of reviewers and critics acceptable, but what may seem unnatural in the literary sense has always been my natural mode of creation. Just as I have written in all genres since the seventh grade in my quest for different ways to affect readers and audiences, within each genre I have always sought new or different combinations of fictive elements. A major example is the fifteen-year history of the re-writing of my first novel, published as my second, *Cassandra Singing*. I wrote that story first in 1954 as a short story, then adapted it as a different narrative in a one-act play, then simultaneously worked on it, revised it, as a novel and a play, produced several times, later as a radio play, then as a screenplay at Warner Brothers in 1971 after publication of the novel in 1969. The characters, the narrative, the locale, the techniques, and the style changed radically not only as demanded by the different genres and by major changes in those genres over the years but by the effects of changes in my life and by my creation of other works during that period. The characters are so alive for me forty-five years later that a sequel begs to be created.

The structure of Lucius Hutchfield's narrative in these four novellas follows the chronology of my own life: two years of adventures in the Merchant Marine; a few weeks getting my little brother off the chain gang; my reading about an old Appalachian woman who claimed to have had a child by Jesse James; and my two years as an adolescent usher at the Bijou Theatre in Knoxville, Tennessee, my hometown—all the events, people, and settings transformed in the Pleasure-Dome of my imagination.

I was nineteen when I left the University of Tennessee to live the life of a writer in Manhattan. Tired of working in White Tower hamburger joints around the city, I wangled seaman's papers and finally got a ship Christmas Eve, 1952, out of Seafarers International Union Hall in Brooklyn, and shipped out of Hoboken, New Jersey on the *Seatrain New Jersey* that carried box-cars to Galveston, Texas. There a local seafarer told me the story of a girl who replaced her brother as leader of a motorcycle gang after he was killed in an accident. That so inflamed my imagination that I thought of her through other voyages, to Panama, Aruba, Chile, Hawaii, and throughout two years in the army, where, in Alaska, I began writing about her, calling her Cassandra.

Just out of the army, I married Roberta Young of Ames, Iowa, and we moved to San Francisco, attracted by the romance of living the lives of the Beat Generation. My creative writing teacher at San Francisco State Teachers College, Walter Van Tilburg Clark, author of the celebrated novel *The Ox-bow Incident*, liked my novel-in-progress, *Cassandra Singing*, but given the fact that I could not finish it in time to serve as my graduate thesis work, he suggested I expand into a novel "The Hero and the Witness," a seafaring novella that I had finished. I changed the first person, journal format to third- person. Much longer, it was published as *The Beautiful Greed* in 1961 as my first novel.

In 1978, out of my concept of the world's one breathing, I conceived, with supreme naiveté, a sextet of novels called "The Adventures of Lucius Hutchfield": first, a shorter *Bijou*, based on my two years as an usher in Knoxville; second, "The Hero and the Witness," the Merchant Marine setting; third, "My Intellectual Life in the Army," now in progress as a memoir; fourth, *Brothers in Confidence,* based on my two brothers and me as two different types of conmen; fifth, "The Activist in the Ivory Tower," derived from my early years as a teacher in an Appalachian teacher's college; sixth, "Bijou Dream," in which Lucius returns to the Bijou in 1970 en-route to Hollywood to write an adaptation of his first novel, but never leaves the theater.

The Beautiful Greed is narrated in the third person, central intelligence point of view (I prefer Henry James' term): everything is filtered through Lucius' perceptions. "The Hero and the Witness," the novella version, is told in Lucius' first person journal narration. Out of my conviction that the author's choice of the point of view technique determines the reader's essential experience, I wanted readers to experience that major difference, from the novel version, along with differences in characters and events, so I submitted the novella version to *The New Orleans Review,* where it was published in 1977.

While Robbie and I were still living in Knoxville, where I was finishing my undergraduate degree at UT in education, majoring in history and speech, the prosecutor in a small Georgia town telephoned to urge me to help him keep my little brother John off the chain gang. He liked John, as did the five people he conned into accepting bad checks. I went down there and conned all his victims into dropping charges, so that the strict judge let him go. But having passed checks across state lines, he was arrested by the FBI.

Twelve years later, living in the Bishop's palace while serving as assistant editor of *The Kenyon Review,* I was inspired by my friend of the San Francisco days, the poet Jack Gilbert ("David, I bet you could write a story a day") to write a story for each of five days. Just as I finished the final scene of John's story—in which the big brother, called "Traven," escaped from a Texas prison, arrives, claiming to be a lawyer, and cons the judge into releasing little brother—my big brother came rolling up to my house in a car filled with carnival dolls, my elderly cousin, and a tall, scary stranger traveling with him. "Traven" was published in *The Southern Review* in 1968. (I have changed the title to "To Play the Con"). My many public performance readings of it have gone very well.

I was teaching creative writing at Louisiana State University as writer-in-residence in Baton Rouge when Tony Bill called me from Warner Brothers wanting to adapt "Traven" ("To Play the Con") into a film. But his partner came up with Paul Newman and Robert Redford in *The Sting*, and that killed the deal. When *Cassandra Singing* was published the next year, I got another call from Tony, bringing me to Hollywood where I was the last writer-in-residence on the Warner Brothers lot.

Meanwhile, Peter Mayer at Avon wanted to publish "Traven" as a paperback, but finally decided it was not long enough, so I ended up incorporating some quite relevant material from my long-time work in progress, *Bijou*. It came out as *Brothers in Confidence* in 1972 and as the first half of *Pleasure-Dome*, published by Bobbs-Merrill in 1979.

The second half of *Pleasure-Dome* was a major revision of "Nothing Dies but Something Mourns," first published in 1968 in *Carleton Miscellany*, the swift writing of which was inspired by my learning that Georges Simenon, French novelist, wrote each of his many short novels in eleven days. Sitting in a wicker chair under an oak tree on Hot Holler Road in Deep Gap, just outside Boone, North Carolina, where I did my first teaching job, I wrote the first draft of "Nothing Dies" in 11 days. The characters and locale have returned to haunt me so lingeringly that I am now into a sequel, a full-length novel called *The Wreckage of Dreams*.

The essay version of "Marble Goddesses and Mortal Flesh" was written two years before the publication of *Bijou*, while I remained under its spell. Lavishly illustrated, it took up almost the entire issue of *Film Journal*, published in 1972, with the subtitle: "Notes for an Erotic Memoir of the Forties." I drew upon the material in that memoir to write the novella "Bijou Dream" in 1990. Lucius returns to the Bijou, finds it a porn house, buys it, re-opens it to show the movies of the 1940s, it fails, the backstage part of the theater burns, and he retreats into the projection booth, where he tape-records his obsessive memories. The first three novellas are dramatic narratives; this final novella is more a drama of consciousness, a meditation. Re-titled "A Demon in My View," after Poe's "Alone," it was published, in a much shorter version, in *The Southern Review* in 1989 and reprinted in my fourth collection of stories, *The Last Bizarre Tale* in 2014.

I, no less than Faulkner, suffer no lack of material, not to mention no episodes of writer's block, discouraging, I ought to have cause to expect, anyone's supposition that my inclination or compulsion to compress, expand, recast, and reprint elements of my fiction is to get *something* published. Going on 84, I am deep into seven book-length works of fiction and nonfiction in several genres simultaneously, carried along out of "the world's one breathing" upon a single, unbroken flow of creative energy that "may at first achieve true time."

FOR THIS COLLECTION, I have revised all four novellas. I have made minor changes in the style of the first three and major, and rather thorough stylistic changes in the final work. To enhance the unity of the collection, I have made the names of the characters consistent with *Bijou*, making also the names of places in that novel consistent with these novellas. For instance, Cherokee becomes Knoxville. "The Hero and the Witness" was the first, short, version of my first novel *The Beautiful Greed*; it differs from the novel by being in dated journal format in the first person.

The original versions of the novellas appeared in the following publications, which are gratefully acknowledged.

"The Hero and the Witness"

    The Beautiful Greed, Random House, 1961

    "The Hero and the Witness." *New Orleans Review* 4, no. 3 (1977): 206–16.

"To Play the Con"

    "Traven." *Southern Review*, NS 4 (April 1968): 346–91.

    Brothers in Confidence, Avon Publishers, 1972

    Pleasure-Dome, Bobbs-Merrill, 1979

"Nothing Dies but Something Mourns"

    "Nothing Dies but Something Mourns." *Carleton Miscellany* 9 (Fall, 1968): 245–88.

    Pleasure-Dome, Bobbs-Merrill, 1979

"Marble Goddesses and Mortal Flesh"

"Marble Goddesses and Mortal Flesh: Notes for an Erotic Memoir of the Forties." *Film Journal* 2 (September 1972): 2–19.

"A Demon in My View." *The Southern Review,* reprinted in the short story collection, *The Last Bizarre Tale,* 2014.

David Madden | BLACK MOUNTAIN, NORTH CAROLINA, 2017

The Hero and the Witness

DECEMBER 28, 1951

The *Polestar* is two days out of New York Harbor now. We're sailing south along the coast, maybe even parallel with Tennessee. I've decided to keep a journal of my first trip after all.

Nothing has really happened yet, but I have to go back a little and tell what *seems* to be happening.

You can't learn to be a writer by writing freshman themes on "My Summer Vacation." Just reading about life and being tested on paper isn't enough. So I left the university before the end of the term. I used to day-dream a lot about going to sea. All I had to do, I thought, was go to New York and sign on a ship to India, like Larry Darrell in *The Razor's Edge*. I started hitch-hiking last May. I'd never been out of Tennessee before. New York fascinated and scared the hell out of me. All I had was thirty dollars and not much sense.

When I found out how complicated and difficult it was to get on a ship, I had a vision of living on the Bowery, sleeping in a room full of bum-laden 50¢ cots, but I kind of liked the idea.

At the seafarers' union in Brooklyn, a Mr. Cobb offered me a trip-ticket, the lowest priority you can get. I was all set to go to India. But after a week of sitting around the hall, trying to act as nonchalant, as bored as the old men, as quietly cocky as the young ones, it dawned on me what a wait I would have.

So I got a job as mail clerk for Bambi Baby Foods. The office was on the top floor of the Empire State building, but after a few days the glamour of that building wore off. One day we all stood at the window and watched through waves of heat the arrival of a massive new passenger liner, coming into New York Harbor from its maiden voyage.

On Saturdays I'd go down to the battery and watch the ships and ride the Staten Island Ferry. I was waiting for Christmas. One of the old sailors told me nobody likes to ship out at Christmas. Most men go on the beach for a big drunk or a visit with their families.

But a week before Christmas, I got fired. The girls had sweated out the summer without a fan, their thin dresses sticking like Scotch tape to the hot leather seats. Now they were doing overtime without pay. They liked me, so it was easy to organize them to resist. I organized myself right out of a job. As I left the office, I yelled, "Worker s of the world unite! You have nothing to lose but your chains!"

That's what the seamen had done and they had a very fine union. The Eugene O'Neill days are just as dead as the Herman Melville days. Nobody can slap you around anymore. The longshoremen are different. Mobster Tony Anastasia has them scared shitless. Christmas Eve, they were holding an election. The seafarers' union had offered to include the longshoremen.

The hiring hall was empty. Everybody was out with placards, walking the streets of Brooklyn, earning priority credits on their shipping cards. I went out, too, in one of the union cars, squashed between two men who looked like wrestlers. I ambled on one side of the street and glared at Anastasia's gangsters on the other. There was snow on the sidewalks and we were freezing in the wind from the ocean. A young mother placidly pushed a baby carriage through the sinister mob.

Finally, what looked like a regiment of men came marching down from the voting place. "Here they come," somebody behind me said. Watching them come, I got mad. I hate to fight. I can't anyway, but thinking about it pissed me off. Here we were trying to free them from Anastasia who was taking the food from their babies' mouths and they, all those big, husky brutes, were letting one man no taller than me scare them into fighting their own liberators. Man! I felt like beating the living crap out of every one of them.

But when they got to the corner, their marching feet hissing and stamping like a locomotive on the frozen snow, I turned and found my corner empty, except for me and my cold, red fists. I know I would have stayed there and plowed into all of them and maybe they would have felt how stupid they were, pulverizing a little runt like me, even if the little cop on horseback hadn't ridden up between us, revolver drawn, yelling, "First bastard steps off that curb gets his ass blown to kingdom come!" The regiment did a sharp column left and dispersed.

The next day I read about the bomb Anastasia had hidden in the hiring hall the day before. Somebody found it in the "head." But the day after Christmas, I got a ship. The S. S. *Polestar*. I'm a wiper. I didn't know what I was supposed to do, but I was raring to do it.

The next morning, wearing my new leather jacket, green turtleneck sweater and engineer boots, I got on a subway to Brooklyn. It's a horrible, helpless feeling to be on an express to Brooklyn and it turns up in Yonkers. Like when you're going under ether and can't fight the damn stuff. But I wasn't late. I was as nervous as a cat on a—as a whore in a—as a leaf trembling in the wind.

It was still dark as I strode over a network of railroad tracks among some warehouses. The snow was deep, falling thick and fast. Brooklyn near the pier looked grim, masses of black and white, blurred by the swarming snow. But the air was almost warm. Suddenly, there was the ship! A great big son-of-a-bitch, tall as the Empire State building. I was surprised and nervous, being there all alone. The steep ladder shook, knocked against the side of the ship, as I climbed, my suitcase so heavy it nearly pushed me back down. At the top stood a dark, hooded shape, covered with snow, like a statue.

"That you, Peron?" The strange accent threw me. Maybe I was on the wrong ship.

"No, it's me," I said, facing him.

"Who the hell are *you*?" He blew breath smoke in my face. "Santa Claus?"

"No, sir, I'm the new wiper, Lucius—"

"Hoping you was that damned Peron."

"Are you the captain, sir?"

"Trying to get wise with me?"

"No, sir. What do I—?"

He looked around, trying to see through the snow. "Hey, Bill!"

A bearish, heavily-coated shape emerged from the snow. "How's the watch, Dane? Throw that spiked snowball at Peron yet?"

"Wise guys all over this ship! Hey, take this new wiper to the Chief Engineer."

The thick, faceless figure waved for me to follow him. When we got into the passageway and I saw him in the light, he looked like a comic snowman. "Merry Christmas," he said, sarcastically, but laughing. "My name's Bill Boroshov."

"Mine's Lucius Hutchfield." We shook hands. Then he turned and knocked on a cabin door.

"Who is it?" The voice sounded drunken coming through the wooden door.

"Got your new wiper here, Chief."

"Well, tell him to go wipe himself. Peron come aboard yet?"

"Not yet." Silence. Then Bill yelled, "Merry Christmas and a happy Yule, Chief!" snickering into his fist, poking my ribs with his elbow.

"Rot in hell, you Russian smart aleck!"

Bill laughed as he tugged an iron door. "Come with me, Lucius. Get you settled down."

I followed him through a maze of doorways, passageways, and steep, narrow staircases. "Doesn't the captain meet you on the dock to sign you on?"

That really made him laugh, slapping musical vibrations out of the green enameled iron walls as we walked. "Well, man, all I can say is, don't spread it around this is your first ship. This crew's just waiting for somebody like you—especially if Peron bitches loud enough to get hisself signed off."

"Who's Peron? I mean, isn't he the dictator of Argentina?" That made him laugh all over again, much louder. Some of the fo'castle doors were open and men looked up from bunks, chairs, and washbowls, casually glancing at us, faintly curious. They looked tired, moody, a little mean, but somewhat meek, not at all like they were waiting for someone like *me*.

"When I first signed on this junk bucket in San Francisco, I couldn't pass any of those fo'castles without everybody yelling, 'Hey, Bill, how's the boy!' But now, after a two-year trip around the damn world, they're all like rattlesnakes, coiled up with nothing to strike at but their own stinking asses." But he smiled and talked in a jolly voice. I knew I'd have to take a lot of kidding at first. "Here's your little love nest, Lucius."

The iron bulkheads were pale green, the deck, dirty red. In the iron room was a double bunk bolted to the bulkhead, a desk, also bolted, two lockers, a wash basin and a chair. A clothes line, slung across the fo'castle in front of the port hole, sagged under a pair of stiff, paint-saturated jeans a single paint-pocked tee-shirt, and a long red rag.

"That's Peron." With a flourish of his hand, Bill presented the soiled garments. He went over and spoke to them. "Aren't you gonna say hello to your new bunkmate?" Then he said to me, "He speaks only Spanish lingo when he's nervous." Then he spoke to the garments again, "He's gonna take the place of your ol' buddy Mike." Bill laughed so hard he had to sit down, bending over like he had a cramp in his stomach. He was a young husky fellow with a very pleasant face, very black, curly hair. I liked him right away.

"Who's Mike?"

He told me about the wiper I am replacing. Mike was the worst drunkard Bill had ever seen. Used to lay in his bunk all day long, and after the whiskey was gone between ports, he'd drink shaving lotion, and he got so mean even Red Crane, the chief engineer, was afraid to disturb him. And he hated Peron with such intense nausea that he had threatened to slit his throat in his sleep if he ever came into the fo'castle again. So Peron had slept topside on a canvas cot half-way from Israel to New York, until the Atlantic cold was more fierce than Mike's eyes.

"Why does everybody dislike this guy?"

Ignoring my question, Bill said, "And this Red Crane, your boss, that's another joker you gotta watch. He wasn't just drunk. He was playing with his hobby. Got the largest collection of filthy pictures you ever saw. I mean, nobody's seen 'em but he has this huge scrapbook and he's always pasting little pictures in it. Peron seen 'em but he won't come out like a man and tell you that's what they are. Him and Crane sit in there and look at 'em till they're blue in the face. I don't want to give you the wrong idea, but they're real buddies, if you know what I mean. All Peron talks about when anybody'll listen is mostly hisself, then hisself and 'my wi-ife,' as he says it, and then hisself and Red Crane, and it's got so the only one listens anymore is Crane. Crane speaks Spanish. It's sickening to listen to 'em."

"What's the matter with Peron, anyway?" I was convinced that everybody, even good ol' Bill here, was prejudiced because Peron was Spanish.

"You'll see. What's really wrong with him it takes a while to see. You gotta observe it, you know what I mean? See, I watch these guys. I like to study 'em, you know? People are interesting to observe. Take my mother. Russian, you know, from Russia. She's real old fashioned as hell, see. Trying to get me to marry this girl in our neighborhood. Full of Russians. I ain't no Russian, and the girl ain't neither. We're goddamn Americans, by God. But the girl has Russian folks too, so it's all arranged. Except I ain't even hardly talked to this broad myself. You know? I mean, people sure are interesting to observe."

"That's what I know."

"You said Peron might not come back."

"Yeah. Well, he's trying to negotiate. See, he's always negotiating—every port we hit. He negotiates the hell out of me. Trying to get a visa into the states so 'I can be with my wi-ife.'" It really tickled me the way Bill laughed when he talked. "She's a damn nurse, a high-class one to hear him talk it. And beautiful? Man, his wi-ife! But he don't show no pictures. Yeah, she's about as beautiful as his back."

"His what?"

"You oughta see his back—well, his face, too. But his back is swarming with huge scars from pimples, you know. It's like looking at the moon through a telescope. And his face is a real walnut. I mean it really is, man. So you better hope he don't negotiate hisself off this ship. I mean, I don't want to scare you but these guys are coiled up inside like rattlesnakes, dying to riddle some poor guy. Can't hardly blame 'em, though. We been on this ship two years. Around the damn world. We been counting on signing off this Christmas. But now we got this cargo of provisions to take to Tal Tal, Chile. Damn earthquake down there. This is what they call a goddamn mercy mission. Somebody's gonna need mercy before we get that far. Not a soul in the Union Hall to replace us, see? Have to be off your nut, like Mike, with his stomach full of Aqua Velva." He almost never stopped laughing at that. I tried to laugh, too, because I liked him even though he was scaring the piss out of me. Then he had to go on watch. "Gotta relieve ol' Dane."

After a while, I went up and stood on the fan-tail and looked at the Manhattan skyline. The buildings of Wall Street broke slowly through the dissolving gray of the morning and the thinning snow. Then the snow stopped, and the sun came out. I watched a taxi coming from a long way off toward the pier.

I didn't know why, but I was sure Peron would be in it. Two men got out but I correctly identified Peron. I couldn't see the face clearly, but a marked difference in his manner of getting out, standing there, talking, shaking the other man's hand, dressed very dapperly in a brown double-breasted suit, a Homburg hat, spats planted arrogantly in the grimy slush, a yellow kid-gloved hand carrying a shiny leather briefcase, a gold-tipped cane tucked tightly under his arm, assured me that this man would have a back pitted like craters on the moon. If he'd been in a movie though, he would have looked like a foreign, sophisticated counter-spy or an emissary arriving to restore order. The other man got back into the taxi, which took him away.

As I watched him ascend the steep, narrow ladder, his bearing still regal as the ladder shook against the bulkhead, seeing his face now, thin, sharp, pitted, swarthy, with a Van Dyke beard, I reminded myself that I had resolved not to give in to the talk nor even allow *him* to aggravate me, always to remember that prejudice and the extreme need of these men for a scapegoat was behind it all. Because already I vaguely felt something obnoxious about him—the impenetrable serenity of his haughty air.

More curious than nervous, I returned to the fo'castle. A short, thin, naked man stood with his scarred back toward the door. His fancy clothes had vanished. Before I could back out, blushing almost, he turned and we faced each other. He was the skinniest man I have ever seen in the flesh. But the horrible thing was not the acne scars and the shrunken face, the pale, almost lovely blue eyes, the bones showing under his skin, the huge rotten toe-nails, but that tremendous dong, hanging like a bell-clapper, nearly to his bony knees.

He smiled, spoke in perfect English, with only a mild Spanish accent. "Ah, here you are. You had better get ready for work. Red told me to tell you, to take you under my wing, and show you the ropes. We sail at noon, you know."

I went in, annoyed by the slight resentment I was feeling, for he seemed amiable enough. But I couldn't speak to such incredible nakedness. He took the jeans from the clothesline. They were stiff as a sheet of tin, but he got into them with loud rasping thrusts of his scissor-like legs. Turning my back to undress, I saw my suitcase on the lower bunk.

"I moved your things. The upper bunk is mine."

"I thought that was Mike's old bunk."

His eyes bulged, his lips tightened. "Do not speak to me of that monster!... I can see you are an intelligent young man. Well, I welcome you to this ship." He put out his hand. I shook it. It was like touching the entire nakedness he had now covered with the paint-pocked work duds. He wore the red cloth like a sash. "I have had to live for two years among these vermin. They have absolutely no culture. They are worse than uncouth. A drunken horde of filthy whoremongers. Perhaps you are different. Red Crane is the only gentleman among them. He is an officer—not like these scum with whom I am forced to cohabit. You will like him. You will like me, too. I am very easy to get along with. I come from pure Spanish nobility. Oh, they have their feeble, childish jokes. But my name is Jack Santos. I am an exile from the Peron regime. Someday I may assassinate him myself."

He continued his monolog as I undressed, talking fluently, not in a loud, pompous voice appropriate to his rhetoric but quietly, in a cultured baritone. But it was odd after all Bill had told me to hear him call friendly greetings, in a slight tone of benevolent condescension, to men passing in the hallway. And all the time my own nakedness was unfolding. I quickly, nervously got into my work clothes.

"You cannot wear that heavy shirt." He pinched the red fabric. I didn't like that at all. "You will roast like a pig."

I put on a white tee-shirt and followed him out the door. He locked it. "There are thieves among these men. You have to watch them."

Down the passageway, he opened a steel door. Hot air like a wool blanket flew into my face, covered my body. When I stumbled backward to avoid the scorching air, he laughed. Some men laugh like a horse, galloping—he laughed like a fox terrier, trotting. His teeth were perfect and white.

He stepped inside, reached back and took my hand. I shuddered at the first contact. He drew me inside. The door slammed shut. We were on a red steel cat-walk, steep ladders dropped down through three landings into the midst of a huge steel room, swarming with pipes, and at the very bottom were six colossal turbines. The noise and the heat seemed to pulse and pound together. My tee-shirt was soaking wet before we reached the lower stage. I wondered if I would be able to take it. Looking at skinny Jack Santos, alias Peron, I felt challenged.

Jack led me to a huge red cage constructed of iron wire diamond shapes. He introduced me to Crane, who was messing around among some nuts and bolts. Tall, stocky, the silent type, except for his red, crew-cut hair, he reminded me of John Wayne. After all Bill had said, I was surprised to hear him talk so affably, smiling irrelevantly now and then as he yelled my duties above the clamor of the turbines and gave me some advice. Just as I was beginning to suspect Bill of malicious gossip, Red Crane said, "And mostly, don't believe everything you hear on this ship. You have any problems or anybody try to give you a hard time or get you into one of these nasty little arguments between cliques, you come see me. Stick with Jack there—he's had it rough. Okay? Now let's see how you can paint, kid."

I didn't like the "kid" stuff but he seemed to be the kind of guy you can respect and like, even if he is your boss.

So I went over and knelt down beside Jack Santos among the large paint cans and brushes. He talked a blue streak close to my ear as we mixed the paint but the noise was so hellish all I could do was nod and smile. I followed him to where some ladders and planks were rigged up among a network of pipes as big around, some of them, as my own body. The men we passed gave me friendly smiles. I was beginning to feel fine, to get the feel of the ship.

But when I looked behind me, I saw a trail of red paint like blood all the way across the immense engine room, and Red Crane was stalking it towards us. He didn't even look at me. Swiftly, but almost casually, he lashed out with the back of his hand and nearly knocked Jack's head off his shoulders. Jack gave him a quivering but weirdly genuine smile. "Clean it up!"

Impulsively, I strode over to Crane and looked up at him. I was so mad, nervous and scared, he didn't hear me the first time. I repeated, "You can't slap him around, sir. This is a union ship."

He smiled calmly, said, "Don't believe everything you hear." He walked away, turned, yelled, "Get to painting, kid!"

I got to painting. The salty sweat that drenched me, stung my eyes.

At coffee break, I went up to Jack. He was leaning on the rail, smoking, gazing at Manhattan.

"By God, Jack," I said, shivering in the bright, cold air. "I'll call a special meeting. We won't let that bastard knock you around."

But when he looked at me, I saw a smile fade from his scar of a mouth. "Red Crane is my friend," he said, indignantly, and moved away from me down the rail.

Dane, a big young man with a mane of blond hair and a smooth Nordic face, came to the door of the mess hall, looked out. "Hey, Peron! Your ship mates want to know if you're too good to have coffee with us. We want to drink to your return to your ol' buddies." He sounded serious, but he just had a lot of control because when Peron didn't answer, he closed the door and I heard a muffled laugh like a jackal.

As I descended again into the heat and roar of the engine room, the ship began to move.

I was about to starve when lunch time came, but I went on deck first because we were moving out of the harbor. There was the Statue of Liberty right smack in front of me, as green as the WWI soldier in front on my old high school in Knoxville. I sneered at the Empire State building, hoping my old boss at Bambi Baby Foods was watching from his top-story window. I felt free as a dolphin.

The mess hall was full of men. Puny Christmas red bells and green streamers decorated with flies hung limply from the ceiling. Bill called me over to sit with him. Boris, the southern oiler who had smiled at me in the engine room, was yelling at someone in the galley, who was cursing him from out of view. A young, handsome Mexican with a comical face, black mustache, bushy black eyebrows and oiled, pompadoured black hair, leaned on the serving counter, looking out at the men in the mess hall, a cigar between his big, white, grinning teeth. "Hey, Beel, that Peron's new sweetheart?" He nodded toward me as I sat down beside Bill.

"Yeah." Bill laughed, looking across the table at Jack, who was washed and combed now, eating slowly, his head bent over his plate. Then to me he said, "Don't worry about Babe. He's a wet-back from way back, but he's a lot of fun, man."

Boris, a fat fellow with pale skin and large white hands, yelled to Babe, "Hey, you tell that bugaloo son-of-a-bitch of a chief cook I want some decent goddamn food or I'm gonna cut his liver out with a pair of rusty nail clippers!"

Babe grinned.

As Boris continued to issue a steady, boisterous deluge of obscene verbal abuse, I imagined the cook hiding behind the range. I didn't dare look around. Then a tremendous clatter shook the floor and I heard a scream of shock as I myself shook.

When I turned, I expected to see my first dead man, even though everyone was laughing quietly and the cook was laughing loud like a banshee.

But Boris, startled, cursing, had jumped to his feet. A large iron pot wobbled against the bulkhead.

The cook, a small man of about fifty, his steel-rimmed glasses steamed, was holding to the doorjamb, laughing, pointing at Boris, who quickly jumped at him, "You bugaloo bastard!" chased him out among the hatches.

Jack looked up at me, said quietly, sneering, "Disgusting—just like little children. They make me sick."

Boris came back in, cursing but smiling with silly glee. I realized it was a ritual joke.

The others were laughing without enthusiasm. "They're real buddies, those two rebels," said Bill. "They go on drunks together in every port. Chief Cook always pulls that on him—sneaks up and drops that pot behind Agistone's chair."

Boris frowned, seemed to be looking at me as he walked over to the table. But it was to Jack that he spoke. "What are you laughin' at, Peron?" Jack hadn't laughed at all. He didn't even look up. "You think that's funny?"

"Someone better peek up the pot, gentlemen," said Babe, between his horsy, cigar-biting teeth. He grins all the time.

"You heard him, Peron," said Boris. "Start pickin'."

Without expression, Jack looked up at the man glowering over him.

"Sluefoot" Ryder, the red-faced Swedish bo'sun, had come limping into the mess hall. He picked up the pot and laid it like a bomb between Babe's open palms. As he slumped down beside me, he said, "Let's have a little peace and quiet, brothers." Ship's delegate to the union, he called everybody brother.

Boris strode cockily back to his own table, laughing.

"You the new wiper?" Ryder asked me. I nodded, smiling. "Sea sick yet, kid?"

"Not yet. Guess I will be." But I was sort of sick about something.

"Anybody taken you down yet to see the golden rivet?"

"No," I said, suspecting a joke, but trying to show polite interest.

"The Bo'sun's a horny ol' coot," said Bill. "Better steer clear of 'im."

Bill and the Bo'sun laughed and I thought it a good idea to laugh, too. All the laughing made me apprehensive.

"Peron's going to sic Red Crane on you, Boris," said Babe. He was friendly seeming when he teased anybody, but I didn't know then that it could get on your nerves—he did it all the time.

Bill asked Herman, the hairy messman who looks more like an ape than any ape I ever saw, for more chow, but Babe wouldn't give him any until he'd teased him about the marriage Bill's mother had arranged. "Someone told me she was Peron's grandmother, Beel. How about that, man?"

Bill pretended to be mad in a moody way.

Then Dane came in, very dirty from working on deck, frowning and brooding about something. But when he saw Jack getting up, his face brightened a little. He said to Jack as they passed, "Hey, Peron, I found Mike last night in an alley in Brooklyn—his guts cut open. He said he's gonna come back to haunt you all the way to Tal Tal, Chile. Thought I'd better warn you, pal."

Jack glanced at him through his pale blue eyes and walked out of the mess hall.

"Hey, Herman!" yelled Dane, staring at the warped blackboard where the menu is scrawled. "Give me some of that slop—whatever the hell it is. Didn't they teach you how to write down in Mexico, Babe?"

"I was the president, man," Babe said, grinning. "No time for learning the finer things in life."

Dane looked up at the Christmas decorations, sneering. "When you gonna tear down that junk? Supposed to be funny?"

"You in hell, sweetheart. Christmas every day and twice on Sunday here, man."

Everybody was quiet and moody next day and nothing happened, but yesterday morning when I went up to the mess hall at 5 a.m., this is what I saw on the extra blackboard next to the one with the menu, "Use Dr. Peron's special skin lotion for lovelier complexchun, just like his wi-ife, Evita Peron."

I watched the men come in, sit down, look up and see it and laugh, quietly. Babe leaned on the counter, grinning, playing with a medallion on a chain around his neck.

When Bill came in, Babe winked at him. It was Babe's handwriting, but you could read it plainly now.

Then Jack came in, jauntily almost, smiling to himself, rubbing his hands together, looking neat even in his paint-smeared outfit. He sat down across from me and looked up, pretended not to see the "advertisement."

"And what weel Dracula have?" Babe asked Jack, rubbing his hands like Boris Karloff.

Herman aped over and asked Jack for his order.

Jack mumbled something.

When Herman laid the plate before him, Jack yelled, "I did not order this garbage. I will not stand for this." He pushed himself to his feet and walked out, his bearing dignified.

Babe said, "The customer ees always right."

As Dane came in from the deck, I saw Jack at the rail, looking out at the rough Atlantic Ocean, the legs of his trousers flapping in the wind.

"That Peron shouldn't talk to his elders that way," grunted Herman, reaching for my plate.

I stood on the fan-tail, watching the moiling water, watching the gulls dive at the slop Herman threw overboard, before I had to descend into the inferno to paint the red decks beneath the labyrinthine pipes. But as I stood at the rail, from inside the galley came a prolonged, then subsiding clatter. Boris exploded through the galley door, the little chief cook lunging behind him, wielding a meat cleaver over his head, yelling, "You bugaloo bastard, I'll cut you up and use you for tripe, by god!"

It is night now. This morning there was another "advertisement,"

"Wife for hire. See Peron for detail."

I think he's asleep now, lying up there naked, a copy of *Black Mask* detective stories like a roof over his groin. His bearded face is as placid as the green bulkhead. Somehow it reminds me in this midnight light of the faces of Jesus on those ten-cent store calendars—except for the pock marks.

JANUARY 1, 1952

Hell of a way to face a new year is all I can say. Not just *him* this time, but me, too. Him in the morning at breakfast and me at dinner. I suppose I still like Babe and I think he likes me and didn't mean it the way he does with Peron. Or is there really any malice in any of it? It makes the men laugh. They are uncoiling, relaxing. And Babe likes to make people laugh more than anything. He even teases Bill about that arranged marriage deal. But the laughter is strained, forced.

Every morning, there has been a new "advertisement." This morning it said, "Dear Mama, Please come home. I ain't had a bath in three months. Your illegitimate son, Peron."

Peron doesn't even sit down anymore. He just strides into the mess hall past the blackboard without looking, draws himself a cup of coffee, goes out on the fan-tail, and stands by himself. He doesn't even speak to me anymore because he sees me with Bill and Babe and we're laughing and he thinks it's about him when really they're kidding me about how I'll act in front of my first whore when we get to Panama. But I don't volunteer to talk to him anyway. The harder I try to fight it, the more I dislike him, and the "advertisements" are witty sometimes, but this morning was too much.

I said to Babe as I went out, "You shouldn't throw off on his mother, man."

"What you say?" Squinting his shoulders, he presented his huge open hands to show his innocence. "You think I write those terrible words. I only write the menu, man." The way he said it, I had to laugh.

We're in the Gulf of Mexico now. It doesn't seem any different except it's getting warmer because we're near the canal zone. In the engine room, the heat mixing with the paint fumes and the noise nauseates me. I lean against the bulkhead and slap on the paint and think of the girls there will be in Panama and of the girl there used to be in Knoxville, and I worry about the draft and think of going back to college, and feel homesick. And the fireman or the oiler or Boris comes by and yells a thought in my ear, and I nod, and it's all weird but kind of nice thinking about it after you're out of there and it's night.

Before dinner, at five, we what they call "blow the tubes." Peron and I take turns standing on a paint bucket and pulling these chains. Cleans out the tubes. The steam furnaces would blow up if they weren't cleaned. We're called wipers because we go around and wipe oil from around the huge nuts on the turbines, but that takes only about 10 minutes.

Usually, Red Crane supervises the blowing of the tubes. Just stands there silently to make sure it's done. But today, Boris took over for Crane. Peron was naked to the waist, that red sash tied around him, pulling his guts out on the chains, the sweat glistening down his pitted back.

Boris always likes to whisper some tidbit in my ear. "Ain't he the most putrid sight you ever did see? I can just see him and Red Crane in Crane's cabin, porin' over that big o' book full a dirty pictures."

"Aw, Red's married. To a beauty queen, he says."

"Don't mean nothing. Ol' Red come home one night and found six Brooklyn teenagers in his wife's bedroom, waiting in line." The image made me feel sorry for Red. "Peron told me. He used to try to get friendly with me, coming out from Israel. He's probably a damn Jew to boot." I thought of Boris lynching Negroes, even though he's sort of a nice guy. "You know Dane? Boy, he hates both their guts. Look at those putrid clothes—paint like crap on a chicken coop."

I was glad it was my turn to blow the tubes.

Both Peron and I have to hang our raunchy work clothes on a line in the hot passageway to dry out the sweat. When everybody was passing by on the way to chow, Boris yelled, "By God, Peron, you better hang them slop rags som'mers else! Damn if I ain't gonna toss 'em overboard, if I have to smell 'em an' look at 'em *one more cotton pickin' time!*"

We finished hanging our clothes up and went on to chow.

What was on the board this time nearly burned the skin off my neck, I got so mad. "See the Professor's mother for a good piece of poontang." Peron got a charge out of that, because "professor" means me.

Out in the passageway, I took an axe from a red case on the bulkhead.

Babe was leaning in his usual way on the serving window counter, a big-assed grin on his Mexican face.

I screamed almost incoherently, "Babe, you better erase that goddamn blackboard. I'm telling you! Or I'll plant this axe right in the top of your skull!"

He tried that innocent routine while everybody laughed, but I kept yelling bloody murder, so finally he came slowly from behind the counter and wiped off the board with his apron. I warned him not to do that ever again and then I replaced the axe, and sat down across from Peron who was getting up to go, and I went through the motions of eating like I had everything under control.

But Bill whispered to me, "Let me give you a clue, Lucius. Don't ever try that again. That Babe could have sliced you up before you could bat an eye."

Boris and the chief cook went into their routine, cussing each other for fun, and just when I heard the iron pot crash upon the floor behind Boris and the cook go into gyrations of laughter as Boris shrieked in exaggerated surprise, Peron came running in and yelled at Boris, pointing his finger at him, "I am going to report you! You had no right to do that!"

Boris had thrown his work clothes into the Gulf of Mexico. Babe and Bill laughed and so did everybody else and so did I.

Bill came in just a while ago as I was writing this down. He likes to talk about books and art and different things I'm interested in, and he listens to what I say as though I were a professor, which is what he has everybody calling me, and I kind of like it. I was telling him about the economic situation in India when Dane ambled in, wanting Bill to play some poker. But we kept talking and Dane listened with that sullen frown on his brooding face.

"All that book learning—it's a bunch of bull," he said, with utter contempt. "You ever been to India? Well, I have. I've been all over the world, Professor."

So we argued a long time, and I discovered that all he knew about India or any other country was where all the bars and the whorehouses are. He got mad when I pointed it out.

Yelling at me, he backed out of the fo'castle right into Peron, who was coming in with a satisfied smirk on his face. He pushed Peron slam against the bulkhead and stormed away to the poker game.

"They cannot abuse me," Peron said, whimpering. "I have been to see Red about all of you. He is going to force the union delegate to take action. You will see."

JANUARY 2, 1952

This morning at breakfast there was another "advertisement," the filthiest of all.

When I came up for coffee at the morning break, there was an announcement on the board, "There will be no more filthy signs on this goddamn board. This is an order. Red Crane, Chief Engineer."

With a big grin, Babe pointed out the sign to each man as he came in. "You see that, man? No more of this funny business, now."

JANUARY 3, 1952

We are going through the canal tomorrow. The pilot comes aboard tonight. I swam in the bay today while the ship is anchored. All the men watched and laughed, leaning on the railing, asking me how the water was.

Some of us have army cots on the upper deck for sunbathing. Peron was sunning near my cot. He told me there are sharks in the bay. He didn't laugh, but I knew then why the others had laughed.

Tonight we're going to sleep up on deck because it's too hot below.

JANUARY 4, 1952

We went through the locks today. It's magnificent to watch them work. But the main thing that happened today was Dane threw water on Peron's cot. Peron thought *I* did it.

When I came up to the upper deck after dinner, my own cot was dripping with water. I was just about to plow into Peron when Red Crane came up and said that if all we could do was fight, we'd have to go below and work in the engine room. Going through the canal we haven't had to work. The heat is worse than the breath from a steel furnace.

JANUARY 5, 1952

The captain received orders not to stop in Colon, Panama any longer than it takes to re-fuel. So the men are very angry and silent except for occasional bitching. It's eleven days to Antofagasta, Chile, which is where we have to go before Tal Tal, the disaster village. Bill says it's going to be much worse than the trip down from New York. Not only the men but the ocean, too. Sailing in the Atlantic was smooth for this time of year, so I haven't been seasick yet. We sail at daybreak when the pilot comes aboard again.

JANUARY 6, 1952

I couldn't crawl out of my sack, I was so weak. Even Peron lay up there convulsed. During the night, I had to hold on to keep the sea from pitching me onto the floor.

Red Crane came and braced himself in the doorway. In Spanish, he spoke very angrily to Peron. Peron pleaded. Finally, Red pulled him out of the top bunk and let him fall sprawling naked on the deck of the fo'castle, cursing him in English. I knew he wanted me, too, but I didn't care.

Peron was dressing obediently in his good double-breasted, pin-striped suit. We hadn't had to work since Boris threw his only work clothes overboard just before we entered the canal. Sick as I was, I almost wished I had the strength to go below just to watch him paint in his new suit.

Then Red started in on me and I dared him to lay a finger on me. He laid all ten of them on me at once. That was when I finally threw up—all over his shirt. He was so surprised he just stood there staring at his belly, delicately flicking at it with his nicotined fingers.

Bill was standing outside. He yelled at Red, "Okay, Crane, that's all, man! The damn ship's delegate's going to hear about this." Then he came back again with "Sluefoot," the bo'sun. Bill tried to help me into the bunk but we kept slipping in the puke on the floor and Peron, standing behind Red, ready for work but dressed for church, laughed quietly at the sight.

"Sluefoot" was damned mad at Red. He stalked out, saying, "Bill, round up the men. We're going to have a special union meeting right now."

Red told Peron he could go back to bed.

I was too nauseated to go to the meeting. Bill came afterwards with some crackers and soup and told me about it in detail. The men had decided that a report to the union about Crane would be made when we returned to the States. Also the men voted that Peron was an agitator, causing discontent on the ship.

I got even sicker. Above me, Peron lay moaning, dressed in that suit, pretending not to hear.

Then Boris came in and told Peron he'd have to go to work. Peron got up, staggered behind him to the engine room.

At about four o'clock, the Pacific was still not passive, but I felt less nauseated. Just so I could see Peron working in his suit, I dressed and went below and offered to help blow the tubes. Perched high among the hot pipes, Peron was painting. When he came down to the chains where I stood waiting, carrying his brush and paint bucket, he had paint all over his face, his hands, his hair, but not one drop on that suit. Still neatly creased. Sweat stains only here and there.

Boris was supervising again but Red Crane walked past us and reached up and patted Peron on the shoulder as Peron pulled the chains, standing tip-toe on the empty paint can. Damned if I don't believe tears of gratitude came to Peron's eyes. It made me feel low-down.

After Crane was gone, Boris went over to Peron and yelled for him to pull harder. Peron pulled and huffed and puffed so hard and fast that when the ship hit a high wave and lurched, he lost his balance and fell flat upon Boris. My stomach flopped like a beached fish, I doubled over and missed what happened while they were together on the deck, but when I looked up, Peron was up and brushing off his suit when Boris hit him. He swung again but Peron ducked. He ducked about twenty times, Boris swinging wildly and the ship rolling. It was the most interesting thing I ever watched—like modern dance. Then on the last miss, Boris crashed into the paint cage and fell back like a bull dog in a cartoon—out cold.

The ship's delegate brought the captain down and a lot of us were there when they helped Boris up the steep, narrow steps.

I told them exactly what I'd seen, but I couldn't swear who had started it, and I couldn't.

The captain said to Peron, "Whole time you've been on this ship you've caused nothing but trouble. I think a few days in that paint locker would do you good."

There's no brig on this ship and all the fo'castles are occupied, and the sea was still too rough for handcuffing him to the rail. Except for the engine room heat, the paint cage wasn't so bad. But the whole idea was repulsive even to some of the guys that were satisfied.

But Bill told me that Dane, Herman, and Babe weren't satisfied. When Herman, the ape, went down with some food for Peron, Peron threw paint and Spanish curses at him. In the night, Dane, Herman, and Babe went down and sang to him, lullabies and jingles about Dr. Peron's special skin lotion, and taunted him about his wife because now the captain has decided to pay Peron off in Antofagasta. That means he won't get back to America with a visa to visit his "wi-ife." But they came back to the mess hall, looking glum and still unsatisfied.

JANUARY 7, 1952

I got to feeling sorry for Peron and ashamed of myself, so I took him that copy of *Black Mask* detective stories he's been reading all during the voyage.

He was sitting quietly on a paint can, wearing only his shorts, dripping sweat. Back in a corner of the huge cage, his suit hung neatly from a pipe. But it seemed like he was still wearing it, he looked so dignified and invulnerable.

JANUARY 15, 1952

The monotony of the sea, the regularity and the routine, the painting, the maneuvers of the men in their pathetic efforts to kill time, has been much worse since Panama. Or is it that I am getting used to it and the mystery has worn off? I know all the men now and they're friendly in their surly manner, though they sometimes get nasty when they kid me about my way of talking about things, calling me the Professor, sometimes sarcastically. And I know a great deal about the ship and familiarity is breeding boredom.

But he's there when I go down every morning. Nearly nude, brown, scarred, bony like a starved turkey, sitting there reading *Black Mask* or staring into space. And even that is no longer unreal seeming, or outrageous or weird or even interesting.

This morning, I came up out of that hot hole dreading the dreariness of the gray sky and the gray sea. I casually looked out and the mountains were so sudden and steep and gigantic that it seemed we were moving in among them. The stark Andes in the land of eternal twilight—looking like the Smokies, only nude. That sight made up for everything.

When I went down below, I even tried to tell Peron about it but he, as always, merely looked out of the cage right through me.

He talks to Red, though. Red will come along and offer him a cigarette and they'll smoke together for a while and chat in Spanish and Peron will even laugh and slap his naked legs. Somehow I get the feeling that Boris, watching, is jealous of Peron. I wouldn't doubt he has a secret respect, liking, admiration for Red. I guess I like Red, too, in a half-assed way. The other day, I even asked him if he would talk to the captain, try to get poor ol' Peron out of that chicken coop. "Don't worry, kid. He likes it. Believe me."

Sailing coastwise, we will be in Antofagasta in the morning.

JANUARY 17, 1952

I woke up yesterday morning feeling the stillness of the ship, hearing harbor noises, but the steel rattle of a locker was what woke me. I rolled over and there was Peron, naked as a jay bird, leaning over the sink, washing his famous face.

I wasn't glad he was out until I suddenly remembered he'd been in that cage at all. But odder than that was the way he spoke when he saw in the mirror that I was awake. "Well, Lucius, my friend! Ah, you see, it is a beautiful morning, and soon we will be ashore and having a fine time." And then he began to whistle. The thing about people is, you never know.

While I dressed, he kept whistling and chattering gaily. In the flood of it, he reminded me that he is a political exile, an aristocrat of good family and breeding, has been a museum curator, a teacher, and an official for an oil company in Arabia. Almost made me sick, listening to him brag. For a second, he got serious enough to offer his friendship. "Let bygones be bygones."

What the hell could I do but shake his hand? After all those hours in that sweltering engine room, his hand was cold and clammy. Next thing he did was invite me to join Red and him for dinner. He wouldn't let me refuse politely, so I accepted. Then he sold me some pesos cheap.

"Is the captain letting you stay on the ship?"

"No," he said curtly, sadly. "But I have many friends here. You will see. I will join my wi-ife in New York. You will see."

I began to feel a chummy, though repulsive, feeling between us, so I tried gently to explain to him why the men have treated him so badly, to point out how he might cease to antagonize them. But he didn't hear a word, went right on talking with egotistical bombast. I began to feel smothered.

We were anchored in the bay. Red was supposed to meet us later. Dressed in his suit, debonairly holding his cane and his briefcase in his gloved hands, he rode the launch with me to the dock.

We rode into Antofagasta in the same taxi. In the post office, where we stopped for him to mail letters to his wife and to some officials, I saw Bill, Dane, and Babe and started talking to them and when I turned, Peron was gone. So I went with them, hoping Peron wouldn't be mad, because I'd bought some dirty pictures from the cab-driver who kept jazz-talking me with "man," "crazy," and "cool," and I was afraid Peron might report me to the customs.

I thought I'd have to wait until dark before they would take me with them to a bordello. But they started off right away in broad daylight in an old taxi that rattled my guts. Dane knew where to tell the driver to go—a very grimy section of town by a dirt road, dust all over, and creepy dogs crawling across the street that was cold black shadow on one side and pale sunlight on the other.

I imagined all of us getting slugged in bed and missing the last launch at midnight. But I was more scared of the whores. Not that I've never—well, no use going into that. It's Peron coming in later that matters.

A little old thin woman let us into a roofed-over courtyard, balconies and ornate balustrades. The huge room was full of chairs but no girls. I leaned in the wide doorway to the dance hall, my hands in my pockets, and waited. Then another old señorita came up to me and pulled me away from the door-jamb and showed me the ragged spot on the wood where my leather jacket had taken off the fresh green paint. That made me start feeling self-conscious about all the engine room paint on my boots. Dane and Babe had ambled off somewhere with drinks the woman had brought, but Bill was kidding me all the time.

I couldn't believe it when I heard it. A loud clattering bounce of aluminum, then one long shriek, partly a woman's, and immediately the banshee laughter and the raucous cursing.

I got to the room just in time to look over Babe's and Dane's shoulders and see Boris, naked and white as a peeled Easter egg, his cock bouncing stiffly, as he chased the chief cook around the bed where a tiny young girl lay bug-eyed, scared out of her naked skin at all of that suddenly going on.

"Man, he timed it just right!" said Babe, admiringly. Boris chased the cook all over the house.

Whores were on the balconies now, laughing their asses off. Then they started lazily down the stairs and I kind of backed away a little.

Just when I was getting set with this one young girl named Macarena, and not minding her teasing me about the "pintura" on my boots, that goddamned Peron had to come barging in, debonair as hell. Well, it's a free whorehouse, but it looked just like he was intruding all over the place. The madam knew him right away and they smiled back and forth at each other, talking as though they were on the ballroom floor of an embassy. He was looking for Red, even seeming a little angry about being stood up. Bill tried to make him believe that Red was at another whorehouse but failed.

After a while, I couldn't stand it anymore, watching Peron's way of making out with all the girls, and the one around my neck was getting me to where there was only one thing to do, so I picked her up and carried her up the stairs like I was Rhett Butler carrying Scarlett. What happened in the room was something else. All I can say is, I was a lot scareder than I thought I was.

When I came down again, it was getting dark outside! Through a grimy window, the town looked like it was rolled in a puny, sickening wreath of smoke. The sun was dead red on the mountain crests. For the first time, I felt very deeply the sense of being far from home without a tongue in a strange country.

In the loud, raucous music below, Peron in that damned suit was dancing on his knees from one seated whore to another, tee-ing each one off. He went at one girl so frantically she got a little hysterical, and it was not until then that anyone did any more than watch him with contempt.

Red-eyed drunk, Babe told him to keep his filthy hands off the women. "You think I want to touch a woman you had your hands all over her?" Then he cursed Peron quietly in Spanish.

Bill went upstairs with a huge, lovely woman, and Boris and the cook were pissing drunk together in a corner, so they couldn't have even seen Peron. But Dane was stone sober, hardly responding to the women, staring intensely at every move Peron made.

Then Red came dashing in, all dressed up in a blue new suit and a cocky trench-coat, with a few drinks in him and a gay, happy but arrogant air about him. I have to admit it, he looked great.

When Peron, on his knees, drunkenly begging the hysterical woman's forgiveness, not meaning a word of it, saw Red Crane, I thought he'd have convulsions of joy. He waddled all the way across that gleaming, waxed floor on his knees, his arms out, yelling, "Red, Red, my friend! my friend!" to where Red stood in the doorway, taking off his gloves. Peron took his hand feverishly and kissed it, seemingly sure we and Red would take it as a drunken, whorehouse joke, but it was obvious he meant it.

Red was annoyed, but he tried to laugh it off.

Then Dane said, quietly, "Kiss him, Red."

Red stepped back abruptly, looking at Dane. "What did you say?"

"Nothing."

Red went over and stood in front of Dane. "I said, 'What did you say?'"

Dane gently laid the whore's hands aside, rose slowly and said, quietly, "I said, 'Why don't you kiss him?'"

The fight started there, instantly, but it stumbled and spilled and fell and rolled and jolted, exploded out the door, into the courtyard, into and across the street, and even into another house, ending in a dimly lit kitchen on a damp concrete floor, roaches on the wall, a public-type urinal behind a screen. They stood there in that sickly light panting, limp, bleeding, staring at each other.

Peron had disappeared.

When I heard the car out front, then the boots of the police in the concrete hallway, I tried to get over to Dane, to get the dirty pictures back that I'd loaned him, but it was the first thing they found when they searched him. I could have said they were mine, but he had them, that's all they cared about. Dane gave me a look as they dragged him and Red away and stuffed them into the tiny police car. Something about the olive wool uniforms, all those shiny brown leather belts and holsters, their high boots and snappy caps scared the living daylights out of me.

As we moved toward the ship in the launch last night, I thought, well, at least I won't see Peron again. Now maybe things will be different. I just hope the Captain will get Dane and Red released.

Leaning over the rail, picking my teeth after breakfast this morning, I saw a launch approaching, Peron standing stiff as a poker, dressed as dapper as on that first day in Brooklyn, holding the shiny briefcase and the gold-tipped cane with professional aplomb. I felt a sense of inevitability. In some way, Peron would always be with us.

He climbed agilely up the drop-ladder and set off with a springy step and jaunty air along the deck to the captain's cabin.

He bought some work clothes from the slop-chest, and we painted that day as we sailed down the coast to Tal Tal, which means night bird, the final destination.

They had turned Red loose. He didn't speak to Peron or even slightly look at him, but he spoke amiably to me. "It's a shame about Dane, isn't it?" He really meant it. "Those Chilean tanks are cold and ridden with lice and rats."

In a way, I was glad Dane wasn't on the ship, but I shuddered, thinking of crawling lice.

At dinner, the captain came to the mess hall for the first time since I've been aboard and said, "Men, Jack Santos will *not* be molested again on this ship. I'll handcuff to the rail any man who abuses him."

When the captain left, Babe, leaning on the counter, said, "Okay, men, you hear the captain! No more this monkey business. From now on Peron—I mean Señor Santos—is the guest of honor on this sheep!" Then he started in kidding me about what the whore told him happened, or didn't happen, when we were in her room. But he didn't have his mind on it. He was watching Peron without a glimmer of humor in his vivid, dark eyes.

I do not speak to Peron and he does not speak to me. He's lying up there naked, looking like he always does when he's asleep. No doubt about it. I loathe the man.

JANUARY 18, 1952

Tomorrow, at dawn, we arrive in Tal Tal with rations for the earthquake survivors.

Just as I was dropping off to sleep last night, Peron suddenly started talking to me in the dark. This is what I remember. "I have lived, intentionally, an ambiguous life. I have thrived on lies, on masquerade, on calculated deception. Why? Boredom. Because three years ago, I realized that I had done everything I ever wanted to do, all in one insane rush, one fury of devouring, and that I could no longer become excited or amused or glad about anything. Boredom is worse than hell. . . . But the worst of it is, I am afflicted with a terrible nostalgia! . . . The lies and the less than lies—they all amount to the same ambiguity. You will see. . . . As much as my indifference to everything will allow, I have tried to protect you. I have been a hero to you and you have been my witness. But now you must create your own life. You must be in control."

JANUARY 21, 1952

The night before we reached Tal Tal, I was passing Herman's fo'castle, and I heard Boris, Babe, and Herman talking.

I am jealous of Herman, the ape. The men never sat with *me* in *my* fo'castle. Bent over the drinking fountain outside the door, I could make out only a few details amid the drone of their secret tones, but Peron's name bobbed up like a target.

I walked away quickly, looking for Bill. In the passageway, I met him, he was on night watch, wearing the heavy coat with the hood, and he carried a bunch of chains.

"Bill, you're the only one I can tell. I think Babe and Herman and Boris are plotting something against Peron. I mean, it doesn't sound too good."

He looked at me. "Man you better come in with us, now," he said, with an ironic, hissing laugh.

I was shocked that good ol' Bill could be in on it, standing there shifting the bunch of chains with a steely rattle, staring at me, grinning like Babe.

"I'm not afraid of you guys," I said, walking fast to keep up with him.

Bill stopped outside Herman's fo'castle. "Man, we could shuffle you like a deck of greasy cards."

"Aw, Bill, you ain't like these other guys. I always thought you had a real feeling for people."

"I feel for Peron. I feel for him in the dark, man. Dane's my friend. Now, you can come with us, if you want to make it up to Dane."

I didn't want Dane's friendship. Compared with Peron, Dane amounted to very little, good or bad. Now I was afraid for myself.

"You forgot what the captain said?"

"I been handcuffed to the rail before. Look, if you don't come with us, you'd better go to the dayroom and read your goddamn books, Professor."

I wanted to go, to try to make it not as bad as it would be, but instead I went to our fo'castle to warn Peron. He wasn't there. But his new paint-pocked work clothes were on the line and his towel was off the rack.

I ran down the passageway to the shower. Peron's voice, singing what sounded like a Spanish folk song, came out with floating steam through the open door of the shower room. But when I heard them coming with the chains, I ran back down the passageway and out on deck.

The sky was clear, the air mild and cool. Stars shone against velvet purple. Rough waves thrashed the ship. I stumbled over a loose rope beside one of the hatches.

The wheelhouse windows were dark. I couldn't see anyone in there. Panting, cursing, sweating, I ran up the ladder. I hesitated at the captain's door till I saw in my mind what they'd be doing to Peron, and my fist shot out. "Captain, sir!" No sound on the other side. I knocked again.

Then I ran down the passageway to Crane's cabin. The door stood open. Upon a desk lay a huge scrapbook, open under a bright lamp. Impulsively, I stepped into the cabin and glanced at the photographs. The snapshots were of children with toys, of Crane mowing a lawn, of Crane sitting on the grass beside a woman, and one of him holding a string of fish beside a mountain stream. My face burning, I ran back down to the crews' quarters.

Feeling guilty and afraid, I sat in the dayroom. An old seaman was playing Chinese checkers alone. He didn't want me to play with him. Nobody in the dayroom spoke. They were aware of something, but most of them seemed to have no real knowledge of what it could be. I sat against the wall and stared at the rivets in the iron and at the ceiling where paint had cracked and curled.

Peron had let it come to this. But it was not all his. I had crossed Dane myself, yet Peron stood on the spot alone.

When I thought they'd had time to do it, I went back to our fo'castle, guilty and ashamed. Groping along the bulkhead for the light switch, I felt for a brief moment that Peron hadn't even returned from Antofagasta, that the conspiracy was something I had imagined or even hoped against him, and that the light would fall on an empty room.

But I saw him instantly. He'd been watching me in the dark, and our eyes met in the sudden light. Naked, he lay chained to my bunk. Blood dripped from his body upon the floor. I grabbed at my stomach.

But bending over him, I smelled the breath-taking fumes of paint. The idea of blood persisted. They'd gagged him with his sweaty red sash. Lying across his groin was a glossy magazine advertisement in Spanish for Aqua Velva aftershave lotion. His hair was wet, beads of water glistening. In spite of the gory trappings, it didn't look bad until I saw the blankets on the floor. I'd heard of that kind of beating. The blankets had kept him from bleeding as they flailed him with the chains.

I gently pulled the red rag from his mouth.

He didn't speak or sigh. He didn't look at me again. Even after I'd loosened the chains and thrown them violently into the corner, he still stared at the ceiling.

"I'll get the captain, Jack." I was almost weeping.

"No." It was clear, like a command. I obeyed.

I sat down, but he didn't move, so I got up again and started to go. My foot kicked against a book. It was mine, torn to shreds, and under the bed were all my other books, ruined.

I went up on deck and saw the lights of the little village of Tal Tal, burning weakly. Above the steep, high, desolate Andes, stars shone lucidly. The ship's engines stopped. We were there.

I went up to the upper deck and lay down on one of the cots in the cold and looked up at the stars and thought of home and watched the smoke from the stacks drift across and smudge the stars, and I cried a little, I must admit.

When I awoke yesterday morning, the sun was very bright and sweltering hot. I went to the rail.

Huge black oar boats pocked with white guano were coming toward the ship in a wide formation. I watched them come up alongside and cluster. Dark silent men in old clothes stood in the boats, waiting, looking up against the sun at the deck where the crew was slowly but steadily active unloading the hatches. Then the crates were lowered into the boats. There was no dock on the rocky shore but on the white rocks black figures of women and children stood, waiting, looking out toward the ship. Some houses were still burning amid the general ruin the earthquake wrought, no flames, just smoke rising into the bright hot air.

I was startled to see Dane, his face black with grime and his shirt stuck to his back with sweat, climb up out of one of the hot hatches.

Bill told me Dane had been released soon after the ship sailed from Antofagasta and come by train to Tal Tal and boarded in the night.

But when I saw Peron walk swiftly on deck, with the stride of an ambassador late for a major meeting, I wasn't surprised at all. Not even that he was dressed in that immaculate suit, that shiny briefcase riding at his side in his bony, gloved hand. On his neck, beneath his Homburg, were flecks of red paint.

He deliberately passed me very closely, his shoulder almost touching mine, saying, "You must be in control."

When the Tal Tal men in the boats saw him standing at the drop-ladder, they paused in the lifting and settling of crates and looked up at him. He waved, almost a benevolent gesture, and they began to cheer, "Bravo! Bravo! Bravo! Bravo!" The poor ignorant bastards recognized him as a Spaniard and thought that he must be a Chilean official, the mysterious authority responsible for the coming of the ship, for the gifts of food and clothes.

They cheered until he had descended, with suppressed difficulty, the shaky ladder into one of the black boats, until he had brushed dust from the knees of his creased trousers, until the boats all started back, heavily laden, his in the lead. He stood up in the boat and did not look back at the eyes that watched him go.

Last night, we sailed from Tal Tal, going to Valparaiso.

I heard "Sluefoot" tell someone that the company had contracted another shipment at Valparaiso, destined for India.

I heard someone else say that there will be no shore leave at Valparaiso, and that India is a long, long time and a long, long way to go.

All the men know it now and they are very quiet and surly again, like snakes coiled.

Bill does not talk to me now except to say, "Pass the sugar, Professor." But I remember what he told me when we first met in Brooklyn.

This morning, I was standing on deck at the rail during coffee break and Dane passed me very close without looking at me and a length of greasy chain he was carrying struck my hand and I dropped the cup into the rough waves. I think it was an accident.

The fo'castle seems very empty tonight without Peron, lying up there naked, the *Black Mask* across his groin.

To Play the Con

Did I ever tell you about the time I tried to get my little brother off the Georgia chain gang? Oh. I did . . . Okay, I *will* tell it again.

I had a wonderful summer all set up. I'd persuaded the parents of this old girlfriend of mine Gayle Savage from our acting days at the University of Tennessee that while they were "doing" Spain, they'd be smart to let me stay in the house to keep the windows open. So I had a mansion on Kingston Pike all to myself, and I was happy to be back home in Knoxville. I was late finishing my master's thesis on Henry James because I had gotten side-tracked by my novel set in Knoxville, but Berea College hired me with the understanding that I would finish the thesis before September.

The first thing that hit me was my mother. Coming down the gang-plank of an excursion boat after a Saturday night excursion, she tripped and broke a leg. So I had to taxi her all over Knoxville in the sleek blue, broken-down Buick Streamliner I had bought in San Francisco to cross country, because it suddenly hit me that I was getting too old-looking to hitch-hike.

We were over at grandma's for Sunday dinner, along with a slew of relatives, when we got this call from Blairsville in the Chattahoochee mountains of Georgia. It was me that answered.

"Lucius, they gonna throw me on the chain gang." Bucky's whine was vibrant with outrage.

Hell, it made *me* mad, too. After three years in the federal penitentiary, looks like Georgia could forgive and forget. But, no, they were out to clear the books of those old charges.

"Prosecuting attorney said he might can drop the charges, if the people I passed them checks on will settle for restitution."

"Hello, Lucius?" somebody said, in a deep, lush drawl, "Your brother could use a little he'p." Turned out to be the prosecuting attorney, Jack Babcock. I asked him how much it all came to, and he said, about one thousand dollars. Knowing I couldn't get a spark with two nickels, I said I'd see what I could do.

He said, "One problem."

"What?"

"They all want Bucky's ass. They wanna be able to take a Sunday drive down the highway and see where Bucky's cut the grass."

"Didn't I read about some boys on that chain gang that busted each other's feet with sledgehammers because they'd had more than they could take of that kind of life?"

"They run that story all the way up yonder?"

So I asked him what I *could* do.

"Those people he passed the checks on, they're human. Bucky says you gonna be a teacher and all—respectable citizen. Maybe if they got a look at his brother and talked to him. . . ."

I said, okay, and told him I'd see him, and got Bucky back on to tell him to take it easy, I was on my way.

After I hung up, I wondered what the public prosecutor was doing trying to keep Bucky off the chain gang. Then I remembered that it was Bucky's talent for worming his way into people's confidence that got him in this fix in the first place. A talent trained to performance by our older brother, Earl.

As for the thousand dollars, all I could scrape up was a hundred to show good faith. My folks are all more or less poor, so all they could fork over was the gas money. And I was broke, with no money coming in until October when I'd get my first check from Berea College, and by that time Bucky'd have shackle sores on his ankles. Daddy got Momma to turn loose of a dollar, and he threw that in as his share.

For the hundred, I crossed over to some kin we have on the other side of the tracks in Knoxville. Bakery kin. Millionaires, with a horse in every derby at Churchill Downs. Kin who left the mountains before we did, rich already off moonshine, who bought into a big bakery, then bought out the partners. I never cared much for money myself, but I always wanted to meet those Hutchfields on an equal social basis—they standing on their bank books, me standing on a Pulitzer Prize. But now I had to jump the gun, go to them begging, like I was fresh out of the holler.

I used my daddy's name to get in the office—it worked like a password on the secretary, who remembered him well—because when his daddy was killed in the saw mill and his momma died of cancer of the breast a year later, the wealthy Hutchfields took pity, and every time Daddy came around the lumber yard, they'd slip him a fiver, but never a job. Daddy has the same arrangement now with the government: it slips him a twenty each week out of sympathy for his chronic failure to find work.

Great uncle Lucius Hutchfield didn't bat an eye when I told him my daddy named me after him. But when I told him the story of Bucky's life, and showed him a picture, which favored Daddy—the big Clark Gable ears, the grin that said, 'aw, hell, all I need's a few bucks'—it wasn't long before he was taking me on a tour of the bakery, watching me toss down donut holes. And when I walked out the gates, I had a check for a hundred.

So four flats and a new carburetor later, I had passed through one of the worst rain storms ever to hit the Smoky Mountains and was in Mountain City, where Chet Atkins grew up, the first town Bucky hit, with a list of victims in my pocket.

I parked in front of the Mountain City Family Department store, the same feeling in my stomach I had when I played Biff in a college production of *Death of a Salesman*. It didn't take long to see what they'd do to get a little business. They'd even take a check from a stranger passing through. I was tempted to test this impression, but remembered that Bucky already had.

Mr. Overby, the proprietor, leaned against the counter under a big, spread-eagle fan that hung from the high, pressed-tin ceiling. Mrs. Overby camped by the cash register. As I imagined Bucky viewing this little tableaux, *his* thoughts ran through *my* head. Or were they Earl's? Because according to Bucky's version, our big damn brother, Earl, was the one got him into this.

Mr. Overby wants to know if he can help me.

"Sir, my name is Lucius Hutchfield. I'm Bucky Hutchfield's brother."

By the cash register, Mrs. Overby stirs. "And here I was trying to match you up with some folks from around *here,* cause soon's you come in the door, I knew I'd seen a likeness of that face before."

Then Mr. Overby squints against the glare of noon sunlight in the doorway and walks around me so he can get me in focus, and when he does, he says, "Bucky waltzed in here dressed fit to kill and tried on four suits and took one, and cashed a payroll check—under a false name."

"But I bet you favor your mother." Mrs. Overby's black and white polka-dot rayon dress shimmered in the light.

"Folks *say* I do."

"Because I think it was your walk more than your face. Something about the way Bucky waltzed in here made you drop your guard and like him right away."

"I'm after his ass, myself," says Mr. Overby.

"Fred, daddy's old sign's goin' back on the wall if you don't curb your tongue."

"Well, it was the biggest I was ever took, and it just scalds my cheeks to think about it."

"I was in the army at the time, sir," I said, "and then I had to go on with my education, and now I'm about to start teaching, or I would have been here sooner to let you know that I'll do everything in my power to pay you back."

"You gonna make a teacher?"

"Yes, ma'am."

Mr. Overby squinted his eyes, suspicious. "That state investigator told me *you* was a con man, too."

"That's Earl, my older brother."

"How come *you* ain't a crook, too?"

I tried hard to fascinate *him* with an answer to a question most people seem to find fascinating.

Then they ask me if I'm a Christian, and when I tell them how I was saved in a tent on sawdust when I was a kid, they invite me to supper.

For such a tacky store, they had a fine modern ranch style house, but what Mrs. Overby puts on the table is good ol' country food.

We're sitting around talking, and glancing at *Gunsmoke*, and I begin to tell about Bucky. "He's a year and a half younger than I am. Earl's two years older. So while I was looking up to Earl, I was looking down at Bucky. Used to have to take care of him while Momma was working in ready-to-wear in Miller's and

Daddy drove an ambulance with General Patton. We passed most of our lives in movie theaters, soaking up dreams and nightmares.

"What I wanted to tell you is about stopping off in Reno, Oklahoma to visit Bucky on my way out to get my master's at the University of San Francisco. They wouldn't let me through the gate because it wasn't visiting hours, but when I talked with Bucky's psychiatric counselor on the phone and persuaded him it would do Bucky good to see his brother, he put in a call to the gate. It's one of the biggest federal penitentiaries, where a lot of the mob leaders end up, but it looks like a state university, and Bucky was an impressionable pupil.

"Watching the door for Bucky to show, I kept seeing him come through all the different doors in all the different places from the time he was nine. The juvenile detention home, the institutions for wayward children, Nashville reformatory, and now here he was in the big time, like the prison where I visited Earl outside Chicago when I was in the army, en route to Alaska.

"Well, here come Bucky through the door, grinning and waving, and he gives me a shake and a hug, and we talk about old times on the streets of Knoxville—the smell of the bakeries (which was right there in the three-day-old donuts I brought him) and the factory smoke and the movie theaters. . . . Ah, well, let's not get into that. He was just so sad, it hurt all the way 'cross the desert to San Francisco."

"Let's do without *Gunsmoke* one night." Mrs. Overby twisted the knob.

Mr. Overby sunk in his chair like he'd been wounded.

"Anyway, as I say, I stopped off in El Reno, Oklahoma where they'd transferred him because they said he was cured of his 'nerves,' as he called it, and ought to learn a trade. How to make brooms. But before he got to fastening on the sweeping part, he flew off the handle and broke some guy's jaw."

But I didn't tell the Overbys that the joker wanted to be Bucky's buddy after lights out. Bucky's got a hair-trigger temper. Good thing the only tools of his trade were a fountain pen and a book of blank checks.

"In El Reno, they had Bucky on tranquillizers and it hurt me to the quick, because he moved and talked like a zombie. What was worrying him was that Georgia had a retainer on him for a whole string of checks he passed on his way into Tennessee. Straddling the two states was what brought in the FBI.

Tennessee was satisfied with the three years, to cover the one check in Athens. But Georgia wants to bring him to trial."

What Bucky had hoped was that Georgia wouldn't want to go to the expense of being there at the gate when he stepped out of the federal pen. But on that bright morning, there they stood.

For one thing, Bucky wanted to track down Earl and get even with him somehow. Earl had just come out of a Texas prison, full of religion, and somehow he had got hold of a Mack truck and a tent and had gone on a faith-healing tour. I hope he's serious.

"You see, it was my older brother Earl that led Bucky astray. How it happened was this—Bucky had been out of the reform school for a year and doing all right, playing ball, in fact, and getting scouts interested in his pitching. He had one problem—an eye that was blinking out on him. How did he get *that*? The scar still shows where Earl hit him with a baseball bat when we were little. Raining hard that day, so we were doing a dry run in the living room, me pitching the imaginary ball, Earl at bat, with a real bat, and Bucky, age three, catching. Earl swung back and Bucky began to scream and hold his head and roll in a spreading puddle of blood. A week later, he slipped while walking a railroad track and broke the stitches. A month later, he fell off his tricycle and busted open the nearly healed wound. So he had a good pitching arm, but one strike against him: a bad eye. And the last I heard he was going deaf in one ear. The prison psychiatrist promised me the chain gang would drive him totally insane."

Mrs. Overby cried and I got to crying, too, and Mr. Overby kept saying, in a friendly way, "I'm gonna have his ass in a sling."

After Mr. Overby had gone to bed, Mrs. Overby told me the story of her life, harping on the theme of childlessness. She made me promise not to write about her in a story.

The next morning, Mr. Overby took me down to his favorite filling station and had them fill me up on his credit card, and as I idled the motor, about to set out for Blairsville, he leaned on the window and said, "You tell that prosecutor, okay, I'll settle for the money, and you tell Bucky, it was just that it hurt mine and Mrs. Overby's feelings so much that he'd do us that way, after we took to him the way we did."

In Clayton, a truck full of fresh peaches was backed up to the curb in front of the courthouse. As soon as I talked with Mr. Crigger, proprietor of the Red

Dot Cafe, I was going to get me one of those sweet Georgia peaches from just over the line, maybe two.

The waitress behind the counter had a bottom like two clinging halves of a plump peach, and when I see home-made peach cobbler on the menu, I order it first. But what I bit into was Melba peaches from a can. I resisted pointing out the irony of it to the waitress because Mr. Crigger, thin as a hopeless T.B. case, is sitting on a high stool behind the cash register looking right at me. Then he's staring. Then he gets down off the stool and lopes on his long legs out to the sidewalk and crosses the street. I got the funny notion he was going for fresh peaches to make me a decent pie.

But a few minutes later, Mr. Crigger comes back and sits down again and does a bad job of acting nonchalant, and a deputy walks in and sits right beside me, no better an actor than Mr. Crigger. The deputy seems aware his performance is weak, but he goes at it with a kind of aw-hell attitude. After I pass him the sugar he asks for and he's got it thoroughly stirred into his coffee cup, he says, "You just passing through?"

I give it to him straight, and he gives Crigger a false-toothed grin. "Hey, Ef, this here's that Bucky's brother!"

"Well, 'i God, I tell you, it was that walk that throwed me."

"Ef thought we'd caught you. Hey, Ef, didn't I tell you they had Bucky in the Blairsville jail?"

While Crigger leaned against the counter with a gleaming coffee urn behind him, I started in on them. But they were awful cynical and tough. After a while, I wasn't following the waitress' peachy bottom, I was sweating. I felt ashamed, guilty, and cheap, like the time I was twelve, ushering at the Bijou Theatre and I walked off the job in the middle of the tenth showing of *The Razor's Edge* and struck out for India and ended up in Atlanta, bumming for eating money. Attention picked up a little when I got to the part Mrs. Overby's tears had cut short—how Earl got Bucky *into* this fix.

". . . . so just when Bucky got the word that his physical defects ruled him out of a career in baseball, along comes Earl, just finished with a stretch in Carson City, Nevada. Momma's sick and has to have a breast tumor removed. She's in the hospital and it's Mother's Day, which Bucky never fails to observe, and she's lying up there worrying how she's gonna pay the bills, and Earl puts his arm around Bucky, and starts in on what a hard life he and Bucky have given

Momma. They owe it to her to take care of those bastards that're worrying her to death with bills."

They salute the Mother-flag as I run it up the pole, and I realize I'm consciously trying to manipulate their responses, so when I got the waitress crying and Mr. Crigger said, "Jo Ann, you get back in the kitchen with that bellering! Can't hear what the man's saying," I knew I had them.

"So," I says, "he tells Bucky about this perfect method of passing checks without getting caught, which he learned from some guy on his cellblock in Montana. He steals a check-making gismo from RCA, and they hit the highway. Earl's method worked fine for Earl. You didn't see *him,* did you, Mr. Crigger? No, he let Bucky pass the checks. So Bucky spent three years in the pen, hating Earl's guts. Before that, all Bucky had done was refuse to go to school (because, as it turned out, he could hardly see or hear) and swipe a few things."

They all shook their heads, and there was good ol' Jo Ann, leaning in the service window, shaking hers.

"Jo Ann was here," said Mr. Crigger, "weren't you, Jo Ann?"

"Yeah, I was here. I been telling you for three years he wasn't a bad kid."

"Bucky caught me on a Saturday night just before closing and I just did have the two hundred fifty dollars to break his check," Mr. Crigger reminisced. "Said he had to get on home, 'cause his momma was in the hospital and he'd already missed Mother's Day, and a more pitiful sight, I never—"

"And you fell for it," says the deputy.

"You needn't rub it in."

"What would it have to be 'fore you could smell what it was?"

"Listen." Crigger leaned toward me. "I almost died of the T.B. last winter, and I know what being shut up in a hospital room is—like a cell—so I say, turn him a-loose. But not before I see that money. Who needs revenge? I got hospital bills to pay."

The deputy went out with me and leaned on the parking meter while I got started, and as I pulled away, I blinked at the red violation flag under the deputy's elbow.

In Hiawassee, thirty miles past Clayton, I pulled into Pap's Service Station, where Pap's eating his lunch out of a turn-of-the-century lunch pail. I told him I hated to interrupt his lunch but that I was Bucky Hutchfield's brother and wanted to assure him that I'd make good the check Bucky passed on him three years ago. He didn't even let me get started on my little softener.

"A body gets what he deserves. Any son-of-a-bitch greedy enough to take in a big check like that from a stranger just for an oil change *ort* to suffer. Well, I did. I suffered two hundred dollars' worth, plus the oil, plus the skin off my knuckles where the wrench slipped on that damned oil pan plug of that car of his. I learned my lesson, so I figure he ort to learn *his*."

"He has been, sir, for three years. And the psychiatrist at El Reno told me that if Bucky went on that chain gang, it would kill him, he'd lose his mind." Then I got it in about the threat of mental illness and how Bucky was right on the edge now.

"Hell, let him *talk* his way off the chain gang. I never heard sich a line as that boy lassoed *me* with, and I ain't about to hear another one sich as that, because I ain't sitting still long enough for somebody's brother to get started." I'm leaning against the soft drink box, absorbing the delicate chill through my fanny. I'm about to break the silence by going, when he says, "Come in here grinning like he was my long lost nephew. Why, if he'd wanted to be saddled with it, I bet he could have conned me out of the whole damned filling station, and my uniform throwed in." Then he laughs and slaps his crossed arms, hard, like he's giving himself a friendly whipping.

That's where I slipped in with the story of Bucky's life, stressing the bad influences, but also the loneliness.

"And talk about filling stations, sir, something about them always drew him to them, I don't know what. Maybe *you* do. Loved to watch the racks go up and shosh down when he's little, and press the button on the air hose. He'd sneak into car junkyards and play all day, trying out the driver's seats and turning the moldy keys and looking through shattered windshields at imaginary six-lane highways. He wandered around a lot, up and down streets and cobblestone alleys of Knoxville, alone, looking for buried treasure in the trash cans. And one time I was on a streetcar and I looked out as it turned around at this little park and there he sat astride the big hat of the Minute Man statue like a little pigeon."

For some reason, that part of the story got to Pap more than the rest, and he says, "Son, I'll have me a talk with that prosecutor, and if he convinces me that Bucky's got it in him to re-form himself and open his heart to Jesus, I'll drop the charges and settle for restitution. . . . Now sit down and have a big orange with me." He splits his peanut butter and apple jelly sandwich with me, too. Then he points the nozzle of his orange drink at me and asks, "They's just one thing I want to get straight. How come your brothers end up convicts and you turn out a teacher and a story writer?"

I tell him all about it, and he loves it, and skips back in out of the sun from filling up cars to turn me on again. When I told him that a blank page can be just as exciting and alluring as an open road, and, provided that page doesn't bear the name of a bank, you won't end up in a cell, he said, "Son, you a card."

I'm in my car, the motor running, ready to head for Blairsville, and I tell him to keep an eye out for my name as scriptwriter on some TV show, and when I say it might well be a western, he slaps the hood like he's putting the seal of certainty on it.

As I'm driving away, he yells, "You get that boy out of there and you bring him by here to see me, you hear?"

Taking the manager of the Western Auto store in Blairsville, where Bucky had cashed a check by putting ten dollars down on a plastic rowboat and requested delivery to 2395 Sweetcreek Road, was difficult at first, but once I convinced him that he wasn't the damn fool he apparently thought himself to be for having swallowed Bucky's story, it was smooth sailing. Louis Carpetti was a bachelor who had volunteered to take the store in Blairsville and put it back on its feet, but he was homesick for the Bronx, and when I started going over the high moments in several of the Broadway shows of the late forties, he was fighting tears.

When I showed up, he was closing the doors, so when we parted, it was in front of the drugstore, where I had a pineapple shake and he had a cherry smash.

By then it was twilight, so I drove around the square and saw the light in the barred windows upstairs over the jailhouse, catty-corner behind the courthouse.

Bucky must have been looking and listening for me all day, because just as I shut off the motor, he shows at the window, grinning, barechested, his pants hanging loosely on his hips, his navel black. "Hey, Lucius, where'd you get that *carrrrr*, good buddy!"

In the soft Georgia summer twilight, I guess that long baby blue body with the silver trimming looked like what he'd dreamed about in his cell, but in San Francisco fog, I got *took* for 500 bucks.

Bucky yells, "Come on up, Lucius!" like all I had to do was simply walk in, climb up.

On the screened-in porch, a woman in a starched cotton lavender dress sat on a slightly noisome rusty glider, snapping and stringing pole beans, dropping them into a black iron pot clamped between her ankles.

Then I see on the floor beside the screen sat a girl of about 15 in denim shorts and a pink rayon blouse that had a wide collar, billowed in the sleeves and fastened tight at the wrists. Two top buttons were unbuttoned, showing her white brassiere, and she was bare-foot, but between her legs she was polishing her majorette boots white.

"Majel," the woman says, "if I was you, I'd worry about them white streaks on the porch before your daddy gets back."

Majel hears me shuffling on the steps and looks right up at me over her shoulder, stretching that rayon over her breasts. "Momma, they's a man at the door."

"Looking for the sheriff, ma'am."

"He's wandering over the county som'mers."

"When's visiting hours?"

"Who you looking for?"

"My brother, Bucky Hutchfield."

Majel jerks her head around and looks up at me.

"Majel, it's Bucky's brother."

She sees I am.

"You come all the way from Knoxville, Tennessee?"

"Yes, ma'am."

"Well, you get yourself in here and go see your brother. That poor thing's been hanging on that window for days, watching for his brother to come. Majel, get up from there and show Bucky's brother where to go."

Majel reaches back, pulls herself up by the screen door handle, and starts slapping off down a dark hallway on her bare feet before I can get the screen open. I stepped over the boots and caught up with her.

"I bet you look cute in those majorette boots."

"By god, I better, if I go all the way to Knoxville to compete in that baton twirling convention, by god, I better look cute, and then some."

In the dim hallway, all I can see are her pink rayon blouse and a silver-painted door that she stops at, and when she stands up on tip-toe to reach something on the top ledge of the door, a crescent of pink panties winks at me in the twilight that filters through the bedroom curtains across the hall. Then I smelled her. "I bet you been practicing all day."

"Now, ain't I? "

What she came down from the ledge with was a long key that she shoves into the lock, and like a baton twirler, gives it a twist and yanks the door open.

She says, "Same key fits the one at the head of the stairs," and before I realize what she's doing, I've got the key in my hand and she's stepping aside for me. "And listen, tell Bucky to watch out for my daddy when he whistles while I'm practicing."

"Don't you reckon it preys on their minds to see you leaping around on the lawn in that outfit?"

"Well, ain't it better than nothing? Besides, I gotta practice with a audience, don't I?"

"Why, sure."

I went on up, and there at the barred door stands Bucky, posing for the thousandth cliché photograph of the prisoner, hands clutching the bars. I unlock the door, step inside, lock it again, and drop the key in my pocket. Bucky gives me a big hug and then we shake hands.

"Well, Lucius," he says, looking me in the eye, "they really out to get me *this* time," with that tone of infinite injury. "They jumped me soon's I stepped through the gate at El Reno. Damned man from the Georgia Bureau of Investigation and Sheriff Thompson. Exri-dited my ass."

"Brought you some stuff." I gave him a bag full of Hersey Kisses Momma sent, a pack of Wrigley Spearmint gum, some do-nut holes, a Milky Way and your favorite magazine."

"Thanks. But I can't hardly read, I'm so nervous."

In Springfield and El Reno, he read all the Thomas Wolfe he could round up, because he knew Wolfe was my hero when I was about thirteen, and though I'd switched to James Joyce long ago, he liked to make sentimental allusions to Wolfe. He tried writing, too. War stories, at first, because he'd been in the

Marines when he was fifteen and got kicked out, and he thought war stories would sell easy. Later, he wrote some things about kids in trouble and asked me to send them off for him and we'd split the profit, because he knew it would make the best seller list since it was all true.

The room stinks of stale pee and clogged drains and dirty, fetid clothes and feet and beds, and more than a century of sweat and mustiness, and from the stove below comes the smell of turnip greens simmering and coal smoke. Smells like poverty, lulls me—the smell we grew up in.

A fat man wearing nothing but a pair of overalls, his arm in a sling, one eye puffed with mosquito poison, walked around, munching on a Moon Pie, sipping a Dr. Pepper that he tucked under his good arm between sips.

Under the windows is a row of cots, and on one of them lies a boy of about nine, on another sits a boy about eleven, who looks at me with mellow curiosity. "Hey, Bucky-boy, that your brother?" yells the older one.

"That one shot his mother." Bucky puts on his basic melodramatic expression. "Yeah, Tom, he's my brother." Then he turns back to me. "Other one's his little brother, Billy."

"You come to get Bucky off the chain gang, Mister?" asks Billy.

"I'm gonna try." I felt silly.

"*I* heard they was going to 'lectricute him," says Tom.

"I let him talk that way," Bucky says, his voice low, full of long- faced compassion, "to take his mind off what they might do to him. She wasn't really his mother—foster mother. She's laying over there in the hospital, and they don't expect her to live. See, Tom and Billy's orphans—I mean the court took 'em away from their real mother, who's a two-bit whore in a little town down the mountain. So the county farmed them out to this old man and his young wife that run a chicken farm, and it was like slave labor. They'd get up at five and work till dark, and what they had to eat was scraps when the man and his wife got full. And least little thing, she'd burn 'em up with a belt. So finally, Tom got tired of seeing his little brother covered with welts, so he slipped out with the old man's shotgun one evening, climbed up on the roof of the chicken house, and told Billy to call the woman out, and when she stepped out on the back steps, cussing and wanting to know what he wanted, Tom let her have it."

"Blamed jolt of it nearly flipped me off the roof," says Tom, who's been straining to hear. "I reckon she'll keep her face slappin' hands *off* my brother."

Bucky tosses a tin-foiled Hershey Kiss between Tom's legs. Billy jumps up on his cot and dives onto Tom's, grabbing for the cigarettes. Tom holds the pack high over his head. "Ut, ut, ut, watch it, watch it, damn it!" Tom slides off the cot and slaps around on the concrete floor bare-foot, dancing around, holding the cigarettes up out of Billy's reach. "Wait, just a minute, Billy, don't grab. Bucky ain't offered *you* nothing."

"Give 'em one." Bucky watches them closely, smiling.

"Okay, stop, just stop pawing at me a minute," says Tom, and starts to take one from the pack but Billy grabs it out of his hands and runs with it and slips in the slime by the open shower stall against the opposite wall before Tom can even get started chasing him.

Tom and Bucky laugh, and the man in overalls stops pacing and looks at me. "They ain't no peace and quiet in this place either," he says, like that's what I came for.

Billy starts bellering, getting up very slowly, the pack squashed tightly in his little fist, cigarettes strewn around him.

"Ha, ha, ha, ha, ha," sings Tom, "lit-tle Billy busted his buh-utt!" Tom laughs so hard he starts to stagger, then tosses himself onto the cot and rocks, his feet kicking in the air.

Billy cries and picks up each cigarette carefully, looking at his brother between each one. "You better hush," he keeps saying. "Better huh-ush."

Then Billy walks calmly over to the picnic table in the corner and picks up a Dr. Pepper bottle from a Royal Crown bench and whizzes it at the cot and it shatters against the stone wall a foot above Tom's head.

I shake the glass off the front of my shirt and it twinkles weakly in the dim light of the three bulbs, speckled with horse flies, that dangle from the ceiling.

Tom, his body frozen in the rocking position, looks at Billy with mock awe and astonishment, then slowly gets up. "All right, by god, all right, by god, now you're going *to get it.*"

"Well. . . . Well. . . . Well. . . . Well, you made me slip and bust my ass, didn't you?"

Tom looks Billy dead in the eyes. "I'm gonna-beat-the–livin'-hell-out-of–you."

Tom chased Billy for almost five minutes, all over the big bull-pen. Watching such a burst of energy was so tiring I had to sit down. The severely carved initials on the top of the school desk I sat on felt like they made designs on my buttocks.

"They should-a drowned the little bastards," says the man in overalls, philo-sophically, "the day they was borned," and he goes into the toilet booth in the far corner, slamming the door. When Billy slams into the partition, the man says, "I'm gonna *kill* me a couple a hellions 'dreckly."

Billy cracks his knee against the iron frame of a cot and doubles over in pain, and Tom catches up with him and starts slapping his head and face. Bucky watches every movement, becoming so absorbed his mouth goes slack and his eyes get bleary and then I realize the performance has *me* hypnotized, too.

"I'll kill your ass, you sonofabitching low-life bastard," says Billy, slugging into Tom. Tom slaps him until his arms weary, and then he walks away, leaving Billy screaming, shuddering on the cot.

"Tom!" a woman calls from out in the yard below.

He goes to the window, panting, red from exertion in the humid air. "Ma'am?"

"Are you beating on Billy again?"

"Yes, ma'am."

"Well, quit it!"

"Yes, ma'am, I will."

Tom had the cigarettes again, lit one, offered Bucky one, then me, but I don't smoke, and then he tapped the toilet door. "Hey, Pete, your momma allow you to smoke yet?

"Better not get close enough for me to smack you."

"She's coming over." He tossed a cigarette over the top of the booth.

Billy had stopped screaming at the top of his lungs, and shifted into low.

"Cry baby," says Tom, passing Billy's cot. He lies down on his own cot and smokes.

Bucky was still in a zombie-like state from all the narcotics they had given him at El Reno and from present fear and nervousness. The charm he had turned on his victims was deeply submerged. I told him what I had gotten done that day, and he had a sullen, resentful, bitter word for each of his victims.

"Now, Bucky, they want to help you. Why shouldn't they want their money, too? *Before*, they were more interested in your hide."

When it finally soaked in that their attitude could keep him off the chain gang, he sneered at their gullibility. That annoyed me.

I began to defend them. I reminded him of the visit the man from Western Auto had paid him. "He said you just wised off at him." Bucky denied it, tried to blame Mr. Carpetti, suggested he and the Judge were friends and out to get him. "He said you called him an s.o.b."

"Liar."

"He said you did, now Bucky."

Bucky looked shocked. "Would you believe a stranger 'fore you'd believe your own broth-er?" We were sitting on his cot and he scooted down a little so he could register his shock more dramatically. He wasn't consciously conning me, he was just reaching for the available clichés. If he detected the slightest blood disloyalty—as he did then—he would go into a profound sulk. You could have sliced the silence with a jack knife.

Pete ambles out of the toilet-booth and lies down in the 40 watt light and smokes.

Billy's whimpering. Tom gets up and goes over and sits on Billy's cot and pats him on the shoulder. "Poor ol' Billy, come on, honey, don't cry, come on now. You hear?" He lights a cigarette and leans over and tries to look into Billy's face, stroking him with one hand, offering the cigarette with the other, crooning, "Don't cry, little Billy boy, don't criiiii." Billy pulls the covers over his head. Tom goes back to his cot.

From under the covers, Billy says, "Wait'll I tell the judge. I hope they *do* 'lectricute you."

"Didn't I say I was sorry?"

Bucky smiles and looks at me. "Who they remind you of?" I pretended not to see it, because I didn't want to go over it. "Me and you, when we was little, and you used to beat hell out of me for something, and then...."

That started it. So I sat at the head of his cot, my back against the stone wall, and Bucky, half-reclined on the rest of the cot, talked in a resonant, mellow voice about our childhood in Knoxville, still pronouncing certain words in the childish way he has. It embarrassed me to listen to it at first, because I am afflicted with a terrible nostalgia. Sometimes I have seizures of nostalgia at night that hurt.

One night I was sleeping in the lush grass by the shore under a beached boat in the Russian fishing village of Ninilchik on the Kenai Peninsula in Alaska, and I woke up to take a leak. As I looked across the water at an extinct volcano, bathed in that strange northern light, an intuition of my whole childhood rushed over me. Now I remember that *Alaskan* moment with a strange sadness and melancholy of its own.

Psychiatrists would say we had a traumatic childhood, and I guess the broken home, the bad environment, and all that, had the predictable effect on Earl and Bucky, but I remember none of it with anything but affection. Earl was nine when Daddy started drinking and staying gone three days at a stretch, so he didn't even have to live through the worst part as a little kid the way Bucky and I did.

But we were depression babies, and Earl and I had to carry our lunches in a lard pail, with our own milk in a Mason jar, and I guess it was supposed to be humiliating. Earl, anyway, realizing that a boy deserved something better, would steal cans of pineapple from the A&P and at the lunch table he would pull them out and, with a big taunting smile on his face like the Joker in Batman comics, he'd open a can with a little stolen can opener and eat the pineapple, smacking his lips, while the well-to-do kids watched in envy.

Earl takes after my daddy—get what you can out of people with as little effort as possible, but if things go wrong, don't blame anybody, don't feel malice, resentment, or hatred. Daddy took to drink, and Earl took to the con game as ways of dealing with life, and both of them take things as they come.

But Bucky takes after my mother, seems like. She had a good life in Cleveland when she was a girl, up till she was about sixteen, then the depression hit my grandaddy who was doing well in the glass business, and they started going down, and had to return to Knoxville, till one day he shot himself, and Momma had to go to work in a cafe, and she met this handsome, soft-spoken easygoing fellow from South Knoxville, and he turned out not to be much count, so she ended up with the attitude that the world had betrayed her, men in particular.

Raised three boys during the depression and the war, while Daddy was in the ambulance corps, and every chance she could, she played the angle that she was a poor little woman whose husband had more or less deserted her. It just so happens that she did put up a good fight and people admired her for it, and Bucky loves her more than anything on earth. Just before he left El Reno, he almost went berserk worrying about her, and they had to let him talk to her on the telephone to pacify him. He was worried about her now because of her broken leg.

Well, the kind of childhood we had, you'd think you'd want to forget, but even when I was six years old, I used to go to sleep after a ritual in two parts. First, I'd review my life until I sensed I was about to go to sleep, then I'd stop, and pick it up the next night like a serial, and then I'd talk to God in a chummy way, and that's how I'd drift off.

So Bucky in his cell stirred all that up in me. "And remember that time we went to the show and the ticket man grabbed me as I ran in and ripped my shirt off and you picked up a cigarette butt urn and threatened to frail hell out of him? He thought I was going in without a ticket but I was so eager to see the next chapter of *Red Ryder* that I just raced on in, and you screamed at him for tearing my only good shirt, and then when I wouldn't leave after the show was over, you started pulling at me and slapping me and I was screaming in the lobby and some man came up and said he was going to beat hell out of you if you didn't quit slapping that sweet little boy—*me*. Ha! Remember?"

I'd never forgotten. I says, "Yeah, and remember," trying to steer him my way, "that creek we always crossed on the way to the show?"

"Yeah. Fartso, the whale."

"The who?" Tom is lying on his stomach, his face propped in his hands, listening to us.

"Lucius used to tell me there was this whale named Fartso—"

"It was Earl told *me*."

"—that lived in the creek and we'd throw popcorn down to him, and I kept trying to see him. That went on for five years, me believing there really was a whale that would give you presents if you were good."

"Hey, Tom," says Billy, peeling the blanket off his face, "you remember that ghost horse you used to tell me about, and you said it was going to come some night and take me and you away from the orphanage?"

"Shhhh," says Tom, "Can't you hear it? He's out yonder eating Mrs. Thompson's morning glories."

Billy jumps up and leans on the sill and looks out through the bars. "Hey, where? Hey, where at?"

"Ahhhhhh. The springs popping in your cot scared him away."

"You ought to heard the stories Lucius used to tell me and Earl when we was little. We slept in the same bed and we'd get under the quilts and Lucius'd tell us stories about Captain Marvel and Zorro and Straight-hair and Fatsy—Laurel and Hardy. They'd forget to put on their clothes in the morning—Straight-hair and Fatsy—and get on the streetcar and these old ladies would say, 'Eow! Butts and do-dos!'"

"Hey, mister, if I turn out the lights, will you tell *us* a story?"

Billy's standing up in his cot, looking at me, his eyes bright.

"Yeah, mister," says Tom. "Tell us a story, tell us a story."

"Hate to get started and have to go. It's dark outside, and I reckon they're ready to kick me out."

"Hell," says Tom. "You could sleep *here,* far as that goes. Folks passing through stay the night here all the time. Sheriff Thompson's a good ol' feller."

"Go ahead, Lucius," says Bucky. "Tell one, like you used to."

Billy giggles and runs the length of the room, leaping into the air to catch the light cords until all three lights and faces blink out and only the bright moon looks in.

Says Tom, "Make it a ghost story."

"Ouuuu," says Billy, and jumps over Bucky's cot and climbs under the wool blanket with his big brother.

"Get ready for bed first."

They shuck off their shorts and snuggle in. Pete's under the covers, too, his back toward us like a wall. Bucky smokes Luckies, and I get set to tell it. I don't know any ghost stories by heart, so I make one up as I go along, about a blood-stained carpet. Billy and Tom are chewing gum, popping and smacking, till I reach a scarey part, and they stop and the gum lolls out on the tip of their tongues in the moonlight. Bucky stops smoking, a long ash on his cigarette, and Pete turns over and looks straight at me, his eyes glazed, and in the pause, we hear cars outside in the distance rumble over bridges, and dogs bark, off in the trees.

Near the climax, a key turns in the lock and slowly, responding to the moonlight and the hush and the smell that softened all his movements, the Sheriff walks in. His head bumps a light bulb, and he's slender, a little bent, and wears a gun, slack on his hip. I pause while we watch him amble to the foot of Pete's cot.

"Pete, I been a-lookin' all day fer that gun. I'm wore out."

"Well, Frank, I been studying that over. No use in you hunting and hunting. Hell, I mize well show you where I threw the damn thing."

"Okay, bright and early we'll go out yonder."

"Shhhhh," says Tom, his finger to his lips. The Sheriff turns slowly and looks at him. "Bucky's brother's trying to tell us the finish of a ghost story."

"Well, I *thought* they was somebody sitting with you all in the dark there."

"Let him tell it, Sheriff," says Billy.

"Well, *I* ain't stopping nobody."

But he just sort of dangles there in the moonlight, so I ease back into the story, and the next thing I know, he's sitting on the foot of Pete's cot, listening. Just as the blood-stained Persian rug raises up and smothers the killer, the Sheriff's wife calls up the stairs for him to come to bed.

"You welcome to stay," the Sheriff says, and I say, thanks, and he locks us all in, and as he's going down the stairs, he says, "Goodnight, Baby Jo," and a voice on the other side of the wall calls out, "Goodnight, Sheriff."

"Goodnight, Baby Jo!" yells Billy.

And they all yell goodnight back and forth, and I figure Baby Jo is a Negro, in a segregated cell.

I took a cot, and Billy was asleep, curled up against his brother, who fell asleep just as I looked his way, and Pete was gone, and Bucky, doped with the past, said, "See you in the morning," and I said, "Night," and in a few 'drecklies night was in us all.

Next morning, a backfiring truck woke me, and when I looked out the window, it was a peach truck, so I sneaked down to the square, using the key in my pocket, and got a sack full.

I left all but one on the picnic table, and quietly locked Bucky in the cell and put the key above the silver-painted door.

The white kitchen door stood open at the end of the hall, and Majel's bending over a round table, taking a last sup of coffee, already setting the cup down as she swings her hip out to miss the curve, and she comes at me fast, the fluffy pompons bouncing on her snow-white boots, the luscious ruffles on her low cut, white cotton, fresh-ironed blouse waving as she bounces, one arm held stiff by a blue suitcase, and I thought she was going to run me down, but she tucks the baton under her arm as she gets to me and gives me a glancing kiss and a flick of her hip as she rushes on, and what she tosses over her shoulder is, "I'd love to give you a *pre*-view, but I'm about to miss my bus to Knoxville." When I get to the porch screen, she's aiming for the open door of a Greyhound bus, twirling her baton like a buzz saw.

I started out walking to look for the county prosecutor's office. Somebody directed me down a steep hill from the square to an old white, wooden house. Grass stood high in the front yard and grasshoppers flew up as I went along the walk. Two black and white spotted dogs on the porch lifted their heads and started raising hell. A window shoots up to my right and a man sticks out his head, says, "Ace, I reckon you and Hoppy want me to dump another spittoon on your heads! Now hush!" in a voice louder than the dogs. His black-streaked gray hair stirred up on his head, his face red as a beet, his eyes swollen, his lips whitish—the look of him makes me turn away, sure I've got somebody's house, not a lawyer's office, but he says, "What *you* want so early?"

And I say, "This where Jack Babcock's office is?"

"It's his bedroom till the office opens. You didn't fiddle around getting here, did you? Bucky goes before Judge Stumbo Monday at two."

"Oh, you know who I—"

"With that face and that walk? Swing around the porch to the side door."

He comes to the door in wrinkled trousers and a white shirt open to his navel, showing a hairy pot, and the smell of him hits me below the belt.

"They all described him by his walk, and when I saw him amble into the courtroom with Sheriff Thompson for the indictment, I knew why. Half-cocky, half-friendly, half-better-look-out."

What I walked into was the image of an old-time law office, full of old-fashioned furniture, and what he pointed to when he said, "Sit down, Lucius," was an old cracked-leather couch. I felt Babcock's warm sleep in the seat of my pants. He went into the bathroom.

And when he comes out again, he has on a tie and his hair's combed perfectly, parted almost in the middle, with a wave on one side, and two cups of coffee steam, as if by magic, in his hands. I take one as he blows at his coffee and lets his broad butt and pot belly sink into the leather cushion.

"How's Bucky?"

"Well, just waiting, sir."

"Aren't we all!" I didn't look at him.

"Bucky tells me you're a writer."

"I do write, yes, sir."

"Jack. I'm Jack, and you're Lucius, okay?"

"Okay, Jack."

"See all them books that's got you surrounded?"

"Law books?"

"Full, chock full of stories."

So he took me on a two hour tour of legal documents containing vivid testimony concerning various sexual exploits from mere exposure to rape, from 1821 to 1956, and then he shows me a revolver he used on a German prisoner guard inside Buchenwald concentration camp, and says, "Write a story about *that*." And running all through it like a thread is Bucky, and I imagined not only that Jack had done a production for *him*, but that I was merely an affable stand-in for a rerun.

Then we steered straight onto Bucky, Jack interrogating me about Bucky's background, till his eyes were misty. "Steam from the cup," he said, blowing on the cold coffee. "But don't depend on Bucky's sad story with Judge Stumbo. The first fact you got to face is that Stumbo's been to the end of the line and come back. The gooks chopped off his son's head in Korea, and if you see a sporty little red Ford convertible, that's all the old man's got left. And second fact is that he's *always* been mean, and he hates my guts almost as much as I hate his."

"Then I'm afraid even to ask you—"

"Askin's free."

"Whether you think he'll let me pay off these people a little at a time over the next year or so out of my teacher's pay."

"Lucius, we may as well kiss Bucky goodbye."

When Saturday morning country people started coming in to see him, I told Jack I'd see him later.

By the time I got back up to the top of the hill, I was dizzy with the heat. The sun glanced off cars and pickup trucks parked rib to rib facing the courthouse and in the outer square facing the stores.

As though duty-bound to authenticate the cliché, old men were parked hip to hip on the benches around the courthouse, talking, spitting, whittling, gazing silently out from the hub of law, order, tradition, and sloth, sitting in the cool, under skyscraper oak trees that spread out so lush at the top they covered the clock-face in the tower.

"Hey, there, Hutchfield, you got any more of them ghost stories?" Through the leaves of a low-hanging, spread-fingered limb of the oak, I saw Sheriff Thompson leaning on the sill of a wide window, smoking, waving. I laughed and waved, he chuckled and glanced around to somebody deep in the cavey-cool and dark of the office and dusted his cigarette on the ground, where no grass grew. His clothes were a little wrinkled and slouchy but he had the ghost of Gary Cooper going for him. Then to his side, suddenly, steps a man in a severely ironed and creased khaki uniform, and a glistening leather belt and holster, and slick yellow hair give him a corseted look, and he waves me in.

"Come to get your brother off the chain gang. Right?" says the well groomed cop, as I come in the door.

"To put it subtly, yes."

"I *told* you he was a card," says the Sheriff. "Hutchfield, this is Mr. McCoy of the Georgia Bureau of Investigation. Me and him was the ones went to Oklahoma to bring back your brother."

"And me and Bucky," says McCoy, "were the ones nursed this old coot back to life. Broke down on us in Kansas City and we had to sit around a hospital room three days before we could come on in."

"Sit around ever' Kansas City bar and strip joint ever was, you mean, while I was *dying*."

"I never heard *this* story," I says, so they tell it, together, with the precision, pace, and thrust of a duet.

"But my advice to *you*, son," says McCoy, "is to turn around and go right back to Knoxville. Number One, that brother of yours is a habitual criminal. Guys can murder once, and stop. They can rob and stop, sooner or later. But you take your check passer or your con man, they don't *never* give it up. So you may as well give up on your brother, now as later."

"Well, I think there's hope for Bucky. I know what you mean, Mr. McCoy. Earl's like that, but Bucky can be saved. Earl can't. Bucky's in it out of bewilderment—always getting the world's signals crossed. But Earl's in it for love. And it's the *only* love he knows."

"This your older brother?"

"Yeah."

"Ain't no love 'tween Bucky and *him*. That long ride back, all I heard was how Bucky was gonna make Earl sorry."

"We all got tickled, thinking up ways he could do it," says the Sheriff, "and it two a.m. on the highway and me sick as a hog in the back seat."

"You know, I once asked Earl, since he never seems to get away with it, why he does it—passes checks and stuff."

"It's the thrill of it," says McCoy.

"That's what *he* said."

"Hell, I didn't have to *ask* him."

"Way *he* put it was, 'You walk into a store and you fox a man into your confidence and you charm the money out of his pocket, and when I walk out,' he says, 'I feel great. It's not the money. Look,' he says, 'I take a chance. When I lose, that's *my* tough luck. Next time, I'll know how to get away with it.' He's never bitter toward—toward you guys, or the people who bring charges, or the prison officials. It's just tough, and that's his attitude."

"I like a guy with a good attitude, don't you, Frank?"

"I pre*fer* 'em."

I didn't go into Bucky's attitude, how he's always, since he was little, felt the injustice of it all. Somehow or other, somebody has sold him out, led him astray, it's not his fault, he can't help it, it all started when he was too young to control it. The evidence in his favor is overwhelming. Besides, that's what he's been told all his life. And he believes everything he's told, by this authority and that—by me, and by Earl, and by books, and by ads, slogans, salutes, pledges, promises, all the home truths. But when he rams his hand into one of those Christmas stockings up to the elbow and the smell of what's in it hits him, he gets that look on his face of awed surprise and hurt.

I say, "Another thing about Earl. One time when he was just out, and I was going to the University of Tennessee, we took a ride through the old neighborhood and parked in front of the house, the one out of about twenty-five that we grew up in, where we lived the longest and had the most fun—the house where he accidentally broke open Bucky's head with a baseball bat— but that's another story—and I says, 'Well, Earl, I hope you've given it up for good.' 'Lucius,' he says, solemnly, 'I've learned my lesson. I'm through. I'd rather die than go back.' I says, 'You know, Earl, the thing that's always scared me is that when the FBI is tracking you, you might take to a gun, and—' By the red light of the semaphore above us, I saw the hurt look on his face. 'Lucius! You think your own brother'd do a thing like that?' He likes to keep his image in as sharp a focus as the next man. At the time, he had a job driving a truck on a run to Texas. It paid well. He even urged me to accept a little loan of twenty bucks. A week later, they caught him smuggling marijuana back over the border."

A Negro boy of about eighteen shows up in the door with a sickle in his hand. "I'm about to cut, Mr. Frank."

"You can't cut those weeds in this heat, Baby Jo." He was the boy the sheriff had spoken to last night as he went down. Turned out, he was an orphan that they let sleep in the jail and do odd jobs.

"I don't mind to cut it, Mister Frank."

"You wait till the sun goes down, you hear?"

"I don't mind to cut it, Mister Frank."

"You want to get a heat stroke?"

"I don't mind it."

"Okay, but when the sun starts to boil, you get in the shade, you hear?"

Baby Jo nods and backs out.

Then I ask them if they want to hear a little story about Earl? "I'd sight rather *hear* about 'em than track 'em down," said McCoy.

"Stick around till dark, and he'll rip off a ghost story for you."

"One time, soon after he was released from prison in—I forget where—Earl was traveling for a magazine subscription outfit, and he was using the district manager's car, going up and over the hills of North Carolina, and it was late and he was fagged out, and he woke up in a hospital bed, with a state trooper sitting by his side. The threat of the trooper focused the picture quickly, and behind the trooper he saw his coat hanging on a hook on the open closet door, with a book of phony checks sticking out of his inside pocket.

"'Driving a little recklessly, weren't you, Mr. Hutchfield?'" says the trooper, noticing Earl's eyes are open.

"'I guess I was, sir,' says Earl. 'I went to sleep at the wheel. I've been working pretty hard this week and I was trying to get home to my wife and kids.'

"'Know what you mean,' says the trooper. 'I was on the way home to mine, too, just off duty, when I saw you writing your name on the landscape.'

"'Will I be okay?'

"'You *feel* okay?'

"Earl says he feels like he could make it on home. Trooper asks him where he lives, and he says Bristol, Virginia, and the trooper says, 'Oh, yeah,' he had a good buddy, used to be a trooper, running one of those *big* jobs where they're constructing the U.S. interstate highway. 'What's his name?' Earl asks. 'Earl Moretz.' 'Earl Moretz!' says Earl. 'Good drinking buddy of mine. In the VFW., right?' Earl asks, because he likes to take risks. 'Yeah,' says the trooper.

"So they chat about good ol' Earl Moretz.

"About an hour later, Earl gets ready to leave, and the trooper says, 'Sorry, but I got to take you over to the courthouse and fine you. Serious traffic violation.'

"'Sure,' says Earl, and he goes to pay his hospital bill. When the nurse says it's twenty dollars, Earl asks if it's okay to write a check, and she says, no, it's not.

"But when the trooper, who's known her since she was a baby, says, 'It's okay, he's a friend of Earl Moretz, the check's okay,' she says, 'Then go ahead.'

"'Could I make it for a little over the amount,' says Earl, 'so I can gas up my car and get on home?'

"'The trooper says, 'It's okay, isn't it?' and she says, 'I reckon.'

"Then the trooper tells Earl he'll have to sit around the police station until nine o'clock (it's just seven) till the judge comes in. Earl says it's his kid's birthday and he promised to take him to a ballgame, and couldn't the trooper take the check and give it to the judge? Finally, the trooper says okay, but let's see if your car works okay, so he took him over to the filling station, and that pulled in five more guys, and they all had another hour of Earl Moretz, while they got the car to running, and then Earl wrote a check for the trooper to give the judge, and got change from the trooper's own pocket, and then wrote a check for fixing the car, and got change, and when he passes the city limits, he has one hundred dollars in cash, and a large charge, and three more years in a North Carolina prison waiting for him."

"And you'll be telling the same story about Bucky 'fore long," says McCoy. "What your big brother's got is contagious and your little brother is infected with a full dose of it."

"Bucky, hell," says the Sheriff. "What about *this* one? Here I should be out scrounging around a cornfield for that gun Pete used on his wife, and 'stead of that, I'm listening to bedtime stories at high noon."

"What *I'm* trying to figure out is what you doing here in the first place," said McCoy, "less you expect to work on the judge. . . . Hit it, didn't I? Well, forget it, son. You'd have better luck with that statue of Judge Stumbo's great-grand-father about to fall off his horse in front of the courthouse. Am I right, Frank?"

"I'd *swear* to it. *You* all make yourselves at home. I'm riding," says the Sheriff, like it was an all-occasion exit line.

"And not only that, what you got a lawyer for, if you gonna do the tear-jerking on your own?"

"What lawyer?"

"The one up from Florida."

"That's one more than I know anything about."

"Maybe your momma hired him since you left Knoxville."

"Not likely, though to get Bucky off that chain gang, she *could* have done *any*thing."

"Well, this lawyer came to see me this morning down in Gainesville where I'm based, and he was wearing a white Panama suit with a wide-brimmed Panama hat, driving a white 1942 Lincoln Mercury Zephyr in mint condition. Fellow with black hair and a mustache and a cigarette holder. And carrying a shiny, shiny briefcase."

"That's pretty good, Mr. McCoy, pretty funny. You're not a bad con man yourself, but you don't expect me to believe anybody'd be seen in public look-ing like *that*, do you?"

McCoy laughs and slaps me on the shoulder. "You really *are* a card, ain't you?"

In the downstairs hallway of the jailhouse, a young man with numerous little waves in his red hair was talking to the Sheriff's wife. He wore a flowery tie, held a red-leather Bible, and sweat from his armpits molded his white shirt to his ribs. They blocked the silver door, so I stood to the side while they finished talking.

"Way I done, I went up there like I'd just come to see Bucky Hutchfield, because he sent word he wanted a visit from a preacher, but I seen it was a good chance to *talk* to them *boys*." He's very solemn, as though standing in a church he's built with his own words. "But I kinda drew them into it, and before I left, I had them all three down on their knees, giving their hearts to Jesus. Sister Edna, it was a blessed thing. If they'd just let Jesus in sooner, maybe none of this misery would have happened."

"Well, law, when kids ain't got no mother. . . ."

She smiled at me, then stepped aside so I could reach the key on the ledge. I went on up, ready to behold an angelic scene—Bucky, Tom, and Billy on their knees, sanctified. But before I reached the door, I heard springs bouncing rambunctiously, and then there's little Billy humping his cot sixty miles an hour, yelling, "Give me some poontang! Hey, preacher, get me some poontang, please, preacher!"

Bucky and Tom were laughing at him, doubled up on their cots, and Pete is just fading into the toilet booth, slamming the door behind him, disgusted. "Heatherns!"

"Hey, Lucius, you missed it, buddy!" says Tom, running to me. He did a perfect imitation of both the preacher, who turned out to be a student from the seminary ten miles down the pike, and of Billy. He acted out the preacher working on Billy for ten sweating minutes, inviting him to get washed in the blood of the lamb, and Billy nodding his head, finally saying, "Yes, sir, preacher, yes, sir, I want to be washed whiter than snow." When he asked Billy if he could get him anything, Billy said, "Please, preacher, all I want is me a red Bible like the one you got." And Tom acted out how Billy, as soon as the preacher shut the door downstairs, yelled out, "I'd rather have some poontang!"

That got Bucky and me into a long story about the three McAnally girls that Earl and Bucky and I used to play jungle with back in Knoxville down along the Tennessee River, and how we'd take turns being Tarzan and Jane and Boy and Cheetah, and how there were always two left out—Bucky and Millie, because they were too little. Then Bucky told how they would give up and go off and play Tarzan and Jane all by themselves.

Bucky was happy with the young preacher's promise to drive fifty miles up to Chattanooga to see Reverend Dunlap, a preacher who used to visit Bucky when he was in jail up there, waiting to be picked up by the Tennessee Bureau of Investigation to stand trial in Nashville years ago. Reverend Dunlap, he was certain, would drive down and try to soften Judge Stumbo.

But when I told him what Jack and the Sheriff and McCoy said about the judge, and when I reviewed the possibilities, Bucky started to cry. Because he had lain on the cot for a week, imagining me driving up to the rescue, getting him out of there.

I lingered with them until almost dark, then I went out and got them some hot dogs and a big orange apiece, and then to pacify Bucky, I put in a call to Knoxville to see how momma was.

Momma said she was doing okay, except that the cast was heavy and her crutches hurt her, and she wished she could go dancing. Then she asked if I thought she ought to come down to Blairsville. I told her I didn't see that it would do any good. She said, "But don't you think if I come down there on crutches, they'd see how much Bucky's mother believed in him, and maybe they'd. . . . Well, you know. . . ."

I told her I knew exactly what she meant, but that I had all angles pretty well under control.

I felt guilty locking Bucky and the kids in and going to the movies, but I was bone weary, worrying about Judge Stumbo's personality.

I was about to open the door of the screened porch when Mrs. Thompson called to me from inside the house. She held the telephone out to me when I came into the room.

"It's your daddy—long distance from Knoxville. Barely make out your name, he's so sloppy drunk."

He was drunker than that. "Lucius" was about all I could make out, and I've had years of practice, trying to net the little silver fish that leap up out of the muddy stream of his drunken gibberish. The penalty for falling for the lovable drunk notion is that you've got to hold still for a lot of unlovable flotsam.

As he let it flow, I remembered the bright Sunday morning a cop car pulled up in front of the house and Momma had to take her bathrobe out to it so Daddy could get from the curb to the living room without the neighbors seeing he had on only his shorts and a hangover. The cops had found him under a viaduct, stripped of all but his shorts, into which he had probably peed in fright as drunks were stripping him.

As Daddy's voice rose and fell on the phone, crooned and crowed, I remembered the year after he came back from the war and Momma had divorced him as hopeless—the nights when he would stand out in the streets or up on the railroad tracks that rose on a clay bank above our house and call for me. "Lucius! Hey, Lucius! Ho, Lucius! It's you daddy, son!" And Momma'd finally say, "Go out to him, and pacify him, Lucius," and I'd go out at two a.m. to pacify him, and end up gathering material for stories, because as the track chilled my tail, he would tell about the way it was when he served under General Patton. He had a theory that Patton was really murdered, because so many people thought he was a sonofabitch, and he'd kill anybody that said he was.

Then he'd tell the story about sitting under a tree cutting his toenails with a bayonet and limping quickly over to the aid-tent when he stuck himself, and starting back for his boots just as a mortar shell shivered the tree to bits, and somehow I always connected that with Patton not being a sonofabitch. He mourned his failure to live up to such luck.

"Son," he'd say, "if I could write stories, we'd *all* be rich."

Finally, he passed out on the phone, and I hung up, and I drove down to see *War and Peace*, showing in Dahlonega at the drive-in.

Coming back, passing Jack's office, I saw a light in the window, showing through the mist. Craving company, I pulled in the driveway.

The inner door was open, so I saw him through the screen door, feeling behind the law books. He turned, a bottle in his hand, his fingers about to turn the cap, then he saw me, saluted with the bottle. Suddenly, the two bird dogs are at the door, standing rigidly, their noses to the screen, their teeth bubbling with spit.

"Ace! Hoppy! Don't you eat that boy! Sit!" They wiggle-backed off and sat, and I went in.

"They pissed off at me cause I quit hunting. Have a drink." I did. "Sit down." I sat on the leather couch and he stood in front of me. "So you want to know why I drink. I didn't *used* to drink. Know what I *used* to do when she kicked me out? I'd drive out to that little island in the middle of the intersection of Highway 19 and 76, right under the blinker, and park. Smoke me a cigar in the dark. Then I'd come here and sleep. Some people—well, most anybody around here would think I was crazy." He took a swig from the bottle. "You know, sitting there, like that, out in the middle of the night, smoking a White Owl. Sometimes at two-thirty in the morning, mist fogging up my windshield, car filling up with smoke. And *drive*—I love to drive at night, you know? Just, by God, drive on down to Atlanta if I have to. Get it out of my damn system.

"Because if I didn't, I think I'm capable of doing a little harm. That's why I come straight *here* now, and don't go no further, and bring along these gentlemen to watch me. *They* know what I'm up to before I do it."

"You're like us, Jack—me and Bucky and Earl. Always got to keep moving, us Hutchfields. Between us, we've covered every town in this country."

"Hell, I rode the rails in the thirties. If I wasn't tied down to the law, I'd walk out. But see, we lost our kid, and we can't have no more, so I got to overlook the way she treats me, don't I? The only thing wrong with *her* is me. Now, listen, you the only one I ever told about the traffic island, because you a poet, see, just like me, hell, by God, I'm a poet, too. Hell, look at Edgar Allan Poe. You listening?"

"I'm listening," I said, like it's the first time I ever said that to anybody.

"*I'll* give you something to write about. Hell, I'm a character. Folks all the time say, and not to be funny neither, 'You know something, Jack, you're a real character.' Why, if I was to tell you my life story, you wouldn't believe it."

He told it, and I believed it. Because I had heard it *before*—in Knoxville, New York, New Orleans, San Francisco, Denver, in the army in Alaska, at sea, en route to Panama, to Chile, and other points east, west, north, and south. I reckon some people are born listeners and some are born tellers, and some, like me, are double blessed and damned.

Toward the end, his sweaty red face started working and writhing like a can of worms, glistening in the light, and pretty soon gushing tears and slobber. I was a little uneasy when the bird dogs started tail-thumping and whining, glancing at me like it was my fault. Then he went to sleep, and I climbed the hill and crossed the square to the jail.

Hanging from a tree near the screened porch below the jail, a truck tire swing looked awful still in the streetlight, and I smelled the juice of the weeds Baby Jo'd cut, and the honeysuckle vines clinging to the side of the porch.

As I stepped up to the screen, a voice says, "Look out! Here he comes, with another ghost story," and as he took a draw, the tip of his cigarette lit up the Sheriff's face. I opened the screen and there was somebody sitting with him on the glider, his face, his bare arms and feet pale in the filtered moonlight. "Me and Pete's having us a beer. Old lady's sawing logs, so we thought we'd sneak down a few. Bite the cap off one, Hutchfield."

"No, thanks, Sheriff."

I fell asleep on my cell cot that night with an image of Majel, sitting on the front seat of that Greyhound bus in her costume, her legs apart, lapping up the miles to Knoxville.

The next day was Sunday, and all I did was sit around the jail with Bucky and Billy and Tom and Pete, eating peaches. I got Henry James out of the car and tried to read in him a little just to keep in shape, but the kids kept distracting me with their antics and their wild, rich talk, so, deciding to "try to be one of those on whom nothing is lost," I shut up *The Sacred Fount.*

But I couldn't relax, worried about the judge's reaction when I offered to pay for crime on the installment plan.

So I went out and put through some phone calls to Bucky's victims, hoping I could persuade them to agree to that arrangement. I had given them all the impression they would get the full amount tomorrow.

Mr. Overby said he was going to have Bucky's ass in a sling, Mr. Crigger said he had hospital bills to pay, and Pap declared that suffering was good for the soul—look at Job and what it did for him—and he wished it on all his friends, including me. And the Western Auto man said the company expected him to make an example of Bucky.

Since I'm not effective on the telephone, I didn't try any kind of plea.

When I got back at about twilight, Bucky was lying on his cot, gazing glassy-eyed at Tom as he chased Billy with an R C bottle, and Pete's bare feet showed below the toilet partition, and from down stairs the aromas of Sunday dinner—green beans, corn bread, and fried chicken—drifted up.

"I just been laying here worrying about momma."

"Well, that's fine. She's probably awake worrying about you. And Earl's probably lying awake trying to figure a way to con somebody out of some change, and that'll be something else to keep Momma awake. String all the nights like this together and what do you get, Bucky?"

"What the hell you mean by *that*?"

"Nothing. And don't give me that hurt look. Goodnight."

"Well, by god, you can go off and let them throw me on the chain gang, if *that's* the way you feel about it! Hell, I ain't begging *no* damn body!"

"Shut up and go to sleep." I stormed out of the cell in a huff.

I walked a while, then I drove around town, and I even parked on Jack's traffic island under the blinker, and later passed his place, but the light was out, and then I parked outside the jail and walked some more down the streets of the town, and when I got back to the square the moonlight had soothed my nerves.

On the corner in front of the courthouse, the front of my baby blue Buick streamliner was jacked up over a U.S. mailbox, one light smashed, the other glaring at the moon, the four doors slung wide open, a rear tire flat.

When I got up to the cell, Sheriff Thompson was squatting between two cots, petting Tom with one hand, and Billy with the other, the two kids lying on their stomachs, the rough blankets over their heads, crying worse than I had yet heard them, and in the past two days they had hurt each other at least twenty times. Bucky leaned against the wall, squatting, too, trying to tease Tom, in a sweet way, out of crying.

Under the weak electric light, Pete stood, one hand clapped over his mouth. I went up to him and asked him what was going on, and just then somebody kicks me in the tail. The first time in my life anybody *ever* kicked me in the tail. As I turned, thinking it was Bucky, Pete let his hand fall from his mouth, and it and his hand were bloody. Pointing his finger at me, the Sheriff says, "And *you* left the damned door open."

"I was mad at Bucky, I guess I forgot—"

"And *that* big hog," he says, pointing at Pete, "got mad at the kids and blabbed what I told him. Does it hurt much?"

"Yeah," whines Pete.

"Good."

"What happened, Sheriff?" He turns his back on me and tries to console the kids.

Bucky came over to me and told me that the Sheriff had heard from the hospital that Tom's and Billy's foster mother had died of the gunshot wound, and then Pete, out of spite, told the kids, and said he heard that Judge Stumbo was going to send Tom to prison and Billy to another foster home, so the kids tried to run away in my car.

"Some idiot failed to lock you all in."

The racket eased off a little, and I said I'd go sleep in the car.

"No, by god!" says the Sheriff. "You're spending the night in jail!"

After everybody was settled and it got dead quiet, I said, "Bucky . . . Bucky . . . Bucky."

"Yeah, what?"

"I called up all those people a while ago and tried to get them to agree to let me pay them a little each month, but they said they had to have the cold cash tomorrow." He didn't say anything. "Bucky . . . Bucky . . . Bucky. . . ."

I wanted to lull him to sleep with a solution, as, in our childhood, I often lulled him to sleep with a story. But I had no solution and he was beyond the consolation of a story.

Then I got an idea, a verge-of-sleep idea that blended into a dream. To get the cash to pay off his victims, I could pass some bad checks in Chattanooga. With the completion of my dissertation, I would move progressively into a state of academic rigidity: tenure, marriage, kids, house, new car, the whole show—a bomb. But by passing the checks, I could save my brother, who, it was dead certain, would go berserk, plunge into a deep depression that could get him killed on the chain gang, where there were so many hair-trigger possibilities.

And besides, I always wondered what it would be like to have unlimited time to write (and I wondered, too, whether I had my brothers' talent for controlling life, at least for the duration of a con), and as I fell asleep the names of Cervantes, Milton, Dostoyevsky, Genet, and other great prison writers chimed in my mind.

But when I woke the next morning, my mind was on the judge. The Sheriff let me out before the others were awake, and I went up and backed my car off the mailbox, then went into the courthouse to work on Judge Stumbo.

The judge's secretary's long black hair, with a pompadour, took me back to the forties. In her blue skirt, white sleeveless blouse, spike heels, and stockings with a lustrous sheen in the dewy morning light, she had a hard-life, country-come-to-town prettiness, and misty eyes. That always does it for me—misty eyes.

"I'm Lucius Hutchfield," I said, as though using a password. It didn't pass with *her*. "Bucky's brother."

"Who's Bucky?" She lay outside the charmed circle.

"He's to face the judge this morning, and I'd appreciate a chance to talk to him."

"The mood *he's* in, you'll wish you hadn't." Putting it as a challenge that way makes me eager to get to him. But her brassy manner and loud voice, contradicting her misty eyes, make me nervous.

"Is he in there now?" I nodded at the closed door.

"Yes. And be glad *you're* out *here*. Now get out, and I mean that in a nice way, because I'm doing you a favor, Mr.—"

"Hutchfield. Listen—"

That's just what the judge was doing—listening to her loud mouth. Because the door cracks a foot and he's standing in it, five feet high, showing an expression long ago set in concrete that was now beginning to crack.

"Did you say he was Bucky Hutchfield's brother?" He seemed to speak without opening his mouth.

"Yes, sir."

"Get out of here," he says to me.

"That's what I told him, sir." She ripped a sheet from her typewriter.

"But, sir, I must talk to you before two o'clock." Desperate, I blurted out the theme. "The chain gang will kill my brother!"

Judge Stumbo nods from the waist up, his eyelids slam shut three times with gavel-like finality.

"But the prison psychiatrist said—"

"Never *believed* in psychiatrists."

"Please, sir, I'm just trying to be my brother's keeper—"

"You're a fool."

"Well, sir, the nation needs teachers, doesn't it? And I'm trying to become a teacher, but I left off work on my dissertation to come down here to—"

"This nation don't need another educated fool."

"Sir, please, sir, just let me tell you the story of Bucky's childhood, and I think you can see—"

"I've heard too *many* stories. Besides, I lack imagination."

"Sir, at least think of my mother—"

"I have no desire to think of your mother."

"Sir, what can I say, what can I do, what can Bucky do, to convince you—?"

"Your brother has only to be born again and live his life over in a different way. As it is, he goes on the chain gang." The crack in the door closed before I could open my mouth.

But then I got to laughing. It was a great line. "Hey, he's really a very funny judge, isn't he?"

"I thought it was funny, too," she says, throwing her carriage, "first time I heard it."

But when the morning sun hit me in the face on the courthouse steps, I wasn't laughing. I had only five hours to work a miracle. Then, although I had just experienced a failure to the contrary, I realized that my last thin chance was to approach the victims *personally* again, and beg them to accept monthly payments. An even thinner chance on the other side of that was that the judge would accept their decisions.

So I hopped into my Buick, started off and swerved, wobbling, into a service station, having forgotten the flat. They also patched up the radiator and pounded hell out of a few other places, as if beating the car to submission, and I set out for Hiawassee with only five dollars left of the hundred I had when I left Knoxville. I headed for the other end of the line so I could gage my time as I worked back toward the deadline at the courthouse.

As I drove along, I half-decided that if I had no luck by the time I got to the third victim, I'd start cashing checks in the next town. Time passed quickly as I imagined the effect of such a move on my life. At least, I could finish the novel I was working on.

Mr. Overby squints against the sunburst where I'm standing in the doorway of his store. He seems puzzled. "He just left."

"*Who* just left?"

"Your lawyer—Bucky's lawyer. Mr. French."

"Huh? Listen, I just came by to talk to you about the money Bucky owes you and try—"

"He just paid it off. You s'pose to meet each other here?"

"Hold it, Mr. Overby. What's going on?"

"Mr. French just paid me, see." He pulled a check out of his big wallet, thonged to his belt at the hip. "And I signed his paper."

"What paper?"

"The affidavit saying I don't want to see Bucky prosecuted, I'm satisfied with restitution, plus the interest for three years, like it was a loan. And a big plus feature of the agreement was that I get to keep the money even if Judge Stumbo sentences Bucky anyway—which he will."

"So you get your money on the hip and Bucky's ass in a sling any way the cookie crumbles, huh?"

"Yeah." He grins, delighted with the justice of it all. "Plus, *plus*—I sold him three brand new suits, one his size, and two Bucky's size, and about a hundred dollars of this and that."

"What did he look like?"

Then Mr. Overby gives me the exact same description McCoy of the G.B.I. gave me, each item in the same order, right down to the shiny briefcase. "I'm gonna get *me* a briefcase like his."

Then Mrs. Overby comes in and carries on about what a handsome, dashing, though oddly dressed, fellow Mr. French was, and she made me promise to bring Bucky by to see her, and I had to promise again not to put her life story in a book.

When I walked into Mr. Crigger's Red Dot Cafe, he's up on that stool smoking a big cigar with a two-inch ash.

"You just missed him."

I ask who, and we go through the whole routine, the description of French and all, the gist of which is that Mr. French came in and treated them both to Crigger's best porterhouse steak (since Crigger didn't know what French meant by Chateaubriand), and over their steaks they came to an agreement, and Crigger settled for Mr. French's terms, which were the same as Overby's.

I drove up to the pumps where Pap was white-washing the island. He looks up, double surprised to see me. "I know," I says, "I just missed him."

"By less than five minutes."

"Driving a classic 1942 white Lincoln Mercury Zephyr in mint condition, right?"

"With brand new rubber all around. I unloaded four new B. F. Goodrich American Classic Wide Whitewall tires on him." He gave the island a sloppy slap of white wash.

"Did you get a cigar out of him?"

"Smoke it after lunch. Ought to last the weekend."

I scratched gravel to catch up with Mr. French, but jerked to a stop at the edge of the lot—out of gas. I didn't have any money left. Out of the goodness of his heart, Pap exchanged a tank of gas for my spare tire, my hubcaps, and, since I wouldn't need it without the spare, my jack. He said I looked faint and shouldn't go without my lunch, so he threw in a pack of stale peanut butter crackers that I almost choked to death on before I got to Blairsville.

I had the feeling there wasn't much point in going back, certainly no need to check the Western Auto man. If it was humanly possible, this Mr. French would get Bucky off.

In a "no parking" zone in front of the courthouse, aligned with the walkway, was parked the white Lincoln Mercury Zephyr. I parked behind it, confident Mr. French would take care of any fines.

In front of the drugstore, a greyhound bus was discharging passengers. The driver reached his hand in, and the first thing I saw was a prize-winner's red ribbon bobbing on Majel's breast as she stepped down in her white majorette boots, the pompoms swinging. She sees me getting out of my smashed-in Buick and smiles and waves. I wave back, then go on into the courthouse.

The Lincoln Mercury Zephyr, though white, reminded me of the Green Hornet's car in the chapter play Earl took me to see the day Bucky was born. Momma wanted us out of the house to spare us the shock of birth. Earl held my hand, and as we went over a bridge, he told me about Fartso the whale, who lived in the creek below. If I threw him a nickel, Earl said, Fartso would tell his gremlins to bring me a Buck Rogers gun. "Give it to me," he said, "and I'll throw it in."

Later, watching the Green Hornet's car force the bad guy's car to swerve and smash into a gas pump, I wondered for a minute how it was that Earl hugged *two* bags of popcorn when he had thrown *both* our nickels into the water. Twenty years later, it suddenly dawned on me.

Dawn's rosy fingers goosed me as I stepped into Judge Stumbo's outer office and saw Earl hefting a dangling lock of the secretary's long black hair that took me back to Joan Crawford in the forties. As if verifying the testimony of witnesses, Earl's wearing a white panama suit and hat that bring the sunlight indoors, and green-tinted glasses, a mustache, a pink shirt with a white tie, and two-tone, brown and white shoes, and in a chair lies a shiny briefcase with H. F. on the gold clasp.

He doesn't see me, and he's saying, "Not many girls can wear such long hair and get away with it, but if you lived in New York, you'd be setting a style, brown eyes."

Her misty blue eyes look up at Earl, and she's forgotten, like many other girls, what the hell color her eyes really are, and a feeble smirk is her only attempt to control the situation.

I stayed quiet, dangling in the doorway.

I'd come in at the climax, because she gets up and goes into Judge Stumbo's office, and Earl turns and glances right *at* me, as though we had been together all morning and I had just stepped in after a brief trip to the John. So I try to match his cool.

The door opens, and the secretary steps aside to let Earl pass. She leaves the door ajar, so from where I stand, I watch Earl walk up to the desk and put out his hand at such a distance that the Judge has to get up and reach across his desk to shake it.

I can't catch all the conversation, but I see the affidavits come out of the shiny briefcase and the Judge take them and peruse them, shaking his head negative. ". . . . willing to pay the court costs," I hear Earl say, his voice becoming louder, stageworthy, as he builds the scene. "I realize that in a case like this the court costs are what some people might regard as exorbitant, nevertheless, we're willing to lay it on the line today, sir. Settle it out of court, if possible."

"Sir, everybody has been at me to handle this case out of court, but I don't handle, sir, and you may as well save your techniques of persuasion until court convenes—in exactly ten minutes. Now, if you will excuse me. . . ."

I stare at the back of Earl's head as he remains seated, very still, and the judge stares at Earl's face.

"Pardon me for staring, sir," says Earl, "but isn't that—?" Then I see the color photograph of a young man in a Marine uniform. "I *thought* the name was familiar. Judge Stumbo. That name kept nagging at me all the way down the highway. That's Joe, isn't it?"

"Why—yes, but—what's that got to do with Bucky Hutchfield?"

"Nothing, sir." Earl rises, still looking at the picture. "Nothing."

Then, he jerks himself into a posture of efficiency, puts out his hand so the Judge has to get up again and reach out to it, and as they shake, the Judge says, "Mr. French, what were you about to say?"

"That I knew him. The machine gun—"

"Who told you about Joe?"

"*Told* me? Let me tell *you*, sir. I was there." The Judge's other hand reaches out and the four hands clasp in one fingery knot. "All *I* got to show is one bullet wound, but poor Joe. . . ."

Then I remember the scar under Earl's shoulder blade. In Texas, a prison guard bent over a water fountain and his pistol fell out of its holster and fired.

"What are you people doing out there?" says the Judge. "Mr. Hutchfield, your lawyer will be with you in a moment." He pushed the door shut. "Now, sir. . . . What did you say your first name was?"

Muffled through the door come a few phrases: ". . . died in my arms . . . I was delirious at the time . . . didn't know him well, but . . . last words were, 'Candyman, Candyman.' . . . That mean anything to you, sir?"

At the word 'Candyman,' the secretary frowns slightly, then, slowly, smiles cunningly, then shrugs, stops pretending to work, and sits back, her arms folded, listening with me.

"Candyman Joe's nickname for his father?" I ask.

She smirks and nods her head. "How did *you* know?"

"Imagination," I say, and nod *my* head.

Twenty minutes later, the Judge comes out and says, "Mrs. Harmon, would you please write out a check for a hundred dollars? Mr. French needs some expense money to get back to Florida, and I'm afraid he can't cash a check locally, him being a stranger passing through, but they'll cash one with *my* signature on it. And here's his check to cover court costs. We've settled it out of court, so strike Bucky Hutchfield from the docket."

We all shook hands and the Judge hurried out to court, thirty minutes late, content with Earl's promise to return and spend a weekend with him some time shooting grouse.

Smirking, Mrs. Harmon turned to me. "Show Mr. French the jail."

"If there's a florist in this town," says Earl, posing in the doorway, "expect a dozen roses within an hour."

"I won't hold my breath."

As we're going down the steps toward his car, Earl says, over his shoulder, "See you in jail," and I see there's a ticket on my windshield, none on his. I follow in my car, which I want *near* me up to the last minute. In the short drive around the square to the jail, I notice the new tires on Earl's car, the suits hanging neatly in the back, the boxes of other stuff stacked in the seat, and I imagine all the checks he passed this morning, and hope each of the recipients got a cigar at least. And then I think, yeah, everybody but me.

By the time I climb out of my wreck of a car and reach the screen porch, Bucky is already out there, a grin stretching from one of those big ears to the other, and Sheriff Thompson is folding a piece of paper, probably a note from the Judge. And right quick, there's Majel, draped in the doorway, decked in her outfit, the prize winner's red ribbon still dangling, and I see in her eyes, even in the shade of the porch, that when she looks at Earl, she sees Miami in full splendor.

I stayed outside in the broiling sun, while Bucky manfully shakes hands with Sheriff Thompson and hugs his tearful wife.

Earl gives the Sheriff a big cigar, then loads his own pearl-handled cigarette holder and feels for matches until the Sheriff lights it for him, then lights his own cigar.

They all step out into the sunlight, shaking hands, and Earl even reaches for Majel's, and when her shoulders twitch as if by a small electric shock, I figure he's tickled her palm.

I follow the parade toward the cars, Majel cavorts and tosses her baton into the sun and it spins and sparkles and Bucky runs ahead and jumps behind the wheel of that white classic Lincoln Mercury Zephyr like it was Santa's sleigh.

"Follow *me*," Earl says to me, as he gets in beside Bucky. They take off as though they have a motorcycle escort. As, in every sense that matters, they have.

Just before I pull away from the curb, I look up at the window where I first saw Bucky two days ago. Behind the silver iron slats stood Tom, his arm around Billy. They didn't wave. They didn't move.

At the intersection where the caution light blinked in the sun's glare, I took the highway less traveled by, the one that offered a short cut over a curving route to the state line.

Earl and his chauffeur, Bucky, were borne along in their dreamboat down the super highway toward the horizon.

This was eight years ago, and the last time I saw Bucky was when I was in Idaho a few months ago for the world premiere—as the producer called it—of my play *Call of the Wild Goose*. A little theatre group was trying it out for us, and I had gotten leave from the University of Montana (I *didn't* stick at Berea after all) to be in on rehearsals.

Opening night, a terrific snowstorm hit, and television cameras were set up to shoot first nighters—Boise high society—as they came in out of the blizzard.

Three came in and one stepped back to hold the door open for a fourth, and in walked a tuxedo with you-know-who inside, and that grin, transported from the Sheriff's porch.

On camera, Bucky was asked why he had made the trip up from Dallas in this terrible blizzard, and he replied, with a jut of his chin and a look of amazement, "Well, you don't think I'd miss my brother's play, do you?"

What he missed, of course, was the character *in* the play, who resembled himself—at least in *my* imagination.

He was driving a classic 1941 green Hudson, one of only a few hundred made that year. Living in the car, he travels all over the United States, constantly on the move, from one brief job to another, living by his wits, but apparently keeping out of trouble. He's been living that way for eight years, and I've taught in almost that many colleges, by choice, and he always shows up at least once or twice a year from a thousand miles away, and a few days later, he leaves, usually in a rain or snow storm, and I get a card several days after, saying, "Dear Lucius: Well, I made it to Tucson, okay. On my way to San Diego. All my love, your brother, Bucky Hutchfield." On the back is a color photograph of an Indian in full costume or a buffalo, for my son's sake.

And if you'll just be patient, I'm sure Bucky will come knocking at that front door before you have to go.

Since Blairsville, Earl's served three short stretches, in Soledad, California, Carson City, Nevada, and Parchman Farm, Mississippi. But now *he's* going straight, too, living and working in Toronto, where he's married and has a family, and runs a tabernacle of the Holiness church. His wife sings, and he scorches sinners alive with his visions of hell, and then leaves them in Jordan. Well, who can tell? Maybe, even if it's a con, maybe he does some good.

Because Earl's the oldest rat in the barn. Earl sold us *all* a bill of goods. Not just the judge, the victims, the sheriff, but in the beginning, back home in Knoxville—me and Bucky. With that Merchant Marine outfit, standing like that at the front door with the September sun around his head, a nimbus of light, evoking far off places, far *out* episodes. I never told you about that? Then listen.

A smoky-red October afternoon. Me and little Bucky and Earl playing marbles under the Indian cigar tree with a bunch of tough kids and somebody says to Earl, "Okay, Big Chief Chew-tabacca, shoot!" and Earl stands up, hitches up his knickers like Humphrey Bogart and spits tobacco juice bulls-eye into the ring and says, "You all take it easy, you hear? I'm going swimming." And we all laugh like hell as he walks down the street, his pockets bulging with marbles, into the autumn sunset, by god.

Thirteen years old at the time, and went off with only a dime to his name. Didn't see him again until a year later, in September, when I looked up from reading *Smilin' Jack*, and there he stood at the screen door with the sunlight behind him and a merchant seaman's cap cocked back to show his pompadour. Says, "Shhhh. Wanna surprise Momma," as if he didn't have many more years to do *that* in.

This one ends the summer before my first novel came out, and it'd been eight years since I had seen him last, in Blairsville. He'd just come from working in a Mississippi cotton patch, under the gun. And here *I* was, the first in the family on both sides to graduate from high school and even on through college, and making two thousand a year teaching at a big university, and a novel coming out, and a clean record in the home-town and the FBI files, and—You know, I didn't want to show off and make him feel bad, I wanted to make him feel part *of* it, so here we were: two brothers having a reunion at Grandma's house—sort of the home place, you know, because Momma moved all over the city of Knoxville when we were little—and Earl was out in the back yard, ablaze with flowers, and he was lolling in the hammock under the mimosa trees, and smoking this fat-assed cigar and wearing the baggy clothes they let him out in. Swinging in that hammock, raising a cloud of Dutch Master cigar smoke, grinning at me.

So I sat in this white kitchen chair Grandma'd propped up the curtain stretchers with, and tried to make him feel a part of it all.

When I told him about the teaching job, he says, "Listen, kid," in this Yankee accent he picked up and stuck to since his first trip to New York, "what you waste your time teaching English for? Why don't you become a doctor or a lawyer where the *big* money is?" It tipped me off balance, and I made some lame excuses, and he says, "What's this they tell me about you got a novel going to be published?"

"Yeah." I broke out in a face-aching grin.

"Listen, kid, you better watch out for these editors. They'll try to cheat you out of what you got coming to you. I know. What you need is an agent." Well, I was still feeling the reunion scene, so none of this soaked in. I was thinking, here's where I'll make him feel he's a part of it all, and not just a three or four time loser con man fresh out of prison. He was still kinda thin and hollow-eyed, you know. But 'bout that time, he says, "What's it about?"

"'Bout when I was in the Merchant Marine."

That made him give the hammock a good swing with his dangling foot and look at me squint-eyed through the cigar smoke. "Kid, when were *you* ever in the Merchant Marine?"

Just before they drafted me into the army, I told him, but didn't remind him that I used to send him money orders for stamps and Bull Durham from ports in Savannah and New Orleans and Chile, then later from Fort Jackson, nor how he used to sign his letters, "Jesus is the only hope for today's youth," knowing the censors would get it back to the parole board. I won't stress the fact that *I* believed him. "Whatever made you go in the Merchant Marine, kid?"

I got choked up a little because I was about to grab him with it. "Well, Earl, remember the time . . .?" Then I filled him in on our childhood and the time he showed up in the merchant seaman's outfit. "And you told me and Bucky all about New York and shipping out to Panama and the West Indies. Remember, Earl? It got Bucky to running off from school and taking little trips that finally landed him in a detention home. It stirred up the wanderlust in me, too, but good little ol' Lucius, you know, stayed home, and dreamed about it, and saw movies about it, and wrote novel scenarios projecting himself into it, and read Joseph Conrad, and finished high school first. Then I went to New York, worked at the White Tower hamburger joint by night, sat in the Brooklyn union hall by day, till I finally got on a ship to India day before Christmas. There was this man on the ship we called Peron because he was from Buenos Aires who kind of reminded me of you. In my novel that's coming out, *The Hero and the Witness*, he turns out to be a strange kind of hero, in a bass-ackward way, and I'm his witness."

Earl braked the hammock with his foot, and kept it still, one eye squeezed shut against the smoke from the Dutch Master hanging in the corner of his mouth. Then he gives the hammock a little push, takes a long draw, spews out the smoke, dusts the cigar, and smirks: "Why, kid. I ain't never been in no Merchant Marines."

I heard a mimosa blossom drop. "But—"

"But, hell," Earl said, "I just wore that outfit so I could hitch hike across country easier."

*Nothing Dies,
but Something Mourns*

"Is this a fancy which our reason scorns?
Ah! Surely nothing dies but something mourns!"
BYRON | *Don Juan*

"All out for the middle of nowheres."

Before Lucius opened his eyes, he heard the piano tuner spit out the window.

His stinging eyes scanned the lushly treed mountainsides for a sign of Sweetwater. "Can't see a thing."

"Nothing *to* see—even when you get there. But you can't miss it. Looks like God just took and threw a handful of houses and stuff up 'gin the hillside."

Lucius backed out of the car, rocked on his quivering ankles, and shook his head like an underwater swimmer, trying to focus his eyes, sore from grit and windstrain. The old man had stopped on the edge of the road where the sky seemed to look up. Lucius walked around the front of the car to the driver's side.

"See that fresh muddied road behind you that drops off into nowheres?"

"Yeah."

"Just follow your nose. Got your bag?"

"Didn't have one." Lucius looked at the piano tuner's nose, blue-veined, like a relief map of the mountains.

"Tell me something, boy, where'd you *get* that shirt anyway?"

Two-toned blue, whirling stitches, some country music singer had abandoned it in Manhattan, where it hung on the "Unclaimed" rack and sold for twenty-five cents. "Got it from a Peruvian ditch-digger."

"I want you to hush." The old man laughed at that.

"Thanks for the ride. If you ever take a trip, call the nearest Trailways Station. I handle tickets to all points not on the map."

"Never said what you was going to Sweetwater *for.*"

"Look up a friend of my childhood."

"Wouldn't be surprised if I knew him."

"Me neither. Name's Jesse James."

The piano tuner's laughter echoed among the trees, but he didn't settle for a gag. "Anybody in particular you want to see in Sweetwater?"

"The old lady who owns the Blue Goose Hotel."

"They say the old lady's dead." His hard frankness rejected everything Lucius had said. "Claim that newspaper story killed her—like a shot in the back."

The old man pulled back onto the highway, headed toward Cold Mountain, where he intended to tune an old lady's piano in which the last chord had died thirty years ago. Something like that was what Lucius had in mind himself. And the melody he hoped to play would give some impression of what it was like to lose one's virginity to Jesse James.

As the piano tuner's car curved down the long mountain slope, his lights illuminated a billboard painting of Dan'l Boone, one hand sighting into, seeming to salute, the West, the other holding a long rifle. YOU HAVE PASSED THROUGH BOONE WHERE "HORN IN THE WEST," THE WORLD'S GREATEST OUTDOOR DRAMA IS PERFORMED NIGHTLY. On behalf of Boone in his grave, Lucius turned over.

Standing in the middle of the highway, listening to after-rain drip from the leaves nearby, Lucius felt like a hick in Times Square. Here as there, the only direction to look, if you wanted to see anything, was up.

On the red clay road, he could see down, too. The sky was clear with evening stars and a full moon was overhead, but on the mountain ranges below, masses of thick clouds and films of blue mist moved. The mud road disappeared around a bend where dark green trees and bushes were thick. He followed it, though it would lead him only to the grave of the woman he had come to listen to.

At the bend, the foliage above the road broke and Lucius saw, far ahead, the Blue Goose Hotel. He felt cheated. He had come all that way to be told that she was dead. In possession of a few enticing facts and misleading rumors, he confronted a task of the imagination. He would have to conjure up what had been left unspoken. Perched in the moonlight, the Blue Goose Hotel was huge—and maples and birch and dead trees framed it solidly and many miles of mountains surrounded it. Like a fire tower, it looked down on everything.

The road did not show anywhere between the bend where it seemed to stop and the hotel it doubtlessly passed. Not even the roofs of other houses showed near the hotel. It seemed the sole reason—and it seemed enough—for the stars' and the moon's glow. The clouds and mist below were a stream, broken by green boulders. In those milky depths, a legend had hooked him and fished him out.

Around the bend, a cornfield lay. In the moonlight, it looked purposely well-illuminated. Someone stood among the dry husks and the crooked and kneeling stalks. "Hi, neighbor," Lucius started to say, realizing that some clichés might just as well remain undisturbed, but he let his hand fall when he saw clearly in a different slant of light that the figure was the skeleton of a scarecrow. Vines of morning glories curled and coiled around the stalks. He smelled honeysuckle. Up here on the roof of the world, everything came a little late. While fruit and flowers rotted and then shriveled on the plains and in the valleys below, they were bursting into ripeness in the mountains.

Through the low-hanging leaves of an oak, he saw moonlight glance off a jagged pile of rocks, powdered with silicon. Walking under the tree, he saw a red brick silo, rocks piled high against one side.

He passed the black doorway of the silo. Shafts of moonlight falling through the broken roof showed that it was empty.

Though he had known it would be, he didn't see clearly until now that the Blue Goose Hotel was blue. On a tower at each end, weathervanes and lightning rods caught and shot moonlight into the trees. If the rods and vanes reminded him of TV aerials that was his own fault. But he hoped there would be none on the houses he expected to see around the curve. An abutment of the mountain abruptly cut off the hotel itself. He caught his breath with a sudden rasp that echoed in the trees—a giant, orange grasshopper, huge as a Mack truck, blocked the road.

For an instant. Then the cloud on the moon thinned, and he saw why the road was new, the mud gummy. The grasshopper became a machine with a long arched backbone. Tires taller than Lucius, and a scooper that carried the dirt raked up by the little bulldozers surrounding it, they stood now in the new, tall grass, some of their blades bearded, others bright steel in the moonlight.

Beside the road, pieces of rusted machinery lay in the grass. "Togetherness," he whispered.

The road behind him, the dense wall of vegetation before him where the road stopped, standing in the circle of yellow and orange machines that seemed to have come to an ironclad but silent understanding about him, Lucius *felt* alone.

Going around a tool shed, he stepped onto a path and climbed until he came out on a gravel road where moonlight shone on a sign nailed to a wood rail fence.

SWEETWATER

Population 1850—102

1952—73

Seventy-four, Lucius thought, if you count the ghost of Jesse James. Jesse and Frank rein their horses, lean, bones aching, in their saddles, and look at the sign and then at each other, and Frank says, "May as well."

Sweetwater was just as the piano tuner had said—flung out with a flick of God's wrist along the side of the mountain, tipped like a well spout, so that in the road a man would always be either trudging up, or trying to keep from running down, slipping on ice or mud, or stirring up dust. The dozen or so buildings leaned as though rolling with the earth on the 23° inclination of its axis. Nothing kept it from being, there in the moonlight, an evening in 1880 at about eight o'clock, until Lucius saw the first building on the edge of town.

A faded sign insisted on what his eyes refused to believe—FROZEN CUSTARD. A cracked oilcloth banner hung from the roof of the shack— GROWING WITH THE TOWN—TOURISTS WELCOME. Rain had washed the three large windows. They gleamed. Grass and blackberry vines grew along the walls and tapped on the glass in the faint breeze, and streaks of dark brown dirt marked the once white walls that sun and thaw had cracked and peeled. No kids had broken its windows. Squatting forlornly, it stubbornly awaited the arrival of a batch of tourists, or were hopeful that the machines around the mountain would rescue it. Lucius ate some of the shriveling blackberries and flipped a nickel onto the counter at the dispensing window. "Here, pal, buy yourself a cigar," he said, and started up the hill.

Some elderly voices on a porch high above the road stopped as Lucius felt himself seen. Ivy entwined on wires strung from the porch floor to the ceiling all along the front to the steep steps like the strings of a harp screened the porch. Maybe they sat talking about the night the two horsemen entered town. Maybe Jesse James, a little dizzy from the dribbling wound, heard a swing- creak, too, heard it stop suddenly and the wood crackle as a fat old lady in a sundress—Lucius saw her as he came nearer—leaned and looked down into the road. And if someone didn't snap off a light and a gray fringed head didn't appear ghostly behind a pane, he may as well forget the whole thing. As he passed the eighth house, one did. He had the feeling that he was giving the cues, until he realized that the books he had read, the movies he had seen, not to mention the life he had lived, had called them often before.

But the light had not *snapped*. It had faded on the window quickly to black. Along the steep road the glass insulators on the stiff arms of the telephone poles gleamed in the moonlight, wireless.

In front of The Sweetwater Trading Post, two men sat on a bench. They watched him go by. Passing the hotel without a glance, Lucius hoped they would be partly satisfied.

A chimney and the charred foundations of a house that had once faced the hotel rose out of the meagre rubble where Lucius sat on a rusty barrel under a young walnut tree and gazed at the hotel, wishing the old lady's ghost would turn on a light so he could focus his courage. Beyond these ruins and the hotel, nothing but trees and space, and, below, lower mountain ranges.

Cracked stone steps led up to the hotel. Beginning at the towers in the front, balustrades ran around the three-story building, and the verandas sagged. A wide, glassed-in porch and two large glass doors fronted the middle section. Lucius imagined the way it would look at sundown certain evenings in September and how the color would turn at twilight tomorrow. In the moonlight now, the glass was cool blue.

The view below and above was steep. In the milky stream that was rising now from the valleys below, the hotel seemed anchored. 'It seemed to rock gently like a clipper in a bay.' Sitting on the barrel, rust scaling off when he moved, he knew that what he would imagine would be no different from the way it would be if she had been alive to tell it. If she *would* have told it. But underneath his desire to hear it, he felt a strange itch to know the truth, even as, knowing a scrap of it, he was already turning it into fiction.

On the ride down from New York, he had felt certain that though she had refused to give the story to a local newspaperman—who had gone ahead and printed the rumors alone—she would have looked into Lucius's eyes and given it to *him*. She would have recognized him as one of her own kind. And she would not have been able to keep silent.

Affecting what he hoped resembled a saunter to the eyes that watched him, Lucius moved into the young trees. Before he could abandon the affectation, he tripped over a rock. Feeling around on the ground in the dark, he felt a slight depression in the earth. Then his fingertips stroked chiseled marks on an upright stone slab. He remembered Jesse's grave in Kearney, Missouri, and the marker, like a curbstone in the weeds. He leaned against a tree awhile, looking at the side of the hotel, and then he walked slowly toward it.

As he vaulted over it, the balustrade swayed like the limb of a tree. The porch received him without a mutter. He walked along the side to the rear, glancing into the small chambers through lace-curtained windows. In one of them, Jesse read the Bible by the moonlight through the window, and in another, Frank read Shakespeare, his favorite.

At the back door, he knocked lightly, paused a few minutes, then turned the porcelain knob. The door hinge whined like a cat. Entering a creaky hotel booked solid with ghosts on the roof of the world, he was in his natural element. The scene was different, but the element, created at will, was always the same. Their eyes would have met—she would have known that at last someone had come who understood.

He moved from room to room, tapping lightly at each closed door before opening it. In the middle of the ballroom, he paused a moment, as though the waltz had just come to a stop in *him*. In the lobby, where the register book was open and moonlight puddled the chairs and sofas, he stopped again, the creaking in the wood did not stop. It was all right if she was following him, because *he* was following *her*. Did she think he was someone she had been expecting all her life —someone who, now that she was dead, had finally come?

In one of the bathrooms, he let down the seat. The wood felt warm. On a Sunday morning, with the sun on his belt buckle, Jesse James reads the St. Louis paper—his own letter to the editor, castigating him for defamation of character, signing off with "Yours respectfully, Jesse James."

Lucius pulled the chain. A bird flew out of the water chamber over his head and crashed repeatedly against the window pane. He opened the window and watched the bird fly straight into the moon, now ringed with clabbered cloud and a reddish glow, and vanish in light.

On the second floor, in the west wing, he opened the door on a room like all the others, except that she was in it, sitting right at the sill in full moonlight in a wicker rocker, lowering a Coca-Cola from her lips. The green bottle, half full, poised in front of her, she asked, "Jesse?"

"No, ma'am," said Lucius, finally, a painful ache in his chest, holding hard to the knob, believing and disbelieving in apparitions.

"Who are you?"

"Lucius Hutchfield."

"That means nothing to me."

"Me neither, most of the time. Guess that's why I'm here. I hope I didn't frighten you."

Her gray hair hung long and thick behind her head, thin around her face. The hair, and the eyes, were the only things he had not already imagined. The dated shoes, the dated dress, but not the hair and the eyes. Her gaze, fastened upon him as he stood framed in the door, seemed to scrutinize him in microscopic detail. He had expected her to be able to see the outside world only dimly. She folded her hands and looked out the window. When he saw that the hands trembled and that the veins were swelling, he realized with panic that she was terrified, that she was apt to scream on the instant.

"Please, don't be frightened. I'm harmless."

"You have no right."

"I'll go, if I'm intruding." Lucius turned as though he were leaving. "Don't you want to know why I've come?"

"I care neither where you've come from nor where you are going."

"That leaves me dangling. For a moment anyway. Long enough to tell you why I've come. Will you listen and stop trembling like that?"

"You've no right."

"It'll take less time than for you to finish that Coca-Cola." She looked into his eyes. "I got hold of a story about you. Some hack reporter in Boone claims *you knew* Jesse James." As Eve *knew* Adam.

She stood up, straight, and walked past him out of the room. She had looked into his eyes and it had made no difference.

Lucius followed her into the hall. She moved very slowly, very strong, like a figure on an urn.

"No, look, Miss Ransom. I want to do it right. I just want to sit in the lobby with you and let you tell it. You don't have to—tell—I don't expect you to tell about—I mean, just tell anything about him that comes to you."

They were on the stairs, dark, windowless, although the lobby below was white. He took her elbow to help her down, but when he felt the bone tremble, he jerked his hand away as though a moment's more pressure would snap it.

"I'm not a newspaperman. I hate that stuff. I understand how you feel about that. Look, when I was a little feller, I saw a movie about Jesse James. I played Jesse James with my two brothers Earl and Bucky and kids in the neighborhood even after I was too old to play legends, and it's like I was raised with him, but I want to lay my hand on a part of the legend where I can feel the blood still beat. I understand how you feel. It's personal. Well, that's how I take it, too. It's something I have a need of, that I can't explain, but that you, you surely, can understand. They've buried him under a slush of clichés. It takes two to resurrect—one to call forth, and one to witness."

She opened the glass door on the left of the glassed-in porch and turned on him. The look in her eyes made him step aside. If she lived ninety percent of her life in the past, the other ten percent was, for Lucius at that moment, unbearably immediate. She wasn't afraid now—rage made her tremble.

"I've come a long way, Miss Ransom." Lies like truth.

"So have I. And a long way to go. You in that direction, if you please, and me in my own."

"Think about it. Goodnight. Sweet dreams."

Lucius stepped out onto the sandstone step and heard the click of the lock, like a pistol cocking, at his back.

Hard cold creek water on his pulses and dabbed on his eyelids exhilarated him.

In the silo, he lay on dead cornhusks and looked up at the moon through cracks in the roof. Listening for snakes and running his hands over his body, imagining black widows, kept him awake until he was too weary to sleep.

Then he listened to Sweetwater Creek flow by the silo at the bottom of the path, and when the frogs were quiet, he even heard sand under the foundations of the silo trickle down the bank into the water. The blasting and the rumble of the machines had loosened the weak foundations. Though the machines had been motionless for weeks, the earth still moved.

His intention was to transform what Miss Ransom told him into a fiction *Lady Fair* would publish. In that magazine his first published story had appeared, with illustrations by Dali. Too much James Joyce, not enough Jesse James? He had come to wonder if that couldn't possibly be true. He thought, "Of course, I have not done, seen, felt, read, experienced everything, but I feel that way. Having felt everything, I now feel nothing—except a tinge of nostalgia for life in general, life by a full moon. The unmoonlit life is not worth living, said Socrates Hutchfield as he watched the first rocket signal its landing on the moon."

Loris Blackburn, the love of his life, had once written to him that he belonged with Keats, Shelley, Byron, and Swinburne. "You mean," he had replied, "I should be dead?"

The only person he had not failed, if he could only believe her intensely enough, was Loris Blackburn, the girl he had lost to an insurance salesman. It occurred to him that in the Age of the H-Bomb, she had made an appropriate, if not a good, choice.

Leaning against the sink, he had opened the envelope from Loris Blackburn, postmarked Knoxville, Tennessee. No letter, just a clipping from the society page—Loris Blackburn Underwood pouring tea from a silver urn in an arbor where the Dogwood Garden Club had had a successful meeting, ushering in the new season. She wore a white dress, a bracelet on her wrist, a string of pearls around her neck, a smile on her face, and a black patch over one eye. Scrawled in purple ink across the white tablecloth—"There's more here than meets the eye." And Lucius knew that behind the patch, the lovely blue eye was unblemished. In context, it was a gesture with more style than Lucius had been capable of in years. She had often told him that the only thing that made life bearable and sometimes blissful for her were the secret letters that had passed between them over the years, from suburbia to "far out." Her gesture bore witness to both the fruits and the futility of the vicarious impulse.

Folding the picture to slip into his pocket, he had noticed the headlines on the reverse side—DID JESSE JAMES PASS THROUGH SWEETWATER, NORTH CAROLINA? "Fact or Fiction?" He had read the article, then he had folded it and slipped it into his pocket.

Lured, he impulsively got into his unreliable car and drove all night until it broke down in Boone. The repair job would take a day or two. The piano turner's car, though, was fit to travel and Lucius was welcome to a lift to Sweetwater, not far off.

At an altitude where the air was thin, the appetite was ferocious, he hoped to get drunk on moonlight, get high on honeysuckle.

Lucius wondered whether the Blue Goose Hotel was real or an image in a dream he would have after he fell asleep. Drowsing, he tried to distinguish between things he had dreamed and things he had actually done. It was more an addiction than a habit, and he had long been hooked. Hunger and sleeplessness blurred the distinction. But it had never mattered before. It wasn't liable to now.

Shining through the breaks in the roof of the silo, the moon, he thought, fell on one of the few remaining romantics. But if it had once been a symbol of romanticism, the moon was now a symbol of the lunar age of space. Had the moon always had two faces, and had it now turned the other one?

THE CATERPILLARS AND BULLDOZERS had not moved during the night. They waited. The weeds and the wild flowers did not diminish the machine's arrogant aura of purpose. They had a job to do, and would do it quickly and efficiently. As soon as a way was found to dissolve the human element. Lucius sneered, shook his head, spat on a blade as he passed.

Four old men sat on the bench in front of the Sweetwater Trading Post. They turned looks of suspicion on him. They were dressed up, on their faces the gray pallor of funereal solemnity. Maybe she had died in the night, or killed herself, walking in the dark. Or maybe it was Sunday.

Staying on the side opposite the hotel, Lucius walked on up the hill. At one house, an old lady in a rayon black-and-white polka dot dress moved slowly down the steps, side-ways, carrying a covered plate, and another woman stood on the porch, shading her eyes against the sun, trying to see something in the direction of the Trading Post. Both stopped and watched Lucius pass. Suspicious and resentful, they looked straight across the road at him.

The church door was open and its bell began to ring. In Kearney, Missouri, adolescent Jesse James stands up and asks the congregation to pray for his wayward brother, Frank.

In the woods, Lucius searched for the gravestone that had tripped him the night before. Giving up, he headed deeper into the trees until a blaze of roses three times his height stopped him. A rose bush had entwined itself around a pine tree. They must have started from sprigs together. The roses had grown profusely and the weight of the bush had deformed the pine as it reached for more sunlight. But its needles were dark green and the sap smelled strong and pure. Younger rose vines grew from the ground at the outer rim of the tree where the branches had sagged under snow and roses. The vines were pulling the branches even lower.

Through a narrow gap, Lucius eased in under the tree. He put a petal in his mouth and rolled its velvet surface over his tongue. Morning sun sifted through the thick weave, and hues of green, red, brown pulsed in the light. "I knew," said Lucius aloud, "as I stood there in the morning sun under the coolness of the trees, that this freak of nature was the most beautiful thing I had ever seen. And here, so the story goes, stood Jesse James in the moonlight one September night in about the year 1880, winding his gold watch, taken, it was later learned, from the wife of a judge who had unfortunately bought passage on the Mammoth Cave stage."

The roses and their thorns were so inextricably part of the tree that climbing the pine, Lucius felt as though he were also climbing the bush. When he finally looked down through whorls of petals, tiny green leaves, needles, thorns, and crusty bark from a limb near the top, his cowboy shirt was frayed, the backs of his hands were scratched.

". . . So one day Jesse and Frank James came to Sweetwater, looking for a place to hide out until Jesse's wound could heal. He had never entirely recovered from the wounds he got in the Civil War under Quantrell either. Jesse was an impetuous fellow who did exactly what he wanted to do. So they took one look at the Blue Goose Hotel and knew they'd found a place to rest, rejuvenate.

"They often sat in the lobby and smoked, looking like traveling salesmen behind their newspapers, shoes shined to a luster there in the light of the kerosene chandeliers. They were polite to the guests, they played a little poker with the men, they loved to talk about politics and the state of the nation—about crops and cattle. And they seemed reasonably well informed on the subject of railroads, too.

"But Jesse was restless. One night he took a walk in the woods. The moon was bright. It came through small openings in the trees. He stopped under a pine that had roses growing in it to wind his watch. Glancing back down the path, he saw a lovely girl of fifteen in a long white dress, her black hair like velvet in the moonlight. Humming to herself, she held a sprig of honeysuckle in her small, slender hands. The sound of Jesse winding his watch turned her where she had stopped in the path, and then her eyes were on him."

Lucius saw the roofs of the town, and a group of people crossed the street at a long angle from the Trading Post toward the Blue Goose Hotel where the sun on the windows glared at them. A few women wore old-fashioned bonnets. Some of the men hung back. Lucius was certain, as he watched them mount the broken steps and stand outside the glassed-in porch, that they were paying their first visit as a group to Miss Ransom. But they seemed charged with a mission, and they came, no doubt, to the walls of the fort armed with the best of intentions, all of which, Lucius, the stranger, knew would fire blanks.

The sun was boiling hot, and they stood there awash in heat waves, until one man opened the door and shut it four times before he went in. They turned their backs a few moments, then shifted sideways, glancing through the hotel windows like passengers on a train.

Miss Ransom appeared at the tall front window of the west tower, visible from the waist down. The green shade wavered once at the side and he saw half of her face. He hoped the roses hid him and that she hadn't seen the tree quaver when he climbed.

When the missionaries went in, twenty minutes later by Jesse's gold watch, Lucius started down the tree. Looking up, he saw that a wasp's nest, like a faded Japanese lantern, hung within inches of where his head, spinning images, had been.

Hot chills went through him as he climbed down. Standing on the ground in the enclosure of curving limbs, needles, and roses, his feet humming from the strain, he sucked the blood from his wounds. On his empty stomach, the blood was sickening.

He emerged from the woods just as the missionaries emerged from the wall of panes, heads bowed low. They crossed the road at an angle and entered the church. As Lucius passed, the choir was singing "Power in the Blood."

The good, duped, dispossessed, doomed, old folks of Sweetwater, North Carolina were all in church, marking time with toe taps and fan beats. One day soon they would make way for the course of empire, and join the 14,000 Indians of the Cherokee nation who had made way for *them*.

Under the eyes of Zara Jane Ransom, standing in her tower, Lucius would take a last and loving look at the town Jesse James had passed through. He would leave Miss Ransom's privacy enshrined. He would enter it only through his imagination. At one time that had been more than enough.

Between the Trading Post, the first building on the precipice side above the creek, and the Blue Goose Hotel, the last building on the side where the mountain continued to rise, Lucius stood in the road. Dappled by the shade of a maple, looking up the long steep block, Lucius saw what Jesse had seen. Nothing seemed to have changed. Along the sides of the road, wooden walkways had probably raised the stroller above the dust, mud, and ice. Cracked, tipped, jutting slabs of concrete that tree roots had disrupted showed where a sidewalk had been attempted years ago on a more metropolitan model. No other attempt at change had left a trace.

Taking a last look, he tried to see Jesse and Frank, dressed like cattle buyers delayed in a little mountain town, walk down the boardwalk. But in the absence of moonlight, he saw only the empty town of eleven buildings deflecting where it could the bright noon sun.

When Lucius was gone, he would see everything, he hoped, in the light the town needed to reveal itself.

"More than any of the others," Loris had once written to him, "your letters enable me to lead the two lives I seem incapable of living separately."

Back home, he could perhaps live both his own pale life and the week in Jesse James' life that had transformed Zara Jane Ransom's.

But as he turned to go, he caught a glimpse of a man on the porch of the house three doors up the hill. He appeared to be shading his eyes against the sun. Enabling him to see what? Lucius turned, saw an old white horse, grazing in a vacant lot beside the store. When he looked again toward the porch, he realized that the man was beckoning to him. The man backed toward the front door, beckoning more broadly. Lucius walked toward the steps that led up to the yard.

When Lucius reached the sunken, flag-stone walk, the man stood in the doorway, the door open behind him, the screen pushed out. "You—looked like—you was—about to—leave—town," the man said, in a high, jerky, taut voice, as though he were on the verge of gagging. "Come on in."

Lucius stepped inside. At the end of a cool hallway, the back door was open. A few feet from the edge of the back porch, the mountain continued to rise, covered with large-leaved kudzu vines. The wide front door was open. Then Lucius sensed that the man was gone. He seemed to be stomping around on the porch. A shattering fit of coughing convulsed him. Lucius walked on into the living room. The shades drawn against the sun, the room was cool, but in a space between shade and sill he saw the man's legs as he danced in front of the window. Lucius stood in the middle of the Thirties and waited. The man came in, stuffing a handkerchief into his back pocket.

"Pardon me, them coughing fits storm over me like that sometimes. Sit down, mister."

Lucius sat in a chair beside a small round table where a pitcher of lemonade sweated on a carved, brass tray. There was only one glass. The man poured and handed it to Lucius. He caught Lucius looking at his missing thumb as he took the glass.

"Railroading was rough in them days, mister." He sat down across the room. "I ain't the only one noticed you walking around. Reckon you been reading that article." Lucius nodded, sipping the lemonade. "Well, you're looking at the man that helped get it wrote. That young reporter come up from Boone to write about *me*—offered me twenty dollars just to talk about the old railroad—and ended up writing about *her*. He said something about Jesse James being an old railroad man, too—something smart aleck like that, and I let it drop about Miss Ransom, and he took hold like a starving dog on a bone. So if you come to get what he couldn't, you may as well as to stayed home. I told what little *I* know." He noticed Lucius's interest in the room. "Joists in this house is all hand-planed and fitted. Hardly no nails at all. Wooden pegs, hand-turned. My people built nearly ever' house in Sweetwater and the one they didn't build did a swan dive right off the mountainside into the creek. One snowflake too many, they say. And after they sic those wrecking machines on the whole town, I'm gonna open me up a tourist court in Florida. Ain't nobody staying close't by to Sweetwater."

"What's going to happen?" Lucius stepped onto a back porch in the back of his mind and felt the rumble of machines in the loose boards under foot.

"Ever see a picture of that town in Japan we bombed? Hiroshima?"

Lucius looked through a bombsight at the negative of an aerial photograph. "Movies of it."

"Like *it* was—except with a frosting of concrete over it. You come at the right time. Take a good look."

Lucius saw the flash, then the colossal cloud. "A road?"

"Damn three lane highway, the way I hear it—right where we're sitting."

"Why?"

"Boone is a farm town that wants to be metropolized and pull in all the Blue Ridge Parkway tourist trash. They got a outdoor drammer that gyps part of 'em. 'Fore you get to Blowing Rock there's a little toy train that some days a thousand city folks pays to ride. And Blowing Rock ain't nothing but a tourist town—I mean it got borned in the cracked head of some feller sitting in a office in New York. They got three auction houses full of junk imported from all the points of the compass. Some way they're all in on that nightmare, like a half dozen people on one of them telephone a party lines, so they figure, wouldn't it be the berries if we could just hook all our wagons to the same star and ride it to the moon. Way to do *that* is build a highway over the mountains between Boone and Blowing Rock."

"But I came *up* on one."

"Oh, but the new one'll get you there three minutes quicker—and no curves! So what they're gonna do is shove us all down the mountain and burn the houses where they land—wood better than what you'd find in any new house today. Time. They say they ain't got time, because they lost the summer—too many storms—and winter comes sudden and takes a hard hold up here. When she goes, it all goes."

"Miss Ransom?"

"Wasn't for her, I reckon most of us would of been long gone. We would a gone out on the highway you come in on. Lots of 'em *has*. Claimed she give 'em the creeps, and moved out. How far you come?"

"New York."

"And you going back empty-handed?"

"Empty-headed, did you say?"

"Handed!"

"Yes."

"Then you come to the right man. I'm moving out soon. Few days from now. My wife promised that if they couldn't get Miss Ransom to see the truth, she'd go. We got all that money the state give us for the house, but she won't go long as Miss Ransom's on her throne up yonder."

"The truth? You mean about the wrecking crew?"

"Not just that—she doesn't know about *that* or won't believe the sound of it. But the taxes. They got till next week to persuade her to go to the old folks home or the wreckers'll come in and tear it down around her. They've done alerted Sheriff Odom. I figure Odom's trying to do the right thing by her, trying hard as a man can, but they got that law waiting for him to carry it out. And if he has to, my wife says as sure as they's a sun in the sky, we'll bury that lady next day. And some claim they'll bury a few machine jockies before sundown the same day. For my part, they ought to be able to see she's as old and worn out as that mare down by the store that's headed for the glue factory soon's we all pull out."

"Does she know about the back taxes on the hotel?"

"—And her living off what folks send over and leave on the back porch. What? Yeah, she knows about that. But nobody can make it sink in. They hoped she'd sell when she saw that, and go to the poor house, and not never know that they tore down the hotel."

"What about her relatives?" Lucius was glad to have found someone who was willing to talk. Trying to shove away, for the moment, the question, why?

"Not a living soul. But that ain't what I started to show you." He took a small black box from the fringed piano stool and crossed the room and bent over and opened the box. "Know whose watch that is?"

"Yours?"

"What do you mean, mine? Does that look like *my* watch? I got on a *wrist* watch. Only *chain* watch I ever owned got smashed in that wreck on the mountain just before they stopped the run. If ever a son-of-a-bitch ort to been shot—anyway, damnit, this here's the one Jesse James dropped on the road as he was leaving town."

The one, Lucius recalled, mentioned in the newspaper article. "That's very nice."

"Nice? Nice? Goddamn it, that's Jesse James' *own* watch. Dropped it in front of that old brick silo down yonder and I found it when I was just a kid. Listen. Hear it tick? It's still ticking. Now listen here." He pointed the thumb-less hand at his chest. "Go ahead, I don't mind, hell, I don't mind. It ain't in the catching stage, either, so don't rare back like that. Nice? Hell, mister, how much you give me for that damn thing? I ain't got all night. You want me to die standing right here talking to you? You think I want to die in this town, right in the middle of all this dying? Ain't I got a right to die in some place where they's young boys chasing bare-assed girls and the heat's dry and the ocean's cool?"

"I've never *been* to Florida myself."

"Don't tell *me* it's nice. How much you give me for it?"

Lucius stood up. "I'm sorry, mister. I'm just passing through."

"Give me what you can. The wife's afraid to go just with what we've got. She thinks you have to be rich to cross the state line."

"I hope you make it, mister."

"All right, you young bastard."

"Mister, you want to sell that watch or eat it?"

"Well, you forced me into it. I'll *tell* you!"

"Tell me what?"

"About the time Billy the Kid robbed the train I was—"

"Thanks for the lemonade, mister."

The sun was so bright when Lucius reached the steps that he threw his arm up before his face. The watch hit him on the shoulder and skidded down the steps.

"You young tramps don't believe in nothing!"

Lucius searched the hotel until dark before he found her. She stood by the front door when he came back down the stairway, her hand on the knob. She opened it as he walked toward her on the carpet and the moonlight pouring onto the glassed-in porch burst into the lobby as through a sluice in a dam, lapping at Lucius's feet.

"Yes, ma'am, I see it. The door to the Blue Goose Hotel where you met Jesse James about eighty years ago. He's waiting for you now up there in one of those rooms—and I'll bet you don't know which. You never learned which. That's why you go from one to another, more a transient in each than any of the other guests *ever* were.

"I almost left town at noon today. I don't want to hurt you. This is not just a story. I could tell you why I—But I can see you won't listen. And you'll never tell me, will you? You put me right with all other others. . . . I see the door okay.

"I also see you going *out* that door one day soon because you can't pay your taxes, and I see tourists flooding in to see where Jesse slept with you—maybe. Bought by the same joker who thought he hit on a good thing with that frozen custard shack down the road. Or have you ever seen it? I'll bet all the shades are drawn on the town side, so you won't have to be reminded. But if you can't find that room, that joker *can*. Any one of these rooms will do, and the card on the door facing will tell all about it—*his* version.

"One time I was hitch-hiking across country—now this will just take a second to tell—and I dropped down a hundred miles out of my way just to hit St. Joseph, because I wanted to see where Jesse James lived out his last days. The House on the Hill had been moved to Highway 71. It is surrounded by a Jesse James Tourist court, a service station, a dance hall, and a souvenir stand. You can buy hamburgers, beer, soft drinks, and an assortment of plastic mementoes. Nearby is a bronze monument of a rider for the Pony Express, opening the west at ten miles an hour.

"But folks want to see the place where a bullet opened up Jesse James. Stop! the neon sign blazes. See the Bullet Hole! I saw it. It looked like it had been made by a cannon—a cannon out of which tourists have been shot, barbed with their ballpoint pens, their stubby pencils, their greasy lipstick, so that *their* names will be immortal—the lucky ones around the hole, the hordes of others all over the walls and the floor. Do you want that desecration for the Blue Goose Hotel?

"All I want is for you to tell me, the way you want to tell it, and I'll be true to your words in the magazine that publishes it, and it'll be a memorial to him nobody can ravage. *Lady Fair* has already told me they'll buy it. I don't even want the money. I'm saying it's yours for telling me, yours to pay those taxes so you can spend your last days here, instead of in the poorhouse."

The old man with the watch had slipped him an ace, and she had forced him to play it. But he would conceal the joker—the fact that paid taxes or not, the hotel would come down within a few weeks.

She let her hand fall from the knob. Lucius closed the door as they stepped into the wavering flood of light, the pattern of frames on the floor.

"Come after dark, the way you came tonight."

"So you were watching me."

"No. I heard you coming out of the trees. I hear every step in the hotel."

"Whatever you say, Miss Ransom. Believe me I—"

"I want cash."

"Ma'am?"

"I'll tell it every night for three nights."

"Fine."

"But I want cash."

"Well. . . . Well, I'll call my editor, and when I come tomorrow night, I'll give it to you."

"I need three hundred dollars. Not all at once."

"May as well."

"I am ninety-five years old. I may be dead when you come some night. I refuse to accept money for something I have not given you."

"Well . . . ."

"And do not hand it to me. *Hide* it—one hundred dollars at a time—in the hotel."

"Sure. Where? "

"Anywhere. And don't tell me."

"How will you—?"

"I'll find it."

"But—"

"I know the Blue Goose Hotel better than you know your own body."

"I don't doubt it."

"Goodnight. I've forgotten your name. Please do not remind me. It will be easier to forget you."

"Must you deny me my identity?"

"You have done that yourself." She opened the door. "Pass through the reading room and leave by the side."

Walking among the bulldozers toward the silo, Lucius doubted that the editor would send him a penny.

The following morning, Lucius thumbed a ride into Blowing Rock, where he called Willa Sarett, fiction editor of *Lady Fair,* who informed him that the air-conditioning unit had broken down and that everyone was "*pos*-tively roasting, Lucius dahling."

He outlined the story and quoted the old lady's price. Willa Sarett couldn't *pos*-sibly advance him three hundred dollars on a story of that description. If he wanted to take the risks, he could write the story and she would give it a swift acceptance or rejection. Okay?

Meanwhile, Lucius strolled into the Blowing Rock branch of the Watauga National Bank, exchanged a dollar bill for dimes, then strolled out, a book of blank checks concealed in his pocket.

All day he walked the mountain paths around Sweetwater, trying to decide whether the romance of Jesse James was worth risking the reality of the North Carolina penal system. But just before the old man closed the trading store, Lucius bought pencils and Blue Horse tablets. After the sun went down and the moon came up, he sneaked through the woods into the Blue Goose Hotel.

After a rarefied game of hide and seek, he found her sitting in the lobby, where she told it.

Finished, she mounted the steps, stiff as a poker. In one of the letter slots behind the desk in the lobby, he stuck a check for one hundred dollars, wondering how she would react when she discovered that he had gone back on his promise to pay cash through the nose.

At the population sign nailed to the fence, Lucius crossed out 73 with a pencil and wrote 77, including Charlta Ransom, himself and Davis Woodring.

Day breaking in the silo—light and birdsong—woke Lucius and he began to write. Miss Ransom's Bostonian manner of speaking, picked up and preserved unaltered from her affected mother, drew from Lucius a Jamesian style. A legend of Jesse James rendered in the vernacular of Henry James, transcribed on Blue Horse tablets with a number two pencil bearing the legend "See Rock City" and honed to a point on sandstone blasted out of the side of a mountain—thus he preened his bizarre appetite for irony.

I DO NOT KNOW who my father was, but my mother assured me again and again that the blood of Boston gentility flowed through my veins. That may well be, but because of that Boston gentility, which somehow found its elegant way to the servant's quarters of that house which I have always imagined was on Beacon Hill, I wore on my body from infancy until my fifteenth year a faint film of dust from roads that led always away from Boston.

We had always enough money to live well, and as a servant, my mother, blooming out of the Glasgow slums, learned not only how to arrange a rendezvous with the son, but also how to behave like the mistress, and how to behave among men such as the master.

No one we encountered betrayed the slightest doubt but that she was what she pretended to be—a widowed gentlelady with sufficient income to live in the manner and in the towns in which she pleased, and she pleased, it must have seemed to those looking forward to seeing her again—although she was arrogant, stingy, and snobbish—that she was pleased never to visit the same town twice.

My dear mother was convinced that her reputation, although both created and exposed solely within the walls of that house on Beacon Hill, would someday confront her across the lobby desk of some resort hotel, as if her reputation were a physical thing, capable of following her and provided by the devil with funds equal to her own.

This strange routine, somehow, over the years, became known, and the story of the widow and her child, now a lovely girl of fourteen, unmistakably genteel, who moved from one resort to another, did indeed one day await her in a little town on the Carolina coast. There was no mistaking, not even by the girl at her side, the smile and the way the clerk pointed the handle of the pen toward her as she stepped forward to sign the register. With that gloved hand still raised, Charlta Ransom, as my mother called herself, turned and touched my cheek with the tips of her fingers and whispered, "They know." Without a word, I followed her out of the hotel, but what she said to me in the lobby became, as soon as I felt upon me the eyes of those seated on the porch, the two most horrible words in the world.

We crossed the Piedmont and rose into the mountains. In Winston-Salem my mother had learned of a town in the mountains, one of the highest in America, and the following morning when I opened my eyes, I looked down at a sea of clouds and what appeared to be the very spine of the world. I have never known what reason Sweetwater ever had for being. Either something extraordinary or nothing at all could cause men to build a town so high, so perched on the edge. I like to think nothing at all—that it is its own reason for being. It was here when we arrived, it is here now, and in every sense that matters, it will always, like the mountains, be here.

THE BLUE GOOSE HOTEL. When my mother saw that sign, she turned one of her rare smiles upon the town and the mountains. Perhaps her reputation—she said it as one would say, 'my lover'—would stand in the road, the devil's money jingling in his pockets, and smile, too, and turn and go away, never imagining that it was here that Charlta Ransom had decided to spend the rest of her life.

No summer people sat on the porch. A few people sat in the lobby, but when they stared, they stared frankly and honestly. And one man, I remember, stood up, as though that enabled him to see better, while the newspaper he had been holding floated to the floor, carpeted I saw, as I crossed the lobby a step behind my mother, with a rug that bespoke the future of the hotel—it would have to last until the hotel nailed up its windows. But the lobby lacked the bitter aura of the has-been.

The room to which we were shown had its secrets perhaps, but with secrets of our own, we never sought out others. My mother sat on a hard chair by the window and gazed out at the wisps of mist that moved through the tops of the pines. Suddenly, she rose and left the room. That was probably the second and final impulsive act of her life. When she returned near midnight, she stood at the window, her hand resting on the curved back of the chair, and, aware that I had sat up in bed, she said, "You are never to leave this room except with me, after all the lights in Sweetwater are out."

I did not learn until 1928, forty-eight years after our arrival in Sweetwater, that some time before midnight my mother had bought the Blue Goose Hotel. Although she behaved as though she owned it—I often heard her voice in the hall, never stern but always clear—it never occurred to me that she might. From my window, I saw nothing of the town, only the pine forest, the birches, the sycamore, the buckeye, the oak, the cedar, the ferns, the mountains and the clouds below, the clouds, oh, my God, the everlasting clouds, and fields of wild flowers blazing in the distance, snow so prevalent I knew what the North Pole must be like, and a forest fire smoking all the month of March.

But my mother, I sensed by echoes of one kind and another, arrogantly kept at a distance from the townspeople. They were tolerant, but they came to resent her—the tone of voices in the hall changed over the winter, while my mother's remained the same.

In April, a chopping sound woke me one bright morning. An old man going into the woods was all I had seen of a human being out that window, so I stood there in my dressing gown with the sunlight burning through the pane, seeing nothing, the bright sun was so direct. But when I stepped aside, I saw a young man with an ax raised over his shoulder, the sun flashing on the blade, wet with the juices of the pine, his head back, his bare chest heaving. He could not see me now, I realized, because the sun glanced back at him off the window. If I stepped back into the full flash of the sun, I would not be able to see him, either. I moved as though responding to the sun, until the window and the lace curtains framed me again. I knew that for him the sun burned my thin nightgown as if it were mist. He seemed so alone under the pines, but I sensed that *his,* unlike my own, was a sweet solitude that was born with the first stroke of the ax and would linger in his body after the last.

I sat by the window all day long and watched the pines fall around him. A little boy brought him water, an old man sat on a trunk and talked to him and after a few hours got up and walked off, leaning on the cane he had whittled while sitting there, but I knew that the young man was conscious every moment of my face in the window overlooking the pines.

He worked a week, chopping and hauling the pines away. I had a mortal fear of my mother, who taught me since I was old enough to understand the human voice that men were evil and cruel. In our wanderings, she made use of every opportunity to point that out. If a man gripped his wife's arm in suppressed anger, Mother nudged me and pointed with a glance of her cold gray eyes. The female tutors who had come stiffly to my rooms in the various hotels all seemed to have had previous training from Charlta Ransom. I was an impressionable student, and my mother impressed me with everything she said or did. I feared her, although she never struck me until. . . .

I was afraid of the young man who cut the pines, but the fear he inspired was so different from what I felt in my mother's presence that my confusion and fascination made me impulsive and reckless in my daydreams. But my body felt drugged and cumbersome as I moved in the room.

One night the young man threw a note tied to a pine chip through my open window. He could not spell, his grammar was poor. What he said terrified me, but after a while I realized that what I felt was also elation. I answered his note, intentionally misspelling, using poor grammar, but I couldn't resist signing my name with a Spencerian flourish—Zara Jane Ransom.

By July, we had managed to meet on the back porch of the hotel. As I felt the hard thumping of my heart, I knew how a frightened bird must feel. I was startled when the young man emerged from the shadows and crossed the porch in the moonlight and spoke my name, 'Z-Z-Z-Za-ah-ara—Zara,' he said. All he managed to stutter that night was my first name and his own full name, Davis Woodring.

Before the first week in September, he had told me that he loved me and I let him hold my hand, which prevented him from speaking at all. My mother, of course, never knew. Perhaps she drank, and passed her nights in a deep sleep.

Ritualistically, she came to my room every night some time before or after midnight and took my hand, and I went with her down the deserted halls, down the narrow back stairway, rank with an animal odor, and out onto the porch at the rear of the hotel. We always wore simple but elegant dresses, especially if there was a moon, and often she let me get a few steps ahead of her on the path along the mountainside and I felt her eyes on me. In her own way, she was proud of me. Of the figure I presented to the moon.

On one of those walks in the moonlight in early September, she came up from behind me and took my hand and turned me gently around and kissed the corners of my mouth. That brief moment of bliss, the only one we ever shared, ended abruptly with the sharp little shriek that came from my mouth. It was the first time I ever knew that I was capable of hurting my mother, but I had not intended to. And I could not explain that it was not her kiss that startled me—although there is nothing more startling than impulsive expressions of affection from cold people—but the sight of a man, leaning against a tree a hundred yards away, winding, I learned later, a gold watch, at midnight in the middle of the forest. At his back was a deformed pine tree to which clung profusely a mammoth rose bush whose briars twisted and looped among the branches and whose erratic blooms were now opening in the moonlight.

AT NOON, the tale transcribed, Lucius emerged from the silo and found a crust of grasshoppers clinging to the bricks. "Worst this year than ever I remember seein' 'em," someone had said. Whatever juice there had once been around here the grasshoppers had gotten years ago. If those houses, hidden behind the trees, and the Blue Goose Hotel, visibly balanced on the hill, were like the dried husks in the field, the corn was still green and lush in the imaginations of the inhabitants, and Miss Ransom appeared to be the underground reservoir that kept certain juices pulsing. Lucius washed his hands and face in the creek and hitch-hiked to Boone.

In downtown Boone, Lucius responded on impulse to the open door of a phone booth and put in a collect call to Knoxville, Tennessee. He had not spoken in person to Loris Blackburn since the morning of her marriage three years ago to Earl Underwood, "a sweet guy." She had finally made the decision that a life of quiet desperation was to be preferred—slightly it must be admitted—over a life of spectacular disintegration. Soon after making this decision, she had made another, concerning a husband, children, a car, a mortgage on a ranch house (the ranch itself consisting of other ranch houses), a church of *his* choice, a convenient shopping center, and, ultimately, the secretaryship of the Dogwood Festival. Lucius picked up the phone in a flush of sentiment, but when he told the operator it was a collect call, he knew he was going to hit her for a loan. To cover the checks. He hoped that the actual voice of the hero would have such an impact that she, his witness, would respond.

"Hello." She was grunting. "Doran! Hello."

"I have a collect call from—"

"Pardon me, please. No, Doran, no, no, no, honey. Drop it, honey. That's— Pardon me, please."

"I have a collect call from a Mr. Lu—"

"Doran! Doran! For God's sakes! Hello, whoever it is, please call back, my little girl is trying to plug in the TV!"

Loris Blackburn Underwood, responding to the impact of other things, pitched the phone into its cradle.

Lucius wished her well, and, his car still mysteriously failing to yield to wrenches, hiked back to Sweetwater as the sun sank and the mist in the valleys rose.

From fading twilight until deep dark, Lucius searched for Zara Jane Ransom. Finally, he heard her voice through the walls, coming from one of the rooms, telling him to leave the hotel and not come back. He had deceived her. Cash. She had insisted on cash, and he had left a check in a message slot behind the lobby desk. He thought and spoke quickly and regretted it immediately. He had heard, he told her, that a stranger in Boone was convinced she had a cashbox full of money hidden in the hotel. If she was robbed, checks could be cancelled, cash could not. When she unlocked the door and let him in, she didn't appear frightened. Simply convinced of the soberness of his argument.

In the middle of her story, Zara Ransom stopped talking and laid her hand on the window sill, quickly but softly, as she might have laid it on Lucius's knee to quiet him. He listened with her, hearing nothing. She did not seem certain. "What is that sound? It stays in the distance. Before, it was always in the daytime." She put her hand back in her lap, under the folds of her dress and continued.

After she finished the telling, Lucius said, "It's probably just a rumor—about that guy that thinks you've got money hidden in the hotel."

Tomorrow night, after the end, the final installment, he would tell her it was only a joke. Nobody, he would tell her, had the heart to rob the sweetheart of Jesse James.

That night, he slipped Exhibit B in the case of Watauga Bank vs. Lucius Hutchfield under the carpet on the stairs, wanting to discover just how much better she knew the Blue Goose Hotel than he knew his own body.

"Hi, neighbor," Lucius said, to the skeleton of the scarecrow as he passed.

When he stepped over the sill, someone inside the silo slapped Lucius's face. Unable to see, he threw up his hands. Whoever struck him was part of the dark. Someone slapped at him and kicked at him rapidly as he backed away from the door. He stumbled over a rock and fell backward.

A body fell on top of him, kneeing him in the groin. Reaching up to catch hold of his attacker, Lucius's hand caught hold of a breast. Even through the dress, his thumb felt the nipple vividly.

"You get out of this town, you hear me, you get out of this town, and you stay out!" She slapped at him.

He caught her around the waist and pulled her down to him. His arms moved up her back until he could hug her tightly. Her hair hung about his cheeks and he could hardly catch his breath, the scent of cheap jasmine perfume was so profuse. "Who are you?" For some odd reason it struck him as a stupid, pointless question.

"If you don't leave, the *next* time, I'll use something more than my fists!" She yelled into his ear, breaking away from his embrace.

She rose, kicked him in the ribs, and ran off down the road.

Lying in the silo on the straw, he felt thankful to the woman. She had introduced an element of risk. Physical risk. It went well with the risk he had introduced himself—the checks. He slept the sleep of the somewhat absolved.

The next morning, Lucius wrote Part Two of the *Legend of Jesse James and Zara Ransom* in the voice of Miss Ransom.

AGAIN, THE FOLLOWING NIGHT, he was there, but hidden by a limb of the pine tree that touched the ground, laden with roses. Walking behind my mother, I looked for him. One can always see well enough in the dark when there is something to see. His solitude seemed like mine, as though it needed another solitude to make it bearable. I thought I heard him breathing at the same moment in which I was most conscious of the scent of the roses, but I heard something behind me and turned with my mother to watch a deer leap out of some ferns across the path.

I never thought for a moment that he had come there to wait for *me*, yet I was certain that he would be there the following night. Although there was a fine drizzle and water dropped from the leaves and clouds hovered around the moon like a hand, he was there, the toes of his shoes protruding from the roses and needles. His coat-tail, flung back where he had his hand in his pocket, showed through an opening in the leaves.

The following night, a rose lay on a stump beside the path. My mother stared straight ahead. I caught it in my hand as I passed, and when I lay on the bed an hour later and opened my hot fingers, it was bruised. I pinned it to my nightgown and the mingled smells of the rose and of my own body kept me awake until dawn.

The next night, he was not there. I hung back, trying to see through the moonless darkness and the foliage, but my mother called to me to hurry before the rain caught us, and I stumbled up the path to the summit.

From a ledge 3,000 feet above sea level we had a view of the Appalachian mountain ranges. We often drank from the spring that fell into a natural fountain shoulder high before turning left across the path and stepping onto the ledge. That night, my mother drank first, and as I bent close to the sound of falling water, I sensed, even before she grasped my wrist, that my mother had stopped abruptly, then she turned.

I turned, my mouth wet, and saw him. He stood on the ledge, facing us, the sky violet and endless behind him, the mountains like furrows below him. The clouds having passed, the light from the quarter moon shone on his face.

He bowed solemnly. "Good evening, ladies. Please forgive me if I startled you. My name is John Howard."

"Mr. Howard," my mother said, "this is a private walk. If you must walk at night, be good enough in the future to take the paths on the other side of town."

"But am I likely on the other paths to encounter ladies so charming as yourselves?" He did not bow again, but tilted his head slightly, and new shadows enhanced the glow on his face. When he smiled, my mother put her handkerchief to her mouth, took my hand, and walked swiftly down the path.

I wept that night, knowing our walks would end until Mr. Howard should leave Sweetwater.

The next day was incredibly hot. I walked about the room in my undergarments with a damp cloth in my hand and the dead rose in my hair.

At noon a pebble struck my window pane. Davis Woodring stood below with a note in his hand. I pretended not to see him.

That night, the air was cool as I sat in my dark room by the open window, looking down into the clearing Davis had made with his ax.

Two men, one taller than the other, stepped off the porch below and walked among the stumps. I heard the murmur of their voices. The shorter man sat on a stump and drew on a cigar, revealing Mr. Howard's face. Suddenly, he rose, stood before the tall man, spoke quickly and sharply, and then strode off toward the forest, flinging his cigar high into the air. I felt much nearer him when I saw that he limped.

The tall man shook his head, turned slowly, and returned to the porch. I heard the swing creak as he sat down and swung.

I was still at the window when Mr. Howard emerged from the trees, far to the right of the path. He passed directly below me, and just as he disappeared, I coughed. Stepping backward, he came into view again, his head back, his face dark. "Zara?"

I closed my eyes for a moment, trying to stop trembling. When I looked again, he was gone.

An hour later, I heard a soft knock at the door. I was too terrified to open. He knocked only once more. Then I heard his footsteps on the carpet in the hall and listened for a door to open. But the sound of his footsteps faded.

The next day, I stayed by the window, but he did not come.

When Davis Woodring came, I leaned back and hid behind the curtains. I felt guilty and ashamed. I knew what he felt, and I knew that my mother was wrong—cruelty was not a special quality of men, and perhaps even in men it was sometimes regretful.

When midnight came and Mr. Howard still did not come, I knew that he was torturing me, and I suffered all the more intensely.

My mother came to say goodnight. I stayed out of the light because I knew that I looked sick and that she, she certainly, would know immediately what ailed me.

That night, when he knocked, I felt the vibrations against my bosom and stomach, and even in my knees. "Zara?"

And I said, "Yes," and opened the door.

He walked past me across the room, very slowly, and sat where I had sat all day. Standing against the closed door in the dark, I knew that he felt the warmth of my body on the red velvet of the cushioned chair.

"Please sit with me." He rose and put out his hand.

I took his hand and sat where he had sat. Still holding my hand, he reached for the hard chair and pulled it over and sat on the other side of the window.

"We can't talk," I cautioned him.

"We don't have to."

We held hands a long time, and then he got up and held both my hands and kissed each corner of my mouth just as my mother had done on the path that first night. He pressed my palms against his cheeks and left the room.

The next night, he slipped a note under my door, and at 2 a.m. I slipped out and met him in the spring house.

"It's chilly in here," I told him.

No moon, the woods dark, we moved among the trees and vines very slowly to the ledge, aware of miles of mountains below us in the absolute dark.

We sat down there and talked for a long time, until one faint spot of red, like a blemish, appeared on the sky.

The following night, I lay with him in the enclosure of the rose tree. It was the first and last time in my long life that I ever felt blissful pain and ecstasy.

The following night, he began to teach me courage. I had told him how frightened I had been of him, how terrified I was of people, of my mother above all.

He laughed gently. "Every man in this world lives in mortal fear. Some men avoid it, some men embrace it. Let's say only that I've never avoided it, and that the minute—no, the instant—I do, I'll be dead the next."

When I told him that I had never been out of my room in the daytime, had never seen Sweetwater in daylight, and at night only through the trees as my mother and I climbed the hill behind the Blue Goose Hotel, he became so angry he stuttered and slammed his fist against the trunk of the pine-rose tree.

I told him that one ride in a buggy through the town would satisfy me, that it would be almost like Boston.

He put his arms around me. "At noon tomorrow I will be waiting in front of the hotel with the reins in my hands and if you don't come out on the porch sharp at noon, I'm driving on, and not coming back."

He didn't say another word to me that night. I lay awake until dawn, quivering, because I knew I could never open that door, much less ride with Mr. Howard through town.

At eleven-thirty, a knock startled me. I had spent the morning praying he would come, and that I would be able to persuade him to forget his reckless notion. But a stranger stood in the hall.

"Are you Miss Zara Ransom?"

I told him I was and he asked permission to come in and talk to me. "I'm Mr. Howard's brother."

I let him in and stood by the door. "If my mother—"

"I know. I'll be brief as possible. It may hurt you, but it will hurt less than the future will, if you go on seeing my brother. What would you say if I told you he is married and has children?"

"I've never thought about it."

"Think about it now."

I had never really lived in a society, and did not have the thoughts, the fears most young girls perhaps had.

"I can see by your eyes that it means close to nothing to you. Perhaps you're too young to understand what that can mean. Well, I packed my bags and my brother's in case I'd have to tell you and then tell him that I had to tell you, so—"

"Tell me what, Mr. Howard?"

"That's just it. Our name isn't Howard. It's James. We're from Kearney, Missouri. My name's Frank."

I couldn't speak for a few moments. I saw a man's eyes between the brim of a hat and a red kerchief over his mouth and chin.

"Where is Mr. Howard—Mr. James now?"

"Like a plucked goose, he's sitting in front of the hotel that's named after him."

"Thank you for coming to see me, Mr. James."

"It's your own business what you do about it—yours and Jesse's. *My* horse is saddled. I've got a wife and children, too. The difference is—I ain't forgot it. Good day."

I opened the door for him. He was a real gentleman.

I put on the dress I was wearing the night he first saw me. I opened the door and went into the hall. I was not afraid. I was going for a buggy ride with Jesse James.

For the first time since the night my mother and I came to the Blue Goose Hotel, I descended the stairs into the lobby. It was full of people, waiting for dinner. As they all watched me cross the lobby and glide toward the door, I held my head high, imitating my mother's carriage. Jesse James waited for me outside.

I glimpsed my mother's back where she stood just inside the dining room. A waitress saw me and dropped a handful of forks, because although she had never seen me, my resemblance to Charlta Ransom struck her.

Jesse must have seen me, even from where he sat in the sun as I walked across the cool, dim lobby. He was at the door when I reached it.

He lifted me into the buggy, and as I waited for him to climb in on the other side, I saw Frank James smoking a cigar in a rocking chair, his feet on the rail, his saddle bags leaning against the rungs.

Then I saw my mother on the porch, but we were down the drive and almost on the road before she called to me.

We rode up and down the street four times. Jesse bought me a transparent apple from a farmer whose wagon was full under a tree.

When we entered the drive to the hotel an hour later, I was even less afraid than before, because I realized something about fear. I had ridden brazenly with my lover up and down the single street of Sweetwater, unafraid of my mother, or these strangers, because I knew Jesse James, the most famous and daring outlaw in all the world, was at my side. But not until we entered the drive did I remember that no one but *I* knew who he was.

Frank James was not on the porch.

As Jesse held the door open for me, tipping his hat to the ladies in rockers, I glanced back at Sweetwater and saw Davis Woodring, walking uncertainly up the drive.

In the lobby, Jesse bowed to me and strolled into the dining room as I ascended the stairs.

When I opened the door, my mother laid her hands on me and beat me until, tasting blood in my mouth, I sank to the floor.

ALL DAY, UNTIL DARK, until time to sneak into the hotel to listen to the final episode, Lucius stayed near the silo.

Again, she made him search for her in the dark. He was "it." Without the moon, he had to *feel* for her. Finally, he stumbled over her feet where she sat on the ottoman.

"Did I ever tell you about the time Jesse came through Knoxville?" Lucius wanted to give Zara Ransom something of Jesse James, even a compassionate lie, blended with something true. She did not speak. "There was this famous detective named Bligh that wanted to hunt Jesse down. One day Bligh met this very good-natured traveler at the Baltimore and Ohio railroad station and they got talking and Bligh set him up to a cup of coffee, and in the course of the conversation, Bligh declared that as he neared retirement age, his one wish was that before he died, he could at least meet Jesse James. The next day, he told several friends about the fine gentleman he had chanced to meet. Few days later he got a postcard from Baltimore. 'Dear Mr. Bligh— You have been quoted as saying on more than one occasion that if you could only meet Jesse James, you'd be content to lie down and die. Well, Mr. Bligh, you can now stretch out, lie down and die. The gentleman you met the other day in the R. R. depot of Knoxville was Yours Sincerely, Jesse Woodson James.'"

Telling her story, Miss Ransom mentioned the silo, and when Lucius said, "Ah," so faintly he didn't realize it was audible, she said, "I imagine you have been to the rose-pine tree, too."

"Yes, ma'am."

"Do you promise on your sacred honor to leave town and—" She stopped and sat very still, her head tilted, her eyes flickering from side to side.

"What's—"

"Ssshhh," she said. "Listen. Do you hear it?"

"Hear what?"

"That strange noise again?"

"What noise, Miss Ransom? It's only my breathing."

"I heard it only in the daytime at the end of spring, day after day, and then it stopped, and some nights in July, I have awakened with that strange rumble in my head. Don't you hear it?"

Lucius listened with her. He heard only the locusts, but he realized what she meant. The resentful silence of the bulldozers found expression in their dreams under the moon, and the echoes of that nightmarish roar reached the ears of one of the doomed even after the moon had gone into the clouds.

"No, I can't hear a thing, Miss Ransom."

"Why do you lie to me? I can see in your eyes that you hear something."

"Probably the cars on the highway. Please continue your story. Jesse James and Davis Woodring are about to draw on each other."

"Do you promise—?"

"Yes, on my sacred honor—to leave town when you've told your story."

"Forever."

"Forever."

"No. That is all I am going to tell you."

"But, Miss Ransom, did you or did you not go away with Jesse James?"

"You do not have to give me another check. I didn't realize until I saw them standing in the road just now, again, after all these years, so vividly, what a sacrilege I have committed in telling you *anything*."

"But Miss Ransom, isn't there some kind of sin against telling a story up to its climax, then getting up and walking away?"

"I realized something else in the same moment. I'm finally beginning to understand why you're here. So when I say I am not going to tell you any more,

I'm not being mean-hearted, for by stopping here, I surrender it all to your imagination."

"Thank you, Miss Ransom. I understand. You are a very kind and wise lady. You know, I was telling a friend of mine just recently that I had *not* done, seen, experienced everything, but that I *felt* as though I had. That, having felt *everything*, I now felt nothing. I'm glad you believe so strongly in my capacity to feel again that you—"

"No. No, you don't understand. You are cursed with consciousness, young man. Perhaps that saves you from lunacy. But, no, you see, I don't think you've *ever* felt anything."

He heard her dress move as she stood up in the dark. As she climbed the stairs, he didn't move.

After a while, he had control over himself again. Then he realized that *that* didn't speak well for him either. He went to the top of the stairway and counted the steps, down to the thirteenth. He felt under the carpet for the check he had left the night before. It was gone. "I'm leaving the third check, Miss Ransom," he said, in an even voice, knowing that she would hear him. His legs were weak as he descended the stairs to the lobby.

He went to the kitchen. Her wonderful good hearing no doubt caught him there. He took off his shoes and went into the dining room where long ago places were laid for dinner. At the place where Lucius imagined Jesse James had sat after that noon buggy ride, where he had sat with fork in hand when Charlta Ransom, her hands ringing and aching from the blows she had given her daughter, entered and strode across the room to his table, Lucius lifted the plate and placed the check in the white circle that he could not see but knew was there on the dust-laden tablecloth.

In Sweetwater Creek, he washed his hands and his feet. In the dark silo, he ate Pork and Beans from a can with the fork he had taken from the table where Jesse James had sat.

Then, by the light of a candle he had bought for the purpose, Lucius wrote the incomplete final episode—

MY MOTHER HAD NEVER LOCKED the door to my room. She trusted more in the certainty of my captivity in her own personality than ever she would have trusted the lock on a door. But she stood over me a moment as I lay on the floor, and the realization must have come to her that now I was a woman of fifteen, and the time had come when it was necessary to shake the fist of authority in my face and to put me under lock and key. Perhaps she realized later, too, as I did soon after she left the room, that she had taught me that cruelty and destruction may be the province of the male but it was ground upon which a woman might occasionally stand to advantage.

On my feet again, I went, of course, directly to the window. A man walked off the porch from below, carrying a shotgun. Through my tears I mistook him for Jesse James, but when he raised his face, I did not recognize it. There were so few faces I could have. But Davis came around through the grass at the side and stopped a few yards from the man with the shotgun, who turned to face him. Half an hour later, Davis went away.

During that hour, I learned later, my mother sent for 'John Howard' and ordered him to leave the hotel immediately. His bags would be packed and brought to him in the street. It was not the gentleman, 'John Howard,' with his limp and his polite smile, but Jesse James, who laughed in my mother's face.

"Madam, the way you treat your daughter, you should be horse-whipped."

He informed her that he had paid in advance for his lodging and he would gladly depart early the following morning.

But when he went through the hotel asking for his brother and was told that he had ridden out of town an hour ago, he went to his room.

The sheriff was on the porch when he came out. They shook hands because the sheriff liked Mr. Howard and was glad he had come out of the hotel before he could reach the lobby to carry out Charlta Ransom's request.

"I'm going to meet my brother. We plan to rob a train tonight."

The deep laughter I heard all the way up in my room where I lay on the bed crying must have been the sheriff's.

I did not know that Jesse James had left town. At one-thirty a.m., a pebble struck my window pane and I was startled out of a dream of love. The aura of the dream still hovered over my mind as I looked down into the yard and saw Jesse, wearing traveling clothes, stand astraddle the prone body of the man with the shotgun. The shotgun was broken in the middle, as the man himself seemed to be, and lay with two shells at the man's feet.

I opened the window, and the way Jesse opened his arms, without a word of encouragement, so confident that his open arms were enough, and because

I was still in that interrupted dream of love, I jumped from the second story window and he caught me in his arms. And his fervent kiss ended the dream.

I walked blissfully at his side across the grass to the gravel drive and down to the road where the same buggy waited.

He took the reins in his hands and looked at me. "Is this what you want, Zara?"

"Yes, Jesse—*you*, all my life."

"Who told you my name—?"

"Your brother."

"Then it's a good thing for him he left me here alone. He told me he would leave if I took you for that drive at noon today, and I didn't believe him. I thought those saddle bags and that act of sitting on the porch, wearing a frown like Jove, was to scare me. . . . I reckon he knew he'd *better* git. . . . He tell you anything else?"

I lied.

"Anybody else know who I am?"

"No."

"And you would run away to one nowhere after another with a man who tempts death and the devil every day?"

"Yes."

Jesse snapped the reins and the buggy moved slowly down the hill past the dark houses in the soft dirt of the road.

Just out of town on the old road (that has grown over with weeds now, I suppose) stood a silo. Davis Woodring jumped out of the doorway with a pistol in his hand, and grabbed the reins and stopped the horses.

He stuttered the name "Mr. Howard" and vowed he was going to kill him—a horrible animal sound, the spittle from his mouth spraying my cheek.

I begged him to put up his pistol and turn loose the reins so we could go on. I told him that Mr. Howard and I were going to get married. In the moonlight, I saw that Jesse James' knuckles were white from the hard grip he had on the reins. He would reach for his gun, I thought, if I weren't beside him, and he would kill poor Davis Woodring for my sake. I did not want anyone to get hurt.

"Let us pass, mister," said Jesse. His lips did not seem to move.

"Move again and I'll shoot you where you sit," Davis stuttered.

"You don't hold that pistol like a man that's ever used one. You might hit Zara. Now be so kind as to let us go on our way."

"I ain't done much shootin', Mister fancy Howard, you're right, so get down from that buggy and step in that silo, so she won't see me do it."

"What claim you got to such anger, sir? Do you know this lady?"

"I do. She's my sweetheart. You shut up."

Jesse looked at me very slowly. "Has this man known you as I have known you?"

The click of the pistol as he cocked it made us both turn toward Davis.

"No. No, I swear."

"Get down or I'll fire."

Jesse gave me the reins and got down, and Davis was on his side when he stood in the road. Davis led Jesse around the back of the buggy and I pleaded with Davis to put his pistol away, that I never loved him. "But let him go and I'll go with *you*, Davis."

They were at the side of the road and the black doorway of the silo was just behind Jesse and he was in black, so all I saw was his pale face under the hat.

"I'm set on killing him and I'm going to kill him. Get in that silo."

"If you're trying to show her you're a man, mister, this is a certain way to show her the opposite. Uncock that gun and give me a chance to reach for mine and *then* show yourself a man."

Davis looked at him a long time. Then he slowly released the hammer.

"Just allow me my coat unbuttoned, and I'll call you, even despite your having the ups with the gun in your hand."

Begging them to stop did no good.

Jesse unbuttoned his vest and the watch-chain winked in the light from the creek.

"You ready?" I realized for the first time that there was a tremor in Jesse's voice—the sweetest, kindest voice I have ever heard.

"If you are," Davis stuttered.

THAT NIGHT, lying on the loud corn shucks, Lucius did not worry about snakes and black widows. He worried about the effect on his readers, readers like Loris, of learning that Jesse James didn't run away with Zara Ransom after all. But wasn't the ending up to him? Lucius decided to sleep on it, to dream through it.

He woke before daybreak. The candle was a puddle of tallow. He waited for light. When it came, dimly, he began to write, and after a few hours, he set fire to what he had written and warmed his hands.

Lucius was sitting on the bench in front of the Sweetwater Trading Post when the old man came down the road and opened the unlocked door.

"What fer you this bright and early morning?"

"Bottle of milk and a poke full of oranges."

"What's the matter, your bowels stopped up?"

"You might put it that way."

"Stick around a few more days and them bulldozers'll clean you out plumb through. Behind them drawn shades we're *all* packed. Everybody got 'em a truck hired and ready to go, a few steps ahead of the tractors. Guess no harm in telling you, a stranger, all this, since you seem to take a liking to this town."

Lucius looked around at the merchandise and couldn't believe that in several days the old store would "disappear from the face of the earth." Was that expression too strong for what would happen to a little country store, to a small town like Sweetwater that no one ever heard of? Nothing to compare with the town in Peru that disappeared under volcanic lava within minutes? *People* had died there. Perhaps that was the difference. But Lucius imagined this old man in Arizona, and the old man with the fake Jesse James watch in Florida, and others living with children they had not seen in years and had mercifully forgotten, and others sitting against the walls of public buildings in strange metropolises. And he wondered if the people in Peru hadn't the better deal.

The old man talked without a tremor of the impending shove over the precipice, but between that evening five days ago when Lucius first saw him and this bright August morning, he had acquired a ghostly pallor such as one might retain after recurrent journeys across the landscapes of nightmares.

Lucius took the paper cap off the top of the milk bottle and drank long. He wiped his mouth. "Who you selling your merchandise to?"

"What you offering me?"

"Me? Nothing, I—"

"Just as likely you as anybody else. This is all old country store merchandise. Nobody I know would want stuff on his shelves that come from a store that took a swan dive off a mountainside, anyway. Spooky feeling. I used to worry bout that adam bomb, but I don't no more. What's it gonna bust up that I give ary damn for?"

"So you gonna leave it all and—"

"And one of these first days I'll just walk out and get in the car and let my son take me on som'mers. I ain't the only one's leaving stuff behind. But I guess we all got things we won't part with for the world. You cut me off from my old coffee grinder an' see if I don't cut out your blamed heart fer it." The old man hugged the large old coffee machine, a murderous glint in his eyes that made Lucius feel as though he had threatened the old man's grinder.

Outside, Lucius looked at the town. It had been so long since he had felt anything intensely that the anger he felt now turned the milk on his stomach sour. But it was such a general hatred for all the destructive forces he had ever observed or engaged in that he was weak with a sense of helplessness.

He walked toward the Blue Goose Hotel, intending to eat his breakfast under the rose-pine tree. Then he would climb it for one last look.

Someone raised a shade and looked up and across the road at the Blue Goose Hotel. The woman turned quickly to someone in the room. A man wearing suspenders was soon at her side. Lucius followed their gaze.

In the bright morning sun, Zara Ransom stood on the steps with the multi-paned glass front blazing behind her. Lucius did not recognize her by what he had seen before. Now she was dressed in white organdy, a blue sash, and blue ribbon trimming a wide straw hat. Lucius did not see that old woman who had told him the story of a young girl's romance with Jesse James. He saw the girl herself, pausing before the glass facade as though waiting for a gentleman in a buggy to come up the gravel drive. Not until she moved, going down the broken walk to the steep stone steps, was it apparent that she was a very old, decrepit woman whom the sun might kill at any moment.

A cluster of flies sipped at Lucius's orange scented hands and a sweat bee bit the corner of his mouth.

He ran to the store, but the old man was already out front, looking up the road, shielding his eyes against the sun like an Indian Scout. Lucius stood at his side and saw that the glare of the morning sun had turned the white goddess into a shimmering moth with flecks of blue.

"Somebody's got to stop her."

"Where's it any of your concern?" The old man stared at Lucius.

The old people appeared on their steps, the men in good coats, and the women wearing hats.

Another grandfather appeared in front of the store.

"She looks like a woman that's finally got holt of the means to get what she wants," said the storekeeper.

"But where would she get three hundred dollars for them taxes? Rob a bank while we're all asleep?" asked the second old man.

"No use to go near her. The way she come out of that hotel and stood on the steps I vowed to myself wouldn't nothing do no good."

"Yessir," said the second man. "I may as well send word to my son that it's finally time."

When Miss Ransom, walking, down the middle of the road, got within a hundred feet of the store, Lucius stepped back behind the men and, unnoticed, reached behind him, opened the screen, and backed into the cave-like gloom of the store. Between the heads of the men, he watched her pass, the hat and parasol hiding her face.

"Well, I didn't get a look at all of her face." The storekeeper pointed at Lucius. "Did you?"

"Who needs to!"

"Sure as the world she's headed for the courthouse in Boone, a-walking it!"

"Can't you stop her?" They just looked at Lucius through the dusty screen until he saw himself clearly.

Those million readers of *Lady Fair*, sitting under hair dryers, looking like Martians caught and clapped into gas chambers, were waiting for Lucius Hutchfield to provide them with thirty minutes' diversion.

With this sense of mission, he left the two natives of Sweetwater and turned onto the old road that would soon be the newest thing in time-savers or time-killers. The caterpillars and bulldozers sat like ruins capable of coming instantly alive and devouring everything in sight. He picked up a rock, spit on it, and threw it through the windshield of a bulldozer. It made no response.

In the silo, the Blue Horse tablet on his knee, he wrote almost compulsively, imagining endings to the legend.

THEY WERE JUST ABOUT TO DRAW their guns, when Jesse James said, "Just one thing you may like to know before I kill you, mister. And that is that you have the immortal honor of dying at the hands of Jesse James. Reach!"

I screamed, "Jesse!"

Davis dropped his pistol as though it hurt his hand and then threw his arms into the air, shouting, "I'm unarmed!" without a stutter.

Jesse James laughed at him, a Colt revolver in his hand. The tone of that laugh froze me to the marrow. I jumped down and flung my arms around Davis' waist and pleaded with Jesse not to kill him.

"I don't see any reason why I shouldn't."

I told Jesse I wanted to marry Davis Woodring. I told Jesse that I knew he had a wife and children, and that I couldn't live with guns and killing.

Davis told me that *he* couldn't live with *me,* reminding me daily that he was a coward. I could feel his stomach tremble against the inside of my arm.

"You're no coward, Davis," I said. "You're his equal."

"He's Jesse James."

"No. He's Mr. Howard. When he had to tell you his real name, he became Mr. Howard forever. He told you that to frighten you, because he was afraid himself."

Jesse James laughed. "Go with her, mister. My brother was right. *I'd* probably leave her somewhere, someday, and ride fast as I can to see my wife. I don't admit to being scared, but I'd hate to die, knowing I had broken the commandment against adultery. My momma raised me right. She's just got one arm now, but she'd tear me apart. Get in that buggy before I take a notion to walk over your dead body."

We got in, and Jesse pulled out a money sack and pitched it into Davis' lap. He just looked at it.

"There's enough change to set you up in business up in Ohio or someplace. If there's any love between you, you'll have to make *that* yourselves."

Jesse took my hand and kissed it, and stepped back and slapped the rump of one of the horses.

When I looked back, he was standing in the road in the moonlight, putting his pistol back into his holster, buttoning his vest, blotting out the wink of light on the watch chain. The same pistol Jesse gave Bob Ford, which he used to shoot him in the back in the spring of the following year.

EXHAUSTED, Lucius lay back upon the corn husks and thought of himself as a monk in his cell. Voluntary imprisonment, for the purpose of meditation and transcription, and, if possible, atonement. That was how he would look at it when they drove him through the gates of the State Penitentiary. In the absence of monasteries for agnostics, the penitentiary seemed appropriate. It was one thing to arrange your own punishment, but how did one go about arranging to feel the one thing necessary if the punishment was to be meaningful? Shame. He did not yet feel shame. Only self-loathing.

At seven o'clock the sun began to go behind the mountain. Through the rents in the roof, a mellow yellow glow moved mountains down the curved brick wall of the silo. Where there had been only a thin gauze of green moss the day before, Lucius saw testimony to the fact that he and the snakes and black widows that he imagined were not the only transients in the silo. White chalk proclaimed that "Rufus Noe got Gloria Jones Chery August 18, 1953." Was that worth recording? He looked at it as he had once looked at a crude cave drawing that dated from 964 B.C. Lucius started to rub it out with the sleeve of his shirt, but it occurred to him that the world was a museum without walls, and he felt like a vandal who had refrained.

When it got dark in the silo, he went out and sat in a clearing on the bank of the creek and watched the darkness thickened on the water under the low trees. Then he took off his clothes and waded into the creek. The water was ice cold. When he came to a place that sloped, he ducked under and rubbed his body vigorously. He crawled out and put on his clothes. But he still felt unclean.

Suddenly, the mountains seemed to give out a strange groan that rose from the valley below. He ran up the path to Sweetwater, a siren growing louder. On the road, a red and white ambulance, with a red swirling light on top, raced past him, leaving a film of dust over his face and hands, and he brushed it from his clothes as he walked swiftly up into the town.

People were in the road going up to the Blue Goose Hotel where the ambulance had parked in front of the main entrance. They gave Lucius hostile glances as though he, being a stranger, were an accomplice to whatever had happened to Zara Ransom in Boone. The storekeeper shoved past Lucius, the legs of his overalls rasping together.

When Lucius reached the steps, the ambulance was already edging through the old people back down the drive. He knew that all the houses were empty, that here in front of the Blue Goose Hotel was gathered the entire population of Sweetwater. He counted them at a glance—twenty-five, one of whom was a spastic child. A woman seemed to guard the door. From her comments to the people, who appeared to take turns speaking to her, Lucius learned what had happened.

Miss Ransom had appeared at the tax clerk's desk with three one hundred dollar checks Lucius had conned her into taking for her life story choked in her hand, and the clerks had decided to tell her for good and all that no amount of paid taxes would save the hotel, that a four lane highway was coming through, and that she would have to go to the poorhouse or to stay with relatives if she had any. So Lucius would *not* have to settle into a cell.

She had tried to walk back in the sun, but she had fainted in the middle of Boone, and someone had carried her into the A & P, where it was cool, until the ambulance arrived. They somehow realized that if they did not want her to die, they had better take her back to the Blue Goose Hotel.

Lucius broke through to the woman on the steps. "May I see Miss Ransom?"

"I been seeing you roaming this town for a solid week. In my day, somebody would have shot you by now. We don't appreciate newspapermen—"

"I swear, I—"

"Even her own townspeople can't get in to see her. Ain't nobody gonna disturb her privacy."

Lucius wondered whether, if he got close enough, he would smell jasmine perfume on the woman. He looked at her breasts. She was younger than the others, not over fifty, and looked strong enough, willful enough to jump a man in a dark silo.

Lucius started to ask if any of them knew of anyone who was kin to Miss Ransom, but he remembered something the old man with the fake Jesse James watch had said, "She's the last of her tribe, 'less that little bastard of hers, if she had one, is still roaming around."

At least he could honor his promise. Lucius left Boone, his car in humming fine condition now.

Passing through Bristol, Tennessee, he stopped at the post office. He had found some twine and some heavy brown sacks in a trash can in an alley.

"This wrapped okay?"

"Well, I wouldn't put it up as a model. What's in it?"

"Dust blown off the moon."

The man looked at him. "Okay, neighbor, dust blown off the moon. First class or by air?"

"Vintage 1880."

"Fifty cents parcel post."

"Well, the fact is—it's a manuscript."

"A who?"

"A—Nonprofit rate, okay?"

"Sure. Twelve cents."

Now that he had entrusted to the mails his own fanciful ending to the story, Lucius broke out in a cold sweat. Tomorrow, he would wake up in Knoxville, miles outside the magic circle he had woven round himself thrice, with the sour taste in his mouth of the milk of paradise that fear of hail had curdled in his dreams.

But it hit him just as he reached the far side of Kingsport—a profound nausea that made him turn around in his tracks.

He had to go back. Not to get the truth, then transform it into fiction. He intended to make no substantial changes in the story submitted to *Lady Fair*. The only change, if any were made, would be in himself. Something that would, he hoped, mix well with despair.

No, he was going back in search of the facts, thus declaring a breakdown of the imagination. "To make fiction agile," he had written on the Manhattan subway steps the night of his twentieth birthday, "one must cripple fact."

But now all that compelled him to return was the lust for truth. No, not truth, because fiction, when its images were charged to the highest degree with meaning, was truth. What he wanted were the facts. Did Zara Ransom actually lose her virginity to Jesse James, or did she not? Answer, yes or no. Answer in the broad light of day, not in the moon-flooded lobby of the Blue Goose Hotel. Did Jesse James show a sharp, thin streak of cowardice, as Lucius imagined, or did he not? Did Zara Ransom run away with Jesse James or with Davis? Is Zara Ransom living in the Blue Goose Hotel for its associations with Jesse James or with Davis Woodring?

Now he knew, from the lady's own mouth, how it felt to lose one's maidenhead to Jesse James. But he wanted to know if it really happened. The facts, he knew, would change nothing. After all these years there was no point in believing them. But he expected the facts to give him —especially if they contradicted the dream—a certain feeling he knew he needed, although he didn't like knowing what it was—superiority.

He was breaking the promise he had made to Zara Ransom. The promise to leave "forever" as soon as she had told her story. But with a self-loathing self-righteousness, Lucius took solace in the possibility that she had deceived him. To get the raw material from which he might conjure up the *fictive* image, he had been willing to risk the penitentiary. Were the *facts* worth that? They were not. Yet, in self-ignorance, he had taken the risk anyway.

Three days after his departure, he was back.

The silo was gone. Not a trace. Not even such a shadow as a man made on the asphalt in Hiroshima. More like the way Flash Gordon used to disintegrate objects and people with his ray gun. The bulldozers, caterpillars and tractors were gone. The path did not end at the trees—it went on—a wide swath of red clay up to the old road into Sweetwater where the population sign had been nailed to a fence. But when he reached the road, his shoes full of dirt, he saw no fence, no sign.

Glancing down the hillside, he saw the frozen custard shack, lying beside the creek, the cinder blocks strewn, except for one wall in which a large pane of glass remained, reflecting the early morning sun, winking up at Lucius.

The trading store lay beside the creek, crumpled. All the houses on the same side where the store had stood, including the church, had been goosed off the edge of the cliff.

The hotel and four other houses remained. Clouds of dust, stirred up by the machines, had rained down on them.

On both sides of the sloping road the machines, yellow and orange, their windows streaked with dew, were parked.

"Silent as a tomb," he said, standing on the edge of the cliff. But that sounded weak for what he sensed. No, this town was as silent as a little town "emptied of its folk, this pious morn."

He heard a truck leave the smooth pavement of the highway and hit the gravel. He stood among the branches of an uprooted and fallen tree and watched for the truck to break through the foliage below. The truck stopped alongside the tree. A man in khaki got out and took a leak in the middle of the road. Now Lucius knew, as he watched a look of relief spread like a stain across the man's face, that no one remained in the town.

When the man, buttoning his trousers, looked up and saw him, Lucius asked, "How much did you bring this morning?"

"How's that?'

"Progress."

"Don't get you, buddirow. You fish?"

"I might be."

"That's a hot one." Laughing, the man reached over the side into the pick-up truck bed, and pulled out some fishing gear and started toward a path that once sloped from the store down the cliffside to the creek. "Got an hour yet before we crank 'em up. Fish ever' chance I get.

"Say, you know where they took her?"

"She *was* up at Fair View Rest Home, but she run off." Then the man disappeared over the rim of the mountain.

The bulldozers were parked on the clean-swept cliffside, looking down over their work as though slightly awed.

He searched the hotel again. Standing on the glassed-in porch the possibility came to him that she might be at the tree, hidden among the roses and pine needles. She would, he knew, find a way to play it well to the end.

But only birds stirred when he touched the limbs, catching a thorn in his thumb. He climbed into the pine tree, hoping the wasps would be asleep. Moonlight gilded the wasp's nest silver. Now man, collectively, had lit on the moon. Once a symbol of romance, the moon that had shown on all the harvests in the world's history was now a symbol of the lunar age to come. Now that the romantic moon had gone down, it would never show its face in these parts again. If the world had waited for a banner to hang in the sky, proclaiming the supremacy of technics, one hung there now, glowing with what appeared to be luminous paint.

The bones in Lucius's buttocks ached. Keeping clear of the wasp's nest, he pulled himself up off the hard limb. Standing, he heard the limb crack before he felt it give. His hands still gripping the pliant limb above his head, he swung away from the cracked one and felt with his toes for another limb. As his foot touched a branch, he saw a light flicker in the Blue Goose Hotel.

Through the pines and ferns, the hotel was one smear of misty white and the windows sent flashes leaping among the pine needles. Straining, twisting painfully to get a foothold further down, he saw a light flicker brightly at one small break in the foliage, and suddenly it glowed like a web behind the ferns a hundred feet away—more than one moving light swung through the rooms. Boys camping for the night. A boy and a girl from a resort, looking for a place to make the summer memorable. Perhaps. He squatted on a limb and moved his head in quick little jerks to find holes in the pine-rose tree, and he saw four windows flash with bursting light like a string of firecrackers exploding silently. The searching, darting beams were urgent, delving.

The odor of roses was so profuse in the muggy air he could scarcely breathe. Thoughtless of his footing for a moment, he stepped into what struck him after he hit the ground as thin air. Barbed thin air. Thorns raked his face and arms and ankles and ripped through his shirt, and even his scalp burned as he lay in a tangle of briars, beginning to feel the hurt in his muscles and bones. He tasted blood. Petals of shattered roses drifted down over his head and shoulders and into his lap as he sat up. When he heard the wasps, he panicked. Crouching under the mesh of briars, he lunged. But the lush cocoon held him tightly as the wasps came down on him and clustered on his back. From the trunk of the tree, he pushed himself away again into the briars and pine needles and with one hideous rip broke through, leaving an opening for the wasps. Free, he ran, the wasps in pursuit, a few stinging his back and arms.

All the windows on the side of the hotel toward which he ran pulsed with flash lights, flicked on walls from the wrist. Whatever had gone wrong, he suspected himself.

He jumped from a bank over a ditch and walked down the steep road. In the middle and on the sides of the road and up the hotel drive trucks and cars were parked crookedly. Sheriff Odom's car showed its polish in the moonlight. Men ran off the porch and leaped over the rail, and one jumped out a window.

"Yonder she comes, a-walking!"

Lucius saw a man in overalls and a ballcap standing on the hood of a produce truck point up the road in his direction, and the man yelled again.

Suddenly, Sheriff Odom appeared on the bank above, a beam of light round as a melon in one hand.

As Lucius raised his hands, it was as though his thumbs had flicked switches—four flashlights nailed him to the road in cross beams. Imagining the serious, purposeful faces of the men behind the saucers of light, Lucius laughed.

"Somebody run you through a sewing machine?" asked the sheriff, indifferently.

Cars pulled off the main highway, dipped a moment into darkness, then their lights leapt over the arched backs of the caterpillars and spread weakly over the windows and walls of the hotel, dipped again, and shone on the backs of the crowd as the cars climbed the hill. Many cars were parked in the road already, and tourists and local people walked among them with an air either of having everything under control or of being frankly bewildered at their ignorance of what was going on. Lucius saw a girl in shorts write her name with lipstick along the side of a bulldozer—MILLIE BICKERSTAFF LOVES DALE, CHAGRIN FALLS, OHIO.

The men who had been with the sheriff collected around him and waited for him to speak. He leaned against the front of his patrol car. Now that they knew Zara Ransom was in the hotel, this congregation of strangers behaved just as the townspeople had before she left.

Sheriff Odom tilted his hat over his eyes, bent his head in meditation, and flicked the flashlight on and off.

Lucius was sure that Zara Ransom watched the crowd from one of the dust-powdered windows.

Finally, Odom pushed off from the bumper. "Don't nobody move. This is my problem."

He started up the sandstone steps. But midway, he stopped, stepped backwards, down one step, and removed his hat.

Zara Ransom appeared in the doorway of the glassed-in porch. The crowd on the road and the drive below hushed. She wore the same white dress, and what the noon sun had done for it, the midnight moon now did differently.

Lucius looked at her, the question in his mind. She stared into his eyes as though sticking a needle into a button, and he knew for a certainty that Jesse James had never touched her. That Lucius Hutchfield had.

The silence began among those under her gaze at the foot of the steps and spread slowly, steadily, to the edges of the crowd. The lights of some of the cars parked among the crowd shone bright on the porch. But when the figure in white appeared in the moonlight, headlights went off. Even at that distance, the crowd seemed aware that a legend was bodied forth on the porch, that the figure, which did not demand respect, deserved it, reminding them perhaps that those who do not remember the past are doomed never to imagine and relive it.

Caught in her eyes, Lucius half expected Zara Ransom to fling the three one hundred dollar checks at his feet. He saw that he was not, like the others at his back, a stranger. He had known her, he had ravished her, and the dust on the hem of the virginal white seemed to testify to that act. If that ravishment had occurred in time, it had occurred in a past that had never changed for Zara Ransom and would now never change for Lucius. For no matter where he went, he could never leave Sweetwater.

He wished the sheriff would speak. But he stood there like one of the telephone poles that tomorrow would come down.

A man jerked at the straps on his overalls, as though pounding himself like a post into the ground. Having never been to Sweetwater before, he had the look of a man who would never forget that he had.

Startled by a faint click behind him, Lucius turned and looked into the lens of an expensive camera aimed at himself that hung from the red, sweating neck of a man in a straw bill-cap, Swiss shorts, and sandals. He looked up, winding, and Lucius saw the face of a German. Reflected in the window of the station wagon behind the tourist, Lucius saw his own cowboy shirt, and, once an intruder, he now felt part of the authentic American scene which millions crossed the Atlantic to make.

Eyes uplifted, the crowd seemed to be waiting for a sign from the porch, perhaps a command or a revelation.

She opened her mouth as if to answer them, but a long space of time ticked between the expectant silence and the sound of her voice. "I will come with you in a moment, sir." Presumably, she spoke to the sheriff, although her eyes remained on Lucius. He knew that if he turned away or even averted his eyes, he would never turn again in the direction of whatever salvation remained for him. No one followed her eyes—they must have seemed to be looking at nothing. "I came back to get something that belonged to Jesse and me."

Lucius flinched.

She stepped back and a shadow fell across her eyes before she turned.

For the first time, she had made it public. And she knew that privacy was a thing she would never know again. She knew, what Lucius knew even more clearly and differently, that her story was in the public mails, that he had committed her privacy to the eyes, if not the hearts, of the readers of *Lady Fair*. Now Lucius knew, with a sick thud in his chest, why Zara kept the money. She felt, like many another woman he had known, that she had earned it. So she had, in her own genteel way, arrogantly pronounced the name of her situation.

She disappeared behind the wall of panes, the white of her dress dissolving in and merging with the moonlight that flowed through the warped squares of glass.

Sheriff Odom jumped up onto the back bumper of the patrol car, clapped a large hat on his head, and held up his hands, palms out to the crowd, like the victim of a stick-up. "Ladies and gentlemen. May I please have your undivided attention. Please! This is a very trying experience for Miss Ransom. I ask you, as good Christian folks, to get in your cars and drive away. There's no more here to see. Miss Ransom is just gonna get together a few things and I'm gonna drive her back over to Fair View Rest Home. And that's all they is to it. So do her this one favor." He was forgetting that almost none of these people, many tourists, had ever heard of Zara Ransom. But they were responding. "Don't make her have to see your faces when she comes out. . . . I see a few folks are getting into their cars. Good Christian folks who know how to act. So. . . ." He continued to talk to them, his deep resonant voice getting lower, more soothing, as they turned, some with hands in pockets, some flipping cigarettes over the cliff, toward their cars. Odom remained on the bumper watching them.

Between the starting of motors, Lucius heard locusts and jar-flies.

A Pekingese in one of the tourist station wagons barked and an elderly lady rolled the window up in front of its pug face.

Unable to move, Lucius waited for her to come down the wide front steps. He wanted to see her up close, to see and touch the sharp edge where the virginal white dress, the past, and the gray hair and wizened face, the present, were separate. Now that she was tainted, she might look upon him with at least a glint of compassion.

The red tail lights of the last cars had passed between the bulldozers lining both sides of the road and were blinking on the rise to the highway where the rail fence and the population sign once had been, when Lucius saw a glow of red on the side window of the sheriff's patrol car.

On the bumper, Odom turned and let down one leg in the same motion. Seeing Lucius, he said, "What the hell's *your* name, mister?"

"For want of a better name—Bob Ford," said Lucius, wondering where the red glow came from.

"Well, if you ain't out of sight of this place in two shakes, I'll make hell for—" He stopped, shock in his eyes.

Hearing the crack of wood behind and above him, Lucius turned, expecting to see her step off the porch. The glass panes were red.

THE CROWD RETURNED with the fire engines that came from Blowing Rock and Boone over the almost obsolete highway.

Lucius stood in the crowd and watched the Blue Goose Hotel burn and the long thick whips of water lash the collapsing roof and walls. The multi-paned front had turned him and the sheriff back from the pulsing heat, and they had tried the windows facing the porch, which encircled the hotel, but the force and suffocating density of smoke had made them turn their backs, stagger to the rail, and go finally over the rail, where they had writhed on the grass amid flying sparks. They had heard no human sounds from the rooms.

An ambulance came.

Between the driver and his assistant sat a young man in a tee-shirt. "What's the story?" His glasses doubled the burning hotel. "The old lady in there?"

"I don't know. Why don't you go in and see for yourself?"

"Ha!"

"False alarm for *you*, kid," the driver said to the young man. "Reckon the questions you raised in your article will just have to dandle."

The driver and his assistant, the young newspaper reporter squeezed between, their cheeks and ears red, turned and went away, the stretcher sheets white and neat through the window.

AT DAWN, when the men arrived to operate the bulldozers and other wrecking equipment, the flames were out. Smoke rose in thin, isolated, curling streams from charred and dripping planks and beams. The Watauga County fire engines had salvaged a structure that still turned a few walls toward the morning sun.

A man in a red sporting cap stumbled into town from the woods above the hotel, his shotgun broken over his shoulder, his game bag flapping loosely at his side, and asked Lucius, "What's it all about?"

Before Lucius could tell him anything, the sheriff called to them across the ruins.

"Hey, you two men! How about helping us look in these ashes. Help us find her. These men have got to crank up and go to work."

The wreckers sat on the machines, smoking, talking quietly. Lucius and the hunter and the sheriff and his deputy and several other men moved carefully among the ashes, trying to keep clear of the few walls that still stood, supported by chance alone.

Lucius poked with a stick into smoking mattresses and black upholstery, afraid each thrust would send back into his hand the vibration of a bone. Even so, he was still hoping to find something that would give him the facts. That he still felt the compulsion to complete the factual picture nauseated him.

Her body was somewhere near. He smelled it. When he looked up and saw one of the wreckers looking at him with distaste on his mouth, he knew that he was closer to the machines than any of the operators were. In Lucius, the inanimate, conscienceless monsters had found a will.

When they found Zara Ransom in the ashes, her bony wrist was caught in the charred coils of the bed springs, three coils away from what had once been a packet of letters. A kerosene lamp lay, blackened, at her feet. Around her head lay the fragments of the glass chimney, shattered like the dome of her imagination. The fire appeared, then, to have been an accident. It depended on whether, as the years passed, he would believe his own eyes or vision from another source.

The hunter asked Lucius, "Hold the letters while I work loose the old woman's hand?" Strange that the man had extricated the letters first.

Lucius went down to the creek, away from the smoke and the stench, away from the human, living faces. Were the letters from Jesse James or from Davis Woodring? Did one of them tell her where to meet him? Did one of them—? Lucius suddenly didn't want to know. What he had seen in the old lady's eyes had solved the really important mystery—his own guilt.

He crumpled the charred packet in his fists and sprinkled the flakes of paper into Sweetwater Creek.

Leaning against a birch that the shoulders of animals and men had rubbed smooth, he remembered that the way to any palpable punishment—the checks—had gone up in smoke with the love letters. How sweet would have been the caress of handcuffs on his wrists, this instant. A subtler form of punishment was what he dreaded.

The machines starting up startled him. He had expected the wreckers to turn, eventually, and go away. A final, belated gesture of respect. But if they were going to do it, he would have to watch. He was, he knew, the supervisor on this job.

Only the wreckers and their machines remained. They climbed the drive, gravel and grass sputtering out from under the mammoth, smoking rubber tires. Other machines bounced along the creek below, heading for the houses that had already been pushed over the edge, their windows opaque with dust and smoke, to finish the wreckage.

"Let's get this job done quick, men!" The foreman's yell sounded desperate. "Before the place is swarming with curiosity seekers!"

Paper ashes like charred skin clung to Lucius's sweaty palm, but he did not wipe them off. Standing in the midst of the whirling dust and the concatenation of machinery, with the smell of the charred wood and the exhausts of the machines in his nostrils, he felt for the first time since he came to Sweetwater something besides nostalgia for the romantic world of days gone by.

Lucius Hutchfield Meditates on Marble Goddesses and Mortal Flesh

In the summer of 1946, in Knoxville, Tennessee, in the Bijou Movie Palace, thirteen-year-old Lucius Hutchfield, a sawed off, blue-eyed, lightnin' haired little fucker, stands On the Spot in his usher's uniform, gazing, as if in a trance, into the golden outer lobby, and in the pleasure-dome of his imagination, he watches Billy the Kid walk toward the Tennessee Kid, in a duel, in Helena, Montana—a story he began writing that day in Christenberry Junior High School, certain that by Spring, he will be a rich and famous writer, while on the screen at his back, his hero Alan Ladd says to Veronica Lake, "Every guy dreams of meeting a girl like you. The trick is to find you."

I WRITE IN THE MORNINGS, but that weekend, before my trip to Hollywood, I couldn't conjure.

Idling past the television set, I punched the *on* button the way you pluck a leaf as you stroll under a tree limb, disdainfully switched away from Saturday football to Joseph Cotten talking rather condescendingly to Jennifer Jones, who was acting uninhibited, unpredictable, and I thought, Ah, good ol' *Portrait of Jennie,* but just before Cotten called her "Singleton," it began to look wrong for Jennie, and after a Pepsi commercial, the announcer said, "And now we return to *Love Letters,*" one I didn't remember, so I started to turn it off, but Shelley had wandered in and said, "Let's see how it turns out, Dad."

I trespassed the zone of concentration Marta created around herself reading Simone de Beauvoir's *The Second Sex,* in French, for god's sake, then slowly orbited the house and wandered back into the living room and, with a faint sneer, rather reluctantly allowed *Love Letters* to draw me in. I laughed indulgently at its sentimentality, but then it got interesting, despite the passé amnesia gimmick. That movie's aura overwhelms me *now,* but I forget the details, feel a compulsion to know, so I'm looking for it again, among the stuff I have here backstage in the Bijou.

Alan—Joseph Cotton—used to write love letters to Victoria—Jennifer Jones—for Roger during the war, and Roger won her—the old Cyrano routine. Then one night Roger, drunk and mean because Victoria loves him only as the man reflected in the letters, blurts out that he didn't write the damn things, and beats the fire out of her, and the old lady who is her guardian—Victoria was an orphan—kills Roger. Thinking she did it herself, Victoria loses her memory, spends a year in prison, and when she gets out, she coincidentally meets Alan. Calling herself Singleton, not knowing who she was before, she falls in love with Alan, but knows he is haunted by the memory of someone named Victoria. Alan marries her. But she ultimately traces herself back to her old guardian, who tells her the whole story, as Alan overhears.

Among the 500 magazines I owned when I was usher in the Bijou, I had a copy of this issue of *Screen Romances*. For most of the movies, the pictures were powerful enough to make me feel I knew all about them even before they appeared on the screen. But *Love Letters* was one of the few stories I read, and the only trace of all those movie magazines to survive my merchant seaman and my army years was two covers of *Motion Pictures*—featuring *Gone with the Wind* and *For Whom the Bell Tolls*—and this climactic passage of *Love Letters* that I cut out and kept.

"Slowly, looking straight at her, Alan began to speak words which he knew Victoria would remember now. 'I think of you my dearest as a distant promise of beauty untouched by the world. If I never see you again, my last thought will be that I fought for you and lost. But I fought.'

'Alan!' she gasped.

'Do you think you will forgive me?'

For the first time in this room, and slowly at first, her smile broke through. 'It was terrible waiting for you. But finding you was such a great miracle that anything I suffered seems only a small payment in return.'

And, still with perfect trust, she held out her arms to him.

The End."

On the television, that November afternoon in snow-white Vermont, twenty-two years after I first read that passage and copied the lines they quoted to each other from the love letters onto the end of one of my many letters to my first junior high school sweetheart Loraine, the theme music swelled, the camera pulled back in rhythm to it, giving the feeling of a flower bursting from bud to blossom, and I, standing in the doorway, between my study and the living room, felt that era go through me in an intuitive rush, like a peristaltic rush, and I started to cry, hysterically, and ran from room to room, raving.

At 35, I still have nightmares of carrying papers a day late, sometimes three days, and nightmares of opening night in a college play on the Bijou stage, no lines learned, a desperate lunge into ad-libbing, and dream still of going back to work at the Bijou as an usher after years of being away. That night, though, I dreamed nothing.

I don't like living away from Marta and Shelley, so I wasn't eager to leave our farmhouse in Vermont and spend four months in Hollywood writing a script from my novel, *On Target*, an off-beat detective story set in Knoxville, originally serialized in *Adam*, a second-rate men's magazine. Thrilled to be fulfilling one of the great ambitions of my childhood, I was, even so, feeling nervous dread.

Still, I felt guilty for abandoning work on my fourth novel, and for leaving my creative writing students in the lurch.

Monday, the day before my flight to Hollywood, I got a letter from Momma, who was taking care of Mammy, as we called my grandmother, who had fallen and broken her hip. Responding reflexively to the assumption that human-interest stories interest me as a writer, she enclosed a clipping from the *Knoxville News-Sentinel*. A man was found asphyxiated in his car in the vast parking lot across the street from the Bijou Theater. Snow had fallen the night before, so the police assumed the old man had turned on his motor to keep warm. I wondered, To keep warm while doing *what* in a parking lot? You don't *sit* in a parking lot. The car, a 1947 Chevrolet, bore Florida license plates. So what was the man *doing* in Knoxville?

I didn't realize then that there might be a link between that clipping and the one Momma had sent two weeks before, announcing the imminent demolition of the Bijou, fallen to showing skin-flicks. Published plans were for erecting a new public library on that site. On that spot also Knoxville's first store had once stood, and later a jail, and then, I know now, an inn where Southern-born Union General Sanders had died in the bridal suite of wounds inflicted by a sharpshooter from the tower in "Bleak House" out on Kingston Pike.

The old man on my mind all day, as I drove icy rural roads to the airport, I began to see the picture. Down in Florida, Miami probably, he, too, had read about the demolition of the Bijou. Perhaps someone had sent him the clipping. Why? Had he, too, once worked there? Maybe he'd been the projectionist, during 1946 and '47, my time as usher. He'd retired to Miami. Reading they were going to tear down the Bijou, he'd realized it meant more to him than he'd ever known before. A terrible nostalgia took possession of him and he'd gotten into his car and driven up here. One last look at the old Bijou, grown dim in memory. Driving up, he'd reeled off his years as a projectionist. Maybe he remembered me, in my blue usher's outfit—that blue-eyed, sawed off, lightnin' haired little fucker stationed at the main aisle, On the Spot.

And when he arrived in windy, cold, damp Knoxville, he was shocked to see the block long spread of concrete where the old Lyric theater had stood, and where had also stood Max's Greek restaurant and the Colonial Hotel and the Courthouse Drug Store on the South corner. All gone. The parking lot drops down a very steep hill, each space marked in bright white, a squat little hut smack in the middle. So he arrives Friday night at about six o'clock when the lot is empty, and drives into it, right up to the sidewalk, facing the Bijou, and he sits there staring at the marquee, remembering. Starts up his motor every once in a while to diminish the chill, and all behind and around him the lot fills up, people going to the Bijou, the Tennessee, and the Riviera, the only uptown theaters left now, twenty years later, 1968, while he sits in the iron-cold moonlight, watching his own movie on the windshield, a drive-in movie memory montage, and clouds huddle together, darkening, snow begins to come down, so he starts up the motor again to clear his windshield. After the last show, movie patrons return to their cars, and clear the lot, and the snow covers up their tracks, and the man's car runs out of gas, the battery is weak, and the windshield wipers stop flapping, and snow sticks to the windshield, covers the car.

Bright and early the parking lot attendant's footprints squeak over the solid quilt of snow toward the solitary car.

In the airport, on impulse, I cancel my plane reservations and plot a trip to Knoxville by train, a complicated maneuver, and leave the snowed-in Appalachian mountains of Vermont for the snowed-in Appalachian mountains of Tennessee. A conscious romantic gesture. Although I had hopped freights before I was ten, I'd never ridden a train as a passenger before. At a little shop near the station, I bought a mangled copy of *Of Time and the River* by my childhood hero, Thomas Wolfe, to read the train journey passages on my way to Knoxville where I had once stolen a paperback copy of his short stories from a drugstore when I was thirteen.

In Knoxville, I checked my bags at the L & N station and walked snow-rimmed sidewalks about a mile to the Bijou, where the still slots out front were blank, the marquee stripped to essentials.

FOREIGN FLESH

ALSO CAPTIVE DAUGHTERS

HELD OVER.

For seven years now, the Bijou has been a floozy, showing skin flicks, first "tit" shows, then "beavers," now, as Leo Gorsey of the Dead End Kids would say, "the woiks."

The Bijou was to be torn down for the new library. In the stacks of the old one, white Tennessee marble, I once made love to the Love of My Life, Loris Blackburn, among the W's, Thomas Wolfe approving. The wealthiest Methodist church in Knoxville, I'd been told, inherited the Bijou in recent years and hoped to raze that Tower of Babel, rip out its image-flickering tongue forever, not knowing about the seven-year lease, forced to profit now from porn. Irony is indigenous to Knoxville.

A bouffant blue-haired elderly lady tore off a ticket for me. The lobby has been stripped, flat pink paint slapped over the walls. "Negro Balcony" sealed off. Drapes in the box seats sagging, ripped, pores choked with dust. Seats rickety, like riding a streetcar. Stinks like the vanished Roxy burlesque-and-three features-plus shorts Theater over by the Market House. Out of the men's room on the balcony landing walks, the old "queer," as boys called "the Mad Scientist." Hurt me to hear him called that—and the tone of voice.

The door to my old manager's cramped office was open. A dark, tough Italian sat behind a desk, another like him sat beside it, both filling the room with cigar smoke. Rock and roll music came from the auditorium, having I knew not what to do with what was on the screen.

I asked the manager when the Bijou was to get demolished.

"They delayed it."

"So you're going to stay here a while?"

"Naw, we're pulling out. Our lease is up, and business ain't so hot. Movin' on to Asheville."

"When do you close?"

"End of the run of this feature. What's it to *you*, anyway?"

"I used to be an usher here back in the forties."

"Is that something special to be?"

I conned them into letting me look around. A mark in the carpet showed where the still stand once stood in the inner lobby. Glowing warmly, orange and green, like a juke box, it used to illuminate images of Vivien Leigh, Hedy Lamarr, Veronica Lake, Lana Turner, Joan Crawford. Marble Goddesses, their smooth marble vaginas untouched.

Backstage, a trapezoid of uninflected emptiness. Yellow light over the stage door burned out.

No white or pink panties, concealing tight pussies flaring on the front row, spied from the orchestra pit through a rent in the red velvet curtain, my pulse normal now, feeling no fear of getting caught twenty years later, seeing now only a bank of whiskered faces, lit by the bright exposure of white bellies, quivering asses, and whirling titties. The backstage sex of yesteryear is all now on the screen.

I rented a room right next door in the Lamar House Hotel that occupies a corner of this sprawling building.

I didn't call Mammy's house to speak to Momma and them. I didn't feel pulled toward that vortex. Earl and Bucky might chance to be there, even Daddy, the family embroiled in some new crisis, or the eruption of a dormant old one.

The next morning I bought dark glasses, and walked around.

I remembered a photograph of a corpse on a morgue slab tacked to a bulletin board in the Seaman's hiring hall in Brooklyn. DO YOU NO THIS MAN? An old man, face sagging, the sheet peeled down, exposing his nipples. He had died of a heart attack in the hiring hall one day when I was too bummed out from working the night shift at the White Tower hamburger joint on Eighth Avenue to go in. I was eighteen, waiting to ship out. His face haunted me. I felt guilty for not being able to recognize him and locate his next of kin. Then

I noticed the date. December 3, three weeks before. He would be already underground, in an unmarked grave, nameless.

The next day, Christmas Eve, I got a ship to Tal Tal, Chile.

Imagining the projectionist's body, too, lying unclaimed on a steel slab, I hurried to the Knox County Morgue, hoping to make it before they carted the projectionist away. I didn't recognize him. He wasn't nameless, though. His toe was tagged: Alfred Ford.

I arranged for a funeral.

I was the only person at the Lynnhurst Cemetery on the northern outskirts of Knoxville, where Grandpa Charlie, who shot himself, his mother, Matilda, who died of rectal cancer, and my infant baby brother, Billy, who died of locked bowels, are buried.

I called the producers of *On Target*, told them I was sick and wouldn't be able to show up for another month or so, and they saw no big problem in that.

The demolition was delayed, so I was able to sign a short-term lease, and a week later, I re-opened the Bijou, showing two of my great favorites, *A Song to Remember*, starring Cornel Wilde as Chopin and Merle Oberon as George Sand, and after that *The Blue Dahlia*, starring my old hero Alan Ladd and Veronica Lake, the Goddess who wore her wavy blond hair down over one eye.

The blue dome above the Bijou auditorium—when the lights went down for the first feature showing and the stars came out, filling the sky to overflowing, some brighter than others, jewels, diamonds about to shower down upon me.

I moved out of the Lamar House Hotel next door and set up living quarters in the dressing rooms backstage.

With money from the Warner Brothers option, I gradually restored the Bijou as closely as possible to the way she was in the summer of 1946.

I tracked down some old uniforms and hired two ushers, one of whom, I swear to God, was the spitting image of me at thirteen, and dealt with a slew of tedious details. I had about six months to go until the fall of the wrecking ball.

I've promised the church that owned the property to throw in a few Cecil B. DeMille biblical movies now and then to polish up their tarnished image, so I booked in *The Sign of The Cross*, starring Claudette Colbert and Frederic March.

The old men who lived in the Lamar House Hotel next-door came in, retired railroaders and salesmen and carpenters. Reproached me for "cutting out those risqué movies."

I work in the manager's office on my script of *On Target*, Dashiell Hammett, James M. Cain, and Raymond Chandler hovering over my shoulder.

I continue to show movies of 1946 and '47 and earlier for about a month, changing programs three times a week, going to double features to put as many as possible up there on the screen. *The Postman Always Rings Twice, The Big Sleep, The Razor's Edge, Jesse James, The Maltese Falcon, Love Letters, Duel in the Sun, Frenchman's Creek, The Sea Hawk, King's Row, Rebecca.*

But attendance is very light and sporadic, and as I stand under the marquee, rocking back and forth on the edge of the curb, wearing sunglasses and a mustache, I sense that the people passing feel there is something spooky about the place. Only lonely old men like Daddy—I saw him come in, and hid in the office—come to these movies. I expected my little brother Bucky especially, maybe big brother Earl, to get drawn in. I'm disappointed and hurt that people my own age aren't lured into seeing our old movies. I know, of course, that, like myself, they've seen them again on television, but I imagined them secretly yearning for the old setting, the old standard-sized screen, so I dismantled the Cinemascope screen and installed one of the old square rigs for their sake.

Finally, I was the only patron in the auditorium, and that was creepy because I have never been the only person in a movie auditorium.

So, half of my Warner Brothers advance spent, I closed down the Bijou forever.

I had forgotten about the caves. When I remembered them this morning, I went down the warped wooden steps into the basement where we kept and selected the posters and the photographs to go in the still stands, but found no trace of the iron door that led to the caves. Did I dream years ago so powerfully and vividly that I've remembered—and then forgotten—those caves as if they existed? Exploring, then turning back, running scared, I know that when I was an usher I had sprung my ankle in there, under the streets of Knoxville, somewhere between the Bijou and the Market House, and that was how Doctor Summers discovered I had incipient Freidreich's Ataxia, clawfoot deformity.

And one night, Daddy ran up to me where I stood On the Spot and told me an escaped convict was trying to kill him for screwing his wife, so I hid him in the caves and he got lost but somehow got out and forgot he was ever in there. Sounds like a wild dream. I'll keep looking for that door. Maybe they plugged the caves up somehow, leaving no scar on the wall.

Very reluctantly, Marta finally gave in to my urgent request and shipped every scrap I ever wrote in five crates. They arrived a few days ago—including some artifacts and mementoes—a fat portfolio of my drawings, an album of photos, Loris's hair ribbon, my library card, dated 1947, a whole raft of stuff. It's all back there in the dressing rooms, spread out. My private exhibit.

When I got out of high school and went to sea, Mammy let me use the pine wood quilt chest I used to sleep in as a child when we stayed overnight to stash my movie stills and books and writings in. When she married her longtime secret lover, the fire Chief, in 1948 he brought a beautiful mahogany chest into the house and Mammy moved the pine box out to the coal house that used to be a circus wagon ticket booth that Grandpa Charlie towed home behind his T Model Ford one twilight and that she saw passing her window on the streetcar.

When I returned from the army in Alaska and married Marta, I dug all that stuff out of the box in the coalhouse, and I've stored it into many perishable cardboard boxes over the years. Out of one life and into another, I've pack-ratted all the writings I've saved—and I've saved everything—from one end of the United States to the other—Boston, San Francisco, Charleston, Asheville, Burlington—six teaching jobs in 12 years.

Momma is a gypsy, a nomad, dragging her junk along, from house to house, job to job, city to city, man to man, sickness to sickness, out of her unhappy past into her uncertain future.

When I was a kid, Momma—who still doesn't know I'm in Knoxville—used to wake me up cleaning out her dresser drawers late at night, lights blazing while I was trying to sleep about seven feet away. Scratch, rattle, clink. Some of it she has always stored in the circus wagon coal house at Mammy's, and she used to go down there on the alley three or four times a year to sort out her stuff. Her hoarding disgusted and exasperated me. Not long before my own habit of collecting and transporting and resorting objects imbued with allusions to my life became almost obsessive, I was still pleading with my mother, who was living on a country road outside Cincinnati like a gypsy in her lover's two trailers, surrounded by four rickety out-buildings with leaky roofs containing her belongings, to throw it all away.

With a narcissistic, pack-rat ruminativeness, I had often dipped into, read with fixed fascination the stories I wrote since I was eleven. After five years of not looking into them, I've been immersed in them all this week. I have never read them all in one gorging, but I am now—having arranged them chronologically. Reading these stories is like making an archeological discovery at a familiar digging site—each story reveals a deeper layer in the life of my imagination. As I look over these stories, and old diaries, old letters, souvenirs, play and music concert programs, all space and time melt into an ambience.

I am still wearing this gold-plated, radium dial Elgin wristwatch I bought with Bijou usher money in 1946, but the time it tells with hands and numerals is not the one I go by. I straddle two worlds—adolescent and adult, blurring the distinctions in many ways.

The more lost artifacts I recover, the more melancholy I become, and the more I long to stroke the artifacts I still can't find.

For two weeks, I've been trying to unclog the toilet drain in my backstage "apartment." I've poured burning, smoking chemicals down it, and they just hiss back at me.

I'VE BEEN WRITING all this in long hand. Writing's too slow. And I feel a compulsion to tell it to myself, so today I am beginning to read it over into this little tape-recorder. I'm going to put all my notes on tape, and fragments of thoughts, and descriptions of objects, and I'm going to read some of my old stories and story fragments and scenarios and maybe diary entries and letters into the recorder, too.

Telling it into this tape-recorder is sort of getting back to the way it was when I was a kid, telling stories from when I was three to Bucky and Earl and neighborhood kids and at recess in elementary school, not starting to write them down until I was eleven. Who I was. The kid who told stories to other kids. "Tell me a story." That's all it took, and I'd rip one off, tongue clacking as fast as a world champion speed typist. Then under tons of books, I got away from telling stories. But in the last ten years or so, haven't I given about 200 dramatic readings of my stories all over the country? Now I am telling instead of writing, and even though I am telling only myself, I feel strangers hovering around me, and my own words and the winding spool of the tape-recorder hypnotize me.

Some of the stories from the Bijou time are incomplete because when I was in the seventh grade, I asked my best friend, Joe Campbell, to leave my notebook on my front porch while I caught the streetcar to the Bijou, and the wind ripped parts of them off the rings. In the three file cabinet drawers full of my writings from the Bijou time, mud-stained and rain-streaked pages remind me, and I still feel a sense of loss, an ache, and wonder every time I pass that field, or think of it—in the Merchant Marine in Mobile, Savannah, New Orleans, San Francisco, Venice, Yugoslavia, Rome, and the many places where I have taught—whether some of the pages might not still be in the weeds under the mud, somehow preserved just enough to be legible. I seldom leave the theater. Wondering about that yesterday, I caught a streetcar—a bus—out there. Sad archeologist, I walked around in the sedge grass between the white sides of the house we used to live in and along the bank of the Southern Railroad tracks, kicking at little patches of snow. "These fragments have I shored against my ruins."

Okay, that is just a few things that come to me—warming up—about the stories and poems and plays I wrote when I was a kid. Noticed in my old red diary that I mentioned working on "The Cosgroves of Destiny"—first reference to a story. What the hell that one was about I strain to recall, and I'm left strangely unmoved by the title. No trace remains. Sad.

And classy Marion Cassidy lost the first story I do remember writing, "Blue Waters," a sea story inspired by Goddess Maureen O'Hara in *The Spanish Main*. I based most of those early stories directly or indirectly, consciously or unconsciously, on movies, movies that I was aware were often based on published stories. Many stories I wrote during the Bijou time were movie scripts in disguise.

In the seventh grade, I wrote as I daydreamed. On the Spot, the main aisle in the Bijou, I dreamed while my hero Alan Ladd said to Veronica Lake in *The Blue Dahlia*, "Every guy dreams of meeting a girl like you. The trick is to find you," me unreeling on the dome of my skull the Tennessee Kid in a duel with Billy the Kid, Alan Ladd playing the Tennessee Kid, who is a back-dated version of Lucius-Ladd looking, five years before he was cast in the part, exactly as he did in *Shane*. People passing me by, Hood, the middle-aged, shell-shocked manager, saying, "Keep your eyes sharp for the patrons, Hutchfield." I was both in and out of this world. But where was *this* world? What was *really* happening? What was the real world? The boredom I *might* have experienced or the thrilling adventure, mystery, romance in my skull that made me have to go to the bathroom backstage every hour or so to take a whizz?

Almost thirty radio plays, stretching from seventh grade to senior year in college. "Storm," an adaptation of *Portrait of Jennie* by Robert Nathan that was made into one of my favorite movies with Goddess Jennifer Jones. Had my own radio show in high school. I based one play on the time Duke, my blowhard, hard-to-like friend, got caught stealing a necklace in Miller's department store. Shifted the locale to New York, under the influence of Thomas Wolfe's use of dialect in "Only the Dead Know Brooklyn." I directed and starred in it, playing Duke. An aesthete by that time, contemptuous of radio drama as an art form—fodder for the masses, the average age of the audience about nine years old, et cetera, I slanted the script, feeling I was working beneath my talent. But in college I wrote a modern adaptation of *Medea* for radio, using Robinson Jeffers' adaptation of Euripides as a model.

Very little poetry during the Bijou time, except what I wrote in praise of LaRue, who I loved from afar from the second grade through the sixth, and Loraine, a goddess, and Loris, the love of my life until I met Marta. Reading Poetry with a capital P came in high school, influenced by Edna St. Vincent Millay, Maxwell Bodenheim, W. H. Auden, Poe, Elinor Wylie, Sara Teasdale. I intend to dip into my *A Little Treasury of Modern Poetry*, revised edition that I found under dust in Knoxville Book Store by the river.

Most often, I wrote two types of stories, adventure stories and sensitive artist stories. For the adventure stories—crime and Western and love stories—I even had an agent when I was 14, until I stopped writing them under the influence of James Joyce in the tenth grade. The first serious story was "Seven Frozen Starlings," inspired by a two-page spread in *Life*, showing seven starlings frozen on a telephone wire—I'm looking at it now.

In two weeks, the only screwing stories I ever wrote, one of them pure imagination, the others based on *Of Mice and Men*, I sold to a fat boy in study hall at

Christenberry Junior High for his lunch money—my first sale as a professional writer.

In high school, I started writing, but never finished, "sensitive" stories about my wandering, criminal brothers Earl and Bucky and my melancholy Uncle Luke. I had been in love with Loris Blackburn for three years, and the former goddess Loraine was a good friend now, and Harry was my best friend, and he and I were no longer ushers or both carrying papers again, over in East Knoxville. Reading the early short stories of Hemingway, I picked up the name Nick, which I usually used in stories and sketches about myself, and in some of the ones about Earl, I called him Ben, after Thomas Wolfe's brother in *Look Homeward, Angel*. Now Earl's out of prison after serving three years for con jobs and has a fourth wife and a mentally ill kid and is digging ditches and trying to sweat off a drug habit, and I'm fascinated to see in those stories how I had transferred my own love of Baboo—my little baby brother for whom I had grand plans for his future but who died when he was 11 weeks old, so named because little Bucky could not pronounce "baby"—over to Earl, giving Earl my own fictional name, Nick. Reading Thomas Wolfe about the mystique of trains put that train track just outside the kitchen window in one story, for only one of our houses was near a track.

Daddy's sister, Matilda, though, lived next to railroad tracks across the river in South Knoxville. Before Bucky and I went to the Juvenile Home and two weeks later to St. John's orphanage while Momma was seriously sick in the hospital, we'd stayed with Aunt Matilda—"Waltzing Matilda" was Daddy's favorite song, his sister being the one who raised him when his Momma and Daddy died when he was eleven—and I never forgot the sudden trains, rushing right by the bedroom window, so when Thomas Wolfe came along, dragging his trains behind him. . . . After they tore down her house, the Lake Theater was built on that spot and then Momma was cashier there awhile, and every movie had suddenly passing trains in it.

And then my freshman English teacher Mr. Carson at the University of Tennessee, who also became one of my play directors in the theaters there, told the class to write a theme for the final exam on their plans for the summer. Sneering at the mundane assignment, risking failure in the course, since I'd already rejected three other assigned dumb topics, I wrote "The Call of the

Wild Goose," a biographical essay about Earl. Mr. Carson still thinks it's one of the best things I ever wrote.

I seldom wrote stories in which I was the focal character—that is, after I stopped writing the "future" scenarios detailing my wanderings over the face of the earth in pursuit of the meaning of life, leaving violence and broken hearts in my wake. Wrote one in my own voice in high school though, but focused on Jewel, one of our twenty or so landladies—who was always waiting for her soldier lover to return, and she was very tall and homely in a way that made me imagine an attractive young woman under the surface somewhere.

Then came the explicit autobiography with a grand design, *Children of a Cold Sun*, tentatively titled, about me and Loris, when I was a senior at Knox High, the year before it ceased operation and was broken up into schools at the four points of the Knoxville compass. The only part I really worked on was about the time I ran away from home to Asheville en route to India, inspired by the ending of the movie *The Razor's Edge*. Sitting in the enormous study hall, that had a balcony and buckled, slanting floors, I wrote down the scenario of our future that I day-dreamed on the freight train going up there, then walking the streets of Asheville, and on the bus coming back. Unfinished. Then when I was a freshman—I hated such terms, *I* wasn't any of those, and could never get them in the right order, just as later I always had to ask whether an associate professor was higher than an assistant professor, even when I held those ranks myself—at UT, in my basement room, I returned to *Children of a Cold Sun*, picking up the Asheville runaway narrative where I'd left off.

Late one night about two years ago, the Bijou time began severely to haunt me, as I kept Marta savagely awake till dawn, describing every damned detail, how I longed to run my fingers over the wood and plaster and iron textures, the fixtures, the nail heads, screws, of the Bijou, a variable skin, memory's Braille. Well, isn't that what it's all about—making metaphysical connections with the past? Marta who lives very effectively in the present to go meaningfully into the future, says, "Hell no." But the impact of such seemingly trivial details can shut a man off from the world, even if he isn't living backstage in a condemned theater. The world's logic contracts, and I think, feel, as if I am collaborating with the unconscious of the race in extending a pervasive aura of emotional meaning. Or some such horse shit.

I've been integrating all scraps and notes and fragments and outlines and scenarios, with their completed stories to see how the stories developed from ideas. Reading the scenarios in which I projected myself and Loraine into the future in exotic places—"Two People," "Mood of Hunger," "Naked Destiny," "Destroy the Flame," "The Cosgroves of Destiny," "Now and Forever," like movie titles. What are she and the other kids in those stories doing now? A few months after she broke up with me in 1947, and I'd returned from running away to Asheville, I had the feeling of tagging along after the Buzzard Ridge gang, her three girlfriends and Harry, who were friends before I came along, tolerated now but not wanted.

Loraine looks back at me as I walk quickly down Gay Street toward the Bijou and says, "Stop looking at yourself in the winder glass, poet!" I skipped toward her twice and, trying to kick her in the butt, slipped and busted my ass on the sidewalk. She was so outraged by the attempt, she sank her teeth into my knuckles. I carried the scar for two decades, but when I looked, sitting in Piazza San Marco in Venice a few years ago, it was gone. I mourned for Loraine another year, then she became my friend, then even Loris's friend, too, almost a pal, after a year of being rivals over me, and I would confide in her about Loris and Loraine would confide in me about Harry. Here's that photo of Loris and Loraine holding hands in the middle of Walnut Street, looking back at me over their shoulders, smiling as if conspiring my undoing.

I'm going to stop now and go across Gay Street to the Gateway Newsstand just now to pick up a *TV Guide* to see what old movies are going to be showing on television. Sometimes I watch them in the lobby of the hotel next door.

Watched a Bell Telephone ad, showing the neighborhood street of a small town. "Long ago you went down the street and left a part of your life behind you. . . . Even long ago is not so far away." Inspired me just now to dare to give Loraine a call from the office. Cool, seemed afraid to talk. I imagined her husband in the other room. Her voice the same, though deeper, from smoking, I imagined. Said she'd seen Loris at the Santa Claus parade holding a boy baby in her sweet arms. Loris was heavier, she said, and her daughter was a majorette, marching with South Knoxville High Band.

Tomorrow, I'm going to return to Loris by mail a photograph of her and her sister at her mother's funeral that she gave me the summer we planned to run away to Greenwich Village and get married. When we broke up, I kept a box full of her things—that blue satin dress I gave her for her 16th birthday, pictures, books, her school notebook, career book. The dress is hanging backstage as I tell this.

I might be able to track down Marion Cassidy. In the fifth grade, I'd let her read "Blue Waters," first story I ever wrote, and she kept it to show to her mother, but she never gave it back. She just might still have it.

In the basement of Lawson McGhee Library, I've been reading the *Knoxville News-Sentinel* on microfilm, some of the same issues I used to carry—pulp paper and ink that smelled so fresh—on my Sharp's Ridge route, just before I started ushering at the Bijou. Disguised, because the curator knows me vaguely, I go into the Tennessee History room, and they allow me to glance through some of the photographs of old Knoxville in a collection donated to the archives by a prominent and beloved photographer. The negatives are on glass plates and some of the prints have not yet been made. Some were damaged when the earth walls of the basement of the old mansion where they were stored collapsed during a long rainy season. I contributed $50 to the project. Now they have a high school girl going through the chaos of 5,000 photographs from 1910 to 1949, trying to catalog them by date and subject. Each day I look over a new batch. In books and in commemorative pamphlets put out by dairies and hardware companies celebrating 100 years in business, I find other old photographs of Knoxville sites and sights. And I look at the old Bijou theater programs, when it was a high society legitimate theater palace where they say one-legged Sarah Bernhardt once pranced.

In the past few weeks, I've snapped over 300 photos of Knoxville, using the black camera Loraine gave me for Christmas 1946, and taped them all to the brick walls back stage, along with thousands that I've taken over the years that Marta dumped into one of the crates she very reluctantly shipped to me from Vermont.

I put a return address—a box in the main, marble post office—on that photograph I sent Loris, but I've received no response from her. Sometimes I see her elderly father in Market Square, sauntering along past the vegetable trucks parked along the sides, his thumbs hooked in his back pockets.

The stills of Goddesses of the Silver Screen. Like skin. Magazine pages a different skin texture. The effluvium of old movie magazines on my desk in the manager's office of the Bijou evokes the aroma of girls' hair. Starched blouses of the Woodbury soaped girls were like the new movie magazines on the racks in the drugstore where I used to kneel, waiting for the route manager to dump my *News-Sentinel*s on the curb in North Knoxville. With money from delivering papers, I collected a slew of movie magazines. Knew all the stars' faces and names, remembered the titles of all the movies I'd seen, many I had read or only heard about, and made the lists I am looking at now, but 20 years later, I'm forced to engage now in complex detective work to deduce the titles of obscure movies for some of these old stills.

A girl on my Sharp's Ridge paper route who looked like Vivien Leigh bestowed upon me her collection of stills, some sepia-toned by time, some dating back to the Thirties, as she made a clean breast of things to marry a G. I. returning from the European Theater of War. I wanted the faces of the Goddesses, Lana Turner, Veronica Lake, Gene Tierney, so I stole stills from the basement poster sorting room at the Bijou, *The Postman Always Rings Twice*, *The Blue Dahlia*, *The Razor's Edge*. Put on an exhibit some years ago in the library of the little college in Charleston, South Carolina where I taught drama and creative writing and edited a literary magazine. Everybody was fascinated.

Left most of these stills with the editor of *Movie Heritage*, of which I am still an associate editor, and he sent them here at my request. Some of them I gave Joe Campbell when I was about 16. He wanted them, not because he really desired them, but because I valued them so much. While I was away in New York and at sea, they were stored in Mammy's circus wagon coalhouse in gray flat cardboard boxes, with black tape sides, which I had kept when I used to borrow records from the Lawson McGhee Library. I even bought more stills years later, but mostly stuff for Shelley, *The Wizard of Oz*, *Laurel and Hardy*, who I called Straight Hair and Fatsi.

I've been trying to get them all back now, all the stills, all the magazines, round them up somehow. Put an ad in the *Sentinel* last week for stills and movie magazines of 1946–47. I retrieved none of the actual stills I once collected, but from the two people who responded, I got six magazines, one of which once belonged to *me*. Bucky had written a telephone message to Momma on the back of *Screen Romances*, Gene Tierney and Tyrone Power in *The Razor's Edge* on the front. In the margin of a fictionalization of "The Killers," starring Ava Gardner, I had written, "Life is raw meat slowly cooked by the eye of God." Margins often triggered an impulse to write.

When I was a kid, even before the Bijou years, I used to go to sleep every night after a ritual in two parts—review my life serial fashion and, when I sensed I was drifting off, I'd talk to God, and go to sleep that way. Later, after I'd begun to write stream-of-consciousness stuff and didn't believe much in God and was living intensely in my life and in my writing, the ritual was simpler in form, more complex in content. I'd let my will rest and encourage bizarre, surreal images to show up on the movie screen of my mind. Descriptions of LSD trips pale beside my memory of those imagistic orgies—I reveled, wallowed, it was thrilling, sublime, sometimes frightening. But I was in control of—if not always the content—the method.

Last night I dreamed I saw a newspaper ad for the Bijou-Broadway Theater, announcing Charlie Chaplin on stage, starring in *A Streetcar Named Desire* by Tennessee Williams.

Marta sent, with dramatic reluctance, more of my old books—arrived today from Vermont—the old Penguin paperbacks with the Robert Jonas cover art, his famous knot-hole technique—a shackey house seen through a knot hole in a fence, Erskine Caldwell's *God's Little Acre*—the Mexican abstract of James M. Cain's *Serenade*—the lyrical *A Portrait of the Artist as a Young Man*— are especially exciting to hold in my hand. I never realized back then that paperback books had not been published very long—that the lists were short, the various publishers few, Bantam, Pocket Books, Dell. *Avon* covers were mostly lurid. I set out to own most of the books in the early series, forced by dire need to sell some of them to used bookstores all over the United States, then missing them one day, searched for them again in bookstores, putting the same editions on my shelves again. In one of the sketches I wrote in study hall at Knox High, I described the effect on me of a lurid Jonas paperback cover—Faulkner's *Sanctuary*, a woman in a mauve slip against the background of a pock-marked, wet blood-stained wall.

And here, spread out on the manager's, my desk, are all my Thomas Wolfe novels. Wolfe's epigraph to his book of short stories. "Vigil strange I kept on the field one night. . . ." I used to love to say that line. I thought the line was Wolfe's so I wrote it inside the cover of my first journal, like the ones he wrote his novels in, didn't know until four years later it was Whitman's—one of the few lines of his poetry I ever really liked. I read very little of Wolfe's or anybody else's fiction. *The Short Stories of Thomas Wolfe*, with that brooding picture of him, that marble brow, black eyes staring. How a great writer should look. The one I stole from Gateway newsstand, risking ending up in prison or reform school with Earl or Bucky, to show his spirit how much I loved him, to give the book greater value.

Soon's I got back home from going to Asheville when I was fourteen to visit the house where he grew up, I sat down in my sanctuary and wrote a letter to Mabel Wheaton, called Helen in Wolfe's novels. Here it is, first draft.

Dear Mrs. Wheaton, This letter is very difficult to write for I wish to make upon you a sincere impression of the nature of the important request I wish to make of you, and explanation of said request.

To be brief, and please do not make a decision until you have read this letter with understanding of my motives. I wish to be in your service and in the service of your brother's admirers this summer acting as caretaker and guide of the Thomas Wolfe Home in Asheville.

I am 14 years old, soon to pass the eighth grade. I have held jobs steadily since the age of 9, done housework for my mother since the age of 6. I *will* be a writer. I enclose a picture.

All formality aside, I wish now to express myself in why I want the position, which I do not consider a job.

Of the many admirers of Tom Wolfe I like to pride myself in the belief that I am the most ardent, and most sympathetic, and in many ways my characteristics as a person and as a writer very closely resemble those of Tom, none of which, however, have been directly inspired by the admiration I have for him. In short, realistically speaking, Tom is my hero.

I, like Tom, carried papers as a young boy. I have been imprisoned, so to speak, in my youth within the limited boundaries of a small, stiff-necked town. The world outside, which I came to know only by books and people, fascinated me. I am now extremely bitter toward life, confused and bewildered by it, as well as skeptical of its deity, having been only mildly influenced in this respect by Tom. I thirst for fame, yet not as strongly as Tom, I thirst more for achievement, self-satisfaction, which Tom discovered too late was the real thing he had wanted. Even this I suppose he could not grasp, and I do not expect to surpass him in that manner. I have a story to tell, which is as real, beautiful, ugly, tragic, pitiful, sinful, and as much an obsession for me as the one Tom told so beautifully. Thus there are many things, more than I can tell, characteristic of Tom, that apply to me.

Why is it so important to me that I be caretaker of Tom's home? Aside from the sentimental beauty of the idea, and in a way more important, is the fact that in such an environment, dripping with inspiring atmosphere, more strange and of a more terrible beauty than I have ever known before, I can write, in peace and sweet exile, the novel of my youth which I have for so long yearned and been obsessed to write. I feel the urge is as great, if not greater, as it was with Tom.

The fear that I may seek a thrill in lounging on Father Wolfe's couch, playing the piano, eating at the family tables, or sleeping in Tom's bed, may be freely dispelled. Although I regard the house and everything in it as earthly sacred, with a respectful sentimentalism, I am not a thrill seeker.

Of course, I wish to live in an unused room, being very careful while cooking, and it is for sure that my absence at any time from the house would be extremely brief, for this would be an exile, strict, and unconditional. I shall ask no payment other than perhaps, and this need not be, money for food.

Having visited the home last week, I went away bubbling with the idea that, with all I know of Tom, which is a very great deal, I assure you, I would be, please don't take this for conceit, an asset to the home. I could be on hand to offer any explanations uninformed admirers may wish.

I feel that this job, if you wish to call it that, for to me it is a privilege, would be the turning point of my life, a rare experience and unforgettable asset to the progress of my artistic being.

Please consider this request very closely and with understanding. Words fail me in telling you what this will mean to me. Yours sincerely, Lucius W. Hutchfield

A few years later, I returned to Asheville with a UT drama instructor who directed my play "The Great Wings Still Beating," which won a state contest and was performed in the round at UT, and who was going to Chapel Hill to see about a job. But he drove way out of his way through the mountains, through Hot Springs, to go through Asheville so that he and I—he even looked like Wolfe—could make a pilgrimage to the Old Kentucky Home where our hero had lived as a kid. And in Chapel Hill, we walked the old-fashioned campus where Wolfe had walked and sat in a room where workmen were hammering and sawing in the library and read news clippings, looked at photographs in the Wolfe collection. And the professor took me to the Carolina Playmakers Theater where Wolfe's plays had been performed, one starring himself, and we sat in on a playwriting session. Then he introduced me to the head of the drama department, who resembled a banker more than a man of the theater, with the idea that perhaps they would have a scholarship for old Lucius when high school turned him loose. And I used the same green waitress's order pad to write down my impressions of *that* trip as I had used for the 1947 Asheville trip.

A year later, I adapted to the stage the same section of *Look Homeward, Angel* that Ketti Frings adapted several years later, but the Carolina Playmakers turned it down. I will donate it to the Wolfe collection at UNC.

During Spring vacation when I was in the eleventh grade, I went to New York City for the first time, in the sleek green Studebaker of a young Jewish man who acted in the community theater group to which I belonged then called Knoxville Stage, and when passing through Washington D.C., we stopped for gas, and I called up Mabel Wheaton on impulse, who remembered my letter very well, although she'd never gotten around to answering it because a Thomas Wolfe Memorial she said had then almost been formed, and an official hostess already hired. "Well, you just come on out to see me," she said, sounding just like Helen in *Look Homeward, Angel*, "and I'll fix you up a big supper." But my friend had to keep moving and I slept in Wolfe's Brooklyn that night.

In the Spring of my sophomore year at UT, I made ten tapes of my readings and commentary from modern poets, to be broadcast over the university radio station during the summer, and I included passages from a fire-singed copy of *Face of the Nation*, a collection of lyrical pieces from all Wolfe's work, that I had found a few years before under an abandoned old house, and while The Polestar went through the Panama canal and I painted the engine room in 110 degree heat, a source of solace was the knowledge that my voice, reading Wolfe, was going out over Knoxville.

A decade later, I was asked to come to Chapel Hill as writer in residence for five weeks. I went. I hated it because nobody invited me to visit classes, and I love to teach. Wrote nothing. Except the outline of *On Target*.

So as I walked around Asheville on that first trip, I didn't know those things would happen—nor that I'd seek out places where Wolfe lived in New York and Brooklyn, where he lived in the same room, I was told, from a window in which Roebling, paralyzed with the bends, directed the building of Brooklyn Bridge, the room where Hart Crane wrote his epic poem *The Bridge*. But even back then in Asheville, I felt a sense of rich possibilities, not only in the moment, full of the past because of Wolfe's books, but in the future, too.

I walked over to the Gateway just now and showing *The Short Stories of Thomas Wolfe* in one hand, I put a quarter with a flourish on the counter, and said to the owner, "That's for this book I stole from here when I was a kid."

"Thank you," he said, without frowning. "It'll cost you a dollar and a quarter today."

Elated that he'd not only improvised well upon a potentially awkward situation, but had topped it, I gave him the rest of today's price, even though the book went out of print long ago.

Even now, when magazines on the racks contain stories I've written myself and for which I've received fifty bucks from *Botteghe Oscure,* published in Rome, or as much as two thousand dollars from *Playboy*, I feel the same imbalance in my stance and as I walk out as when I used to steal. Even where I never stole anything.

I've returned to the Knox High library and to the Lawson McGhee Public Library the books I stole years ago. Don't ask me why.

All the bookstores have vanished now. The Chinaman's place, the Knoxville, Matheny's, and the one across from the Roxy were gone when I returned from Panama. Except the Gateway, which makes it mainly on shiny new paperbacks and magazines. And a modest book department in Miller's, where I met an old man who took me to his house and showed me some rare books he bought when the Chinaman's store closed down. Bought Ramsey's history of Tennessee and his biography. "That copy," the old man told me, "has an interesting history. Some looters pulled it out of the fire when Dr. Ramsey's house burned at Mecklenburg during the War Between the States."

"Where's Mecklenburg?"

"Why, at the forks of the Holston and the French Broad River up around Boyd's Bridge. Old Doctor James G. M. Ramsey always said Unionist editor Parson Brownlow—that vile serpent, Ramsey called him—sent a Union soldier to burn it down while he was roaming the South with the Rebels, doctoring the wounded and carrying a depositary as a Confederate treasury agent with him wherever he went. I found that book in your hand in the attic of an old farmhouse over in Ebenezer a few weeks ago. Worth about a hundred dollars but my social security check won't stretch, so. . . ." And he threw in Ramsey's autobiography. So if facts are what I need, I've got them here in this fat, crumbling volume, ferreted out by Ramsey—that vain old historian, Parson Brownlow called him—when he must have thought they were about to perish from men's memories. Called it *The Annals of Tennessee.* But only up to 1800.

I went through the fiction section of the open stacks at Lawson McGhee Library today and looked for books with my name on the card. Of course, they've changed the cards for most of them, but some of them haven't been taken out much in the past twenty years, so I found my name, the last one on two of the cards, the signature very different from the one I wrote beneath it to check out Maurois' *Ariel,* a life of Shelley—who I named my son after—and Dante's *Divine Comedy,* which I never finished. Bruce, the albino usher's name, was on the same card. I wonder, did *he* finish it.

Back then, I never imagined, as the metatarsal bars I wore on my shoes to correct incipient clawfoot deformity clicked on the marble floor, causing heads to look up, that this sometimes gloomy building would become one of the single most important public places in my life, that I would always feel self-conscious, a little guilty as if I was unworthy, inside it, but that I would come in my high school days to feel possessive about it for its magazines, literary reviews, especially *The Kenyon Review, The Partisan Review, Theatre Arts,* books, and classical music records, and as a rendezvous with Loris. And that one day I would walk in and find my name on cards in the catalogue, like runes in ancient temples. And that sitting in the manager's office of the Bijou in 1968, I'd try to imagine what it would be like a few years later on to enter the new library on the spot where the Bijou once stood, and to walk past the spot on the hill where the library will have become only a grease stain.

I see Greer Garson, librarian, trying to shush Clark Gable talking loud in *Adventure*—"Gable's Back and Garson's Got Him," said the preview—and now I see me, a merchant seaman like Clark, standing on a pier in Tal Tal Chile weeping onto a newspaper reporting the execution of the Rosenbergs, who I never thought were guilty of passing secrets to the Soviet Union. Libraries? Yeah, I too have had library experiences, Clark. Making love to Loris on the second tier in Lawson McGhee Public Library, I take up where Clark Gable feared to tread.

Tomorrow, I'll go to Christenberry Junior High School. Maybe I'll find my name in some of the books on the shelves, and perhaps I can con the once sexy librarian into letting me take some of them out. No, she might be dead by now.

Christenberry's closed for alterations and painting, and the young librarian has the key and school is out for Christmas. But the new principal, a very pleasant man my age, whose whole approach seems freer than Mr. Bronson's used to be, but who's worried about the counter effect of some of the older teachers, 60 percent of whom still hang on from my days, said he felt even he had been there for years. "And every year you swear the kids are getting smaller."

Old Knox High is now the headquarters for the city school system. In the library repository in the basement, I look at the old Knox High yearbooks, *The Trojans,* hoping to look into the faces of people I knew at Christenberry. No pictures, the principal told me, were taken at Christenberry itself.

Some of the Christenberry kids transferred to county high schools that started with the ninth grade, so I went out to those schools, too, and looked in their annuals. And looked in the current annual, hoping I'd recognize a resemblance to Loris. Her daughter would be 15 by now.

Going to put an ad in the *News-Sentinel* for Knox High *Trojans.*

Feeling one with my conman brothers, I conned the city repository librarian into lending me one of the old Knox High annuals, so, like the photographer in Antonioni's *Blow Up,* who was obsessed with shadowy indications among park bushes of a murder in one of his shots, I'm looking them over with a magnifying glass at 3 a. m. in my old dressing room where I sleep— *when* I sleep. Demarcations between the rich life before and the neutered present—these pictures. The kids in the 10th grade *Trojans*—name of the football team, of the annual, and name of contraceptives sold in hole-in-the-wall shops in Market Square—come out of the Christenberry past to stand on the front steps of Knox High, looking like well-preserved corpses. Girls from the Bijou time, two years before, are there, too, converging from the four junior high schools. Amazing how many are so keenly familiar. Desire to keep them all alive in my life terrifyingly frustrated. So many pretty girls, such sweet, lovely little breasts. More Shirleys, Ritas, Waunitas, and Dellas than I can remember though.

I admired girls who I never knew, and I was unaware that I was the object of love for some girls. Three I now know about. And how many more hankered for me than those three, who later by chance revealed themselves. One even quit school because she couldn't stand being near me and not be my sweetheart—Oh, yeah, Della Snow—and another was so shy she couldn't speak to me. Ironically, I had felt she was too lovely, good, and pure for me, a misty-eyed, soulful girl. Another girl told me she sneaked into my room and lay on my bed when I was a freshman in college because in high school she'd heard such intriguing stories about me—my shocking beliefs about religion, and the many girls I was reputed to have "done it" with. Bad boy Lucius Hutchfield. How many other phantoms have come and gone, leaving the prints of their sweet fannies on my cot? And I imagined myself in the lives of many girls who knew me not. "Love of others is a reflection of the love one has for oneself. . . ." Opening line of an essay written, after much loving and too little reading, in my freshman year in college, to straighten out the world's crooked ways of looking at love and unselfishness. Selfishness turned on its head became unselfishness, and you couldn't love others unless you love yourself.

All those girls I only looked at, never touched, even socially, and all the girls I made love to. The cliché is irresistible—"Where are they now?" I look into the faces on Gay Street through dark glasses, see flickers of the gone girls, sometimes a woman gives me a startled look of recognition, despite the sunglasses I wear even on dark days, and I don't know her at all. Sad. Sad. "Whatever became of . . ." I say, picking over the shambles of the past.

My memory unconsciously, and my willful romantic vision deliberately, superimposed Hollywood faces—never bodies—upon the girls and women I made love to.

And while I went through long chaste loves, simultaneously with "sordid," thrilling backstage fucks, beguiled by filmdom's fuckless romances, I was concocting romantic sagas in my own imagination, and during the day in Christenberry Junior High, I wrote them all out, one scenario after another, movie events and real events entwined, in almost sexual fervor and intensity of concentration and speed, my arm growing hot as a piston, my fingers aching like a Front Street whore's ass.

Even when I was five, I understood perfectly the love story in *Gone with the Wind*. Older, I began to think of myself as a combination of Rhett and Ashley and I sought and loved girls who were a blend of Scarlett and Melanie, but fucked girls like Belle Watling, thus perpetuating the double standard sanctified by ideal concepts concocted in hot churches and in Hollywood under klieg lights on sets enclosed in enormous barns.

A longtime feminist with my wife, I have escaped the attitudes that the movies taught me about love and sex and the many relationships possible between men and women. Movies taught me what I call my southern purity complex, whereby the woman you love is pure, and above all, yours alone. Lovers repeatedly swear to love each other forever. Sex is an abomination to love. Even so, listening to the ushers ridicule the girls we had screwed backstage saddened me. I respected and cherished them in memory, for they had become part of the grand design of my life, shaped in ideal dreams. And although a little after the Bijou time, I began making love to the girls I truly loved, Loris, as well as the ones for whom I only lusted, I retained the idealistic concept of the loved one as the finest creature on earth, distilled from a metaphysical elixir for me alone.

The movies taught me the strategies of love. I played hard to get. After a break-up with Loraine, I enacted a period of distant hostility, with bitter looks across rooms in Christenberry, passing her in the hall, and on the streets of Knoxville. I experienced a concealed yearning, burning in the eyes, visible in the sensitive mouth, the distracted gaze.

The movies taught me that love was inseparable from grand passions. To prove my love, I enacted irrational jealous antics, until I became a victim of my own conceits. Once, just to test Loris's love, I slapped her, and listened to a mouth full of tears swear everlasting love, so as rationalization, I delight in remembering the time she threw hot coffee in my face to shut up one of my raving jealous riffs. And the time moments after she kissed me goodbye at her front door and her big sister told her she was too young to go steady and Loris whirled around and gave her face a smart slap that I did not see but relish imagining over the years.

An intuition sometimes transfixes me, of all those girls, summer, fall, winter, spring merged into a seasonless moment—thousands of images, simultaneously, of the girls I loved, seen at once separately in each place I met and made love to or simply worshipped them, in all the streets and rooms and theaters, over-populating Knoxville entirely.

one that crawled in the rain, a knife between his teeth, under the circus wagon in Tod Browning's classic horror movie *Freaks*.

From our front porch when we lived almost two years on Dempster, we looked, when the leaves were thin in the fall or all down in winter, or were sticky in early Spring, at the glow, like a red hot poker, of the Broadway Theater marquee a mile away. Big brother Earl leads Bucky and me along the WPA flood-control ditch that cut through the dense jungle across from our house, we hit the smooth path along the bank of First Creek, grassy, and climb up on the bridge on Fairmont Boulevard, and throw grass, flowers, and other offerings over the rail to Fartso the Whale who lived in the creek. Earl told us Fartso was a mean whale—he's probably never read *Moby Dick*, but he cottoned to Monstro the Whale in *Pinocchio*—who had many helpers, like gremlins, and I always thought of Snow White's Seven Dwarfs, and Bucky imagined Santa Claus's helpers. But if you threw him presents, Fartso wouldn't hurt you. He might even help you beat up bullies and give you presents like Santa Claus does if you're good. Bucky believed so passionately in Fartso the Whale, Earl often used Fartso to con Bucky out of his nickel for popcorn, and after Earl ran away with the circus when he was eleven, I perpetuated the Fartso myth as a way of getting Bucky to mind me. "Throw that ol' popcorn into the creek for Fartso and you might get a new Gene Autry pistol with a red pearl handle like Otto's got." And Bucky throws over the rusty rail the popcorn he'd crawled all over the slimy floor under seats picking up in the Broadway.

From Fartso's bridge, we had to cross the most dangerous intersection in Knoxville, the Broadway's neon marquee lights pulsing on our faces. The Broadway sat beside an alley that climbed a hill, at the end of a short block, a branch of the Knoxville Public Library next door where, a poor reader, I pored over Harry Clarke's ultra-bizarre color illustrations of Edgar Allen Poe's stories.

There's my mother, Mildred Pierce, on the screen, making pies to sell to keep food on the table, and that's my Daddy, Frederic March, coming back from serving with General Patton in *The Best Years of Our Lives*, but Daddy ends up a drunk in *The Lost Weekend*, without Ray Milland's Academy Award. I'm the international adventurer, Alan Ladd, in the rain in *China*, pissed off at Loretta Young. Then I'm Cornel Wilde as Chopin playing "The Promise" for Merle Oberon as George Sand in *A Song to Remember*. That's me and my brothers and the other Dead End Kids of Lincoln Park, talking to Bogart, the punk hoodlum, on the slummy docks of East Side Manhattan in *Dead End*. My older brother didn't listen to Bogart as the compassionate corrections officer in *Crime School*, but my little brother listened to my older brother, and while I stood On the Spot as an usher at the Bijou, Lana Turner and John Garfield at my back in *The Postman Always Rings Twice* shoving Cecil Kellaway in his car over a cliff, my conmen brothers are in the state prison and the reform school in Nashville, too far to visit.

As I stood On the Spot on the main aisle as a Bijou usher, I felt steeped in the remembered aura of the Broadway Theater where the pretty ticket girls, older than the popcorn and candy girls, had imagined sweet moments with the men who ripped tickets, or so I supposed. In the cramped lobby of the Broadway, I inhale the whiff of women as rowdy girls slap open the ladies' room door. Entering the urine-Lysol reek of the men's room, I catch my breath. I inhale the dust of the aisle carpet. In August, only a large fan revolves beside the screen. Searching for a seat, I watch Goddess Barbara Stanwyck starring in *Double Indemnity*, a luminous-headed sex-trap, trying to persuade Fred MacMurray to kill her husband. On Saturday, a chapter play. Goddess Linda Sterling starring in *Zorro's Black Whip*. Met her a few years ago at Pomona College, lecturing on avant garde French cinema. Shifting tube of light thrust through projection slots in back wall near the ceiling reflected modulations of light and dark off the screen upon faces in the audience. Melted Milky Ways and Hershey Kisses that shoe leather and bare feet had ground into the concrete. Sweating bodies of children, parents, old people, rows of families—feet, armpits, crotches, soiled clothes coal smoke imbued.

On the screen, everything packed into the kiss. In the audience, the sly sex, the workman's hand slipping down into the starched blouse, the red nailed hand slipping inside the unzipped fly. For nine cents admission, four times through, Goddess Dorothy Lamour in *Her Jungle Love*—three years later, a wet dream, the only Goddess I ever, even involuntarily, desecrated. Sonny and I took turns one Saturday in the Broadway fingering a strange girl from Corbin, Kentucky, visiting her cousin, until, blinking our eyes against the six o'clock August sunburst, we stared at our fingers, turned white and wrinkled, as if we had swum too long in the YMCA's chlorinated pool.

I am sitting on the front row of the Broadway, wads of blow gum stuck to my sooty bare feet, stale blossoms of spilled popcorn nudging my toes. For the second time in my life, I watch Rhett Butler carry Scarlett O'Hara up the wide, red-carpeted staircase, knowing he will make love to her but refusing, out of respect and loyalty, to project on the beaded screen in my head images of that God "doing it" to that Goddess, whom I worshipped above all women, even though deep satisfaction lit up her face as she woke up smiling the next morning, when a dark-haired girl from an old neighborhood comes up to me and asks if I remember her, that time when we were four and I "did it" to her among dandelions one Spring day behind her coalhouse, and I tell her yes, but no, I have forgotten, remembering "doing it" to her cousin, though, blond hair cut straight across her forehead, inside the coalhouse, an ax hanging on the coal dust-blackened wall.

The Fabulous Forties. Hub of my life. The movies and my life—the loving, the writing—always inseparable. Neighborhood Broadway Theater, the hub of the early Forties, of my childhood, all other theaters spoke out of it. Uptown, the Bijou, jeweled navel of the after-Bomb Forties, its facets mirroring all Cherokee's 23 uptown and neighborhood theaters—East, West, North, South. Hub of my adolescence. Fuckless Forties on screen. Fuckfull in the theaters themselves and in neighborhoods surrounding.

The truest, purist Goddesses acted in love stories up on that square screen. In that romantic realm, all their finest qualities flourished. Any departure either intensified their purity or allowed a fleeting sexuality that I felt guilty noticing.

The superficial world of the musicals enhanced the unreality of Goddess Betty Grable, and other musical stars, but because they often dressed, sang, danced in a deliberately provocative way, a special quality of sexuality hovered about them. Most of them seemed to move in a twilight sexual zone. But a group of younger musical stars were so wholesome that they danced and sang in a neutral sex zone.

Comediennes violated the dignity, the aura of purity about the Goddesses. Their antics created a sexual aura that almost inspired sexual fantasies. The exaggerated femininity and the violent antics of homely women in the comedy short films, and their pursuit of men, gave them a quality of aggressive sexuality. Slapstick antics thrust even older women into a sexual context. Some of the older actresses who resembled my mother's attractive girlfriends were outright sexy. And others were like the teacher you hope will invite you to mow the lawn and come on into the house for ice-cold lemonade. As imperfect mimics of the Goddesses, the child actresses who were about my age when I was an usher were sometimes sexy.

When Earl leeringly told me that he heard that Elizabeth Taylor had massaged her titties to make them big enough so she could get the role of the young girl and do the scene in which the doctor opens her jockey shirt to examine her for injuries in the fall and discovered the believable and, for me, incredibly sexual titties in *National Velvet*, the persistent image scalded my cheeks in shame because she looked like a younger version of Vivien Leigh, but I was almost in love with Elizabeth, nascent Goddess, too. And many years later I learned that she goes around the set saying "shit" and "fuck off" with ferocity but a certain lack of conviction, and that while waiting on the set for Richard Burton to stop shooting *Camelot*, she read my first novel.

Most of my childhood, I lived in the Broadway Theater, close to most of the many streets I lived on during that time, close to most of the five paper routes I carried—fired and rehired and fired for missing houses, daydreaming—and I'd rush there after the route. Seeing movies at least twice, sometimes three times—no double features there, from the first movies I ever saw at about two or three years old to the day they closed up and it became a bowling alley, to the day two years ago when I stood inside the burned-out bowling alley and reconstructed for Shelley the layout of the Broadway Theater and we walked around in it, to this very day as I write, and on into the future. I still walk by the shell of her.

I want to tell everything about that time, and I will, but first I have to feed into this humming recorder a great deal about the Bijou. Those were the two most important theaters—the Broadway, hub of my childhood, remaining after I moved out of the neighborhood the essence of that time beyond the Broadway, also, although Uncle Luke, who turned up not missing in the war, pushed my wheelchair all the way from good ol' 2722 Henegar down Atlantic and on down Broadway to see Hedy Lamarr, who I met a few years ago, in *The Strange Woman* that summer I had both legs in casts from the operation to correct incipient clawfoot deformity, and Loris to the Broadway Theater, and I went back, and it seemed strange—and the Bijou, hub of my adolescence, where I met both Loraine and a year later Loris and which had fired me just before Doctor Summers transplanted three bones in each of my feet.

I want to see where the Broadway and the Bijou set in the Knoxville dreamscape, see, too, the other theaters and how they relate to each other.

I turn to the Hammond Atlas to see Knoxville in relation to other towns.

When she talked about other East Tennessee towns, Mammy's voice made a mystery of east and west and north and south.

I want to see where the Bijou stands in relation to where I lived in various houses, on various streets, and in relation to all points of the compass. So the Bijou is the hub, the other theaters spoke outward, because what I felt about the Bijou partook also of the way I responded to the other 20 some theaters. To get to the Bijou from where I lived on the corner of Atlantic and Pershing, I caught a number 2 Lincoln Park Streetcar.

Damn it, the tape broke!

Okay, so the streetcar turned a few blocks up Pershing onto Morelia and hugged the left side of the street, for some reason, leaves flicked the yellow grill over the windows, and I smelled the upholstery shop, whose loading dock set inches from the side of the streetcar. Women in blue and white uniforms, off work at C. B. Atkins's furniture factory where Loris's mother worked, got on a few blocks down. Streetcars! The electric ones showed up on the streets of Knoxville about four decades before I was born in 1933, and the last one entered the car barn next to the Bijou for the last time in 1947, a few months after Mr. Hood fired me from the Bijou.

The Bijou, a jewel movie palace, neither as aristocratic as the Tennessee nor as low class as the Strand on this same street, evoked all the theaters I had lived in during much of my childhood. Every type of movie, except the cheap standard Strand Theater fare. Some revivals. So the women on the screen elicited almost the entire range of my attitudes about love as I watched each movie as usher ten times or more, though in fragments—spaced attention, leaps of concentration, always a kind of subliminal background.

White high-heeled shoes, dark tan legs, white shorts, white blouse, moist large eyes, a pouty, glistening mouth, a white turban—Lana Turner when I first lay eyes on her in *The Postman Always Rings Twice* on my first day as usher. Thrillingly beautiful. I knew as a fact that between scenes Cora and Frank made love, but I didn't experience it imaginatively. What came through was the idyllic scene in the ocean near the end when Frank vows eternal love and proves to Cora that he is not going to kill her in revenge for the way she double-crossed him—he takes her so far out in the ocean that she can't swim back, then helps her swim her back to the beach, but she is killed in a wreck as they are driving home, and the D. A. charges him with faking the accident to kill her.

The Bijou presented roadshows now and then, vaudeville, high class burlesque, plays, *Hamlet*, with the old Polonius who grabbed my ass as I passed him back stage, local amateur talent shows, like the Saturday morning Bugs Bunny Club. Sometimes, two-day runs of plays brought in from UT disrupted the movie schedule, the first play I ever saw, Tennessee Williams's *The Glass Menagerie*, which opened up a whole new world of drama, and within a year I was writing plays, and two years later had won a statewide contest with a one-act mountain tragedy, "The Great Wings Still Beating," reviewed by Luther Langford in the *News-Sentinel*. I was a little resentful of Tennessee Williams when I first encountered his name, but then I'd never really called myself Tennessee Hutchfield on any of my stories—called myself the Tennessee Kid, though, in "Helena Street," where I dueled with Billy the Kid.

Later, I was a little contemptuous that the first *Theatre Arts* I ever looked at had nothing in it about Tennessee Williams, who now is one of my heroes. But *Theatre Arts* became one of my magazines, and I felt as if I were being unfaithful to my fierce love of movie magazines, which were clearly of another world. A few years later, in an old copy of *Life*, which I found at Knoxville Used Books and Magazines store by the Gay Street bridge, I was thrilled to discover that, as an unknown playwright, Williams, too, had been an usher, at the Strand in New York City. Ten years later, I picked up a girl in a Broadway theater, pretending, during intermissions of Eugene O'Neill's *A Long Day's Journey Into Night*, to be Tennessee Williams—partly, it was my moustache and the put-on accent.

A year after Hood fired me, I went to see a talent show at the Bijou and there on stage was a magician doing some tricks with great charm and confidence but almost no audience response. I'd worked for him a week or two showing low-grade westerns in remote mountain areas and quit when he reached for my ass behind the Kodak 16 mm portable projector. We passed each other later in the lobby when the movie was showing again, and I was polite but evasive when he asked me to work for him again. That was the last I saw of him. He resembled my tall, thin, monkey-faced homosexual freshman English teacher at UT who became one of the most important intellectual influences in my life, and who in one half-hour session, six of my stories on his bony knee, taught me more about writing than I was ever to learn later.

And the symphony orchestra played there several times while I was an usher, never imagining in any of my daydreams that in two years I'd be a constant guest at the conductor's house, though usually at first as babysitter to Victor Junior, in the Savage house, featured on picture postcards to show the typical Knoxville mansion. Not until last week did I learn from a book about Knoxville that my great uncle Lucius Hutchfield's house, next door to Savage's, was Knoxville's oldest building continuously occupied as a residence, built in 1821 by Kester Brown, and named Half-Moon Bend.

The Savages became my best friends—Victor Florina, his aristocratic wife, Victor Junior—his tough little boy, and Gayle, his raven-haired daughter, my age, who aspired to be a movie goddess. The glamour of movies merged with the glamour of symphony concerts. Strange to go back stage and congratulate Victor in the very room where two years before I always changed into my usher's uniform. Seemed so long before.

Four years later, I was up on that Bijou stage myself in *Detective Story*, as the reporter confidant of the hero, played by a man who later became one of my best teachers, listening to Prof, the director, give me instructions, and later as the 80-year-old Jewish amateur philosopher Mr. Carp in Odet's *Golden Boy*—the actor playing the title character became a famous Broadway and movie actor. Just before I went into the army I played the pompous Mayor in the French play *The Enchanted*, and a few years later the elderly Vincentio in Shakespeare's *The Taming of the Shrew*—each play separated by adventures in New York, Boston, Washington, and as a merchant seaman in New Orleans, Galveston, Chile, Hawaii, Panama, and by a troubled draftee in Alaska in the army. Rehearsing on stage, I was vaguely aware of a dim figure sitting in the back of the house—a Bijou usher instructed to keep an eye on things as I had been for the first play I ever saw. I acted in three times that many, on the Bijou stage and in Carousel at UT, and after the army I went to Yale School of Drama, where I was in two plays and had one of my own—a beatnik musical adaptation of Moliere's *The Imaginary Invalid*—poorly done.

The girls in the road shows came and went, but the scent of their presence lingered in the dressing rooms where we hung our clothes and goofed off and jacked off and did it to girls who couldn't stay away from the Bijou.

EVEN AS I MADE CLEAR DISTINCTIONS among things, influenced by the attitudes of friends, family, and the general puritanical Knoxville society, in my mind, all the theaters, movies, and people seemed related, emotionally and sexually, blended or overlapped.

"Every guy dreams of meeting a girl like you," says Alan Ladd to Veronica Lake in *The Blue Dahlia*, while, relieved from our posts at the heads of aisles that slope like Knoxville's hills, our feet still aching, stinking, Gale, older than I was, resembling Errol Flynn, and I sit on the dark side of the Bijou near red velvet curtains that hang behind box seats, and Shirley, bigger than either of us, sits between us, not 23 as she had told us but, her protective little brother later tells us, 15 and slightly backward, and she pushes delicate blossoms of hot popcorn through her puckered lips that glisten with lipstick, salt, and grease, as Gale and I, like Errol Flynn and Gilbert Roland crossing swords in *The Sea Hawk*, cross fingers inside her roomy pussy, each of our other hands squeezing a surprisingly small titty. "The trick is to find you."

Seeing Alan Ladd, my hero, my god, on the screen in *This Gun for Hire* thrilled me very differently than seeing the Goddesses, except Vivien Leigh, whom I loved above all women. Maybe if I had seen Alan Ladd short like me and bare-assed I wouldn't have thought him so unreal.

But I didn't see Gale's ass either, the older, Errol Flynn usher, cool, charming, debonair, except when all us ushers, minus Bruce the albino, convened at the Y pool where we swam naked. Gale Blackburn did not bring Errol Flynn to me, I took Errol Flynn to Gale Blackburn. My ideal self, he being 16 to my 14. I haven't seen Gale Blackburn since that late night Brady walked into the Dixie Vim filling station where I sat at the manager's desk, writing, one Sunday afternoon, and told me there was somebody out there wants to see me, in that tone boys used that always got you ready to face an enemy who had come to fight you, somebody who had let you know he was "looking for you."

And there in the back seat, between two strange boys, was Gale in a sailor suit. Brady had got back in behind the wheel and the car was full of boys and smoke and hands and knees more than faces, the only face was Gale's, without the sailor hat, the curly head, the slender face, the Errol Flynn one-side of the mouth smile. I don't remember what we said, I was so excited to see him, and like a movie star come to life, he looked so beautiful, come in from out there, the romance beyond Knoxville, that I'm sure I didn't say much, maybe that I was still writing stories, I think he even asked about that, and about Loraine, and I told him about Loris, and that I had met her up in the Bijou balcony after "our time" as ushers. That scene seems so brief in memory, a shimmering movie still. They were there, and then they were gone, and I didn't even *hear* about Gale after that. A little later about Brady, to discover from Uncle Frank in Santa Fe, where a play of mine was being produced, that Brady was a distant cousin of mine on Daddy's side, as, in fact, I'd already discovered Harry was on Momma's side. Life's cheap and easy symbolism—all men are relatives.

An evocateur of Bijou, Gale keeps coming back in flashes of memory during those long sleepless nights in Washington, New York, Boston, Lexington, New Orleans, Panama, Alaska, San Francisco, Montana, Oregon, Louisville, New Haven, Vermont in the four-story Victorian mansion, when the terrible Bijou nostalgia came over me, and I always see him gliding toward me, slender in his tight uniform, perfect fit, debonair, across the lobby, slow-motion, to spark my cheek with an electricity scuffed off the carpet. So what does it mean to say of someone who has been to you what Gale was to me that you haven't seen him since? How more vividly see somebody than the way I see him? He has been fossilized perhaps, embalmed, preserved, photographed, caught forever on a short strip of film, always there in storage in the film vault of my mind, will come when my will beckons, or come of his own power at times when the context explains nothing. Gale and Errol Flynn weren't so much, it was that I brought to them so much.

I turned off the recorder just now and called Marta to tell her that I miss her and Shelley painfully.

Is the mind a movie projector gone mad, scrambling all the movies, features, trailers, short subjects, comedies, cartoons, newsreels, throwing on the screen across the Grand Canyon auditorium of the years any image that happens to flit through? What happens to all that stuff that gets edited out, that ends up on the projection booth floor, can it be reshot somehow, and reintegrated, can a sequence be unscrambled? It's not the metaphor that matters, but the anguish of not being able to do it. Poetically, the image of Gale is fine, all that he was and meant is compressed into the single image that most expresses his essence, but then why the sadness of recalling him only as a fragment?

Between the Bijou and the tavern next door, on the South side, the street-cars turned into the car barn, and across the street from the Lamar, the little hotel that sits next to the Bijou on the corner, stood the Cumberland Hotel that burned down in 1947, five stories high when I caught the streetcar after usher duty, gone to smoking black the next afternoon where I reported for duty after school.

Directly across the streetcar tracks from the Bijou was the Lyric, green paint scaling, an ancient, enormous, formerly legitimate theater, where *Ben Hur* was once staged with live horses, and operas, plays, pageants, political rallies, then wrestling matches that drew the kind of people who hung around Market Square—and me, every Friday night, after collecting money on my Sharp's Ridge paper route.

Next door to the Lyric—where the dead projectionist stares forever through his windshield—Max's steak house, where Momma was cashier for a few years, and where Marina, Max's daughter, used to work—I admired her from a distance for three years and used her name to name a few heroines in stories. Used to meet Mr. Strange at Max's to discuss the documentary movie scripts I wrote for him when I was fifteen.

From the Andrew Johnson Hotel, a perfect view of the river and the slums and South Knoxville. Had a five-hour talk 'til 3 a. m. with Tennessee Williams in that hotel when he came to his father's funeral, having watched the burial in the cemetery where veterans of all the wars are buried, and many historic Knoxville families, including Parson Brownlow, reviled Reconstruction governor.

Now that all the buildings across Gay from the Bijou have been torn down—to enable the projectionist to sit all alone in his car as snow obscures his view of the Bijou—you can see that the theaters and all uptown stand on top of a long ridge that slopes down at the South end sharply into the Front Street slums and the river, where the houseboats were tied up, where Knoxville began, and where historic Blount Mansion still stands, though nearly a shambles, and slopes at the north end down to the Southern Railway Station, which General Sanders raided in the war. The East slopes were covered with red-brick slums, now cleared for the Civic Center, and on the west slopes on the other side of the Gay Street Bridge are other slums and the L&N tracks. Free to wander all over uptown streets from age 8 on till today, I imagined people and stories, as if it was all one huge reservoir of the imagination, like Venice, I thought, walking along her canals.

On a western hill above the river is the University of Tennessee, where I went to school and where a few years ago Bette Davis shot a 20-second scene, and the library is on the opposite hill, where I discovered "literary magazines." Why do I tell all this to myself when it's all just outside this door? Not out of acute need, but keen desire. "Tell it again, Mammy!" I used to say, and she'd rip off the same old stories, new as new.

Most of the theaters where I spent most of my early life were uptown, within a few blocks north of the Bijou. Even though I fingered or at least smooched girls in most of Knoxville's theaters, the atmosphere of some theaters was more sexually charged than others. Least sexually charged were the two aristocrats, Tennessee and the Rivieria, a block apart in the heart of the business district on Gay Street, where the first-run high-class star-studded movies showed.

A gold-domed, miniature Taj Mahal, the Tennessee—set inside half the ground floor of an eleven-story office building—was a far, far more magnificent movie palace than the Bijou, but too enormous, cold, forbidding, like a temple, a cathedral, walk softly, on the carpets, then marble, then carpets, whisper. A double ticket booth, black and white streaked marble, brass ticket spitter, brass railings, guiding me through six doors into the waiting area, where two marble benches sat, where I never sat. To the left and right, very tall posters work up your expectations months ahead, six on each side. A uniformed ticket lady just inside the door on the right, an intercom telephone on the wall nearby. In the center of the gleaming marble floors sets the candy and popcorn booth, three uniformed girls on duty. Harry's usher pal, laconic Tom, married one of them, blond, and a sweet, delicate butt. Add pursed-lips Preston and you had three musketeers in ushers' uniforms, who, sometimes including me, went off into the dark streets of Knoxville in Tom's Daddy's pussy wagon, a long-assed 1940 Chevrolet Special Deluxe Sedan.

On Saturday nights during the war, enormous crowds waited hours in the two-story high, block-long lobby, steaming bodies crammed together, packed between velvet red ropes, crowds gathered outside around the ticket booth, two aisles kept clear for exits, me brushing with the back of my hand the firm buttocks of girls in front of me during the long "hold outs." Left and right, two wide, oriental-carpeted staircases, marble railings, swoop upwards. When I go in downstairs instead, a marble balustrade arched above me.

Left and right, staircases go down to the lower lobbies, the restrooms, women's outer area looking like a living room, arm chairs, tables, couches, flowers in ornate vases, paintings on the walls, statues standing around. Somehow here more frequently than in the sleazy theaters, I was aware of the man at the next gleaming urinal glancing at my pecker, inhibiting my stream. In the ten-urinal, eight-toilet men's lavatory, the drawings and dirty sayings were more sophisticated, inventive, executed on the best material—the famous Tennessee marble from nearby quarries, marble I proudly stroked as I climbed the stairs inside the Statue of Liberty.

In the main lobby, more paintings, marble statues, antique chairs and sofas, velvet drapes and crystal chandeliers made me, a poor boy, feel inferior but privileged to be there. At extreme ends of the inner lobby, two more staircases rise to the balcony. Six entrances to the auditorium. Four ushers downstairs, four up, a captain roaming, the manager visible if there's a crowd. At one time the Tennessee had 15 ushers, Harry and his other friends, Tom and Preston. Under my leather jacket like Alan Ladd's in *China*, draped over my lap, Loris covertly jacked me off into embroidered handkerchiefs, more sinful feeling because of the ambience of respectable magnificence, as in a cathedral, both of us fearful of discovery, maybe by that woman down the row.

People have a special look about them when they leave a movie theater. The Tennessee gave them its own look. Coming out of the dark theater, where we had heard the swelling music of Max Steiner in *The Big Sleep* above the drone of voices while waiting, down that marbled, spacious concourse, we looked different from the people we watched pouring out of the Riviera, the second best theater in town.

On the same side, a block north on Gay, between the S&W cafeteria, itself a palace, and Clark & Jones Music Store, Walgreen's next down the line, set the Riviera. Without a balcony, the Riviera lacked magnificence, but it was clean, only one long, narrow, steep aisle and showed the first-run movies the Tennessee couldn't fit into its schedule, along with a few high-grade B pictures and most of the great epics—*Duel in the Sun* and *Forever Amber*. There seemed to be an unusually thick traffic in the cramped men's room, and the heavy drapes that hung below the warm orange LADIES sign intrigued me. A fire gutted it in 1950, but they remodeled it, and I can go up Gay Street right now and see *Bonnie and Clyde*. Like most of the women who showed up on their screens, the Tennessee and the Riviera were sexually neutral. I entered them as temples to gaze upon the Goddesses, in their celestial spheres—Bette Davis, Greer Garson, Irene Dunne, Olivia de Havilland, Maureen O'Hara, Paulette Goddard. And on a slightly lower level of perfection, Susan Hayward, Joan Leslie, Geraldine Fitzgerald, Linda Darnell, Eleanor Parker in *Of Human Bondage*, a loose woman and so a tarnished Goddess, inspiring brief, mild sexual fantasies.

Some Goddesses that were built up as newcomers had a special impact— my expectations were aroused and I was receptive but their very newness placed them in a twilight zone of sexuality—Janet Leigh, Jane Greer, especially Jean Peters in *Captain from Castile* and Ava Gardner in *The Killers*. But Jeanne Crain in *Leave Her to Heaven* became a pure Goddess. Some were neutral. I disliked Terry Moore because she seemed vulgar, like some of the junior high prick-teasers. But Patricia Neal was a special newcomer because she grew up in Knoxville and went to Knox High. Her first big role as a Goddess was as Dominique in Ayn Rand's *The Fountainhead* in 1949, a movie that affected my intellect, especially in the army, as deeply as *The Razor's Edge*, that I saw at the Bijou two years after Hood fired me.

On a third level of perfection were the young, soulful, misty-eyed Goddesses, especially Dorothy Malone in *The Big Sleep*. Phyllis Thaxter in *The Sea of Grass*—that Vincent Lawrence wrote the screenplay didn't mean anything to me until I read James M. Cain's introduction to his novel *The Butterfly*, in which he says Lawrence taught him how to write, and gave him the title *The Postman Always Rings Twice*. Nor did the fact that this was one of Eliz Kazan's first pictures mean anything until I learned he was Tennessee William's director. I always sensed something doomed about Gail Russell. She resembled Loris, who never could stomach her. Because of similar looks or aura, I thought of some young Goddesses in groups, especially the MGM girls.

I was merely fond of women whose ethereal beauty transmitted no charge and who were sexually neutral, Dorothy McGuire, Nina Foch, June Allyson, Celeste Holm. I disliked only a few of the neutral women. I tried to like

Claudette Colbert because she was a star, but paradoxically her very sexlessness emitted an aura of sexuality, even though watching her with Spencer Tracy, Clark Gable, and Hedy Lamarr in *Boom Town*, I couldn't imagine her naked.

Coming on strong as sexy women, some of the third level Goddesses moved always in the sexual twilight zone. Evelyn Keyes set off distinct vibrations, but one of the few Goddesses who struck me as overtly sexual and brought me to the verge of fantasy was Gloria Graham in *Crossfire*.

I disliked some of the women who were overtly sexy, seemed lascivious, and exuded raw sex. Some of the sexy ones provoked sexual fantasies *because* they were unlikable, they weren't Goddesses, so I could respond to their sexiness. Ann Blyth in James M. Cain's *Mildred Pierce* I resented for distracting me from Joan Crawford the Goddess with a vivid sexuality that contaminated Joan.

Sometimes I confused two or three of the third level Goddesses with each other, impairing their goddess perfection, but enhancing their sexuality, which had a strange multiple impact. Ann Dvorak and Ella Raines, both tough girls. Bonita Granville and Priscilla Lane were sexy anyway because boys said a neighborhood girl who resembled them had sucked her brother's peter.

Neither Errol Flynn nor Clark Gable nor Tyrone Power nor Alan Ladd in their behavior as lovers evoked a sexual atmosphere, but some of the lecherous actors did, often suggesting something perverted. Peter Lorre in *Casablanca*, Charles Laughton in *The Hunchback of Notre Dame*, Claude Rains, Bela Lugosi, Basil Rathbone, George Sanders, and, oh yes, Zachary Scott in *Mildred Pierce*. So, Lucius, does all this you're taping for all the world to hear mean that everything about the movies, everything related in any way, far-fetched as some might think it to be, to the movies, was, is, about sex? I tend to side with Freud on that, so, yes, I reckon.

Down Gay in the next block after the Riviera just past Kresses and across from the Greyhound Bus Terminal, I see the Strand, another rat house, played all the C class movies and chapter plays first, full of country folks on Saturdays. Uncle Luke ushered there the year before he went to war, so Momma used him and the other ushers as babysitters while she worked during the summer when she couldn't use school. Bucky and Earl and I—Tom, Dick, and Harry, I often thought, sometimes though Groucho, Chico, Harpo—rode the streetcar in from Cedar street with Momma at nine o'clock, and she left us to stand out front until the ticket booth opened at ten while she worked for Mammy, who owned Jane's Café, and the JFG coffee plant where Mammy worked before Grandpa Charlie shot himself was down by Southern Railway Depot, and we could smell it all the way up at the Strand.

The Strand showed all the cowboy pictures. Hopalong Cassidy, Tex Ritter, Roy Rogers—my hero before Alan Ladd—Gene Autry, Wild Bill Elliott—"I'm a peaceable man"—and the chapter plays got first run. *Gang Busters*—the crooks going down that manhole in the subway tunnel during the credits—*Riders of Death Valley*—"We ride, we ride," they sang, —with Dick Foran and Buck Jones, *Zorro's Fighting Legion* starring Reed Hadley, slender as a whip, and a voice so resonant he was also the god-like narrator of "The March of Time" series. Buck Rogers, Spy Smasher—the only serial ever to play the Tennessee—Charlie Chan, The Green Hornet, Captain Marvel, Red Ryder—Little Beaver, played by Robert Blake, one of the killers now in *In Cold Blood*, and I were acquaintances at Fort Richardson in Alaska. Arrogant little twerp. Reruns of older movies. *Scarface*, starring Goddess Ann Dvorak and powerful Paul Muni. The *Sherlock Holmes* movies. Second rate gangster movies. *The Falcon. Boston Blackie.* For 9 cents per boy, Momma had a trusty babysitter.

The cheap costumes and sets and the bad acting and the poor lighting of the cheap C movies made the girls seem more real and so more vulnerable to my sexual craving. And the categories seemed more distinct and acted as a focus on the girls. Westerns. Horror. Cheap musicals. Comedy series. In the cheap short comedies, some of the women were sexy because of the contrast with zanies like Laurel and Hardy, the Three Stooges, the Marx Brothers. Marie Wilson in *My Friend Irma* epitomized all those women. In the horror movies, the most vivid was Simone Simon, on the verge of sexy because she spoke in a French accent in *Cat People*.

The women heroines in the serials, or the chapter plays, as we called them, moved in a special realm, especially Goddess Linda Sterling as *The Tiger Woman*. Around here somewhere is that photograph a famous poet took of Linda and me under a tree in Pomona.

Let's go over, Lucius, one street west from Gay, paralleling. There's the market house—historic, three stories, red-brick, full of consumptive country vendors and fresh butter and meat, dominating the square, farmers' produce trucks flanking the two long sides of the building, flowers on the side where the lower-middle-class stores ranged, vegetables on the side where the lower-class stores stood, the trucks backed up to the curbs, their loaded tail-gates hanging heavy, laden with produce and black walnuts. The police loved to park at each end of the market house, where the fountains were dry. The Market House also served as City Hall for a while, until the fire damage drove it into an old Deaf and Dumb Asylum. Now it is a grease spot only. Momma and I often met for lunch at Nan's little café *inside* the market house. I can see us now.

There was a hierarchy of movie houses in this long block, too. On the west side of the Market House, between little hole-in-the-wall shops where Trojan rubbers, Red Chief chewing tobacco, combs, all brands of cigarettes, cigarette lighters, practical jokes, Milky Way and Mars candy bars, Wriggly chewing gum, and dirty pictures are sold, across the sidewalk from the turnips, spotty shelly beans, and wild cherries, in a narrow hole in the wall, set the Rialto, so tiny it seemed almost a playhouse, even when I was a runt selling newspapers stolen from the bus terminal ramps, yelling, "Errol Flynn Tried for Rape!" and there he was in the still slots and on an outside loud speaker, leading the charge as General Custer in *They Died with Their Boots On.*

A few skid row stores down, past another hole in the wall, the Crystal, the Rialto's twin, both owned by two Italian brothers who opened the Rialto first on Gay in 1914. Then they moved it to Market Square in 1933, year I was born, the year popcorn aroma enhanced movie theaters. On Gay, they'd tried Vaudeville for a few years, but it didn't pay. I heard that two other theaters on Gay were the Queen and the Majestic, torn down before I was born. Then why do I feel nostalgia for *them*, too? Didn't Momma send me a *News-Sentinel* clipping about them in the late fifties? I'm going to stop now and look for it.

Had to go up to Lawson McGhee Library and look at the clipping on microfilm. Gives me a headache to run that machine. Well, the Rialto and the Crystal were literally the "last word" in movie theaters. I never passed the faded posters quickly, I walked slowly by, glancing at the stills that looked wholesome out front of the Broadway but tinted with an aura of sin in this milieu of poor farmers, seedy politicians, peddlers, beggars, blind singers, middle-class shoppers slumming for rock bottom bargains, salvation army workers, hell-fire preachers—a Baghdad bizarre. And as I passed, the voices of Buck Jones, Johnny Mack Brown, Sunset Carson, symphonic background music, the shooting and the galloping reached out to me, and the heady aroma of relentlessly exploding popcorn in these "country hoojer" theaters, mingling with the smell of piss and overworked crotches and reeking feet and the fear of roaches and rats—spine-chilling when I went in barefoot—contributed to the atmosphere of ripe sexuality, crime, and hell-hole evil and diseased flesh.

In the next block up from the Market House's main entrance, across the street from the TVA and the Tennessee State Unemployment Office, set the Roxy, Queen of the Rat Houses, that featured live burlesque to a live band all day. She offers the most stills out front, a triple feature, cartoons, a chapter play, and a half hour of previews. The Roxy's front is a solid bank—an eye-wash—of stills, glossy, rich as eating a whole 25-cent pecan log. She reeks of the forbidden. Momma and decent people in Knoxville say it's a hellhole of sinful flesh and germs. Joe Campbell's Momma, sitting at her Singer sewing machine, casually told me she heard a rumor that my Momma was seen dancing in the Roxy burlesque. The burlesque shows gave me fierce hard ons when I was nine, and left me suffering a severe case of the blue balls. The lingering aura of the girls on the stage affected my response to the girls on the screen. I went to the Roxy in fear and trembling—mainly because seeing the strippers would rot my mind—I could feel my innards boiling and burning, then go slack when Bugs Bunny came on loud and frisky.

My fear of getting beat up in those Market Square theaters and my hope of picking up some tough but pretty country girl—as Earl did, including his present wife—affected my reaction to the women in the re-released B and C grade movies, and the old high class movies that were re-released there, like *Trail of the Lonesome Pine*, starring lyrical Sylvia Sidney, and *Swamp Water*, starring Anne Baxter, sexy because of the erotic swamp atmosphere, and pure and proper Nancy Kelly in *Jesse James*, who I have rediscovered in memory and now see her as a Goddess. In the rat houses, those ladies lost some of their Goddess aura, and I was sometimes shamefully aroused. But those three theaters were so forbidding, I seldom went in, always feeling guilty of some nameless sin. And when I worked for Aubrey the Magician, going into isolated mountain communities and he tried a little grab-ass, he made me feel he'd sneaked up on me in the Rialto.

When he wasn't roaming all over the United States with carnivals, my big brother Earl took the farm girls or the Front Street slum girls he picked up in the Market House or in the Trailways bus terminal to the Rialto, the

Crystal, the Roxy, his natural element. But to see him go into or come out of the Tennessee would disorient me, seem strange. I don't remember him in the Bijou at all except when he won the Al Jolson talent contest doing his fairy at the ball park routine—of course, during most of that time, I reckon he was in the reform school in Nashville or in Brushy Mountain Prison. Or on the lam, as when he sauntered out of the wings of the Bijou stage. The girls in the Market Square theaters and the Strand were big bellied, sported mail-order titties, hairy legs, and wore red socks and pumps, had stringy, peroxide hair, cross eyes, bad teeth, and wore flaming red lipstick, round red rouge spots on each cheek, heavy blond powder, ankle ID chains, and glassy jewelry at ear lobes and wrists. Earl bought them with popcorn, and his salty fingers fingered them in the back row, and I was certain any one of them could give him syphilis.

But the girl Earl has always loved is Erika, the Nazi Colonel's daughter Earl met and married when he was with the occupation forces in Frankfort in '49. She visited me one night, or maybe I dreamed it, when I was in the hospital after the operation on my feet to correct incipient clawfoot deformity. I never saw her again. Nor did Earl, and when I saw Earl again three years later, one of those times just after he was released from some prison, I'd forgotten, when he spoke of her, the nocturnal visit from the daughter of a Nazi Colonel. About a year ago, he told me his hero had always been General Rommel the Desert Fox as Erich von Stroheim depicted him in *Five Graves to Cairo*. I'd thought the fervor with which he convincingly played Rommel in our war games was just talent, but he was his hero. And I always associated him with Bogart or Groucho Marx and a little with Tyrone Power as Stanley, a con man, magician, circus barker, who became a drunk and ended up as a midway geek in *Nightmare Alley*.

I fingered and fucked some girls but did not even imagine doing it to the girls I loved and worshipped until late in the Forties. A similar double standard controlled my responses to girls on the screen. The Goddesses were pure and my "vile" fantasies never desecrated them. But the girls in the low-grade movies were less sacrosanct. I associated the starlets and stars of these movies with the theaters where I watched them. I expected to pick up girls in the low-life theaters every time I went. So images of girls in the low-grade movies entered that frame of mind—of sexual expectations.

I sometimes I miss the actresses in the cheap movies. The Goddesses were so super real for so long in those vivid childhood years that I sometimes feel less sense of loss, but the girls I saw on screens in the Market House galaxy and certain neighborhood satellites, like poor, country real girls, have faded in memory, and sometimes I search impulsively, then compulsively pursue complex detective tracing through picture books for their faces or their names, the way I search through high school annuals to bring back girls I suddenly remember. The girls I met in the dark in theaters and smooched and never saw again—I long to see them in the same way. I try hard to remember their names. Some of them inspired brief, but intensely passionate feelings, not always sexual, sometimes the possibility of a nobler love. Some of the low grade stars turn up on late TV horror shows—Evelyn Ankers menaced in *The Wolf Man*—but the girls in the audiences seem elusive forever. I miss them now, even as I miss Marta tonight.

Knoxville was a voluptuous landscape. I lived and loved girls in all the neighborhoods, and sucked the milk of paradise in each of its theaters.

Each neighborhood, and the way I responded to the girls in them, affected the personality of its theater. The Bijou and the Broadway were at opposite poles, the Bijou almost on the Tennessee River south, the Broadway at the city limits at the foot of Sharp's Ridge north, where it breaks for Broadway going north to Fountain City, both on the same long street since at the South edge of the business district Gay becomes Broadway. Then on out Broadway past the city limit going toward Cumberland Gap—wild in Mammy's tales—stands the new Tower Theater built a year after I was fired from the Bijou—white, ugly cinderblock, no embellishments, except a crying room—something new.

Across Broadway from the cemetery where Charlie Burnett, my maternal grandfather, shot mysteriously while a night watchman at a glass factory when I was three, is buried, and his mother Matilda, five empty plots for the rest of us, near Baby Land, where Baboo, my baby brother lies. The streetcars stopped running that far before I was born, so it was the Fountain City bus I rode out there. I bought illegal firecrackers out there—a forbidden, rural area, lawless it seemed to me.

Still the Tower seemed to be for high class people, and I felt like an intruder way out there, going to see Moira Shearer dance in *The Red Shoes* with Loris out there because she dreamed of being a ballet dancer, Goddess Vivien Leigh starring in *Anna Karenina*, her husband Laurence Olivier in *Hamlet*, especially Wendy Hiller, whose bare back in that stunning evening dress in *Pygmalion* startled me, a sexual jolt, and Frances Drake starring in *Les Misérables*, a Goddess beauty who enabled me to endure annual showings of that 1935 classic in high school.

Re-releases of movies of the Thirties put me in an ambiguous mood about the ladies who starred in them. If I seldom saw them or had not seen them at all in the movies of the Forties, I might elevate them even higher as Goddesses, the way I did Greta Garbo, or feel reluctant to include them into the sacred pantheon, or even be more responsive to their sexuality, Jean Harlow with Clark Gable in *Red Dust*. Carole Lombard, despite her comic vitality, was among the rarest Goddesses because of her beauty, her marriage to Gable, and her romantic death in a plane crash in the mountains.

The Princess was way on out Broadway almost to Fountain City near Norris Dam, a barn of a place that I sometimes confuse in memory with the skating rink behind. Always bright sunlight when I went out there, climbed three long steps from the sidewalk, where I hoped, the few times I went, to pick up a "briar-jumper," but I was afraid the boys who carried packs of Lucky Strikes rolled up in their short sleeves at the shoulder exposing vaccination scars and who wore their collars turned up would beat my ass. The white painted Princess always seemed to glare in the sun like a mausoleum and through the thin walls I heard the skates rolling and twirling and the merry-go-round music of the rink behind, watching Goddess Rita Hayworth dance in black satin dress and long black gloves in *Gilda*. Closed while I was still an usher at the Bijou.

While I was out there, I'd always visit the ducks swimming around Swan Island in Fountain City Lake, where kids had drowned. Drownings, drownings, drownings—Mammy, Momma, mothers, grandmothers, loved to talk about them, not just to warn, but to *tell*—at Fountain City Lake, the Chilhowee Park Lake, people in creeks, rivers, First Creek that flooded each Spring, the public swimming pools. Maybe I went to the Princess a few times with Bobbie and Rosalie Brummett—whose sexy mother, buck-toothed Rita, large eyes, dark skin, and black hair, I loved when they lived out there on a hill in a huge mansion-like house, a hillside of kudzu vines, and a victory garden, living out there before they moved into one of those box-like houses in Oak Ridge, Atomic City.

Coming back South on Central Avenue now, paralleling Broadway, over Sharps Ridge and three other ridges and down into Happy Holler, the Center, the most dangerous theater in Knoxville. I seldom went in, usually crossing to the opposite side of the street or walking fast, rapidly glancing at the stills. But I saw Jane Russell in Howard Hughes' controversial, banned, finally released *The Outlaw*, having missed it at the Tennessee—I'd run away to India via Asheville that week—and in this milieu of sex, violence, and sin, she scorched my flesh, and never afterward had a chance to become a Goddess. I was eager to see Jane Russell, but having seen Robert Taylor, looking beautiful in black pants and black leather jacket, in Technicolor, at the Riviera, I resented Jack Buetel as the new Billy the Kid going in, but ended up liking him better. I hated the many cheap-assed Billy the Kids, Buster Crabbe and others. But Billy never fascinated me as much as that other juvenile hoodlum Jesse James, and Tyrone Power as Jesse was more magnetic than Robert Taylor as Billy.

Parallel to the Center, West into the scary Lonsdale community, the Lee Theater, near Southern Railways yards. One of the neighborhoods I never lived in was Lonsdale, but a few of my girlfriends did. The hills and valleys in there seemed packed with poor, unwashed, sexy girls. I almost never went there, afraid to look anybody in the eyes, the boys looked wild, long blond hair, and loved to fist fight. Their folks worked in factories, mills, lumber yards, the Southern train shops, or lived up hollows on Sharp's Ridge like country people, dirt front yards, baby or dog turd-studded long, gallery front porches. They roamed in junkyards and rode stripped down bicycles, seats jacked-up high. I did see Gypsy Rose Lee in *Belle of the Yukon* at the Lee, and fantasized about her, walking home along the railroad inflamed, excited by her reputation as a burlesque queen.

I very seldom went to the Dawn in West Knoxville out on Western Avenue on the edge of a Negro district, where the Booker T. Theater for blacks made me wonder what they did in there, in that foreign world of hot, steamy, exotic, sexy, frightening pitch blackness.

Swinging back over to the center of Knoxville, at the intersection of Broadway and Central, across from the Flatiron Building, set the Capitol, converted from a poultry wholesaler's that sold live chickens. A faint odor of ghostly chicken shit in my nostrils, I watched Goddess Merle Oberon and Laurence Olivier, standing in heroic, romantic full body profile in the wind among rocks on the heath in *Wuthering Heights*. That movie sent my romantic spirit soaring. Capitol was owned, I learned a few days ago, by the man who owned the Princess and the Roxy, and who also owned some cheap gas stations. Associated all his theaters in my mind with neighborhood poverty and tough boys and foul-mouthed girls. The Capitol opened when I was living a few blocks away on Bearden, going to Christenberry Junior High in the ninth grade, which I failed because I was writing stories in all my classes.

The neighborhood theaters in East Knoxville, where I lived in the most houses, seemed less hostile. The State on Washington Pike was always to me the place where I saw classy Maureen O'Sullivan in *Tarzan and His Mate* when I was three, and stood, that chilly autumn night with Momma and Daddy and baby Bucky and Earl waiting long for the last streetcar, aware of the gigantic swarm of electric wires behind me, sparked into massive electric generators, and across the streetcar tracks, a condemned public swimming pool was closed, snake infested lily pads, surrounded by a wild entanglement of kudzu vines, showing through a vine crawly fence, and Earl, Bucky, and I, feeling the terror of electricity, the creepiness of the jungle, the scariness of the dark, embarrassed Momma and Daddy with repetitious Tarzan yells, Bucky in Momma's arms, I suppose.

About seven years later, while Momma was in the hospital and Daddy was in the army, Bucky and I went to the State on Saturdays with the other kids from Saint John's Orphanage, a large, white stucco building that set on a hill overlooking Knoxville, the Standard Knitting Mill across the railroad tracks nearby, where Mammy worked when she was 13, at the bottom, and the women coming out of the mill in green uniforms made the women on the screen inside seem sexier, and one Saturday Daddy, on furlough, took us to the State to see Goddess Betty Grable dance and sing in *Footlight Serenade*.

And when I was in high school I discovered that the family of Mark McKay, a radio announcer at WKGN, where I was announcer myself during my junior year, and whom I met at the Garret Players, which met in an attic across from the Bijou and the Lyric behind Mitchell's architect studios, owned the State, wealthy from McKay's nursery. Knowing that added to the romantic image of his handsome dark face and the aura of his rich voice.

On Magnolia, the highway to Chilhowee Amusement Park and to Asheville, and on and on to New York, was the Park Theater, white stucco, one of the cleanest neighborhood theaters, where I went on passes from the Bijou, a sister theater in the same chain. Some of the girls who called me up but whom I seldom saw or saw at all were often in the Park. I seldom went to it—not my neighborhood. I was always getting into a fight over there. Boys coming back to Lincoln Park where I was living from over there at Park City often told of big fights, and we planned massive invasions.

Later, I moved to McCalla Street near the tobacco warehouses in Harry's new neighborhood—I'd always associated him with Happy Holler and the Central Theater and Baxter Street where Loraine, Joy, and Peggy lived for a while after Loraine and I broke up. I went to Knox High the year after the operation on both my feet to correct the tendency toward clawfoot deformity. So I didn't go to the Park Theater until I moved out on McCalla, where another streetcar line used to parallel the one over on Magnolia, but streetcars had ended by then and were parked way out on Maryville Pike in a field, rotting, and I carried my last paper route there and the Park was one of my customers. Carrying papers seemed for me—but oddly not for Harry, who loved to play suave—a come down after being an usher and a filling station attendant and a portrait studio coupon salesman.

I'm plotting on a map of Knoxville I got from the Chamber of Commerce, using a red Hi-Liter, the five paper routes I once carried. As the red lines form spokes reaching out over Knoxville in every direction, awe and satisfaction grow in me. The movies advertised in the papers, fresh off the press—exciting to see *what next*. The thick Sunday papers were hell to lug up Sharps Ridge, which I had to climb up and down about eight times from different angles, but the sweet dewy moment was flipping fast to the Sunday Magazine Section to look upon the photographs of movies to come, and the ads with the names of all the theaters. I knew long before Hollywood press agents did that "a movie is first run until you've seen it."

If I didn't get off the number one streetcar at the Park Theater, half-way to Chilhowee Park, but rode on up into Burlington where Mammy was born and raised—"Daddy owned half of Burlington," only a few cornfields in her childhood, "and sold it for nothing"—I could ride the turn-around around a cafe and go back on McCalla toward the heart of Knoxville past the Gay Theater, always foreign and mysterious to me, and its piney varnished paneling front and hovering cedar trees made me feel that the people who went to the show they were better than I was, like an exclusive little club in a solidly respectable neighborhood—nowadays a slum—with the golden lighted, well-kept little stony house library next door.

Realizing that there were that many theaters in Knoxville, so many of them neighborhood theaters, is overwhelming. Have the neighborhoods passed, I wonder, along with the theaters? And now only the Park Theater remains in a neighborhood. Uptown only the Tennessee and the Rialto, and the Bijou, which has survived only because it showed skin flicks exclusively since 1958, ten years, until I rode back to the rescue.

A question I don't dare ask myself is, "Lucius, are you obsessed? In some dangerous way? Perhaps?" Marta refuses to send me anymore artifacts, worried that I may be borderline psychotic.

In the opposite direction from the Gay, West, out across the Tennessee River over Gay Street bridge to South Knoxville, way out Chapman Highway that takes you into the Great Smoky Mountains, outside the city limits, was the Horne, which, like the Tillery out Clinton Highway north, was too far to frequent.

Among the wild ridges of South Knoxville, there were, briefly, only two theaters. Besides the Horne, the Lake, built on the spot where Daddy's sister Matilda once owned a house, where Bucky and I lived a few days when Momma had to go into the hospital and Daddy was in the army, while Momma shipped Earl out to Santa Fe, New Mexico to Uncle Hop's. Trains, shaking the screen, went right past the ticket booth, where for a while in the Lake's two-year history, Momma sat, selling tickets. Betty Field starred in Steinbeck's *Of Mice and Men* there. And I met this one very nice girl in the Lake Theater. Cathleen Ford, lovely, sensitive, honey blond but I was too in love with Loris. Even so, now I hope I will see Cathleen on Gay Street one twilight.

Daddy was born and raised in South Knoxville on the highest ridge crest in all Knoxville. On the bank of the Tennessee, just to the east of Gay Street Bridge sprawled a lumberyard and the Smokey Mountain Slaughter House and the bakery where all his family and later he, and for a while, Momma, worked.

Beyond UT campus, anchoring the strip of eating places and shops, was the Blackburn, neat, clean, compact, cozy, but in a high class neighborhood—a little prince of a theater, whose gentle-mannered manager resembled Leslie Howard as Ashley Wilkes in *Gone with the Wind*. In a little shopping area, at the bottom of the steep hill below Fort Sanders Hospital where gruff Doctor Summers Fitzgerald operated on my feet. I felt a desire to go in there every time I passed it, and I went a few times, I suppose, but felt as though you have to meet certain mysterious qualifications to deserve to feel you belonged there, watching Susan Peters in *Song of Russia*. Susan was one of those goddesses whose sad personal life intensified my response—seriously injured in a shooting accident, she later acted from a wheelchair.

I watched Frances Farmer in *Son of Fury*, re-released at the Blackburn, and ever since I saw a picture of police dragging her away, her panties showing, when she resisted arrest, I have a love-lust for her, and I followed her wild personal life eagerly and hunted down all her movies. She was a member of the Group Theater and married Clifford Odets, one of my favorite playwrights. Her mother had her committed for a while. She told her strange story in *Will There Really Be a Morning?*

Seeing movies advertised at the Blackburn that I'd watched in the Broadway, I felt slightly jealous. I did go there regularly in high school when they started showing a series of foreign or English movies. Celia Johnson having her *Brief Encounter* with Trevor Howard at a train station in a small town in England. Then when I went to UT and lived on Clinch and on Laurel, I went often, hoping to pick up girls. I never did.

Waiting for Marta to arrive from Bismarck, South Dakota, in Knoxville in her drugstore boss's Cadillac, to marry me with her mother and her boss's wife, coming through racial strife-torn Clinton, I sat in the Blackburn watching Jerry Lewis and Dean Martin in a re-run of *At War with the Army*. And a few weeks later, we saw a Greek movie there—title lost to memory—and she said she didn't understand why all those villagers were treating the man with the black mustache and black shirt so brutally. "He's a goddamn collaborator!" "What's that?" I tried, out of my encyclopedic movie memory—she's four years younger than I am—to explain, but when she didn't get it, I responded viciously, "Fuck you!" An isolated incident, as was the time she was wrestling with a set of box Springs inside a U-Haul trailer and pushed it over on me in exasperation with my irritable instructions on how to unload it.

Cumberland becomes Kingston Pike at Tyson Park, and on out, through the vast neighborhood where the rich—my beloved Savage family—are different from us, is the Pike, the twin of North Knoxville's Tower, owned by the same man, built to the same plan, outside the city limits—that seemed strange, and I had to ride the Kingston Pike bus past the Blackburn way out there to see foreign movies. Both were white cinder block, with towers, both outside the city limits, both across from cemeteries, where some of my kin were scattered—and going out there to see foreign movies made me feel intellectual. I made the trips often in high school, my own private distinction, one of the things that set me off, I felt, made me also somehow part of the literary aura. I loved to wander before and after the movie in the hilly cemetery and wrote a poem about it.

Both the Tower and the Pike, at extreme North and West Knoxville, were far off, romantic places for Loris and me. *Bitter Rice* starring Sylvana Mangano—a milestone in my movie history. Speaking Italian, the language of the recent enemy, Sylvana Mangano scalded my whole body, so she had no chance to become a Goddess, and when she raised her arms, revealing whorls of black armpit hair, as she began a torrid dance, I thought good old sex and sin, sin, sin, had come the screen.

So at the time of the Bijou, we lived in North Knoxville, with Mammy's past in East Knoxville, Momma's past in Cleveland, Ohio where she'd spend her girlhood when Grandpa went up there to work in a glass factory. Before I went to work at 13 at the Bijou, I'd already lived in about ten neighborhoods, and in Mammy's house near Christenberry Junior High and Cedar Street—the period richest now in memory.

Although Negroes could attend the Bijou, which had two balconies, the only one in town that did, I never went inside the Negro theaters. The Gem—I always thought of gym—on Vine, in the hot heart of the Negro district uptown, a long block down from Gay, and the Booker T out on Western Avenue in West Knoxville near Knox College, for blacks only, where I saw foreign and classic movies with tall, lithe, intellectual Verna when I was a freshman at UT and saw W. C. Fields and Mae West in *My Little Chickadee* and Jean Cocteau's *Orphee*, but Knox College wasn't a genuine movie theater.

So, except for the Knoxville Theater, that was planned to go up where the Lyric was torn down but never did, those are the theaters of my Knoxville, a town as exotic and bizarre for me as Venice. Aware of all those theaters, an ambience, I stood On the Spot in the Bijou in 1946, the year I turned 13.

Seemed strange that some actors were from Knoxville. Patricia Neal, born up a holler in Packard, Kentucky, but grew up in Knoxville and graduated from Knox High ten years before I did, I was eager to claim as our own, especially when at nineteen she came out as Dominique in *The Fountainhead* and plunged into a torrid affair with Gary Cooper, and going into the Tennessee when I was in high school, I saw her posing for a *Knoxville News-Sentinel* photo under the marquee with the manager, and I got her autograph and promised to write a play for her to star in someday. After a series of strokes, she's come back valiantly from the dead, she speaks with a slur but moves with hobbling magnificence. I visualized her as ideal for the part of the mother in a novel and play I worked on for fifteen years, set up a holler near Harlan, Kentucky.

THE BIJOU TIME ROLLS on from reel to reel, tape number three. Need bigger reels, I reckon.

Foaming atomic mushrooms on Bikini Atoll glared in my eyes as I stood On the Spot that summer, the brassy smell of the flashlight in my hand, imagining that I, my blond hair in a pompadour, was Alan Ladd in *The Blue Dahlia.* The summer before the Bijou, a few weeks after my twelfth birthday, I had awakened Negroes in the Vine Street ghetto, hawking the extra. "Truman Drops Adam Bomb!" The nostalgic fallout from that blast descends forever in the gentle rain of memory.

Three of the houses of my childhood burned that summer. As I delivered Tooley Myron Studio Portrait coupons after I was fired from the Bijou, I passed in happenstance all the twenty or so houses I'd lived in—years later, I'd seek them, as I have been over the past months, deliberately—discovering another empty lot with each pilgrimage, and sometimes new buildings, warehouses, filling stations, university buildings, where my old homes had stood. When I delivered those Tooley Myron Portrait Studio coupons to houses on my old paper routes, my chest ached even then with nostalgia.

But during the Bijou time, not one of the houses was gone, and I felt that like Mammy's house, where I was born, by god, they'd always be there. Walking through the tile factory, having come from portrait coupon deliveries in northeast Knoxville, I felt that I was going through a graveyard, the huge round tiles like monuments to the years of my childhood. Nothing had changed physically yet, but I sensed that the apprehension then would someday become manifested in my outer environment, even as I dreamed of wandering away from Knoxville into the world beyond the Smoky Mountains and Sharp's Ridge. I came to think later that the news I delivered daily in those neighborhoods—if only my customers and I had been able to read between the headlines—was that Vesuvius lava was flowing over Knoxville. The portraits they sat for in the Tooley Myron studios, as well as the ones they refused to pay for, were all like the volcanically petrified bodies kissing, found in the ruins at Pompeii, or that petrified man either in mid-collapse or trying to rise.

Now, looking out upon the denuded ridges of East Knoxville from under the Bijou marquee, I see the massive civic center, surrounded by a desert of red clay that is strangled in kudzu vines, right down to the banks of the Tennessee. The Vine Street district is more leveled than Pompeii, but seeded with new grass, green as the excelsior stuff in Easter baskets.

I go back to Knoxville sometimes over the years, went back last summer, took Marta and Shelley. Vacation. To visit my family and the Savages. Then, almost immediately, returned for the funeral of my favorite uncle—my only active uncle—Luke, who first took me to the Bijou, to see Errol Flynn in *The Dawn Patrol*, a WWI air combat film. And in the streets I look into the faces of the women for intimations of Kathrine Hepburn, Myrna Loy, Hedy Lamarr, Veronica Lake, Joan Fontaine, Greta Garbo, Jean Harlow, Marlene Dietrich, Loretta Young. Some of the Goddesses are dead, some of the girls I touched, too, gone with the theaters, in the same sweeping wind, caught in the lava with my neighborhoods and my houses.

My alma mater, UT, has brought Pompeii to Cornell Street, where I sat on the steep back steps, loaded with presents on my second birthday. Accidental fire has brought Pompeii to the houses on Dempster and Copeland, the trucking company behind our house on McCalla reached out with a lava embrace, a laundry across the street brought Pompeii to the house on Bearden. A filling station brought Pompeii to Central Avenue, a freeway brought Pompeii to Eleanor Street, urban renewal brought Pompeii to the house where I lived on Hill Street, where from my back porch I looked down on the river and the old water tower that I turned into my sanctuary. The Vesuvius blight has hit most of the 20 houses through which my childhood moved like a gypsy, and all but five or six of the 23 theaters where images flashed on the screen and burned shadows upon the asphalt of my brain.

I'm writing a chronology on one of the old dressing room doors. Where I was born, *where* I lived, *when*, girls I loved up close or at a distance, or only screwed, and so on, and on and on.

Anguish at being unable to recall people named, or the real-life model for a fictional character in stories I wrote back then—or to recall a movie I say is great in my early diaries. Looking over the ledger—like the ones Thomas Wolfe wrote in—that I bought in '47, I wonder what year I started it. None of the diaries give the actual year. You son of a bitch, why didn't you keep account of things when you ushered at the Bijou? Stendhal used to ask such questions right on the page as he wrote his autobiography. Never expected back then to give a hot damn in later years about details, accuracy, I reckon.

This anguished feeling of loss evokes the old romantic question. Who am I? What does it all mean? Why are we here? I asked such questions back then, but I look now in 1968 at the moments that generate that feeling, unrelated to the causes that I fight for—for civil rights and academic freedom, and against capital punishment, censorship, sexism, religious bigotry, and the Vietnam War. Who cares? Does anyone beyond me care? Why should they? But don't human beings share this dilemma as surely as we share concern over issues? What is in danger, but oneself and selves like one's own? What is that self but the moments that make it up, moments from the past, as we step furtively over the dark ground of the present toward precipices in the future? The past is what we have, or know we have known, but we know what it is we have not, while the present is a passing over, and the future is a projection—coming attractions. A loving recreation of the past, a splicing of images, a montage of feelings and mostly images, because memory is odorless, tasteless, and touchless. Memory is movies, home-movies, but, for me, mingled with the Hollywood vision of human action.

Seeing movies so many times as an usher, in fragments, though I often saw the whole movie first at the Tennessee or the Riviera, is like the way I see many scenes now and high moments from my life at that time. I see often the old farmer in the ratty hotel room that I shared for fifty cents in Asheville get up to pee often, and *sometimes* tell about it.

Hollywood doesn't dream our dreams for us, it imitates them, and reactivates, stimulates them. What images develop in the chemical wash of millions of girls' brains in sleep, girls sleeping with four sisters and a little brother in Bombay, and a single government typist in Washington in her utility apartment—never showed up then on the Bijou screens of the world. But do now. Movies incite, ignite.

The first movies I saw maintained benign domination over the ones that came later.

And the first girls. A roll call. "My name is Gloria Fletcher." Yes, and one day you were suddenly there in the aisle seat on the back row across from where I stood "On the Spot." After you said, "You have the loveliest blue eyes!" I don't remember another word you said. Though you called me up too often, and talked from your hot house over on Sutherland Avenue in West Knoxville—a mean neighborhood by what I'd heard all my life, and mean to pass through. I never sat with you in the Bijou, never took you out, but you liked to gaze at me from the back row, and listen to my sexy talk on the phone. I think I saw you at Knox High about three years later in the halls and you seemed only faintly aware of me, and I am sometimes startled to rediscover you in a group picture in the *Trojan* yearbook. You're not nearly as important to me as Lucy in Colon, Panama who told me I looked Swedish in my new green wool, turtle-necked sweater and leather jacket and that my blue eyes attracted her. I made love to Lucy, I touched her breasts, she who didn't like men to touch her breasts, until she met me, but untouched Gloria came first, and made me imagine the power of eyes in other ways.

Movies ravish you when you're a virgin. They're not the legitimate experience, they're the I'll-show-you-mine-if-you'll-show-me-yours phase of life, not the legal, serious marriage phase.

Swift's excremental vision in *Gulliver's Travels*? What about Hutchfield's masturbative vision? Narcissus jacking off in the Bijou throughout eternity.

The *auteur* critics seem strident to me, making a mystique out of what was to me a grand commonplace. In the previews, I knew the Capra, the Houston, the Hawks, the Ford, the Lang movies instantly. I knew from the way the Max Steiner music swelled in the previews of *The Big Sleep* that the studio was Warner Brothers. From the lighting in only a few frames, I know whether the studio is Paramount or MGM, and more quickly whether it is RKO or Universal. I didn't know what makes the difference, but I recognized it immediately, back then, even back then.

Not books but movies showed me my life as I was feeling it, searching for it, trying to define, grasp, embrace, extend, create it at that time when I was thirteen. *The Razor's Edge* hit me harder, with less warning, than any other, thrust me, along with real-life contingent happenings, into action. Although no movie exerted a more subtle, long-lasting influence, from age six, upon almost all aspects of my romantic temperament than *Gone with the Wind*, because it put into play the two basic female types and the two basic male types, the two sides, that is, of myself, and I saw that they complemented each other, Ashley and Rhett, somewhat the way Shelley and Byron did. By 1946, Cornell Wilde and Alan Ladd had deposed Roy Rogers, the King of the Cowboys. Cornel Wilde faded long before Alan Ladd, who was reborn in *Shane*. I just learned a few days ago that Ladd played the Green Hornet in the chapter play. But no Alan Ladd movie shaped my long-enduring moods and my very destiny the way the two Cornel Wilde movies did—*A Song to Remember*, about Chopin and George Sand, and *Leave Her to Heaven* that revealed the look of Maine to me, so that Maine became a romantic ideal landscape.

The movie that inflamed my intellect, as *The Razor's Edge* aroused my spirit, was *The Fountainhead*—Gary Cooper as the individualistic architect. His defiant speech at the end set my arrogant artistic life-style for a long time, enabling me to stride with supreme self-confidence through the army as a suspected communist, investigated for refusing to sign the loyalty oath Senator Joseph McCarthy forced upon the army. Here's some of the speech from the novel, from memory. "I came here to say that I do not recognize anyone's right to one minute of my life. Nor to any part of my energy. Nor to any achievement of mine. No matter who makes the claim, how large their number or how great their need. . . . I recognize no obligations toward men except one, to respect their freedom and to take no part in a slave society."

Conjuring up the past is no occasion to be condescending to childhood or adolescence. It's ludicrous the way we try to dismiss what we were before about 18, some people before about 25—"we"—I don't mean to put a chummy arm around all the ex-adolescents of the western world, because I guess my life was extraordinary by the very fact that I was so keenly aware of what I was going through, at that age, during that time, knew it then, that the others around me of my age would abjure, were, in depressing fact, at every moment, abjuring "life" by the very style or lack of style with which they were superficially living life. Everything they seemed to do, think, feel had the look of mutability, something barely sufficient for the day, but hardly sustenance for the future, hardly what even a nomad would choose to drag along "over the desert of life," as I would have put it then. So I guess people who smile condescendingly or even sneer at the discarded self of their adolescence, mean it, but how ludicrous to pretend—no, to *believe,* in many cases—that what they are doing now is the serious endeavor of life, while what they felt then was trivial, perishable, transient. The impressionable age. You damned right. "Be one of those on whom nothing is lost." You double damned right. And when you're thirteen you *are.* Most people don't *lose* what they experience, they discard, bail it out, strip it down, cut it loose. I knew even then how life was supposed to go, and I didn't let it. I knew, or sensed at least, when I was six or seven lying in bed at night on Cedar Street, recapturing my life like a Zorro chapter play, and talking with God, that that was not the way life was supposed to go, was not the way life was going for my brothers, and the kids I played, fought, stole with, and fucked.

Marked off. With my own chalk. The sense of isolation, saddening at times, but avowedly my own doing, and so, at times, exhilarating. Not a withdrawal of the body and its modes of action, but part of the mind and feeling; so that I stole cussed, fucked, fought, took risks along with the rest of them, or ahead of the rest. Shelley, the arrogant schoolboy in Andre Maurois' *Ariel,* was an exaggeration of only a part of me. Not till years later did I realize the full con- sequences of reading that dangerous book about Shelley and Byron and their women. By contrast, the so-called filthy novels adults warned us about had no effect on me whatsoever, beyond a temporary hard-on—Erskine Caldwell, later Henry Miller.

And Byron—"I moved among them, but was not of them"—and Poe were an exaggeration of another part of me.

> From childhood's hour I have not been
> As others were—I have not seen
> As others saw—I could not bring
> My passions from a common Spring.
> From the same source I have not taken
> my sorrow, I could not awaken
> My heart to joy at the same tone,
> And all I loved, *I* loved alone.
> *Then*—in my childhood—in the dawn
> Of a most stormy life was a drawn

From every depth of good and ill
The mystery which binds me still,
from a cloud that took the form. . . .
Of a demon in my view.

And, in the flesh, Riva Tamargo, who, in her Gothic, white mansion in South Carolina, learned and recited all of Shelley, Keats, and Swinburne by heart. The only person I've ever known and loved who actually went long before I did to all the places I imagined going to myself. I was the one who urged her to leave her home, roam the world. Until she met me, she was content to roam like a gypsy within her boundless imagination. Having seen the world, some of it with Allen Ginsberg and Gregory Corso, and Gayle Savage, she settled in India at the age of twenty-four and has lived there ever since, in the mountains, only God knows the exact location. The year she left the mansion, she stopped writing and, like Rimbaud, started living poetry. She is the only really genuine bohemian I ever knew.

So don't sneer, goddamn it, at *The Razor's Edge*, Lucius Hutchfield, until you examine the most recent thing that influenced you. Values. Discriminating sensibility. Contexts and perspectives function within other contexts and perspectives, and the restless, insatiable mind strives to get everything in focus.

Influences can't be measured by intellectually assigned values. My life is not my own. Made in Hollywood, altered later in film studios in Paris, Rome, London, Stockholm, and Tokyo, but mainly, first, and forever, in Hollywood. John Ford, Preston Sturges, Howard Hawks, Mervyn LeRoy—who I have met—Raoul Walsh, Otto Preminger, Alfred Hitchcock, Frank Capra, whose movies taught me basic humanistic values. I am their bastard, I off-spring from reels they set turning. Reaching for the stars, I am the understudy who usurps the stars. Tyrone Power played Larry Darrel in *The Razor's Edge* with much less passion, much less flair, much less soulfulness, and with less vivid memory of the experience, than I did in the fetid halls of Christenberry Junior High, or that time in the cold streets of Asheville. And yet Tyrone himself, the Tyrone of all the roles—Jesse James, the young man, nameless to memory, in *This Above All*—is as real as Gale, the usher I most admired, and Vivien Leigh—though I saw her so seldom—was as real as Loraine, though not perhaps as real as Loris and Marta because by then Vivien Leigh's star had dimmed, or so I felt then.

When I ran away that time from Cedar Street out the highway to Oak Ridge, Clark Gable sat on one shoulder, Vivien Leigh on the other.

Frankenstein, that one-dimensional colossal figure. One-dimensional? He had, for me alone, many dimensions. Scared the piss out of me in the Riviera, in the Strand perhaps, maybe the Tennessee, but came a time in the Broadway Theater when, inspired I think by that scene when he gave the little girl that single flower, in which he was kind, I took him as my friendly bodyguard as I walked home to Cedar Street or to Mammy's through that long stretch of dark, from shining telephone pole to shining pole, and he warded off the Wolf-man, nameless, faceless monsters and killers, and his own former selves.

So don't talk to me, Lucius, about cheap, one-dimensional Hollywood products, concoctions. Kane me no *Citizen Kanes,* blow me no *Blowups, Hiroshima* me no *Mon Amours,* though I bet my love for them can beat up anybody's love. But how to cancel out emotionally what the intellect rejects? A blank screen, like a narrow mind. The projector's always running. Fuck metaphors. *That's* no metaphor, that's my life. *That's* what's happening, man. Gone with the wind—and back again without warning, without reason, without purpose. Like the scar in the crease between pubis and leg at the joint—from the boil I had, walking Loraine, against her will, and Marion, at her own urging, home after Lincoln Park Elementary let out. Always a reminder. Like *that* scar and the one under my eye from running into a clothes line in the army, on my cheek from a blackberry vine. Like the black spot in the palm of my right hand from reaching up to catch a pen on the fly in English class at Christenberry, and the same accident, the exact same spot in Alaska when I was working as a clerk in rations breakdown, although that one didn't leave the mark. The first wound a blue mark in the center of the right hand, where two lifelines meet. And thus, without knowing it, I, in the first half of the eighth grade, first encountered Christ symbolism. But when I became aware of the symbolism, I couldn't bring myself to make anything of stigmata in a story. What does all that have to do with now, with race riots and Vietnam? Assassinations—President Kennedy, his brother, Robert, Martin Luther King. Nothing. Probably.

But the mind is a swamp of trivialities that the undiscriminating mind exalts, the mind ranks death with the lady in a large black hat, glimpsed as I passed a classroom in a Christenberry hallway in a dream. All my life, I've loved that woman in the hat, expected to meet her on the street, for I felt that she was—no one I had known before, someone hovering in my future. No priority. Death. Grandpa Charlie's death. And the woman in the hat. Memory blends, favors now what it slights next. Maybe a life of significance is a war against memory's natural relativity. On the movie screen of memory the absurd view of life is taken for "granite." Remembrance of things past? Who can avoid it? Researches into things past? Few can survive it. If memory is mad, can a man submit to its processes without losing his mind?

When events are happening, what do you see that can be remembered later? *Then,* I was aware of the world opening up, I felt the mystery of life all the time. Even in boredom, in the banal, the routine, the stultifying, I sensed the outer context of mystery and romance and darkness, and fear of the future and a reaching, a longing to go out into it, so that Eugene Gant's feeling in Wolfe's *Look Homeward, Angel* of being prison pent in the bowl of mountains immediately struck me as *my* need.

But what do we really see? If that time, 1946 and '47 was so important to me, "precious" is a word I can't avoid, why can't I remember exactly every detail, what people wore, what off-duty jacket Wade Baliss, the big cop, was wearing that night he shoved the people out of the main aisle when they wouldn't mind *me*? Well, did I notice details *then*? Dark, yes, and only the screen illuminated him, and I often recall that scene, but why not the details? Fabric. I liked him after that, and always liked to see pictures of his lovely daughter in the newspapers years later. But after the Double Cola man shot his wife—Wade's mistress—in the balcony, Wade never came to the Bijou again. He stayed on the force another twenty years, and now he runs, they tell me, a motel in Saint Augustine, Florida. I like imagining the dead projectionist living in that motel. But why so few details about this total human being?

I know these simple-assed questions, but they're haunting, as is the process of memory itself. A gestalt, I guess, we experience a gestalt, and the details pass by because the gestalt can't be broken down into its perceived parts. The whole Bijou experience is one luminous gestalt, charged image, just as all the movies I saw ten times through, though in fragments, seem one single solitary movie, without a name, without stars, without a story, just the imaginative presence of moodiness on the screen.

Without pause, the projector whirrs, throwing on the screen whatever the projectionist has pieced together by chance. I come in, now and then, out of bright sunlight or darkness and sit, fidgeting, watching, sometimes enthralled, sometimes bored, distracted, then wander out, wander in and out, and sometimes for long times, just pass by, the sound of the background music, the voices, superhumanly amplified, as in a time-chamber, coming to us as I pass in the street, alluring echoes, frightening overtones, disturbing discords. Trite metaphor? Fuck metaphor. That's what's so maddening. The projector has a will of its own, and as the conscious will propels, a banana peeling intercepts.

Tell the tape-recorder what you learned today, Lucius, about the Bijou and its opposite pole, my old neighborhood theater the Broadway. OK, when the national corporation shut down the Bijou in 1960, the year Shelley was born, the skin-flick hucksters opening it up needed equipment because the owners had jerked out the projectors, stripped all the accouterments, still stands, everything. So these New Jersey guys heard the Broadway was shutting down, to be converted into a bowling alley, so they trucked the projectors across town for me, and that's what's installed up there now, the Broadway's projectors in the Bijou's projection booth. And get this. Heard tales that the guy who used to be projectionist at the Roxy bought all the Crystal's equipment when it shut down in Market Square and he whiles away his senility showing movies in his master bedroom. *And* I ain't finished. A sergeant from the police force bought the Roxy hardware when it closed up, and he's even more obsessed than the Roxy projectionist is. Top that. Or am I?

How say things are "strange"? In relation to what? What were the norms then in relation to which things are strange now? Because the feeling then was that *everything* was strange? Norms were shifting constantly even back then. To usher at the Bijou was strange because the norm for me was that the Bijou was the place where I saw *The Dawn Patrol* in 1938 with Uncle Luke and *The Man in the Iron Mask* in 1940 with Earl, who resembled the actor in the iron mask. Imagining being locked into that iron mask terrified me. That was the Bijou, the place before I was ushering. And now, what is the norm?

Appearances, surfaces, that's all it all *ever* was, the real and what flashed on the screen, meshed. Am I submerging to *understand* or simply to see once again what my eyes reflected? Even then, *always* then, *especially* then, I wanted to know "the meaning of it all." What didn't Loraine understand? What did I try to tell her that made her giggle, turn her head, smile and roll her eyes? About God. About Byronic roaming. About the romance of poverty. Love of

Man. Evil. Greatness. Fame. In the wind that night, after I persuaded her to go with me to see *The Razor's Edge*—which I had seen first by myself—she would then definitely see, understand, I was certain. The huge oaks blowing, I told her about all my feelings about the mysteries of life in a great rush, my voice like Ashley Wilkes, and even before I knew much about Byron or Shelley, even before their poetry had sunk in, despite the repulsive mouthings of teachers, I *was* Shelley, I *was* Byron. "I moved among them, but I was not of them." And, less consciously, I know now, I was Poe.

I wonder where I first got certain notions, attitudes, and inclinations. *A Song to Remember, Leave Her to Heaven, The Razor's Edge*, I've figured out now, weren't total discoveries. They were incidental, accidental culminations. The inclinations, stimulated in massive and minute ways all along since waking consciousness, were there, and those movies were like suddenly passing a mirror, unexpectedly seeing what our old costume looks like full-view. Even so, *A Song to Remember* did have a tremendous influence on my romantic vision. Revolutionary, bizarre romance, audacity, expressions of will, talent, the brooding genius, sudden bursts of creation. In the summer of the bomb, two major events occurred in my life. I laid eyes on Cornel Wilde and on Maine in *Leave Her To Heaven*. Exactly where? Exactly when? Why do I crave facts? They ignite my imagination.

Maybe they made me ready for Byron and Shelley when I discovered them—when, where, how? *Ariel*, Maurois's biography of Shelley that I am holding in my hand, came in the eighth grade at Christenberry Junior High or early Knox High. I must look in the library copy there to see if I can find my name. Stendhal says in the first draft of his memoir of his youth that he did that kind of compulsive search. George Sand was the prototype of the soul-mate figure who loomed over my life thereafter. Maybe dimly, she stood in the wings long before. But Loris Blackburn would be, I expected, more like Beethoven's or Joyce's wife, firmly docile domestic supporter. I read A. B. C. Whipple's *The Fatal Gift of Beauty* last night, until 3 am, the whole thing, about Shelley's and Byron's days in Italy. No wonder I responded to them. I was predisposed. The vision of beauty in ugliness, of the ethereal, of sexual bountifulness, of nature, of self-inflicted suffering. I never cast myself as a victim, but rather as one who willfully caused things to happen to him, though I felt that to suffer was in the nature of the artistic life. And Tyrone Power on Caedmon records reading

"Childe Harold" revives those old feelings. Mountaintop aspirations. Byron's swimming the perilous Hellespont and the rutty canals of Venice after sheer lovemaking.

Cleared by the Army's Counter Intelligence Corps of being a security risk after I refused to sign a second loyalty oath in the McCarthy hearings days, I was transferred, punitively, to Fort Richardson in Anchorage, Alaska, where I aspired to climb mountains, and did. Not the equipment sort of thing, prior training, with guides, but foolhardy, reckless, heedless, appalling climbs. The mountain I viewed from the roof of Rations Breakdown where I was a supply clerk, and named Mount Verna after a girl I thought I was in love with.

And I met Adriano, a young Italian artist who had been drafted right after he arrived in the USA from Rome, and he had just been released from the stockade, having finished the term of a prisoner he was detailed to guard and who escaped because Adriano refused to shoot him in the back, and we hiked down the remote Kenai Peninsula, and I climbed a marathon mountain above Seward, the side behind where marathon races are run each year, the side that some old fisherman told me no climber in his right mind—what *is* the right mind for a mountain climber?—would attempt.

Do we, did I then, wonder, ask, agonize over what appearances mean, because there *is* meaning—we're taught there *should* be meaning—or because the look, the feel, the smell, the taste of experience is so overwhelming, we can't take in everything, and anguish sets in, and we must give this shadow of experience, this overtone, this sense of loss some stature, dignity, must elevate it, so we dedicate "our better selves" to discovering the meaning? Have experiences, after all, no meaning beyond themselves, their surfaces, like a melody, a flower, a mountain landscape that we thrill to, then we pass on to another and another experience, and what makes us want to make sense of what the senses have experienced? There is something lethal about the show of things, the surface, something like death that the intent intellect or significant emotions must resurrect and embody somehow. Stendhal caught himself writing his memoir in this vein and asked whether it was worthwhile, whether anyone would read it, if not now maybe thirty years later. Is what I am doing like the self-absorptions of Oscar Wilde, Swinburne, Pater, Octave Mirbeau, Lautreamont, Rimbaud, Huysmans, Mallarme, Baudelaire and other decadents? Perhaps. But did they really agonize over it, suffer guilt, doubt?

Nostalgia is saddening because images of a past that has died remind us that the dreamer who experienced them and now dreams them must sadly die. A terrible nostalgia, "a beautiful greed" for experience, and my compulsion to tell a story result in "the persistence of vision," these after-images.

How many times have I watched Rhett Butler carry Scarlett O'Hara up the wide, red-carpeted staircase, or heard Scarlett say, after Melanie's death at the end of the epic sweep of four hours—multiplied by the days of my life, "But, Rhett, where will I go, what will I do?" "Frankly, my dear, I don't give a damn." And at intermission, lines I can't repeat even now without the same aching lump in my throat. Scarlett on the horizon, the blaze of sundown at her back, dress torn, her cheeks dirt-smeared, raising her fists, clutching a just-dug-up radish and its root, "If I have to lie, cheat, steal or kill, as God is my witness, I swear that I will never go hungry again." It's not *what* you say, Scarlett, but when, where, and what happens to what you say. Like that time in that dark holler, after breaking up with Loraine, "I swear that I, Lucius Hutchfield, will make my mark on the world!"

In 1967, I was amused to learn, the Japanese transformed *Gone with the Wind* into a musical that took two nights to perform, just as I had planned to do in Christenberry Junior High study hall.

I'm here talking a blue streak into this winding tape spool but I know I'm not out of my mind. Wife, son, mother, friend, even doctors will testify to that. But I know what they don't know. That I sit here in benevolent quicksand that at any moment may gobble me up, as in Tarzan jungle movies. Outside that door, *The Razor's Edge* is always showing, and the hero Larry Darrell will show up on the screen. They held it over here at the Bijou after I'd seen it the second time at the Tennessee with Loraine just before I ran away to India—studio rain in his face. I know now it's studio rain, but in 1947 I felt it on my own face, real enough to send me to Asheville, bound for India, and four years later to sail actually as a seaman in the Merchant Marine.

Ironic, then, that I don't think I ever got past, until day before yesterday, the opening pages of *The Razor's Edge*. The first sentences were intriguing. "I have never begun a novel with more misgiving. If I call it a novel it is only because I don't know what else to call it. I have little story to tell and I end neither with a death nor a marriage." But then W. Somerset Maugham takes us into Elliott Templeton's arid aristocratic life, no way to dwellingly begin a novel after the movie has so neatly glided over him. But I always had definite intentions of reading it, of course. I've not seen the movie again since—until now, as I imagine it on the screen. I didn't imagine then that I would commit against the novel *The Razor's Edge* the blasphemy of neglect for several years, then of contempt for its popularity almost twenty, until I finally read it, with unflagging interest, fascinated by it not only as a reflector of my own early attitudes but also for its solid craftsmanship. I wouldn't know until then, looking up Herbert Marshall as Maugham in both movies in a movie encyclopedia, that the movie and the book *Moon and Sixpence* used the same strategy of incorporating the author into his own fiction. I never read any of Maugham's other novels either. Knew only "Rain." Although having seen two versions of the movie, the Leslie Howard version made the year after I was born, I always intended to read *Of Human Bondage,* for I almost became, like the autobiographical hero, a cripple. Three surgical cuts to transplant bones in each foot.

Life is perishable in ways the movies are. The impressions, the styles, the look of things, the way of talking and dreaming, projected by the movies and anticipated in one's own life for the romantic future, were like Venice, that theatrical city, that Cecil B. DeMille set, that while she looks eternal over the centuries is slowly sinking into mud, corroding in the saline air, and now in the fumes of pollution. Venice, like Mister Lilly's Pond on Cedar Street, is sinking. Just learned a few weeks ago that the houseboat—scary and mysterious to me as a little boy—on Mr. Tilly's pond had come off the Tennessee River where he grew up. He'd gone to sea, married in New Orleans, returned to find his parents dead, the houseboat sunk, and he'd dredged it up out of the river and hauled it to the half block of land he'd just bought surrounding the new house he had built with his own hands for his bride.

A sense of the war intensified all my responses then, as a sense of the hovering bomb and nuclear winter seems only to dull my responses now. . . . It's running out, the film in my head's running out. Stop now. Blank screen. Film broke.

HERE STARTS A NEW TAPE.

Maybe I'll go back to teaching. Maybe I'll go on to Hollywood. Maybe I won't leave the Bijou. Maybe I'll so immerse myself in the 1940s, pick at sticky loose threads until I become entangled, immolated. Mixed metaphor—that's what memory does. Memory is a stagnant swamp or reservoir of raw material images, film clips. Stirring up the muddy bottom with a stick, a prick? Sex and religion, sex and memory?

Not until I plunged into this struggle to recapture did I realize the sadness of not being able to see Betty Dameron's face. I faintly recall her breath, and now, just now, this instant, the feel of *her* mouth, of *our* mouths, you don't just feel her mouth, but when you kiss like that, *our* mouths. In the fragments of diaries, the name so often recurs on the periphery of my life, and yet no sense of who she was. I know she was there, the name becomes more and more vivid and alive, but the person, the human being, elusive, won't come forth. I want to fuck her back to life, then watch her do simple things in public, walk, go through a door, lean back in a raving tilt-a-whirl at Chilhowee Amusement Park. Kiss all the women my age in Knoxville until I find that mouth. Necromancy, digging up the dead of one's dead past to kiss the decayed lips as though they were alive.

Who *are* these girls duly recorded in my red dairy? I have forgotten their names! How can I forget their names? Debbie, blond, slender, I begin to see, oh, yes, and beautiful, beautiful, too good for me, Jan Simms. "Della" is Della Snow, the Dark Lady of the Bijou.

The summer before I made a half-assed proposal to Marta—"If I *did* ask you to marry me, what would you say?"—I went to a dance at the Teen Rec Hall with a horny friend in UT Carousel Theater who had been with me in the army in Alaska and who became an Episcopalian minister, then vanished from my life, and there I met a girl in the dim light and picked her up. "You don't remember me, do you?"

I hadn't. She reminded me that she was Bonita Sewell and that she had loved me all during the seventh grade, before the Bijou time, and had quit in the middle of the eighth because she couldn't stand being near me, knowing I loved Loraine Clayboe and that she herself was nothing to me. And she'd gotten married that summer and had a child, and now she was divorced, and hated all men. My friend and I took her home where she lived in the River Street slums, in the area where Earl and his German wife had taken an apartment in 1947, and I kissed her in the back seat, and never saw her again.

Backstage a few nights ago, I lay awake most of the night, trying to remember the name of a girl I saw in a dream, a name I've not forgotten in twenty years. She had looked dreamy in the dream, very big and luscious and sweet-faced, faintly cocky, and I'd called her Willa Gibson—secretary of a magazine I had once worked for—and Wanda Gibbs, who used to stare at me in the Broadway and follow me on my paper route. She looked like Frances Langford the singer. Knowing it was neither Wanda nor Willa. Then suddenly Waunita Gibbs. I said aloud, "I want to see her again before I die." More than any of the other girls like her that I fucked, except Della Snow. Waunita Gibbs, whose face I see always behind that wire fence at the Municipal swimming pool, out on the sidewalk, with the shitty, snot-streaked kids moiling around her, her face as she spoke to me. Harry pretending not to know her, sitting on the edge of the pool in red trunks. I don't remember her so much from when we fucked. Her breath was sweet, her mouth was sweet, her body was warm, sometimes scalding hot, her pussy stank. I didn't only feel sorry for her, guilty that I used her, I lusted for her soul, urging her not to fuck us, because Jesus wouldn't love her if she did. Yet, I did.

I'm holding in my hand my first attempt to describe my first meeting with Waunita.

Nick—that's me—was sitting in his easy chair, the one with an arm missing, smoking a slim cigar, Robert Burns, as he read *Look Homeward, Angel,* when into the grey light of the room. . . .

Later on, at UT, I tried again.

CHILDREN OF THE COLD SUN

By Lucius Hutchfield

He heard someone walking carefully through the front rooms. Cocking sideways in his chair, he looked through the door of his "sanctuary." That red face idiotically gleaming, gleefully appeared in the kitchen doorway and let out a familiar shrill, soprano giggle. Jerking his thumb in the fit and bending his knees as he scrambled forward on the bright linoleum still wet from the mop, Harry, in the wiggling of his giggle, said brokenly, "She's here. We got her out here, by God! Come on!"

"Hell," said Nick, grinning. "I'll bet."

"No shit, by God. Come and see."

"Where?"

"On the damn front porch."

Nick followed Harry into the dark living room. A shape on the porch beyond the shaded French door moved black and ragged.

I just now found another version. During a rest period at clerk typist school in the army at Fort Jackson, South Carolina, I sketched the scene yet again.

> Nick had been writing at his desk in "the sanctuary" for more than three hours now, rewriting, cursing the typewriter and merely sitting, thinking. He stared at the high shelf of books and when his eyes came to *The Portable Thomas Wolfe*, inspiration fired by memories of Tom's stories and immortal feel of things, things about which Nick yearned to write with clarity and inhuman understanding, he once again put his fingers to the typewriter keys and began to compose, letting his thoughts and feelings more or less filter through his melancholy mood into the final stage wherein words began to appear on the white paper.
>
> And it was at one of these moments that he heard someone moving silently through the outer rooms of the house, where no lights were burning. He pushed back his chair with a noisy scrape and leaned to the doorless doorway, his heart pounding. And Harry entered at that semi-bowlegged gait with a grin on his face typical of his more foolish moods. That familiar laugh so utterly animalish when out of place, as it was for Nick at this moment, was loud in the stillness of the untidy kitchen. Nick detected from the gibberish flow of Harry's laughter-saturated dialogue that he had a girl outside.

Hovering around the Broadway Theater, neighborhood atmosphere of sex and sin. After Sunday School, during church, when I was four, the preacher's fourteen-year-old daughter lured me into her cool, dimly lighted basement across the alley from the church, fiddled with my do-do-pee-pee-so-so, the loud sermon a hum in the sun outside.

Coming home after watching Marlene Dietrich in *Destry Rides Again* kick the slats out of Una Merkel in a saloon brawl, the fifteen year old girl who "took care of" us dashes through the house to the backyard and pisses hard, sparkling in the September moonlight into new-mown grass and wild onions. Rosalie. Dali, too, loved the memory of girls pissing, three, one a sister—or was it two sisters? I'm eager to go to the library and look it up—lifting long skirts on a bridge in Figueres, Spain. At six, showing two girls my pecker, and watch me pee, standing in the WPA storm ditch.

A girl older than I was lured me into the bushes where our gang stashed Milky Ways and Luckies that we swiped from a store shut down during the depression, and she lay down with her other two sisters in a row, spread-legged, bloomers around their ankles.

In the alley behind the Broadway, peeking through a crack in the frosted glass high above the toilet, listening to an elegantly dressed woman who came in resembling Joan Crawford and ducked fast inside a stall, piss hard and flush loud.

In the jungle behind the Broadway, where a bowling alley now stands, under a tree limb that undulates like Sabu's python in Kipling's *Jungle Book*, trying to poke through Janis's bloomers that she won't take off, an older girl, whose frequent innuendoes in fifth grade geography have led us to this crusty red clay where ants are driven among sprawly dewberry vines.

Living in ten different neighborhoods, most of them close to the Broadway, us boys always stealing, fighting, cussing, smoking, jacking off under railroad trestles, waiting to hop freights to swim in the country. Pounding our pork in caves on Sharp's Ridge. Corn-holing each other in Boys Club camp near Norris Dam.

Greeting or reviling each other at a running distance with "creaming" gestures—snap fingers, point thumb at prong.

Discovery of a bloody Kotex in a rusty trash barrel in an alley, victorious as Victor Mature dragging dinosaur meat back to the cave in *One Million BC*.

Dropping pencils, looking up nice girls' dresses.

Patrolling the front rows of the Broadway glimpsing Technicolor bloomers, as Ann Sheridan in *Kings Row* waits for Ronald Reagan to discover his legs have been amputated. "Where's the rest of me?"

While the burlesque show's going on at the Roxy, the lady manager sits behind me like a teacher, tilted forward, trying to decide whether I'm playing pocket pool. I'm only picking at the scab of a defunct boil through a hole in my corduroy knickers pocket.

"Doing it" to and fingering some girls, I worshipped others from afar, girls who, like the Goddesses on the screen, I never thought of doing it to. The Goddesses did not have vaginas, nor rectums, so they never copulated nor did they perform fellatio. While feeling guilt and afraid of hell for fuckin' and jackin' off, I attributed nobler emotions to the movie stars, the pure, perfect, angelic, superhuman Goddesses. Like the marble and bronze statues of nymphs and satyrs in the Tennessee Theater's lobbies and lounges, the gods and Goddesses on the screen were peckerless and pussyless, smooth, seamless marble and bronze between the legs.

Religion and movies and my own temperament and experiences shaped my sexual attitudes. Sex means Jesus hates your guts if you do it and God, recording the demerits in his big book, rejects you, and the devil, stoking up the fire, claims you. Though I investigated that preacher's daughter in the basement behind the church, and talked of fucking with the dirty boys in another Methodist Sunday school, I was receptive to teachings about purity and sanctity. Got saved, gave my heart to Jesus, in a revival tent on sawdust-littered grass the summer night I saw *King Kong* at the Broadway, not knowing that five summers later I'd be working near the top floor of the Empire State Building—where King Kong fought off airplane machine gun bullets—as a mail clerk for Cloverdale Knitting Company, makers of Nightie Night children's sleepwear.

Thou shalt not commit fornication. Got it. And St. Paul's idea that if you just think about it, you've committed it. Got it. I had thought about it much of the time, and that way of looking at it made sense, in a cosmic way. Love for a girl meant purity of body and mind and a lofty heart. When a boy playing in cars with me in Nathan's junkyard said Joseph did it to Mary to get Jesus, I smeared his ass.

None of the boys I ran with seemed to regard girls the complex ways I did, neither the girls in the neighborhoods nor the ladies on the screen. To me alone, it seemed, women were to be loved, adored, cherished, once loved, loved forever, though you subjected them to romantic fits of temper like Heathcliff in *Wuthering Heights*, Rochester in *Jane Eyre,* and Maxim de Winter in Daphne du Maurier's *Rebecca,* and playfully slapped them now and then to test their love, you never befouled them by word or deed. Nobody around me felt that way, so where did I get the idea? From a movie, or movies? From Ashley Wilkes in *Gone with the Wind*? Not from a book, because I never read a book until I was 13 nor from sermons, well, maybe from the idea of the Virgin Mary, maybe from the idea of Jesus' way of treating Mary Magdalene. Jesus and the woman taken in adultery. Why do I love that scene, why does it make me weep with awe and wonder, even after I rejected the surrounding theology at age 15? Because it's right out of a good movie in which Alan Ladd or Gary Cooper or Spencer Tracy puts down a crowd that ridicules a woman.

I was not among the men and boys who whistled, stomped, cracked jokes, barked obscene noises at the movies when the Goddesses took off even one bit of their clothes. I never wanted them to take off more. Sex was another realm of being, entirely off screen—though as near as the front row seats full of girls. I assumed that in their private lives—though I collected movie magazines, I only looked at the pictures and read a few captions—the stars were pure. I had heard about Hedy Lamarr's teenage nude swim in *Ecstasy* and seen her as the exotic, dark-skinned native Tondaleyo dancing in *White Cargo*, but I never imagined such wild sexual behavior as she recently confessed in her autobiography, *Ecstasy and Me*, which I'm reading now—she loved to bring into play each of her orifices. I befriended her recently when I discovered by chance that she was very down and out. Reading her autobiography in the projectionist's chair. Blasphemy to imagine involuntarily Hedy sitting on a toilet. Not real enough to do it to, strange enough that they resembled mortals so closely. Alive this instant is the moment in the Broadway Theater when I suddenly realized, in horror and disgust, that Vivien Leigh had ears, a nose, and elbows. I'd never imagined she had a vagina, like the one I had my finger in while watching her in *Anna Karenina*. I hear that Vivien Leigh was the most foul-mouthed woman ever to pose for cameras. I was somewhat less disillusioned to realize, in unguarded moments, that the girls I loved most, or worshipped secretly, had ears, nostrils, toenails like ordinary girls.

I was in awe of the unearthly perfect beauty of Goddess Merle Oberon, slightly sexy in *A Song to Remember* because as George Sand she dressed like a man, shattering the norm. Other women I revered for sheer beauty, but I valued acting ability and personality.

The tough, sultry women, despite their aggressive personalities, aroused no sexual responses. Claire Trevor was a little sexy in *Dead End* because of her looks and how people spoke about her, implying that she was a whore and had caught syphilis.

Standing On the Spot at the Bijou, I was aware of the handsome older woman who tore the tickets, and whose hair was cut like Mary Astor's in *The Maltese Falcon* by Dashiell Hammett—great name for a writer—and who had a girlfriend with enormous titties, and I thought maybe they were lesbians, and I was aware of the pretty, cross-eyed woman who sold popcorn and candy and who had a lovely daughter a few years older than I was, and aware of the short woman in the ticket booth who resembled Carmen Miranda, and aware of the Negro girl I glimpsed when the manager's door stood ajar and he was speaking to her through a door behind him—that door right there—and imagined Hood trying to mess with her. I wish I could see her face now.

The Vine Street district was the Negro counterpart of Market Square, and the Gem was their theater—distinctly separate but in a rich ambience of associations. The Bijou, owned by the same company, combined the two settings by opening its second balcony to Negroes, who entered on the side, through a toy entrance similar to the Crystal's, with its own ticket booth, still-rack and popcorn, candy counter, and I sensed pretty Negro girls climbing, climbing to the peanut gallery, sitting high, snug, up under the blue dome—built beneath the bridal suite of the overarching Lamar Hotel, the room where Union General Sanders died of his wounds and maybe the one where my Daddy sleeps now.

And part of the atmosphere of suppressed sexuality was my awareness that as people packed the theater on Saturday nights, looking at Joan Crawford inspire John Garfield to play the violin in *Humoresque*—the outer lobby packed, people waiting to get in—the projectionist on hot summer nights wore only his jock shorts inside the projection booth, set in the middle of the first balcony, tiers of seats on two sides, three rows just under the apertures. Imagined them sitting in there at a school desk reading *True Detective* and *Field and Stream* or jacking off watching the images they projected. Concealed eunuchs of the gods and Goddesses. But one of them looked like Zachary Scott, suave, and, I imagined, lured women into the hot booth where he had set up a canvas army cot.

Hood steps up behind me On the Spot, says, "See that couple over there. Tell them to stop smooching or leave the premises." Was he a Baptist preacher on Sundays when the theater was dark? I can't believe I actually did what he told me. That year, while I was a run-away in Asheville, they arrested Hood in Atlanta as he stepped down off a Delta flight, having stolen a week's Bijou revenue.

And in that darkened, smoldering atmosphere, I stood On the Spot, imagining screwing girls who came in or girls at school, a hard on, unaffected sexually by the Goddesses on the screen, except maybe for moments like the one in *Duel in the Sun* when wild Gregory Peck goes to wild Jennifer Jones' room. I wrote a similar scenario to that movie, more explicit scenes, that the Bonny

Kate Junior High principal, Mr. Bronson, confiscated when he found Loris, two grades below mine, reading it—or Lilli Palmer in *Cloak and Dagger* hiding in the back of a truck with Gary Cooper and some other men, wearing only a slip, raising a machine gun toward the back and where a Nazi soldier is about to lift the canvas flap, or sultry Joan Bennett as "Lazy Legs" in *Woman in the Window*, saying to Dan Duryea, "Jeepers, I love you," and it's subtle as a Mack truck how she shows it—oh, and luscious Jane Russell getting in bed to warm the flesh of Billy the Kid who is seriously wounded and freezing, and suddenly a patron walks up to me On the Spot and I have no pockets in the fancy uniform to conceal the hard on inspired by images of real girls my imagination has been conjuring up.

Errol Flynn aka Gale, Sonny Tufts aka Brady Goosy, Gale's shy cousin, and my own, as it turned out, and Ray Bolger aka Elmo, the chief usher, and Alan Ladd aka Lucius Hutchfield, down in the orchestra pit looking through a rent in the red velvet curtain up at the girls on the front row, their legs jacked up on the wooden railing, their faces, tilted back, lit by modulations of black and white, Technicolor less often, showing the whites of their eyes in a trance, feeding their faces with popcorn and candy, watching a stark close-up of Gary Grant kissing Ingrid Bergman in *Notorious*, and we shiver, seeing black hair or brown curling out from the tight bands of their panties. And we are euphoric for an hour, making visits to the tiny bathroom where, oddly, the toilet sits on a dais.

I went back at least once each shift to jack off. The way dreams were registered on my eyes, flesh took a pounding for the runaway riot of my imagination.

And we find an underground passage in the defunct Lyric Theater facing the Bijou across Gay and look up the ventilating grills in the sidewalk where women wait for streetcars, some wearing no panties in Knoxville's sultry August.

And "closing house," we open the exit doors in the second balcony, where we find used rubbers. From the fire escape, looking down across Cumberland Avenue into the rooms in the Cumberland Hotel, where whores—we suspect—undress, one of them dying in a fire later that night that burns the historic hotel to the ground as we slept in our own homes. I didn't understand why her death did not make the boys sad, as it did me. It's a parking lot now. I park my rental car there.

And Errol Flynn walks over to me, scuffing his feet on the red carpet, and I forget, he touches my cheek, a spark startles me. When he's off duty, and has taken a girl backstage, he steps up behind me, shoves his finger under my nose, says, "Sniff."

Behind the screen, next to the enormous black speaker, up on a stack of hairy tow-sacks full of raw popcorn, no, it was down in the basement by the enormous fans on top of posters advertising Katharine Hepburn menaced by Robert Taylor of all people in *Undercurrent*, the usher staff, Gale, Brady, Elmo, and me, train-fuck Della Snow one snow blizzard night who used to sit across from me in Christenberry library and make pornographic gestures and spread her legs when I dropped my pencil and write "I Luv Lucius Hutchfield" in all the opinion books, and I ever since have ached to know where she is and to see what she looks like now.

What did you say to me? What did I say to you? We must have said something. Yes, you whispered in my ear, "The bird of Time hath but a short while to flutter, and the bird is on the wing," and were no longer the girl I knew before. Your pussy was scorching hot through the Trojan rubber and that put the seal of sin on it, and now I realize Gale, Brady, and Elmo had worked up all that friction in you with rubbers, and I took your hand, helped you walk, sore from fucking four boys, led you through the pitch dark to the stage door ramp and the weak yellow light, Errol Flynn waving you on viciously, afraid Hood would catch us, and you have haunted me for decades, my handing you to Errol Flynn and Sonny Tufts, you slipping on the ramp, busting your knee, as you reached for their grasp, and they shoved you out into the December snow turned into rain. They called a girl like you a whore because you fucked, but now I know you were lonesome and liked to fuck, just as they did, except *they* weren't lonesome. Now from the projection booth, I stare at the blank Bijou screen, wishing I can see your face there, but it's dim, I see only a light sprinkling of pimples, but know that you were pretty underneath the look of sin you had about you and you were voluptuous, your body and clothes reeking of poverty and sin. "She said she would go with us only if she could see you, Shorty." That hurts. Move on.

Loris and I shared special places—a deserted dock on the Tennessee River, neglected Tyson Park, the upper level stacks of the public library. I gave her exotic new names—Gypsy, from her olive skin and dark eyes, Anna Livia from Joyce's *Finnegans Wake*, "Anna was, Livia is, Plurabelle's to be." Zadalia, for its mere sound, Melinda because she aspired to be a ballet dancer. We made special vows, like the one Joseph Cotten made to Jennifer Jones in *Love Letters*. "I think of you, my dearest, as a distant promise of beauty, untouched by the world. If I never see you again, my last thought will be that I fought for you and lost. But I fought." Estranged, I struck the Byronic pose of aloofness, of melancholy isolation, of the exiled lover. The lover goes away to forget, wanders the earth, and the beloved, going in search, experiences many adventures and perils.

Thank you, girls, thank you, for everything. I felt guilt for what I saw, and felt, for what you gave, or did not give, but was it not good? Was it not life-lasting? Will I never cease loving pussy as portal to the known-unknown, and the girls who have them, especially those who love to share them? I have always loved you, girls. I may have seldom talked dirty about you, never contemptuously, never to put you down, never to degrade you for the sake of degradation, always feeling you were—as James M. Cain has tough guy Frank say of sluttish Cora in *The Postman Always Rings Twice*—somehow "holy." But to me you were not whores, even in Galveston, Panama, Honolulu, Antofagasta. Celebrate! Masturbate! Rejoice!

I'm strangely afraid to remember these people, as Doctor Frankenstein—I finally read Mary Shelley's tale a few days ago—was afraid when the monster got out of control. I am afraid that I will not be able to shake them loose once I have resurrected them, that Mr. Hood will never get on that plane to Atlanta with the ticket receipts and cease to be manager of the Bijou but be condemned to live in the labyrinthine basement like the Phantom of the Opera.

I am afraid that I will have to create completely that Negro ticket seller who haunts me, so that she will follow me always when I leave this office, because only in my mind's eye will she exist. I killed her, I killed her in the summer and fall of 1946 and the winter of '47 when I failed to see her. I am obligated to create her, because she was there, and because someone must inhabit the booth and sell tickets forever. Like meeting a girl in the dark and making love to her in the dark and, not seeing her *then*, *never* seeing her. And I am haunted by all those Negroes who sat in the second balcony for hours, came regularly each day, while I stood far below, and we watched the same Alan Ladd and heard him speak, and yet did not see each other face to face.

I WILL CRAWL through the woods of Knoxville, the isolated oases of kudzu vines and sycamores, honeysuckle, briars, sedge, wild flowers, on, no, not on my hands and knees, on my belly, naked, scratch, bruise my skin, upon my knees on rocks and roots to burning flesh, lacerate my nipples, konk my crazy bone, a hurt like coming, exquisitely unbearable, what coming prolonged too long would be, I will walk naked down every tree-lined street after all lights are out, and glance in the ghostly car windows, and eyes will look back at me, women, pussies streaming below their raised skirts, men, dribbling dicks, girls, the taste of peter in their mouths, looking up to watch me pass, milky in the night, and I will wander through front doors in houses among the rooms, out the back door, down the dewy lawns, along the trash can alley, into the back door, then the next door, doors, doors, while they sleep, while they dream, butts rubbing noses, soles, blank-faced, watching me from under the covers at the foot of beds, the little children innocent as maniacs in sleep, the little babies, some few days exiled from the womb, collapsing in their mother's beds as the body sinks in repose, folds, slowly, very slowly, like the Tower of Pisa sinking, leaning, collapsing, or the steps of Venice, going down, down under water slime, the dishes clean in the racks, gleaming in the moonlight through the kitchen window over the sink, I am he who gets up in the night to take a piss, I will piss in their toilets and not flush, and in their dreams creeks will flow, twinkle in the light the wind shakes as light leaks through the leaves, and I am he who gets up in the night to drink from the dripping faucet, I will stick out my tongue and let it drip, I have all night to let it drip, I will lap till morning, and stick my tongue in faucets and let the women lie safe, their pussies, their assholes relaxed, pulsing with humming blood, and I will hear them murmur in their sleep of lovers and lacks, I will step aside as they walk in sleep, back up, press my naked body against the cool wallpaper, the moist wallpaper, as their moist warm bodies pass, their eyes open, seeing the dream they walk in, blind to me, and I will have a hard on most of the time, but I do not molest, I, too, am a dreamer, I will only look, my eyes will reflect, I will not even be a poet and imagine their lives, they will remain anonymous as sleep, safe, secret, and I will be secret, I walk where secrecy is, I want to feel the emanations from their skin of secrecy, I want to witness the one-third of their lives they lose each night, all of them, all over Knoxville, up and down every tree-lined avenue, along the city's seven ridges, across the hills, and listen to night watchmen tick around and around the clock in their little looking, watching spaces, inside fences, inside walls, among the goods, stacked, ranked, rowed goods, dead watches, rifles rooted in darkness, dresses hanging on sagging racks, candy swelling the cases, ice cream crystalizing, chairs with open arms they may not let down, crouching couches, fire extinguishers on alarming walls, and I will climb willow trees and watch nurses return home late in moist shoes and wish them well and I will sit in silent trains round-housed in the Coster Station's defunct railyards, I am in the night he who sees everything while everybody sees dreams, he who is there, standing in the doorway of the bedroom, but who is not seen, who lingers a moment, then goes away.

Our lives are traffic-snarled with such wanderers, who come, and we see them not, who see, and in whose eyes we do not see ourselves.

SAD, SAD, VERY SAD, to say that yesterday a fire got started backstage somehow. I think the work lights got too hot, too close to the stills I had taped to the brick wall and they caught a curtain afire. I'm living that time and telling that time in the projection booth only now.

Rescued the tapes, but everything else is destroyed, all my childhood manuscripts, my clothes, my books, everything. Death. I had intended when I leave here to go to Hollywood, to haul it all to UT's Special Collections Library where the manuscripts of my published works are housed. The city will certainly condemn the Bijou and in a month or so, they will tear it down, and once the funds are available, they'll build the new library on this site. Meanwhile, it will serve as a parking lot, so that three of the corners of this intersection will invite cars to park. The old Market House is a parking lot. Some people charged arson in that case. Maybe that's what happened here. Mea culpa? My terrible nostalgia lit the fire. Or somebody who wants to run the parking lot perhaps. I don't really give a rat's ass *who* did it, *why,* or *how.* It's done. What I should have done for myself was done *for* me.

But only on a physical plane. It's still all on these five rescued tapes. Five. Now I have two recorders, and I'm on the new one. Running on batteries. I think I'll try to keep on telling about that time, as if I were seeing it on that screen down there on the stage. The screen is scorched a little but somehow it escaped destruction—asbestos, I reckon—but it's darkened almost to black. The dressing rooms were destroyed. I sleep here in the projection booth, dreams and all. Stage floor almost collapsed. Seats black, walls black, curtains burnt to a few strings of wispy gauze. A hole in the domed ceiling above the second balcony. March wind roars around in the dome above which General Sanders died in the bridal suite. "I'm glad I was not shot in the back." They boarded up the stage door so it wouldn't be an attractive nuisance to kids, I reckon, sealed exit doors, front doors. The first balcony, where the projection booth sets, sags under the weight of the collapsed second, Negro balcony. No electricity. Candle light. Inner light.

Standing On the Spot in the burned auditorium this morning, the smoke still rising through the rents in the ceiling, where now, from the projection booth, I see the big dipper, I thought of the other burned theaters. The Broadway, where I stood with Shelley one day, five years ago, when he was five, wearing a cowboy outfit, pearl-handled pistols, a large red hat. The Broadway was a bowling alley when it burned, but the fire had reduced it to the ruins of a theater, a rent in the ceiling there, too. Looked like one of the bombed cathedrals I'd seen at the Broadway in movies and newsreels during the war.

And the State Theater across from the Standard Knitting Mill burned. And the Princess in Fountain City. And the Roxy. And the Crystal and The Rialto. They say the old Majestic before my birth burned, too. And the Gay in Burlington. And the Horne. And the Capitol.

I don't have much of the Warner Brothers advance money left. Eatin' pork 'n' beans—now as—I—talk. Sometimes the projection booth—is like a cold—iron box and the two big projectors are as cold—to the touch as a derelict pump handle. The booth is as hermetic as Marcel Proust's cork-lined room, though I can look—out through the two projection apertures at the auditorium and up at the patch of sky. And Poe, the necromancer, is with me—here, too.

On a new tape, I have told, in strict chronological order, the time when I ushered here. It's as if I'm trying to exorcise a bad experience. But at the time I enjoyed it all. Why does it seem malignant today? Am I trifling with things that seem trivial? I have a feeling that I am delving into something that is beyond me, because it is too much a part of me. Does that mean that I add up to a trivial human being? Or a malignant?

When I look down there and try to imagine old movies on the scorched screen, I see stills of comic book type drawings. Late at night, I watch old movies on a little portable TV set an old man in the Lamar hotel next door sold me cheap. When he moved out, he complained that the permeating smell of burnt leather seats suffocated him, the hotel itself untouched. I'm getting a few books of movie pictures from the Nostalgia Book Club sent to me care of General Delivery, and I've ordered some films from Castle Films, three minute, silent 8 mm clips from such old movies as Bette Davis as a killer in *The Letter*. And Bogart, Cagney, and Bette Davis anthology reels. What little money I have, I spend on such things. And I've ordered some reel-to-reel tapes of the old radio shows from a man in Utah who has hundreds. "Who was that masked man?" "The Shad-ow Knoooows. Heh, hed, heh." *The Green Hornet, Superman, Gang Busters*. I'll play them here in the booth, or over that new P. A. system back of the screen that I run on pirated electricity from the hotel on the other side of the wall. My voice coming out of the new speaker I installed to magnify my voice, my past, coming from behind the screen, may jar the balcony loose, or the whole structure may simply collapse while I'm sleeping.

I've been going out every day for the past week in sunglasses, taking 8 mm home movies of Knoxville. When they come back, I'll show them on the toy eight-millimeter projector that I got for three dollars from a junk shop on Vine Street, hang a sheet on the projection booth wall with masking tape.

They say that in 1948 somebody once asked John Gunther, the world traveler, "What's the most beautiful city in the world?" Without hesitation, he answered, "Paris." Ugliest? Without hesitation, he answered, "Knoxville, Tennessee." He hadn't seen it since 1946. Now it's called "The Dogwood Capital of the World." But for Gunther and for me, it's the old Knoxville that lives, its ugliness, for me sometimes painfully beautiful.

Early Sunday, I walked my old paper routes, ugly neighborhoods if you have no sense of beauty in decay, and shot home movies, but not of the most beautiful thing I saw. Following behind the paperboy, walking down a steep path beside a house, I looked down into a room through an open window not even screened. A blond woman, her face nestled between the man's neck and his shoulder, her arm around his neck, lay hip to hip against the man, whose left hand lay over her pudenda, his fingers curled into the blond hairs that showed between his fingers, his right hand resting gently on his doo-lolly, soft, long, floppy. Cheeks of her fanny, like two buds, glistening with cum. Her toenails painted red like her fingers. The morning sun highlighted his black hair and struck the brass bedrail, and one hand, as I watched, twitched. The woman's breasts were big but her areola, nipples, were tiny and brown as poster paint, with golden hair around one, under which her hand lay. I saw only the corner of her closed mouth. The man's mouth was wide open as if in awe.

April 1947, walking along the slopes of the ridge, having seen *Leave Her to Heaven*, set in Maine, I had imagined Maine to be my paradise on earth, that romantic landscape, the natural expression of ethereal states of mind and emotion that I hadn't even lucidly experienced yet, but when I did, it would feel the way Maine looked. And then I was almost jealous and resentful and afraid and exultant at the mere shadow of India that fell upon Maine when I saw *The Razor's Edge*.

But I didn't abandon Maine. After the operation on my feet that summer to correct incipient clawfoot deformity, I projected Loris and me into a future life together in a scenario, "The Angel of Angel Hill," retitled "The Angel of Green Bay," set in Maine. And the locale of other scenarios later that year, actually or spiritually, would be Maine. Sometimes I was a fisherman, but always also a farmer, mainly a writer or a painter. And there I had the Angel girl I had wandered the earth looking for, and I had the great good place, and I had the inner Larry Darrell peace, and I produced fruits of the earth and of the imagination. Because of Maine, I loved "Renascence" by Edna St. Vincent Millay, written when she was only 19 in Camden.

> The world stands out on either side
> No wider than the heart is wide.

But I couldn't have imagined back then that in five years I'd walk away from my job in the White Tower hamburger joint on Eighth Street in Manhattan and, wearing a brand-new leather jacket and new boots, and with money my mentor Victor Savage had handed me across the counter—the scene dominated by all the Savages, in evening clothes, just come from *Carmen* at the Metropolitan Opera, Victor, conductor, composer, his wife, Florinda, daughter Gayle, Victor, Junior, the boy, squeezed between cowboys from Madison Square Garden where the Roy Rogers Rodeo was galloping—money to go to Maine to die, having just broken up forever, never to be free of her, with Loris. Met with her for the last time at the table in the Gold Sun Cafe at the edge of Market Square where I used to sit with the Bijou Boys and later with her, many times, while looking longingly at the waitress who, as I once told her, looked like Elizabeth Taylor.

Ogunquit, Maine, in the fall of 1953. And wandered into the woods, followed by a lovely collie. Walking there I did not imagine that the winter after those autumn weeks of dying in Maine, I would finally ship out of Brooklyn, destination Chile and India. In Maine, the romantic feeling was more intense, hurt more deeply, and at the same time it reached out more extensively into the future. Marta and I drove a limping Chevrolet from San Francisco down to Big Sur one Sunday to see Henry Miller, whose *Tropic of Cancer* I had read in high school in the Obelisk Press edition Victor Savage had smuggled out of Paris, and Miller told me there was no such romantic place as I had imagined Maine to be, but that I ought to take a look at certain parts of Idaho, of all places.

Well, I once had something like the great good place with Marta and Shelley on a farm just outside a small town in the Blue Ridge Mountains. When my first novel, *The Sea Within*, came out, a picture story about me circulated all over the South, depicting me at work in a crude shed, and Marta lugging an oaken bucket of water in one hand, cradling baby Shelley in her other arm. Actually, the daily bucket she used to fetch water was plastic, which broke in the middle of the living room floor one day, but the wooden ice cream freezer bucket looked more authentic in the photograph. She didn't plow, like the girl of my dreams, but she churned butter, baked bread, and picked raspberries. She is the woman of the ideal Maine vision, though not completely—who *can* be? "A distant promise of beauty untouched by the world."

Coming down from a tour of Nova Scotia, with Marta and Shelley, I saw Bar Harbor for the first time, the loveliest part of the trip. Not until this moment has it occurred to me that the images I saw in *Leave Her to Heaven* which created a long-lasting mystique were probably filmed somewhere in California.

Well, on down off Sharp's Ridge, I walked over to Cedar Street where I stared into the dishpan of water and slime that's all that's left of Lilly's Pond. That unforgettable houseboat of his, vanished.

Took a moving picture of the lot where Mammy's Jane's Cafe used to stand that now looks no bigger than a good place to play marbles—where the Chief met Mammy, coming over from the huge fire hall on the opposite corner.

Shot the old Lawson McGhee Library, named after a local pilot killed in World War One. The setting of my first published short story, a craven imitation of Thomas Wolfe's poetic prose.

Got some good shots of the juvenile detention home where I used to visit Earl and Bucky. Last time I was there, though, I came on an education class observation assignment from UT. The teacher, a big fat, smelly woman, told me the sad story of one of the kids who came there to school and was allowed to go home at night, as Bucky was.

As an education major, I chose to observe at Lincoln Park Elementary. My old severe art teacher told me that day that she had kept all the love notes she intercepted from me to LaRue, the child Goddess I loved for five years there. Fulton High, where Loris graduated after we broke up. And up the highway at the high school for Oak Ridge, the Atomic City, also to visit and report on. I should read those reports into the recorder, but that can wait.

Lucius, I wish you could shoot the slums on the hills behind where the Lyric used to stand, but it's all demolished, as if vanished, and the new Civic Center and the new Public Safety Building dominate it now, where a few years ago I took the Chief, near blind, and he waited an hour and never did get to talk old times with his old fire department buddy. Sad going back to the car in the vast parking lot spread over that red clay hill, but the Chief told me First Creek, that empties into the river below us, was the same one that curled through North Knoxville where I used to swim. Such simple things that I don't know. What else, even now? I wrote a story set by First Creek down there across the bridge on River Street across the river from the slaughter house called "In the Summer They Slaughtered Cattle" and used the title later for a play about me and Harry and them and Waunita. Now no slums there either to shoot, gone, too, the ramshackle houseboats that were often the setting in my stories.

On down the river, past the marble-cutting factory, the old brick kilns still stand, abandoned. For many years, I didn't know what they were, wandering down there among them, and when they told me, the kilns as a melodramatic locale inspired a story, the first I ever published, "Alice Entombed," about an old bum who goes in to the library to get warm, and, as a protective maneuver against the severe looks of the librarian, discovers and reads *Alice in Wonderland*, which he steals so he can finish it by the light of the kiln fires.

Other bums think the book is full of money and kill him for it. Wolfian rhetoric. "Draped in the tattered flag of the vagabond which had met with the fury and the chemistry of time and unrecorded distance, from sun-blasted and moon-swollen travel he for the unrecounted instance had emerged from darkness into another strange prison of stone and imprisoned light." Occurs to me now maybe the kids who edited that women's college journal published that story as a joke. But it moved one girl, Letitia, to romance me at the arts festival I attended there.

That time. North Carolina. I'm seized again with the old terrible urge to get on a jet plane to Asheville to stick my hand in the cranny in that brick pillar that holds up Thomas Wolfe's house to see if "Helena Street," the first story of mine I ever got typed up, and the paperback edition of *The Razor's Edge* that I stole from Gateway are still stashed inside. I imagine black widow spiders nesting in the pages or a snake using it for a bed. Or maybe it's disintegrated, or someone found it and imagines how it got there. One of my lovers who was going through Asheville offered to check, but I told her to preserve the mystery. When I stuck them in there, I was confident nobody was likely to see them. Not even me, as it turned out. I'd intended to retrieve them.

Several times over the years, I hitchhiked through Asheville, forgot, and years later I had to lay over in Asheville airport but didn't have time to go into town. The urge to look seized me even in Venice. But now I'm almost afraid to look. I like to think they're still there, though, as in a timeless vault, immured, as the dining room in Wolfe's house is immured in one of my stories and in my description of the small Blue Goose Hotel in a tiny mountain town in another part of the mountains of North Carolina.

I made a deliberate and relatively systematic attempt to tour, like a tourist, my own hometown, *Knoxville* by Betsey Creekmore in my hand, only a few months after I looked with similar close scrutiny upon the history of the stones of Venice, James Morris' *Venice* in hand. Winding through the man-made caves under the Castle Sigroi built on the Bock in Luxembourg, whose typography is similar to *Knoxville*, I remembered the caves under Knoxville, dug out, some say, by Union and Confederate troops as they took the town, back and forth, from each other. Awakening in the a. m. in Luxembourg seeing red in the sky on the horizon miles away, I remembered the red in the sky when I wandered the outskirts of Asheville, lost, and was terrified by the sight, thinking it was another war starting, an atomic bomb blast, or the end of the world, and smiled there in Luxemburg, knowing it had been only the dawn, but I went back to sleep a little scared, and in the morning decided it was the iron foundries of the Ruhr.

Tried to find that unfinished little church on Sharp's Ridge where I used to go to with Loraine and them, but found no trace.

Digging into the *History of Tennessee* by my old history teacher Stanley John Folmsbee, I found all kinds of parallels. In 1821, an Indian named Sequoyah, who lived near Knoxville, became the first man in history to perfect an entirely new phonetic alphabet or syllabary, his purpose, to provide his people with a written language. At 18, I was trying to do the opposite, invent a new language only of syllables that would enable me to create an alternative world to Knoxville.

Took some movies of the island airport for private planes. Where I made love to Loris on a few humid Sunday afternoons in the bordering jungle. Not knowing until a few days ago, digging into history, that the white house on the hill, to the side of the ugly, scary red brick buildings for the blind, like the ones at the insane asylum, was built by Josephus Daniel, whose cousin Edgar Allan Poe, used to visit him there, riding in a buggy under the avenue of trees Josephus had designed, and that still hung over the road in 1947 where Loris and I, that much more in love, caught the streetcar back over the river and on to Lincoln Park where her mother was poised to pounce on her for running with that terrible Madden boy.

I haven't even gone by to see the Savages, as I have on every visit home over the years, but I read on the society page, Victor's guest-conducting in Barcelona, so I went out there and took some movies of that grand house and the wild garden that slopes down to the river, remembering the summer Marta and I lived there, she wrapping meat in a packing house, while the Savages were in Normandy, and I was writing a libretto re-conception of *Electra* by Euripides for Victor and tried to get Bucky off the Georgia chain gang, and the boats would come around the bend, shining their lights into the living room.

We lived in another professor's house on the river in Louisville a few years later when Shelley was three and the lights from many more boats on the Ohio flooded our living room, and floods came and the boats foundered in the fog among the trees just below the house, so I never forgot the first sight of that ghostly beam in the Savage living room, thinking then of Frederic March as Mark Twain, steering down the Mississippi in perilous fog.

Couldn't get a movie of WKGN in the Park National Bank Building where I was announcer. They're way out the highway near the Savages' now, so it's not the same. At only 16, I announced the *Night Watchman Show*, apprentice to Big Bob, who let me take the show on my own, while he brought girls up on the elevator and screwed them in Studio B, and I got fired for playing Tchaikovsky's "Romeo and Juliet Overture" dedicated to Loris on what was supposed to be a request show for country songs like "Honky Tonk Angel." Youngest announcer ever to work at WKGN, about three years after I met Mark McKay.

I told Gayle Savage about him, and she deliberately looked him up and they became lovers before both of them moved to New York at separate times. I'd met Gayle when I organized a small drama group at Knoxville High in rebellion against the official Knox High Masquers. And I told her about the time I looked down out of the tower by the river and saw her lie down naked on a slab of marble and offer herself up to the Moon god. And nobody could beat her doing the Tarzan yell. She became the greatest female friend I have ever had. With Gayle, I visited Mark McKay on the set at NBC, where he was directing a live drama with Maria Riva, Marlene Dietrich's daughter. Maria liked me and wanted me to meet her mother, and I did. Gayle's flamboyant romance with McKay went on for three years, until Mark moved to the west coast and ended up directing morning quiz shows. For many years, my brief encounters with Mark McKay made me think of him as an ideal intellectual, atheist, and temperamental romantic artist. In time, he became a snobbish, intolerant, egocentric jerk, but thanks for the memory.

On out Kingston Pike highway is the tower of "Bleak House" where the sniper spied Union General Sanders riding on a white horse and shot him, and I shot views of the cars passing by from up in that tower. I didn't know back in 1947 that the hospital where Doctor Summers corrected my tendency to claw-foot deformity was named after General Sanders, nor that the Yankees made a valiant victorious stand there against General Longstreet, digging a moat all around the hill, filling it with sharp stobs, and drenching the denuded hillsides with water that froze into one solid sheet of ice, and that in the moat, two hundred Rebels were shot or impaled. But I see it now. And a year later, I learned about James Joyce's romantic tower in Dublin, and later Robinson Jeffers' tower that he built himself at Carmel, California, and still later William Butler Yeats's, and but came to loathe the derogatory cliché of the writer in his ivory tower.

Got a shot of old man Rafferty, who folks have always said, since I was five and could take it in, is a millionaire, but dresses like the bums Daddy lays around drunk with. Over the years, I have come to recognize such old men as the cliché image of the irascible old Deep South type politician. I am so dissipated now that what I see in the soot-blackened, water-streaked lobby mirror bears a resemblance. Thought a bus was going to run over the old fellow while I was shooting him, realized when he hit the curb and sauntered on under the Bijou marquee and on down toward the courthouse that I should have broken my visual concentration to warn him, thinking in a flash of Margaret Mitchell on Peachtree Street, one summer evening in August, 1949, stepping off the curb in front of a taxi, driven drunkenly, recklessly, by a man who posed cockily in front of his cell bars as the man who killed Margaret Mitchell, the internationally celebrated author of *Gone with the Wind*, who, to me, looked a little like Vivien Leigh.

Before I started talking back to myself into the tape-recorder, I went backstage just to look around again at the work of fire. Risking a fall, I eased down the narrow wooden steps to the basement, feeling under me the steel stairs in the engine room on the *Polestar*. Painting the hellfire hot engine room of the Polestar going through the Panama Canal about four years after the Bijou time, I didn't remember painting the Bijou. When I walked into a whorehouse in Antofagasta, Chile, and the girls laughed at the "pintura" on my shoes, I had forgotten the girls in my classes at Christenberry Kate laughing at the paint on my trousers, which I deliberately wore as an emblem of the hard work I had done on Bijou walls and doors, now fire's undoing.

All the Bijou Boys, except Bruce the Albino, lying on tow-sacks full of raw popcorn backstage, snug against the speaker, when Texas City blew up in Pathe News, and we went to the wings, a few at first to watch it burn, and the ones that didn't go, lay listening to our verbal report of what we had seen, the bodies, like the frightening mushroom of the "Adam" bomb, like the George Raft and Bogart movie in the oil fields, *Manpower*, the hero moving in on the roaring fire close enough behind a tin shield to toss nitroglycerin on it, snuff it out, like snuffing out a candle. And when I sailed coastwise to Texas City on the Seatrain New Jersey, loaded with railroad boxcars carrying similar chemicals to those that blew up years before, I saw an anchor embedded in a grain elevator, and didn't remember where and when I had seen the newsreel.

At General Delivery, I found, in a huge packet of mail Marta sent from Vermont, a clipping of a review of my first novel, *The Sea Within*, by a former writing student from my Montana days which he had found stuck in a book when he was packing to move. "Lucius Hutchfield is probably the hardest working writer in America. He works hard because he knew he had to be a writer. He knew it when he was a boy and played along the river in Knoxville, Tennessee. He still talks about the wild dogs that ran there, and the feelings he had when he heard them running and barking along the river when it was night and everything was still. He knew then he was going to be a writer because he wanted to tell about the river and the dogs and the way he felt about them." *What* dogs? My memory is blank. I just got back from going out there to take a look at them, roamed up and down five miles in each direction from the Gay Street bridge, taking movies where dogs still run and bark, but only in my student's head.

THE HOME MOVIES CAME BACK TODAY and instead of the sheet hanging here in the projection booth, I've been trying to watch them on the scorched screen. One shot is of a movie display board out front of the Bijou. NOW PLAYING. Nothing but white blanks where the stills used to go. Home movies.

Up here in the projection booth where I sleep on a canvas cot, I daydream of fucking all the ticket girls and candy counter girls and the older women and some of the regular patrons. Till then, I jack off. Semen, like the silver images, flows.

The projectionists were the unseen, seldom glimpsed aristocrats of the little Bijou realm. From one routine dream world, the projectionist withdrew into another. *Argosy, Official Detective, Western Aces, True, Look*, perchance to dream, one wire in his brain still alertly connected to the bell that warned of the end of a reel. He kept the dreams rolling for the multitudes, smoothly. If not, they cut him up momentarily with ridicule, wisecracks, the likes of which one yearns to hear in these days of focus negligence.

Now that fire has driven me into the projection booth, and I am more and more often afraid to go down the sinking stairs, fearing a total collapse, it occurs to me that I have always sought some sort of "sanctuary" or been thrust into some sort of cell. I have gone from that circus wagon coal house and various converted chicken shacks and private rooms and caves and towers, and the involuntary languishing in cells as a student, a soldier, a seaman, to this projection booth. A monk driven by circumstance and self into a cell—like Martin Luther's cell in Erfurt, where I stood in awe.

"Time out of time."

Last year, as I climbed above Verona, following the inside of a great fortress wall, above the ruins of the Roman theater, I realized I had been looking at Italian ruins and antiquated buildings and streets all my childhood in Knoxville. I felt an almost nostalgic excitement seeing the ruins of castle-like buildings in Knoxville and houses along Kingston Pike, in Cherokee Hills and Sequoyah Hills, derived from intimations I had absorbed, flash by flash from movies, old paintings, drawings, from magazines, especially the *National Geographic*, newsreels of the war ruins, too.

Do I really want to recapture, understand that time? I'm deliberately, consciously distorting, I'm not telling when and the way events happened, not trying anymore to get things right, I just want to put myself *through* that time. That time is *on my mind,* keeps me awake. Images projected twenty years ago. What reason, what point, purpose better than that?

Like my fellow Knoxville native, James Agee in the sharecroppers' house in *Let Us Now Praise Famous Men*, I want to describe a feeling about the very texture of the wood and paint and metal and cloth of the place. I am imagining Agee coming to the Bijou in the early fifties, afflicted with nostalgia. My mania for exact dates, chronological sequence, to complete the record, contrasts with my desire to transform. My story is about a boy who wanted to change everything imaginatively, but whose story the author researched fanatically to get it as it was. Like that time near Boone, North Carolina when I tried to tell the truth in a long story about that woman who told a reporter Jesse James knocked her up.

I see now, clearly, the opening of *Rebecca*—night sky, clouds moving across the face of the moon, and romantic, low-keyed, but sinister music by Franz Waxman as Manderley Gate comes into view in mist. "Last night I dreamt I went to Manderley again. It seemed to be me I stood by the iron gate leading to the drive and for a while I could not enter, for the way was barred to me." And we move through the gate as the anonymous female narrator talks. "Then, like all dreamers, I was possessed of a sudden with supernatural powers and passed like a spirit through the barrier before me." We see trees and vines, growing thicker as the ruined, burnt house appears. "Nature had come into her own again, and little by little, had encroached upon the drive with long, tenacious fingers. We can never go back to Manderley again. That much is certain. But sometimes in my dreams I do go back. . . ."

But in broad daylight when I leave this fire-gutted shell, I find the ruins of Knoxville all around, and I feel the same sense of inevitability Joan Fontaine felt, almost, at times, as intensely focused as her vision and voice in *Rebecca*.

Gale Blackburn gliding forever, like a figure on a Grecian urn, across the lobby to touch my cheek, like Michelangelo's God touching Adam's finger across the cosmos on the Sistine Chapel ceiling—a similar action, less voltage, I hate to admit.

Will I go on until the sound of my voice in this booth begins to come only from out there, down there, from behind the scorched screen, until the pictures running amok in my head show up on the screen, and I go down and take my place in one of the charred seats?

Even now, I cannot exorcise Loris, the trusting, misty-eyed innocent. Thinking of her still yet hurts. The possibility of seeing her on Gay Street turns me into a quivering idgit. When I prayed for the perfect woman that night in the empty church, Loris was lying awake a few houses away.

For Loraine I feel only an abiding affection and unqualified good will for a good life with her family. But it was the romantic life I cultivated with Loraine that hovered over my entire seven years going steady with Loris. I close my eyes. There is an outdoor, ly-in movie screen inside my cranium, as if in a boxed canyon, dark cliffs enclosing me, and I say, voice over, "Show me now the time Loris in the early dawn, dressed for work at the Knoxville knitting mill, child labor, crawled in bed with me while I pretended to sleep." Just that one moment as she is crawling in would take hours, days. "I have weeks to watch."

Yesterday, Daddy got his disability check and bought Earl a second hand car with part of it, and they drove, Daddy drunk, Earl high on marijuana, up the ridge in South Knoxville to the old homestead on Pedigo. Daddy asked to buy the place and the man said it wasn't for sale. He insisted on going in and looking around, and the man called the cops. It was reported as a human interest story in the *Sentinel*, and I figured out the rest. I am strangely moved and frightened by this totally surprising action. I had always assumed that nothing really mattered to Daddy except bootleg whiskey. Now, at sixty-three, he is possessed by a dream similar to mine. I want to buy our old house on Cedar Street. One evening in 1946, Daddy and I looked for a house way out in West Knoxville, so we could move out of Mammy's, and missed the last streetcar, and had to walk almost 6 miles, a time of quiet and communion such as I never had with my father before or ever again.

What I had later was late night, sometimes two o'clock drunken monologues, Daddy, pouring images of the war into my head, during the next five years, and always at the center of it, his coming suddenly, driving his ambulance in General Patton's army, upon the Cathedral at Metz in the fog, until I went into the army myself, but saw only the squat Russian churches made of wood in Ninilchik and Kasilof in Alaska on the Kenai Peninsula.

But on a train, going through southern France into the Alps, destination Venice, I saw a cathedral in the distance, across a smoky landscape, and asked the French-German lady sitting across from me, whose bulky husband slept next to me, "Is that a cathedral, ma'am?"

"Yes, that is Metz Cathedral."

I gazed at it, silently, then I said, smiling wanly, as if proud, "My Daddy came through Metz in the war."

The woman raised her hands as if to protect her face and said, "Ah, ze var, ze var, alvays pipple talk about ze var. Terrible. Terrible. Terrible."

The utter sincerity of the exclamation I had provoked moved me to tears, and I remembered going down the hall from my room on West 53rd street off Third Avenue in 1951, opening a door to what I thought was the bathroom and a very old woman, a refugee, rose slightly off the edge of her cot, waving her arms protectively, shrieking, "Nein, Nein, Nein!" as if the Gestapo had come again.

About Earl and Bucky I've learned a few things from Marta's telegraphic letters—including COME HOME, SHELLEY MISSES YOU—things she gets from talking to Momma and Mammy on the phone—they think I'm already in Hollywood—and their letters that Marta sends on. And I spy on them a little. Watched my brother Earl the ex-con following a county gravel truck along the winter-rutted streets and turnpikes of Knoxville. Having spent most of his life behind bars, he's out there now, scattering gravel.

The first day out of prison back in '57, Earl met in the Crystal Theater and the next day married Sallie, a string bean blond of 15 from Lone Mountain, where Harl Abshire the desperado of the Depression days was born and raised. Mammy and the Chief have raised their son, her own relatives have raised their daughter. His *new* wife, a customer at Cas Walker's cut-rate grocery, where Earl worked the first year out of a Tennessee prison, the last one, runs him off when he comes around the house out in Lyons View, because she collects on desertion. Their new baby is named after Earl.

In Knox High, when Earl was in a military prison for selling an army camera in Belgium, not knowing that one of them still had reconnaissance film in it—or so he claims—I started, by the winter light coming through the many tall windows in the auditorium study hall, "The Wild Goose," a story about Earl, beginning with the night he suddenly appeared, a fugitive, on the Bijou stage and won the Al Jolson contest. I didn't finish the sketch. Nor three or four others about him I started later on.

Marta, in a P.S. all capital letters and three underscores wrote that Bucky buzzed through Vermont a few days ago, so yesterday I walked past Mammy's, in disguise, and sure enough there was a strange, vintage 1941 green Hudson Traveler Six Sedan that could only have been Bucky's choice. He's been out of prison now almost seven years, roaming the country, living mostly in California, near Hollywood, but for extended periods in Cleveland, Austin, Canada, Florida. He shows up every few months, each time with a new dog, a different second hand car. Just passing through, he arrives early in the morning and departs into snow or rain storms on a tank of gas I put in his car, with sometimes a few dollars I gave him in his pockets. He was married once, had twins who died, and who haunt him, as Baboo haunts Momma, and me.

And so does another of Bucky's dead, Emmett, the low IQ lummox, who emerged twenty years after his death at 21 in a negative I got developed last month just to see who the tall figure in it was. Bucky drew a raging soldier at the bottom of a half-finished story of mine, that I erased back then in anger, and a few weeks ago sketched back in. I wrote sketches about Bucky, too. Living in a basement room on Clinch, in the middle of my sophomore year at the college, just before I went into the army, I wrote, out of a mood similar to the ones that kept me writing up in that tower by the river until scary dark, my second sketch of Bucky called "The Idiot Who Follows You," about his wanderings with Emmett.

And Uncle Luke haunts us still—the way he did when he was reported missing for almost two years—more than his death 10 years after he turned up one day at the screen door, grinning, AWOL. Got book-keeping training and became Tax clerk at City Hall. Three years ago, after he'd become a worse alcoholic than Daddy, Luke told the story of his homecoming to the family at Christmas, tears in his eyes, of how he had hidden in Mammy's bedroom and they had sent me in there, not knowing who waited for me, and how I had leaped into his arms and hugged him hard, and that Christmas, full of the telling, Luke had impulsively hugged me, very hard, painfully hard, crying, and I was shocked and startled because Luke was almost always moody and remote, even under his moods of happiness. I loved him, and wanted his approval, but never got it when I expected it, when I felt I had earned it, by becoming a teacher and a published writer.

And just the other day, I saw the Chief out in the yard trimming the rhododendron bush for next Spring. He was one of the first men to clear land, forming up the fire department for Oak Ridge, a made-up city, where they worked, top-secret, on the atomic bomb. Blind now, almost totally. One day, a few years ago, I walked him down to the corner of Broadway to get his lawn mower fixed, and while the man was working on it, the Chief was approached by an older man, a little, skinny fellow, dressed up, wearing a jaunty, colored hat, and the Chief hadn't seen "that old boy in years," he told me later, but called him by name, which I've forgotten, and said to me, "This old feller here, Lucius, run the first movie projector in Knoxville on Gay Street."

Anchor to all our wandering lives, there was not just the little house with its trees, the old oak cut down as a threat to the new roof, its changing trees mimosa and apple, but the woman in the house, who did not change. Part Cherokee, Mammy remained the merriest and moodiest of women any of us ever knew. Even as Earl and Bucky went in and came out of various penal institutions, to return to strange houses or apartments where Momma lived, and as I, after high school, began to roam all over the U.S., the one place that remained for us all was "good ol' 2722 Henegar Street."

I once sent Mammy a Christmas card in a big mayonnaise jar from the Gulf of Mexico as I was entering the Panama Canal on the Polestar, and some man found it and she received it on New Year's Eve the following year.

Uncle Luke could never leave her for long, and lived most of the time in that back room where I had slept with Earl and Bucky during the war. I went by there the other day just to try to catch a glimpse of her, and there she was in her long-cherished housecoat reaching into the mailbox.

And Momma, too, kept coming back to good ol' 2722 Henegar Street, from roving to Nashville, Chattanooga, Cincinnati, Columbus, where she danced with a good many boyfriends, moving in for a long stay sometimes. I can see now, without diminishing my exasperation with her erratic behavior, that the woman in the soapy kitchen of my childhood, of whom I expected so much, was only a child herself. Adults, parents, are only aged children, playing seriously, glumly, and, when they can manage it, joyously.

Well then, was it serious play when Grandpa shot himself, and the family told it as murder all the years of my childhood, until 1947 when Mammy casually said he wasn't shot by an enemy as he washed his hands in the glass company bathroom, but that he'd shot himself because he'd failed in St. Louis, had had to return to Knoxville without any of the fine things he'd accumulated in the big city up North, including the new piano Momma never got over the loss of, and had had to take a night watchman's job in the glass factory where he'd once been a foreman. I felt no resentment toward Mammy and Momma for having encouraged me to intensify the myth of his murder over the years, to handle his empty holster as if it had belonged to a victim who, like Jesse James, had laid his gun down a moment to free himself to perform an ordinary act— Jesse to hang a picture, Charlie to wash his hands. I merely saw my grandpa in a different light, and thus all the rest of them—Mammy, Momma, Luke.

But when Bucky heard the truth, he resented the deception, as if it had somehow diminished him, as if it perhaps explained his own thwarted upbringing. To Earl, it *seemed* to make no difference at all, even as the myth had been perpetuated, and that somehow helped to explain his cynical attitude about other people, his own isolation as a man whose day-by-day survival justified every act. When I wondered what effect his father's self-destruction had upon Uncle Luke, my imagination made me feel even greater compassion for him.

But not until now have I used that knowledge to understand Momma's relationships with many men, usually alcoholics like Daddy, and life in general. I often wondered, what kind of life did she dream for herself up there in St.

Louis, living a very normal, middle-class life in the Roaring Twenties, before her father lost everything, brought the family back to the past, shot himself, and she got stuck in Knoxville, married to a charming but weak young man who happened to come into the drugstore next to the old Majestic theater on Gay street one day and order a strawberry soda?

I've spent most of my life as God's spy, witnessing the behavior of my folks, one episode somehow related to, but still separate from another, one crisis snarling at the heels of another, and then Mammy's casual admission that grandpa Charlie shot himself gave me a means of re-experiencing, reinterpreting the past. What else, I often wonder, do I now *not* know? Am I an orphan, adopted by these people? Prefer not to be. Am I the son of some other man than the alcoholic I affectionately call Daddy? Rather not be.

Back *then,* the Bijou time, all life seemed to be *my* raw material, broken down into intimations of Knoxville neighborhoods, and the family of the world. In these settings, I consumed movies, magazines, comic books, radio shows, plays, advertising, circus, vaudeville—books belatedly, not until I had written more than I had read. These I filtered through my own means of expression. Daydreaming, long narratives in serial fashion, telling stories to Bucky and Earl, kids in the neighborhood and in the orphanage, to kids at school on a rainy day, to Mammy, to the Bijou boys, to Loraine, and Loris, drawing, comic strips and faces mostly, writing poems, stories, and scenarios for novels, plays, radio plays, screen plays—all genres, during the Bijou era.

The movies, advertisements and other media inspired in me, all of us, our own versions of the American Dream, simultaneously providing the con man techniques for achieving that dream. The effect of all these forces is clear in Bucky's life. And I tried to see my own effect on Bucky's and Earl's and Momma's and Daddy's and Mammy's lives, and dreams. In our pursuit of the American Dream, Bucky was a true believer, Earl was a nightmarish atheist, and I was an agnostic of the dream. And we are all con artists, each in his or her own way, but each influenced by the others, by their life-styles, by their techniques, deliberate and unconscious, so that the more I think back on it, Earl seems to resemble Momma most, Bucky Daddy, and me Mammy.

Born and raised in poverty, escaping it with certain talents and will power, witnessing the others trapped, except maybe Mammy and the Chief, but still, *in it,* I retain an attitude that can be described only as the romance of poverty.

"I love those old buildings," Saul Bellow told me, as we rode through the slums of Cleveland. Camus wrote something like that, too.

Somehow, I have always transformed. As in many pen names. Something magical. Since I had read no books all through until Erskine Caldwell's *God's Little Acre* at 14, and knew nothing of the literary world, I can't remember how I got started so early with pen names, for the first story I wrote was by "Cidney A. Chesterfield." I changed my pen name often, as if each new name were a rebirth, a new identity, a Phoenix renewal of power. And in re-naming Loraine as Raine in my scenarios and Loris as Livia, after James Joyce's character, and the many other girls throughout the years, even Marta, whose family called her Martha, I felt possessive, as if mystically I had been in on their creation.

Am I trying to see the pattern? I am immersing at the risk of immolation in a certain time—the year and half when I was a movie usher at the Bijou, the charged image that electrifies so much else. But it's beginning to make sense in spite of my absolute freedom to wallow.

I've retreated from the News of the Day ever since I closed the theater and moved back stage and now into the projection booth. But news has filtered in that Martin Luther King and Robert Kennedy have been assassinated. Riots in 125 cities. The Tet Offensive. Heart surgery miracles. The Columbia University sit-in. The Paris revolution. Resurrection city. The Pueblo seized. Hovering over all, the threat of nuclear winter.

Since I rented the Bijou, Judy Garland and Vivien Leigh have died. The *Saturday Evening Post*, which had a story of mine in galleys, has folded. The world of the movies and of books was at such a romantic distance back then— infinitely remote, even though I knew for certain, as Thomas Wolfe did and as Norman Mailer knew, that one day I would be famous. Now, James M. Cain, author of the novel version of the movie showing on my first day as usher, *The Postman Always Rings Twice*, is a friend. His praise of *On Target* pleased me, even though it's the least artistic book I've ever written. And other heroes of that time, Walter Van Tilburg Clark—more because of the movie than the book version of *The Ox-bow Incident*—and Robert Penn Warren became friends. I have everything I ever wanted or dreamed of, except great fame, and I don't yearn very intensely for that anymore.

I'm considering leaving the Bijou and going on to Hollywood, finally, to write the script for *On Target*, an entertainment, as Graham Greene would say.

Going to Hollywood where all the gods and Goddesses are dead. I wonder which children of the giants will be cast in the movie.

Maybe I will destroy these tapes and home movies before I go, toss them over the Gay Street Bridge into the Tennessee River. I don't know. Maybe. Let's wait and see.

SITTING UP HERE in the projection booth, darkness surrounding. Bodies of darkness sit in each fire-flawed seat. Each seat has felt the butts of thousands and took into its grain, its gloss, the smell of assholes and pussies and balls and stealthy farts, and all those fabrics have shined and worn the leather, the hinges of the seats like the hinges of bodies sitting down or getting up or straining to lean as lovers kissed. My coat over my lap, Loris jacked me off into her delicate handkerchief or mine, snot dried. This multitude of flesh, of mingling odors, so strange to romanticize them, even the screws into the floors, holding down the seats, the strain on them of weight and release, and people climbing over them. Does that matter? If not, why do I think of it? Where does it fit? I crave to lick into the secret crevices of every inch of the Bijou, like a lover licking even between the toes of the woman he adores, like the brass of those bars I push or pull to open the exit doors, lick the burnt out red exit signs. Hearts, they pulse very faintly as Knoxville bodies repose in a dream, heads beguiled, bemused, subdued, immersed, while the eyes too, took, took, image after flashing image, the persistence of vision, the insistence of vision, the violence of light, the message of the eyeballs, felt in the brainpan, of licking, loving, thrilling, frightening, nerve-tingling, spine-chilling, cock-hardening images, palm-sweating images flash, flash, flash, magnified, yet mutilated, only the head, only the mouth kissing, only the four bodies sometimes from the knees up, the way we see people through windows while passing, who pass us in buses, sitting by the windows. Who are these strange creatures? The rose stage door light I installed has burned out again. Hedy Lamarr, on the set of *Dishonored Lady*, stopping writing her autobiography to open her trailer door to one of her latest lovers. The parts of the theater I've never even seen, or looked at closely. I will get up now and wander through it, in the dark, the dark I started to tell about before, the dark here where I write like near blind James Joyce with a large pencil on large sheets of paper, the backs of old posters, I may take to the lobby walls before they tear them down, the dark of the love-nest balcony, the dark stairwells going down from the third to the second lobby, stroke the dark candy case where the immaculate bars of candy and packs of gum set in formation, and the silent popcorn machine, its glass dome, like Snow White's glass dome, and the handle of the popper dark, stiff, round, smooth, slip my mouth over it, and the ticket box, dark black in the black dark, and slowly stick my hand, arm, elbow up to the armpit down in there and feel the spider webs, and run my hand over the railings, the many, many smooth railings, wooden, and brass, and over the rough walls and the smooth walls, and feel under bare feet the dark carpets and take my time, forever, it will seem like loving forever, and make love, make long, lingering, licking, touch-love to all the theater, naked, go naked, and rub my nipples over the smooth and the rough and feel the leather and the wooden seats under my naked buttocks, and gently rub my back against the red velvet, black in the dark, drapes, and sit on the front row and try to see in the deep dark the screen define itself against the smothering, softly smothering, sweetly smothering dark, and think of eyes, your own looking up from the orchestra pit to see your balls resting gently on the leather cushion of the seat, eyes that see even in the dark, eyes that once had the silver screen's reflection lighting up the pink and blue and black panties of girls on the front row and even middle-aged women, shoes off, stocking feet jacked up, eyes uplifted, head thrown back, fingers gripping four tiny buds of warm popcorn and coming up to the parted, puckering lips, the hot tongue lolling the blossoms, melting them in the mouth, and the salt at the back of her throat, and the hulls packed between her teeth, yes, one of them gold, and climb the rickety steps on the sides of the stage and walk over the splintery steps, where feet have pounded dust into the cracks and the grain and hobble through the dark with a splinter in your foot, in your ass, in your cock, and wander among the dressing rooms, taking the ghostly lightbulbs into your mouth, licking the mirrors, feeling the cold porcelain door knobs against your belly button, and on down into the cave of the basement, the smell like the woods where you used to go to jack off with Palm Olive soap, which you kept hidden in the honey suckle woods, go down in fear of the rats in the coal bin, climb inside the huge furnace, cold furnace, and squat on the grate and look through feral eyes at the sooty walls of the furnace belly-stomach, and come out blackened with soot, suffocating, soot in your nostrils, coal dust, flinty, sharp, and lick the bricks and open that black door to reach the fan doors and feel your way over the wobbly, warped plank that runs above the deep drop and open the very tall fan doors and look a moment out at Knoxville and close the fan doors and turn and walk back and kiss the fire singed screen and embrace the amplifier, the voices, the voices that passed through there, Alan Ladd, "Every guy dreams of meeting a girl like you," Vivien Leigh, "If I have to lie, steal, cheat or kill, as God is my witness, I will never go hungry again," and the sounds of war, of rain, of thunder, of ships at sea, of trains, of birdsong, of elephants, of spurs, of hooves at the pass, of muffled hooves and tanks on the desert, of hawks and vultures over the dunes, of music in the harems, in the honky tonks, in the nightclubs, gliding with Rita Hayworth as Gilda, singing "Put the Blame on Mame, Boys," and as you wander, trying to merge your body with the bodies that came, were there, just as *your* body was there, a moment ago in the balcony, and is now in the pit, on the stage, trying to merge your mind, memory, with the images real and reflected, you will walk with yourself when you were thirteen, with Gale and the ushers who came and went, the projectionists, the patrons, and Mr. Hood, and all the girls who came to *see,* and all the children who came to the Bugs Bunny Club to sing or tap dance or see and listen, and the strippers and the magicians and, the UT players, yourself, as Mr. Carp in *Golden Boy*, as the old Mayor in *The Enchanted*, as Vincentio in *The Taming of the Shrew*. They will gobble you up, they will lick you and stroke you and cover you with ghostly spit, like spiders embalming a fly and you will hang suspended in, forever, in, forever, in, and forever, in their minds, and